Y0-BRO-078

Dear Reader,

We are extremely excited and proud that many of our favorite Arabesque romances have come to life on BET. In fact, giving these wonderful stories a new way to affect and delight audiences is the reason why Arabesque and BET merged in the first place. However, books and movies are very different, and at times, we have had to adjust parts of the stories in order to make them more visual and "TV friendly." While we recognize that these few changes may come as a bit of a surprise to fans of the written word, we are confident that the movies are wonderful in their own right.

Thank you for being part of the Arabesque community. And don't forget to look for made-for-TV movies on BET! You won't be disappointed. . . .

Kelli Richardson
Vice President and Publisher
BET Books

LOVE LETTERS

There's nothing like a love letter to express desire and romantic intentions. Please accept Arabesque's love letter to you in the form of three novellas by beloved Arabesque authors Rochelle Alers, Donna Hill, and Janice Sims.

LOVE LETTERS

Rochelle Alers
Donna Hill
Janice Sims

ARABESQUE
BET
BOOKS

BET Publications, LLC
www.msbet.com
www.arabesquebooks.com

ARABESQUE BOOKS are published by

BET Publications, LLC
c/o BET BOOKS
One BET Plaza
1900 W Place NE
Washington, D.C. 20018-1211

First Printing: February, 1997
10 9 8 7 6 5 4 3

Printed in the United States of America

CONTENTS

Hearts of Gold

Rochelle Alers

To Peter—for a love that is profound and complete, and

*Patricia Bradley of Roosevelt Field, Long Island,
B. Dalton Booksellers—my unending gratitude.*

The Man

The look in your eyes, my sweetheart and bride, and the necklace you are wearing have stolen my heart.

—*Song of Songs* 4:9

One

Resting her palms atop a highly polished natural oak conference table, Kenyon Bryant leaned over and scrutinized the head shots and composites of a half dozen black-and-white glossy photographs. The images of four young men, ranging in age from nineteen to twenty-three, stared back at her, their expressions revealing cockiness, arrogance, confidence and awe.

Concentrating intently, she pulled her lower lip between her teeth, finding it hard to believe that the incredible voices on the tape she had listened to earlier that morning at a recording studio belonged to them. Their smooth, melodious and mature voices seemed more appropriate for men twice their age.

Mark Crayton, their producer, had negotiated a multimillion dollar contract with a major recording company for the quartet, then promptly subcontracted Kenyon to oversee their personal financial interests. Mark had been in the entertainment business long enough to see too many of his clients light cigars and cigarettes with one hundred dollar bills one day, then within a few years file for bankruptcy.

The telephone rang, breaking into Kenyon's concentration. She pushed several strands of chemically relaxed hair behind her left ear. Moving over to her desk, she picked up the receiver.

"Kenyon Bryant."

"Even if you didn't identify yourself, K.B., you still couldn't disguise your voice," teased the beautifully modulated deep male voice on the other end.

"And neither can you, James Earl Jones sound-alike," she

teased back. Jesse Parker, or J.P. as most of his friends called
him, turned heads even before he opened his mouth; stylish and
always impeccably groomed Jesse was a modern-day Renais-
sance man, and as Mark's public relations and marketing person
he was responsible for the success of many of the clients who
signed on with Crayton Creations.

"You're going to have to teach me to say 'park the car in the
Harvard yard' like a true Bostonian," Jesse continued with his
teasing.

"Why would you want to talk like a Bostonian when you enun-
ciate like Avery Brooks?"

"You've got a point there, Miss Bryant. But what good does
it do for me to sound like Avery if you won't give me a play?"

Staring out the window at the bare trees gracing New York
City's Central Park, Kenyon smiled and shook her head. "You
know I don't sleep where I eat, Mr. Parker."

Jesse's seductive laugh came through the wire. "I thought it
was one doesn't—"

"Don't you dare say it," Kenyon interrupted. "What's up,
Jesse? I know you didn't call me for a date."

Jesse chuckled again. "Believe it or not, I did. I'm holding
two very coveted tickets to a showing at a Madison Avenue gallery."

"Who's the artist?"

"A cousin. She needs all of the support she can get."

"I don't think so, Jesse. I'm on to something new. Mark has
handed me four young mavericks who just signed a contract for
more money than any of them could hope to earn collectively in
one lifetime if God hadn't blessed them with the most incredible
voices I've ever heard."

"You must be talking about III-D-Tee. David, Darrell, Deacon
and Tyrell. That three is a Roman numeral three."

"The same," Kenyon confirmed.

"I haven't had the pleasure of hearing them, but I've met
them."

"What do you think, Jesse?"

He emitted a snort. "They are going to need a lot of work.

Only one can string a sentence together enough to sound articulate. Two need major dental work, and all of them require an intensive course in deportment."

"How much time do you have to get them ready for their first video?"

"Six weeks."

"That's not long, Jesse."

"I've been known to work miracles, sweetheart."

"Whatever you do, please make certain they don't refer to women as hos or bitches."

"Don't worry, darling. I emphasize that even before I introduce myself."

"Now, Mr. Image Maker, if you work a miracle with these four, then you and Mark can name your price for any client you represent."

The was a pause before Jesse's sonorous voice came through the line again. "Back to why I called you, honey."

"Jesse," Kenyon moaned.

"That's my name, beautiful."

"Don't you ever give up?"

"It's not a date, Kenyon," he said quickly. "You advise me in what I should invest in, and I want your opinion if I decide to pick up a few pieces tonight."

"I don't know *that* much about art," she argued.

"You know more than I do, Kenyon. Ah-h-h please, baby, baby," he crooned in his best Barry White impersonation.

Kenyon glanced at the clock on her desk. It was almost four o'clock and even though she worked out of the office she had set up in the spare bedroom at her Central Park West apartment, she made it a practice not to work beyond five o'clock. But that didn't mean that most of her days began at nine, because they didn't. Many mornings found Kenyon in her office before the sun came up.

What do I have to lose? she thought. It had been a long time since she'd attended an event that wasn't business related. If it wasn't a business breakfast or brunch, then it was a business dinner meeting or dinner party.

"That's not fair, Jesse. Why did you have to go there and do Barry? What time is the showing?" she asked, relenting.

Jesse's rich laughter caressed her ear. "Six."

A smile softened her lush mouth. "I'll go, but remember this is *not* a date."

"It's not a date, Kenyon," he repeated. "I'll pick you up in front of your building at five thirty."

Kenyon replaced the receiver on its cradle, her gaze fixed on the landscape beyond her tenth-floor window. Winter had put in an early appearance in the Northeast even though the calendar said early December. Cold, blustery winds had swept the trees bare, turned the grass a pale gold, and frigid precipitation occasionally blanketed the sidewalks of Manhattan with a covering of light snow.

Thanksgiving had come and gone, along with the Macy's Day Parade, and now the city was in the full throes of a frantic holiday season. Mentally Kenyon promised herself that she would put up Christmas and Kwanzaa decorations this year.

It had been a long time, too long, since she had been caught up in the excitement of holidays. It was as if Thanksgiving, Christmas and New Year's were ordinary days in the year for her.

Lately she discovered the only thing which elicited a spark of excitement was a new client. As a financial analyst she threw all of her energies into creating financial portfolios that yielded maximum earnings on her clients' investments.

In the three years since she had set up her own company, she made two mistakes. Each time the risks she'd taken resulted in substantial losses to her clients. The clients counterbalanced the losses as tax write-offs, but Kenyon never forgave herself for what she called a grievous judgment call.

It had taken her a long time, but at thirty-five she had come into her own as a successful businesswoman, and as long as her business remained solvent she did not think about the time when she had wanted to combine a career with marriage and children.

Dusk threw lengthening shadows across the park, and Kenyon returned to the table and stacked the photographs and papers strewn over its surface into neat piles. She would go to the gallery with Jesse and forget about her clients—just this one time.

After closing the wheat-colored fabric vertical blinds, she turned on an exquisite Tiffany desk lamp, then pressed a switch on the matching wheat-covered walls, shutting off the recessed overhead lights.

Pulling a sweater over her head, Kenyon headed for the bathroom, musing over what she would wear to the Madison Avenue art gallery.

Black! Why not? Everyone in New York City always wore black.

Two

The concierge opened the door for Kenyon, touching the bill of his hat and returning her smile. Her smile was still in place as she walked toward Jesse. He opened the door to a curbside taxi, and she quickly traded the biting December cold for the warmth of the idling vehicle.

Jesse slipped onto the backseat beside Kenyon, giving the driver their destination. Shifting slightly, his dark eyes took in her appearance in one swift glance.

"You look and smell very nice," he said with a wide smile. Kenyon Bryant's thick, black chin-length hair feathered around her face, creating an halo effect. It concealed her high forehead and framed the perfection of her round face and attractive dimpled chin.

"Thank you, Mr. Parker. Anything for a *client*."

Taking her gloved hand in his, Jesse nodded. He stared out the side window, savoring the subtle sensual fragrance of Kenyon's perfume.

Kenyon did not pull her fingers from Jesse's grasp, wondering why she hadn't allowed herself to become involved with him. Jesse Parker was six-one and carried his one hundred eighty-five pounds over a well-conditioned body, which favored garments bearing the label of Umberto Brioni.

Jesse, well bred, educated and astonishingly handsome, had all of the attributes she had been raised to look for; but finding the man with the "acceptable pedigree" no longer had the same significance it held four years ago.

The taxi driver veered sharply off Central Park West, accelerating through a yellow light and heading toward the East Side.

"Slow down, brother," Jesse shouted at the driver through the Plexiglas partition. "We're not in that much of a hurry."

"You want a slow ride, brother—take a hansom!" the driver retorted, increasing his speed. "After I drop you and your lady off, I'm heading back to the garage. Anytime I get to knock off early I take advantage of it. It's holiday time, and every looney tune in the city wants to get into my cab."

Kenyon smiled at Jesse, and he returned it with one of his own. Both of them were more than familiar with the infamous New York City taxicab driver's attitude. The crosstown trip was accomplished in record time, and when the driver pulled up in front of the Upper East Side gallery, his backseat passengers breathed an audible sigh of relief.

Jesse paid the driver and stepped out onto the sidewalk. Extending a hand, he assisted Kenyon as she placed a black suede-shod foot out of the cab, then another. She stood beside him, and he curved an arm around her waist over a flowing black silk, opossum-lined raincoat.

Bright lights, expansive spaces filled with priceless art objects, a string quartet playing a Mozart concerto, and long tables crowded with crudités, fruit, crackers, beverages and hot and cold appetizers greeted Kenyon as she walked into the gallery.

"I see Ruby," Jesse whispered near her ear.

Kenyon rose on tiptoe, peering over the shoulder of a man in front of her. "Where?"

Jesse motioned with his head. "She's standing next to the tall man in black with the dreadlocks."

Kenyon's gaze shifted to her right, and she swayed slightly as her heart stopped beating momentarily before starting up again. It had been four years, even though he looked nothing like the man she had once pledged her future to, but she recognized him immediately.

The man with Ruby Edwards was the former Francis Humphries. The same Francis who had resigned his position as a high-powered Wall Street stockbroker; the same man who had changed his name to Shumba Naaman, gave up eating red meat, lost forty pounds, grew his hair into dreadlocks and set out to fulfill a childhood dream of becoming an artist.

Francis—now Shumba, who had placed a ring on her finger once she consented to marry him.

Francis, and now Shumba, whom she'd loved and never stopped loving.

Jesse's sharp gaze noticed the strange expression on Kenyon's delicate face. "Do you know Ruby?" His hands went to her shoulders and helped her out of the raincoat before he removed his own top coat.

"No," Kenyon replied quietly. "But I do know the man she's with."

Jesse arched a black sculpted eyebrow. "If he is who I think he is, then he's the one who convinced the gallery owner to exhibit her paintings. Give me a minute to check our coats, then I'll introduce you to her."

Shumba Naaman inclined his head to hear what the diminutive Ruby Edwards whispered to him. Large luminous eyes the deep rich shade of warm sherry crinkled in amusement as she expressed apprehension at seeing a noted art critic enter the gallery.

"If he's here, then that means he's a little bit more than curious, Ruby," he replied, trying to put her at ease. Reaching for her hand, Shumba held it protectively within his larger one. "You'll do . . ." He never finished his statement, the words dying on his lips. His gaze was fixed on a tall woman standing several feet from the entrance.

It had to be her, screamed a silent voice inside his head. There was no way that Kenyon Bryant could possibly have a double.

She was the same, yet there were obvious differences in the four years since he'd last seen her.

Her hair was longer. When he was engaged to Kenyon, she'd worn her hair in a short curly style. Now it was straighter, the feathered ends framing her perfect face.

She was thinner, and it wasn't just the slimming black dress hugging the curves of her remarkably feminine body; he remembered the full lushness of her body that had always aroused a dazzling ecstasy he was unable to explain.

And as quickly as the passionate images surfaced, Shumba mentally dismissed them. Four years was not enough time for him to forgive or forget her superficiality.

His gaze narrowing, he watched Kenyon loop her hand over the suit jacket of a tall, well-dressed man and make their way to where he stood with Ruby.

"Here's my cousin," Ruby said. Her rising excitement was evident by the slight quiver in her voice.

Shumba didn't realize he was holding his breath until Kenyon and her escort stood less than three feet away, and what he saw was startling. Kenyon's weight loss made her appear taller than five-nine and the result was ethereal fragility. Her flawless mahogany brown face was chiseled, her high cheekbones more defined, her dimpled chin enchanting, and he admitted secretly that longer hair gave her the appearance of sleek sophistication.

Smoothly he extended his hand to Jesse. "Shumba Naaman."

Jesse grasped the proffered hand, smiling politely. "Jesse Parker." His left hand slid sensuously over Kenyon's back in a possessive gesture. "Kenyon, this is my cousin, Ruby Edwards. Artist extraordinaire." A bright smile crinkled Ruby's dark eyes. "Ruby, my friend and business colleague, Kenyon Bryant." The two women exchanged handshakes.

Kenyon gave Shumba her full attention for the first time. The deep yellow undertones in his brown skin shimmered like liquid gold. Her gaze inched up to his hair, noting the reddish-brown strands secured at the nape of his neck with a leather thong were liberally streaked with silver. His features, almost too delicate for Francis Humphries, were perfect for the six-foot three-inch, one hundred seventy pound Shumba Naaman. His large expressive sherry-colored eyes locked with hers.

She offered Shumba her right hand. "Hello."

He stared at her manicured fingers, then folded her smaller

hand in his. Cocking his head at an angle, he smiled. The gesture was one Kenyon recognized instantly.

"It's been four years, Kenyon. Is hello the best you can come up with?"

Heat suffused her face. "What else did you expect?"

A slight frown marred his smooth forehead. "Something more than a simple hello. After all, it's not as if we were once strangers."

"Four years can make strangers of anyone," she countered.

He didn't know why, but Shumba felt an alien compulsion to lash out at Kenyon. He wanted to hurt her as deeply as she had once hurt him.

He gave her a wry smile. "Anyone but us, Kenyon."

"You're right about that, *Francis.*"

Jesse and Ruby stared at Kenyon and Shumba, both registering the underlying coldness beneath their polite expressions.

Ruby reacted quickly, taking her cousin's hand. "Will you two please excuse us, but I'd like Jesse to see what I decided to exhibit tonight."

"Certainly."

"Of course."

Kenyon and Shumba had spoken in unison. They stood glaring at each other as Ruby led Jesse across the room.

Taking deep gulps of air, she tried slowing down her racing pulse. "I've never known you to be so sarcastic," Kenyon snapped angrily.

"That's because you don't know me. Even when I was Francis you didn't know me." He took a step closer, and the moist heat from his mouth seared her face. "Do you know why you never took the time to know the man you'd promised to marry, Kenyon?"

"Why don't you tell me," she challenged through clenched teeth.

He paused, his gaze moving slowly over her taut features. Despite years of anger and resentment, Shumba wanted nothing more than to take Kenyon in his arms and mold her soft curves to the contours of his body. He wanted to relive both the peace and desire she had once offered him.

"What's the matter, *Shumba?* You can't come up with a plausible explanation," she taunted.

Shumba flexed his broad shoulders under a loose-fitting unconstructed black wool jacket. "No," he said softly. "This is *not* the time *nor* place for a confrontation or closure, Kenyon."

She nodded, lifting a delicate, arching eyebrow. "You're right," Kenyon agreed after a lengthy silence.

They stared at each other, smiling. Their tensions eased. It was replaced with remnants of private memories that made both of them startlingly aware that there was still a tenuous bond that had not been completely severed.

"Let's see if we can't begin again," Shumba said, smiling broadly and extending his right hand. "How have you been, Kenyon?"

For the second time, Kenyon grasped his proffered hand. "Very well, thank you. And you?"

He released her hand and crossed his arms over his chest. Cocking his head at an angle, Shumba's gaze locked with Kenyon's as he studied her face. She was more than well—she was stunningly beautiful.

"Well enough. How's life at Ballard and DeGroot?" he questioned.

"I left them three years ago," Kenyon explained. Shumba's relaxed stance changed, becoming rigid, as a mysterious smile touched her lush mouth.

"Where did you go?"

"I started my own business."

His eyes opened wider in astonishment, and she could see the warm gold lights in their depths. "There was probably a gnashing of many teeth when you handed in your resignation. The word was that you were DeGroot's handpicked protégée to head their international banking division."

"There was no more gnashing and sobbing than when you left Haywood, Field and Rosen."

"What they missed was the *Wall Street Wizard* making millions in commissions for them." His voice was filled with sarcasm.

It was Kenyon's turn to study his grim expression. "Do you miss it, Francis? All of the buying and selling?"

He leaned closer, shaking his head. "No, I don't miss it. And I'd appreciate it if you would call me Shumba. Francis is like the companies we used to work for—they're a part of our pasts."

Kenyon wanted to shout at him that Francis was a part of his past, but not hers. Francis Humphries was who she had fallen in love with.

He had been the brilliant investment broker who earned commissions and bonuses far in excess of his contemporaries during his tenure at a top investment firm. *Forbes, Black Enterprise* and *Money* magazines had featured cover stories and lead articles on the man who had all of Wall Street following his every financial transaction.

Francis Humphries, a Columbia M.B.A. graduate with New York savvy, close-cut hair, Italian designer suits and shoes had swept into the financial arena with the force of a sirocco sweeping across the Sahara; but within ten years it was over. He had come to Wall Street at twenty-three as Francis Humphries and left it at thirty-three as Shumba Naaman.

Kenyon felt the movement of his breathing, and for a brief span of time she remembered why she'd been drawn to the man and had fallen in love with him. Shumba, as he was now known, projected a stunning virility that touched the innermost core of her femininity.

Why, she agonized internally, did he have to change? Why couldn't he have waited until after they were married to undergo his transformation?

Six months—that was all they had before they were to be married when he told her of his plan to become Shumba Naaman.

"May I get you something to drink?" Shumba asked, breaking into her musings.

"Yes—yes, please. Nothing . . ."

"Alcoholic," he finished for her, remembering that she didn't drink. "Don't run away," he whispered, winking.

Kenyon managed a small smile, watching Shumba as he walked across the room. She couldn't run away—not now and not if her life depended on it.

Three

Kenyon stared across the room at Shumba as he ordered her drink. Turning slightly, he glanced over his shoulder and met her gaze, and for a whisper of a second they shared a secret smile; a smile recognized by lovers. Jesse and Ruby approached Shumba, and the spell was broken and the moment was lost—forever.

She was forced to admit that time had been more than generous to Shumba. The forty-pound weight loss accented the exquisite bones in his face and the delicate symmetry of his exotic features.

His hair, which had shocked her once he stopped cutting it, was neatly braided and secured in a ponytail. The profusion of hair ended several inches past his shoulder blades.

Managing a wry smile, Kenyon acknowledged one thing Shumba hadn't changed—his taste in clothes. As Francis and as Shumba he wore the elegant, free-flowing clothing of Giorgio Armani. His black silk banded-neck shirt, loose jacket and slacks floated elegantly over his lean frame.

What had been startling when Shumba had begun his transformation was now sensually attractive, and Kenyon had to admit to herself that she liked the new look. In fact, she liked it a lot.

He returned with her drink, Jesse and Ruby following, each carrying a flute of champagne.

"Seltzer with a twist of lime," Shumba explained, handing Kenyon her glass.

Jesse raised his fluted glass, a wide grin splitting his face. "I'd like to propose a toast. 'To Ruby, and the first of what will become many more showings.' "

"Hear, hear," Kenyon and Shumba chorused, extending their own glasses.

Again they shared a smile. It had taken less than a half hour in each other's presence to fall back into what had been their chant of approval.

Kenyon took a sip of her drink, glancing at Jesse over the rim of her glass. "Did you see anything you like?"

Jesse nodded. "There's a little beauty called 'The Dreamer' I've claimed as my own."

"Excellent choice," Shumba stated. "When I first saw 'The Dreamer' I offered for it, but Ruby wouldn't sell it to me."

"Don't you paint?" Jesse questioned Shumba.

"I sketch rather than paint. Right now I'm sculpting."

"In gold," Ruby drawled.

"Gold?" Jesse questioned.

A wave of deep color darkened Shumba's face. He'd just received approval for several sketches for a line of jewelry for a European designer who catered to private collectors.

"Replicas of ancient pieces," he stated, not disclosing the details of his current commission.

"When's your next showing?" Kenyon asked, surprising not only herself but also Shumba with the query. Her last words to him before she'd walked out of his SoHo loft were that he would starve to death waiting for someone to buy his work.

"You just missed it. I'm not scheduled for another until mid-February."

"Have you sold a lot of pieces?" Jesse questioned.

"Shumba's showings sell out as soon as the date is announced," Ruby offered, grinning broadly at the sculptor.

Shumba's lips thinned in annoyance. He didn't need Ruby as his spokesperson. "There were a few pieces I didn't sell."

Vertical lines appeared between Ruby's eyes. "That's because you didn't exhibit them," she argued.

Kenyon missed the tension between the two artists, saying, "I'd like to see them."

Jesse nodded, admiring Kenyon's enchanting profile. "So would I."

For the first time since Shumba had become an artist, he balked at offering to show his work, and he knew his reluctance had to do with Kenyon.

He didn't know why, but unconsciously her opinion mattered. It mattered because he knew she possessed an above-average knowledge of art, and most of all because the deep feelings he once had for her had not faded completely.

The realization rocked him—he still cared for Kenyon Bryant! And at that moment he was grateful that she was involved with Jesse Parker. He hadn't missed the way the man looked at Kenyon or his possessiveness whenever he touched her.

"When would you like to see them?"

Jesse glanced at Kenyon. "Do you have anything planned for this weekend, honey?"

"No," she replied, "but if it's going to be this weekend, then Sunday is a better day for me."

"How about Sunday, Shumba?" Jesse queried.

Shumba's warm gold gaze lingered on Kenyon's face. "Sunday is fine with me."

"At what time?" she asked.

"Two."

"That settles it," Jesse stated, appearing quite pleased that he had decided to become a collector of art. "Where's your studio?"

Shumba's expression grew hard and resentful. "Kenyon knows where it is." Before she could confirm or deny his declaration, he nodded to Jesse. "Please excuse me, but I see someone I must talk to." He glanced at Kenyon and bowed gracefully from the waist. "Kenyon." Turning, he walked away.

Staring, she followed the direction of his retreat as Shumba strode fluidly across the room. Leaning down from his impressive height, he hugged a young woman whose flowing black smock dress could not conceal her swelling belly.

An icy chill shook Kenyon. She had never given it a thought that perhaps Shumba had married and fathered a child or children, children who possibly could have been theirs if they had married.

Kenyon let out her breath slowly as a tall attractive man shook Shumba's hand while pulling the woman against his body; the woman reached for the man's hand, placing it over her belly in an intimate gesture.

They're a couple, Kenyon concluded, experiencing a measure of relief. Flashing a relaxed smile at Jesse, she said, "Let's see what you're contemplating buying."

Kenyon made her way slowly around the gallery, stopping in front of Ruby Edwards's "The Dreamer." It was an oil on a large canvas, nearly two square feet, depicting an old woman asleep on a bed with one arm dangling over the edge; her lower extremities were encased in a gauzelike fabric. The folds in the gauze shrouding the subject's body were reminiscent of the draped garments on Michelangelo's *Pietà*, and Kenyon concluded that Jesse's cousin was a very talented artist.

Kenyon had grown up with the odor of paint and turpentine wafting from the studio attached to the large house in Oak Bluffs on Martha's Vineyard. Her grandfather, Ellis Kenyon, had achieved worldwide fame as a popular and successful portrait and landscape artist. Her grandmother had related stories of some of the young African-American artists who had sat in her living room with Ellis and in later years went on to achieve their own fame.

Black and white photographs bearing the images of the artists on the WPA Harlem Hospital murals projects—James Weldon Johnson, Malvin Gray Johnson, Hale Woodruff, Beauford Delaney and many more—still graced the tables and fireplace mantels of Dorothy Kenyon's sprawling white house with the wraparound porch on the Vineyard.

After Ellis's death, her grandmother donated a large portion of his work to museums and cultural research centers around the country, the remainder going to Kenyon.

She had also inherited the paintings belonging to her parents when she reached her maturity. The work of Ellis Kenyon was held in trust for Kenyon after the death of her parents. Her mother and father died in a boating accident three days after her tenth birthday.

She curbed the impulse to purchase one of Ruby Edwards's paintings. Her own apartment was filled with her grandfather's work and a few of the other popular African-American artists from Ellis Kenyon's era. The appraised value of the paintings adorning her apartment walls was enough to maintain her current lifestyle for many years to come.

Jesse left his check for "The Dreamer," and an hour after he and Kenyon had walked into the gallery they walked out. The hour had changed both of them: Jesse had come to appreciate art enough to want to begin investing in it, and Kenyon had discovered that the man she had once pledged her future to stirred emotions she hadn't felt in four years.

Jesse noticed Kenyon was unusually quiet on the return trip to the West Side. He studied her profile, her expression impassive, and he wondered if her meeting Shumba Naaman had anything to do with her subdued demeanor.

The taxi pulled up in front of her building. "May I come up?" he asked.

"Not tonight," she replied, managing a strained smile.

"It's just to talk."

"What about?"

"What happened at the gallery." Jesse knew Kenyon well enough to be direct with her.

Hesitating, she finally nodded. "Okay, Jesse. You can come up." The concierge opened the door to the taxi while Jesse paid the driver.

Minutes later, Kenyon and Jesse rode the elevator to the tenth floor. She handed him the key, and he unlocked the door to her apartment.

Stepping into the spacious foyer, he glanced up at the black-and-white oil by Ellis Kenyon hanging over an ebony and gilt table. Facing the table was a flower-decked Biedermeier chest with ebonized and ormolu accents. After hanging their coats in a closet, he made his way to a living room with more priceless paintings. Jesse felt what he always experienced each time he stepped into Kenyon's home—astonishment. The paintings and the Art Déco elements transformed the space from a sophisticated city residence to a magnificent wing that could be in any major museum.

The combining of Art Déco and Neoclassical furnishing gave a sense of age to the apartment, which could have been anywhere in Paris, New York, San Francisco or Los Angeles.

She had redesigned the living room, installing mahogany double doors that allowed the flexibility of opening or closing off the specific areas for privacy. The space had become an intimate sitting room/library that she used for watching television or reading before going to bed.

Jesse walked over to the expansive living room window and stared out at the lights from the towering apartment buildings across Central Park.

Kenyon watched Jesse's relaxed stance, wondering what was going on in his handsome head. "Would you like something to drink?" she asked quietly.

Hands in the pockets of his slacks, Jesse turned and met her direct gaze. "No, thank you. I just want to talk."

She motioned toward the intimate paneled library/sitting room. "We'll talk in there."

Jesse followed Kenyon into the room and waited for her to sit before taking his own plush armchair. The copper tones from the living room were repeated in the library.

Crossing her long slender legs, Kenyon smiled at Jesse. "What do you want to talk about?"

Long, thick lashes concealed the intensity of Jesse's dark eyes as he visually examined the woman sitting opposite him. It suddenly hit him that Kenyon Bryant wasn't aware of the effect she had on men—he in particular.

He had known her professionally for two years, and in spite of his subtle overtures, she had never responded to him. What he wanted to know now was he wasting his time pursuing her.

"Shumba Naaman," he said in a soft tone.

Four

Kenyon was certain Jesse heard her slight intake of breath. Had she been that obvious? Were her deep feelings for Shumba that blatant?

Tilting her chin, she looked down her nose at Jesse. "What about him?" Her voice was soft *and* controlled.

"Why did you call him Francis?"

"I knew him as Francis Humphries."

"So he changed his name from Francis Humphries to Shumba Naaman?"

She nodded slowly. "Yes."

"How long ago?"

"Four years."

The middle finger of Jesse's left hand outlined the curve of his eyebrow. "How involved were you and Shumba?"

Her mouth tightened slightly. "I was never involved with Shumba. It was Francis Humphries I was engaged to marry."

"Do you want to tell me about it?"

Kenyon had never disclosed the true reason for ending her engagement. Not to her best girlfriends, not to her grandmother, not to her other relatives and definitely not to her professional colleagues.

Resting her head against the back of the chair, Kenyon closed her eyes. "It's not that I want to tell you. It's more like I *need* to tell you."

Inhaling deeply, Kenyon opened her eyes and smiled at Jesse. "The man I thought I knew changed right before my eyes. At first he quit his job, then his eating habits changed. Next came his refusal to cut his hair. Within months Francis Humphries died, and Shumba Naaman had taken his place."

Jesse's eyebrows arched with this disclosure. "Did he give you a hint that he wanted to change his lifestyle?"

"No," Kenyon whispered. "One morning he woke up and said that he was going to quit his job and become an artist."

Jesse snapped his fingers. "Just like that?"

"He wasn't ignorant when it came to art," she explained. "Art was his minor as an undergraduate."

"Did you love him, Kenyon?"

"Of course I loved him," she countered angrily. "Do you think I'd marry a man I didn't love."

Leaning over and resting his elbows on his knees, Jesse glared at her. "Did you love the man, or did you love what he was?"

Jesse's accusing question stabbed at her, reminding Kenyon of Shumba. He'd asked her the same question.

"I loved him," she declared, enunciating each word.

"Do you still love him?"

A tense silence enveloped the room, the only sound their soft, rapid breathing. Kenyon clenched her hands until her nails stabbed her palms. She felt as if a dormant volcano had come to life within her and rumbled angrily—the raw emotions fighting for escape.

"Do you?" Jesse repeated.

Biting down hard on her lower lip, she nodded, saying, "Yes. A part of me will always love him."

To her surprise, Jesse showed no reaction to her confession. "Thank you for being honest." Rising to his feet, he stared down at her. "I'll let myself out. I'll call you in a few days, and we'll make arrangements for Sunday."

Kenyon did not know how long she sat in the library, staring out the window. Tears she hadn't shed four years ago fell, distorting her vision. She cried for the love she'd lost, she cried for the pain Shumba had caused her, and she cried for all of the interminable, lonely nights she had spent alone since she walked away from him.

Spent, the flow of tears stemmed, she began the process of healing.

Kenyon awoke early, her eyes puffy from her crying session. Leaving the bed, she walked from the bedroom to an adjoining bathroom. She bathed her face with cold water and followed it with a leisurely bath in a massive sunken tub. An hour later she felt composed enough to begin her day.

Dressed in a white sweat suit, thick white socks, and her hair secured at the top of her head with an elastic band, she made her way to her office. This was to be what she called a work-in day. She had planned to spend the day at home.

Checking the answering machine for messages, she spied a sheath of papers cradled in the tray of the fax machine. As promised, Mark had faxed her the biographical data and net worth statements on the members of III-D-Tee.

Retrieving them and a pen from her desk, she studied the bottom-line figures on each as she headed toward the kitchen. Surprisingly they weren't as low as she thought they might have been.

All of the four held jobs, three lived at home with their families, and one lived with his girlfriend and infant son. None of them had had any contact with the criminal justice system, which she knew would please Jesse. It always made his job easier to "sell" young entertainers if he didn't have to clean up their image.

Sitting down at an Oriental lacquered table in the dining area, she made notations along the margins for each singer. Her small, neat print listed: purchasing property—self and/or family, life and disability insurance, mutual funds which would be conservatively managed balanced stocks and bonds, and a custodial account for the one member's minor dependent child.

It would take her less than a week to research and complete the preliminary investment projections before she met with each member of III-D-Tee for a private consultation. Many times, with approval from her clients, she encouraged the attendance of their parents or significant others. Too often family members placed unreasonable demands on young performers for financial support, resulting in serious cash flow problems for them. Money problems usually resulted in frustration, negative behavior and loss of recording contracts.

Kenyon put aside her project long enough to pick up the newspaper outside her apartment door and prepare breakfast. She sectioned a large navel orange, toasted a slice of cinnamon-raisin bread and brewed a small carafe of coffee. Whenever she worked at home, a light breakfast was enough to fortify her until early evening; however, the dinners she prepared for herself were usually festive affairs. She always dined using her late mother's fine china, silver and magnificent fragile stemware. It was a tradition Dorothy Kenyon had passed on to her daughter and also to her granddaughter.

It was a tradition Kenyon had hoped to pass on to her own daughter. But if she and Shumba had sons instead of daughters, then she would've wanted her daughter-in-law to adopt the ritual. It was something she and Shumba had talked about—family traditions, and he had several of his own he wanted to continue into perpetuity with their own offspring.

Taking a sip of coffee, she wondered why her traitorous thoughts lingered on Shumba. Even if she hadn't seen him the night before, it had been nearly a year since she'd recalled their liaison so vividly. Every Christmas Eve brought with it the realization that she was to have been married on that day.

She and Shumba had planned an elegant candlelight ceremony at the house on Martha's Vineyard where she'd had come to live after the death of her parents. She and Dorothy had planned the wedding with such precision that the two of them were aware of where every vase of flowers would be situated. Dozens of white potted poinsettia plants were on order for the joyous occasion, most to be delivered from a popular nursery in Boston.

It was two years after Kenyon Bryant was introduced to Francis Humphries, eight months after they were engaged, six months before they were to be married and four months before their engagement party, that Kenyon walked away from the only man she had ever loved.

Raising her fragile porcelain cup in a salute, she whispered, "Goodbye, Francis. Hello, Shumba."

She finished breakfast, stacked the dishes in a built-in dishwasher, pushed a button to start the wash cycle, then headed for her office.

Kenyon spent the next four hours checking stock and bond quotes and preparing mortgage amortization schedules on her computer, revising the figures over and over before printing the computations on the laser printer; the telephone rang as she began an analysis of the preliminary investment prospectus.

Reaching for the cordless instrument, she picked it up. "Kenyon Bryant."

"Good afternoon, Kenyon."

She smiled. "Good afternoon to you, Jesse. What's up?"

"I'm calling to firm up our plans for Sunday. I have about fifteen minutes before I leave for D.C."

"Is anything wrong?" She knew Jesse's mother still lived in Washington, D.C.

"No, but my mother is scheduled for an outpatient cataract procedure Friday morning, and I want to be there with her. I plan to be back Sunday, but I'm not certain whether I'll be able to make it to Shumba's by two."

"Do you want to cancel?"

"No," Jesse said quickly. "Give me his address, and I'll meet you there."

Kenyon gave him Shumba's SoHo address and telephone number. It wasn't necessary to look them up because she never forgot them. During their engagement she'd helped Shumba decorate his newly renovated residence.

"Safe trip, friend," she said in parting.

"Thanks, friend," he countered. "I'll see you Sunday."

Less than three minutes after she rang off with Jesse, the phone rang again.

"Ken—"

"Girlfriend!" screamed a female voice. "I did it!"

"Did what, Jeannette?" Kenyon questioned, recognizing her best friend's voice.

"I eloped!"

"Where are you?"

"I'm still in Atlanta. I'll be back next week to hand in my resignation and make arrangements for my things to be shipped here. Then I'm gone for good."

A frown furrowed Kenyon's forehead. "Nette," she drawled, "I'd planned to give you a shower."

"I'm sorry, Kenyon. I hope I didn't put you out."

She smiled. "No. It'll just become a farewell celebration instead of a bridal shower."

"You don't have to—"

"I want to," Kenyon interrupted. "I have to," she added. She'd met Jeannette Hawkins when they both frequented the same after-work establishment, becoming the sister the other sought. "In case you didn't know it, the shower is supposed to be next Saturday at my place."

"I'm sorry I spoiled all of your plans."

"You didn't. You've just changed the theme of the celebration that's all."

She and Jeannette talked for another three quarters of an hour before ringing off. She walked over to the window, smiling. Her best friend had decided to marry the man who had been chasing her for years. Jeannette had balked because she didn't want to relocate from New York City to Atlanta; she didn't want to leave her position at Haywood, Field and Rosen, and she hadn't wanted to sacrifice her independence for marriage. Well, she had just done all three.

It was Jeannette who had introduced Kenyon to Francis when he and Jeannette worked together. Jeannette was to be her maid of honor at their wedding. Now it was Kenyon who would help her best friend celebrate the beginning of her life as a married woman.

Mentally shifting gears, she finished analyzing the figures, then faxed her preliminary prospectus to Mark, ending her workday; she rode the elevator to the lobby and retrieved her mail. After returning to her apartment, she retreated to the library and read her mail and the newspaper.

Night had fallen by the time she went into the kitchen to prepare her dinner. Switching on a small portable television on a counter, she thought about Shumba, but his image was quickly dismissed when an emergency news bulletin flashed across the television screen.

Concentrating on the anchor's words was enough for her to forget about the man she'd fallen in love with—even if it was only temporarily.

Five

Fat wet snowflakes were falling by the time Kenyon walked from the subway station to Shumba's building. Pushing her gloved hands into the pockets of her charcoal-gray mohair coat, she lowered her head, quickening her pace.

She spied the four-story building, sprinting the last few feet to its entrance. Pressing the button on the intercom to Shumba's apartment, she waited for a response. She didn't have long to wait.

"Yes." Shumba's resonant voice came through the speaker.

"It's Kenyon."

"Come on up."

At the sound of the buzzer, Kenyon pushed open the door and stepped into a warm, spacious lobby. Removing her gloves, she walked into the elevator, taking it to the third floor as her stomach churned with anxiety. At any second she would come face-to-face with Shumba, and she wasn't certain how unaffected she would remain.

Would he detect that she wasn't as indifferent as she had appeared the night of Ruby Edwards's exhibition? Would he be able to see that a part of her still yearned for what they had had together?

The elevator doors opened silently, and Shumba loomed in front of her, tall and elegant in a black-and-white striped loose-fitting silk shirt and black slacks. His unsecured long braided hair swept over wide shoulders like softly curling moss.

"Come in please," he said, his golden gaze taking in everything that was Kenyon. "Let me take your coat."

Kenyon shifted her handbag, and Shumba eased the coat off her shoulders. Noting the moisture on her hair, he resisted the urge to wipe it away.

He hadn't realized it, but his hands shook slightly. He was certain he had been ready to see Kenyon Bryant again, inhale her sensual perfume, and possibly touch her delicate body without succumbing to her magic spell.

For years he relived the passion that only Kenyon was able to extract from him. He remembered the distinctive sound of her voice with the Massachusetts inflection, the graceful way she tilted her head whenever she looked up at him, and most of all he remembered her declaration that she would love him forever.

After she'd left him, Shumba wondered if all they'd shared had been a lie, and if they'd married would she continue to lie and say she would love him forever—as long as he was Francis Humphries.

But he had changed. He became a man who lived as he wanted to live and did whatever he wanted to do.

Kenyon tilted her head, staring at Shumba staring back at her. The loneliness of the past four years welled up within her, and at that moment she knew she had made a mistake to see him again. The emotional wounds had reopened, and she was hemorrhaging.

"Jesse will be late," she said breathlessly.

The spell was broken. Just the mention of Jesse reminded Shumba that Kenyon now shared her life with someone else.

"How late?" His voice carried a note of impatience, while a shadow of annoyance crossed his features.

Kenyon was puzzled by his curt tone. "I'm not certain. He's coming in from D.C."

"Do you want to wait for him?"

"I'm willing to give him an hour."

The tension in Shumba's face eased as he forced a smile. He'd made a fool of himself. He sounded like a jealous fool. "We'll give him all the time he needs, Kenyon."

The caressing sound of him whispering her name made her tingle, and she returned his smile. "Thanks."

He leaned closer. "For you—anything." Pulling back, he walked over to a closet.

Shock widened Kenyon's eyes as she watched Shumba hang up her coat. She surveyed his graceful gestures, recalling that Francis had been just as graceful.

Turning, she glanced around the duplex residence. Bleached oak floors, grayish-beige walls and white cotton duck upholstery created a cool, airy atmosphere. An open stairway and catwalk, with its square tubular steel railing, extended the visual space. Floor-to-ceiling aluminum vertical blinds tied together the upper and lower living room windows on the street side of the apartment.

Kenyon recognized the furnishings she had selected: a custom-made Egyptian-style cane daybed beneath the windows, an early Viennese beechwood chair covered in luxurious Donghia velvet, a Charles II English oak chest-on-chest and several Louis XV-style chairs provided a soft counterbalance to the contemporary furnishings.

Shumba stared at Kenyon's slim figure in a pair of navy blue wool slacks and a white cashmere pullover sweater, watching her gaze sweep over the living room. "I've made a few changes."

"You've made more than a few changes." Making her way across the expansive space, she glanced into an area off the living room. Dark green walls, a massive nineteenth-century Austro-Hungarian armoire, an English decoupage potpourri jar and African sculpture set the stage for a moiré-covered French sofa and chairs and two silk tapestries hanging over the sofa.

Moving closer, Kenyon studied the African sculpture. "Did you make this?" she asked, pointing at the exquisitely carved wood figure.

Shumba stood behind her, his warm breath sweeping over the back of her neck. Shivering slightly, she couldn't move. The warmth from his body and the evocative scent of his musk aftershave brought back shockingly sensual memories of their passionate relationship.

Their appetites had been voluptuous, neither holding back from the very first time they shared a bed, and the willingness to share everything and the openness with which they approached all phases of their lives was completely shattered when Shumba announced he needed to "find himself."

He had not given her an indication that he'd tired of the frantic and stressful business of stock and bond trading. Their commitment to an open dialogue was shattered completely the morning he woke her with the announcement that he was resigning his position at one of the top Wall Street brokerage firms.

"No," he replied. "I picked that up on a trip to Benin last year."

"It's beautiful."

"So are you," Shumba whispered.

Kenyon turned to face him, the action seemingly in slow motion. The rich timbre of his melodious voice and the sparks of gold in his large luminous eyes denoted the profoundness of the three words.

Her rapid breathing and parted lips indicated shock, and Shumba decided to press his advance. "Remember what I said the other night about closure, Kenyon."

"What about it?" she asked, finding her voice.

"There wasn't any. You just walked away from me without an explanation."

Her eyes widened in amazement. "Without an explanation," she repeated. "I thought I said everything there was to say at that time."

Tilting his head at an angle, Shumba crossed his arms over his chest. "What you mouthed were empty words, Kenyon. There was no emotion, no feeling."

"I was screaming at you."

"Exactly. You were screaming. And in screaming you were as appealing as a malfunctioning car alarm."

Kenyon felt the heat in her face as the very air around them shimmered like electrical shocks. Reining in her temper, she managed a smile. "You were a lot more genteel as Franics. Being Shumba doesn't give you the right to be rude."

"You think I've changed that much?"

"Yes, I—"

Moving with the speed of a pouncing cat, Shumba pulled her pliant body against his as his mouth swooped down on hers. His tongue sent shivers of hungry desire racing through her, demanding the passion he knew she was capable of offering him.

Caught off guard, Kenyon responded to the passion Shumba summoned somewhere deep inside of her. Pressing her breasts to his chest, she curled her arms around his neck and returned his kiss.

His demanding mouth called out to a hidden, secret ardor that only he knew existed. She pressed her open mouth to his, drinking deeply from the well of passion and desire he had created. The heated blood pounding in her head swept downward, racing through her body and igniting a similar inferno in Shumba's.

There was no mistaking his intensifying desire or his hardness pressing against the apex of her thighs. Shumba was right. He hadn't changed that much—and neither had she.

Her fingers swept through his long hair, the soft thickness of the braids curling around her hand as if they had taken life. Tugging slightly, she pulled him closer, wanting to absorb him within her. There were times during their lovemaking that she and Shumba had actually become one.

Shumba's right hand moved under the softness of her sweater and encountered a softness more exquisite than the finest silk. Kenyon's bare skin rippled under his fingers as they swept up her back. Skillfully and deftly he undid the plastic snap on her lacy bra and released the full, warm globe of flesh into his palm. Muttering a soft expletive of amazement, he released her mouth and captured her breast, his teeth fastening gently around the distended nipple.

Passion fleeing quickly and common sense returning, Kenyon froze. "No," she cried out. "Don't."

Shumba released her, his eyes large, wide, dark and shimmering with a lingering passion. His chest rose and fell heavily under the striped silk shirt as he watched her turn her back.

"Let me help you," he offered when she attempted to fasten her bra.

Kenyon shook her head, her hair sweeping forward around her face. "No."

Ignoring her refusal, he moved behind her and resnapped the plastic clasp. Shumba pulled down her sweater and turned Kenyon around to face him, his gaze lingering her full and thoroughly kissed lips. The fingers of his right hand swept the hair brushing her left cheek behind her ear.

She had become more beautiful that he'd ever imagined. The Kenyon Bryant who walked out on him had been a woman-child. This Kenyon Bryant who stood before him was all woman. She had even responded to him like a woman.

Their lovemaking had always been passionate and satisfying, but she had always approached each encounter with hesitancy. He realized that on too many occasions he had been the one to initiate their coming together. This time when he'd kissed her she hadn't balked. She had given him more than he had demanded.

A slight smile softened his strong masculine mouth as his golden gaze bore into hers. "Have I changed that much, Kenyon?"

Tilting her chin in a gesture that was so familiar to Shumba that he thought that perhaps they never had parted, she returned his smile. "Not as much as I have," she retorted.

Shumba's smile broadened. "How right you are," he confirmed, still experiencing the lingering effects of her passion. "The book is now closed on Francis and Kenyon, and is now . . ."

Her smile faded when he didn't complete his statement. "And is now what?"

He studied the woman he had wanted to and still wanted to marry. The woman he wanted to bear his children. He hadn't thought it possible, but Shumba loved Kenyon with an intensity that made everything else in his life pale in comparison. Even his art.

"The book is now open for Shumba and Kenyon," he began softly. "It's open for friendship and anything else you'd want for us."

Kenyon swallowed painfully. How could she tell Shumba that she still loved him—that she had never stopped loving him? That now it didn't matter if he shaved his head bald, wore a toga, or existed solely on a diet of raw rice as long as they were together.

Extending her hand, she said instead, "Let's begin with friendship, Shumba."

He took her hand, kissing each finger tenderly. "Friendship it is," he whispered against her knuckles.

Kenyon withdrew her hand, feeling at ease for the first time since meeting Shumba again. "Speaking of friends, I got a call from Jeannette the other day."

"I haven't heard from Jeannette in over a year," Shumba confessed. "I've been doing quite a bit of traveling."

"She just got married."

His eyebrows shifted in surprise. "To Raymond Palmer?"

"Yes," she confirmed with a wide grin.

"Now that's what I call a determined brother," Shumba stated, shaking his head. "He just wouldn't give up." *Unlike myself,* he added silently.

There were more times than he could count that he'd berated himself for not going after Kenyon. He remembered the times when he'd picked up the telephone to dial her grandmother's number, hoping to solicit the older woman's support, but each time he replaced the receiver after dialing the area code to the house on Oak Bluffs. And not once had Dorothy Kenyon called him to inquire what he had done to her granddaughter to make her cancel their wedding.

"Smart man," he continued, winking at Kenyon.

"Patient man," she countered, returning his wink with a bright smile. "I'd scheduled a bridal shower for Jeannette for next Saturday, but with her elopement it's now going to be a farewell gathering. I'd like for you to come."

A frown creased Shumba's forehead. "If you'd planned to give her a bridal shower, then why did Jeannette elope? I have to assume she'd set a wedding date."

"She had, but she'd vacillated so many times about setting a date that she didn't trust herself to show up at the church."

Kenyon stared at Shumba, recognizing the faraway look in his eyes, and wondered if perhaps he was thinking about their own aborted wedding plans.

"Will you come?"

"Come?"

"To Jeannette's farewell celebration."

Shumba smiled easily. "Of course I'll come. Where and at what time?"

"Five o'clock at my place."

"Your place?"

"Yes . . ." Kenyon halted. Shumba didn't know that she'd moved. "I moved from the studio apartment a couple of years ago."

"Where do you live?"

"Seventy-sixth and Central Park West."

Shumba whistled under his breath. "Very nice."

She shrugged a slender shoulder. "It's not a two-story loft, but it'll do," she stated, remembering the day they celebrated his closing on the purchase of the two floors in the SoHo loft building. Four months later, after extensive renovations, Shumba moved into his new residence.

Shumba's impassive expression revealed none of the unbidden memories tumbling over themselves inside his head. He had begun his search for a permanent home after his second date with Kenyon. He had known enough women to identify what he wanted in a wife, and with Kenyon it had been the first time in his adult life that he'd met a woman who shared all of his interests while possessing similar aspirations.

Now he wasn't as certain. Both of them had left lucrative positions with top investment companies to pursue their own enterprises, and it was obvious that Kenyon was personally involved with Jesse Parker.

His expression softening, Shumba extended his hand. "Come with me. I'll show you what I've picked up on my travels while we wait for your boyfriend to arrive."

Kenyon's mouth opened and closed quickly. She wanted to tell Shumba that Jesse wasn't her boyfriend but changed her mind. What she didn't want Shumba to think was that she'd been pining away for him during their separation.

"Are all of them sculptures?" she asked, taking his hand and following him up the open staircase.

"You'll see," Shumba said, smiling down at her.

She stopped at the top of the catwalk and stared at a large painting hanging under a recessed light. Streaks of pale color in shades of peach and green splashed across the canvas extended the visual space created by the grayish-beige walls.

"It's exquisite, Shumba." The soft timbre of her voice revealed awe.

He nodded. "Thank you. It's one of my favorites."

Stepping closer, Kenyon examined the artist's signature. The symbols were Japanese characters.

"I acquired it in a barter transaction," he explained. "Hideaki Yamashita wanted a reproduction of an Aztec sculpture I'd done, so we negotiated for what we both considered an equitable trade."

"Still trading?" she questioned, flashing a teasing smile.

Throwing back his head, Shumba laughed a full-hearted sound from deep within his chest, while Kenyon stared at the fall of braided hair sweeping over his shoulders and down his back. Never had she seen a man with long hair appear as masculine and virile as Shumba did at that moment.

Reaching for Kenyon, the fingers of Shumba's free hand swept up the back of her neck. "Let's go, kitten."

Kenyon tensed and he released her. The intimate gesture and his pet name for her had returned with the ease of drinking a glass of water.

They stood, only inches apart, staring at each other. Four years had not been enough to forget . . . forget all they had shared.

This time when Shumba turned and made his way down the catwalk, Kenyon followed silently.

Both of them were lost in the memories of what they'd had.

Six

Kenyon averted her gaze from the room where she and Shumba had once shared a bed and the one which they had set aside as a possible nursery.

Walking into a room behind him, she was totally unprepared for the contents of his studio. Built-in wall shelves were crowded with sculpted pieces from every continent.

"Are all of these yours?"

Shumba gave her a boyish grin. "They're mine. But if you want to know if I sculpted them, then the answer is no." He pointed to a far wall near the floor-to-ceiling window. "Those on that shelf are my creations."

Kenyon barely noticed the busts and totems from New Zealand's Maori and Alaska's Aleutian natives, jade figurines from Southeast Asia, African artifacts and remnants of faded pottery from America's Southwest Native Americans as she stared at a half-dozen exquisitely sculpted pieces of ancient amulets in gold. She picked up a small replica of a woman with a rounded belly.

Peering closely, she studied the precisely detailed features and elaborate feathered headdress. "Who is she?"

"A sixteenth-century Inca queen."

"I hope she was married," she stated, glancing up at Shumba. His gaze lingered on her attractive dimpled chin then moved up slowly, meeting her direct stare. "She appears to be with child."

"She is," he confirmed.

Turning the talisman over on her palm, she read the imprint

on the bottom. The replica had been cast in pure gold. So much for Shumba starving to death as an artist.

Inhaling deeply, Kenyon quickly reached a decision. She wanted the amulet. "What do you want for her?"

Reaching out, Shumba eased the gold figure from her hand. "It's not for sale. I can't sell it to you," he said quickly, correcting himself.

Vertical lines appeared between her large dark eyes. "Why not me?" She noticed his hesitation. "Do you think I won't be able to meet your price?"

Deep color darkened his face. She had openly insulted him. "It has nothing to do with money," Shumba retorted angrily.

"Then what is it?"

How could he tell Kenyon that he couldn't put a price tag on an object she wanted because he still loved her. "Will you accept it as a gift?"

A long, unbending silence filled the room. Anxiety spurted through Kenyon, her heart racing wildly against her breasts. Shaking her head, her expertly cut hair sweeping sensuously around her face, she said emphatically, "No."

"Why not?"

"Why not?" she repeated. "Because . . . it wouldn't be right. Sculpting is your livelihood."

Shumba hid a smile. "What you mean is that it wouldn't be proper." She nodded, and his smile widened. "I forgot how strait-laced you can be. I suppose it comes from being raised by a very traditional grandmother."

"This has nothing to do with my grandmother." There was no mistaking the anger in her voice.

"Then loosen up, Kenyon. We haven't seen each other for nearly four years, and all I wanted to do was give you a gift."

"A gift you could probably sell for five figures."

He leaned closer. "Let *me* worry about my checkbook balance."

She recoiled as if he had slapped her. In the past they never argued about money. "If I can't purchase it from you, then I don't want it."

Kenyon turned away from Shumba, but not before he saw her pained expression. "I'm sorry, kit . . . Kenyon."

"Forget it," she countered sharply, wrapping her arms around her body in a protective gesture. "It appears as if we can conduct business amicably with everyone else but each other."

Shumba stared at the curve of her slender hips in her tailored wool slacks. He didn't want to fight with her. What he wanted to do was pick her up and carry her down the hall to the bed where they'd spent so many pleasurable hours making love. Whenever they made love, the world around them ceased to exist. And he wanted to experience that again. No other woman had ever come close to what Kenyon had offered him.

"What do you say to a barter?" he asked quietly.

Spinning around, she faced him again. "I have nothing to barter with."

"You're in business for yourself. You'll come up with something."

"I doubt it."

"I don't doubt it, Kenyon. You're a very intelligent woman. You'll think of something."

"And what if I don't?"

"Then you'll always have something to remind you of me," he said smoothly, with no expression on his face.

I don't need an object to remember you, Kenyon mused. "I'll think about it," she replied, not committing herself.

Her answer seemed to satisfy Shumba. He showed her the objects he'd picked up during his travels, patiently explaining their origin and what they represented. She was astounded with the wealth of knowledge Shumba had gathered on the different cultures who produced the magnificent pieces stored in his SoHo loft.

His lecture ended when the melodious chiming of the downstairs bell shattered their unspoken truce. Jesse had arrived.

Shumba became the gracious host Kenyon remembered as he served an early dinner of grilled salmon, baked potatoes, a spinach salad, homemade onion bread and a nonalcoholic cranberry punch in the dining room, which had been decorated to resemble a conservatory.

After dinner he lit a fire in the living room fireplace, and Kenyon sat on a Louis XV-style chair, staring at the flames and listening to music while the two men discussed the buying and selling of art.

By the time Shumba and Jesse emerged from the upper level, the fire had died out and the lingering notes on the last CD had just ended. Kenyon came to her feet, stretching sensuously, reminding Shumba of the nickname he'd given her.

Jesse ruffled her hair before pulling her against his body. "You look tired, honey."

Kenyon smiled at him. "What you see is total relaxation. And I have Shumba to thank for that. You've been a wonderful host."

Shumba bowed slightly. "It's been my pleasure. Speaking of hosting events, why don't the two of you come to my Kwanzaa celebration."

She glanced from Shumba to Jesse. "I won't be in town for Kwanzaa."

Shumba successfully hid his disappointment. "Will you be gone for the seven days?"

"No. I plan to return to the city before the new year."

"What about New Year's Eve?"

Kenyon arched an eyebrow at Jesse. "Jesse?"

Touching his lips to her hair, he nodded. "Count us in."

Shumba pressed his palms together and let out his breath slowly. "Very good." He walked over to the closet and retrieved their coats, while Kenyon removed a business card from her handbag.

She handed Shumba the card. "I'll see you Saturday at five."

Leaning over, he kissed her cheek. "I'll see you Saturday."

Kenyon and Jesse rode the elevator to the lobby and were fortunate enough to hail a passing cab as soon as they approached the corner.

She half listened as Jesse talked excitedly about his newly acquired piece of sculpture, unable to totally share his joy because her own thoughts were filled with the smoldering kiss she had shared with Shumba. Trapped by the memories of her own emotions, Kenyon prayed silently for an answer. Should she continue to see him or walk away from him a second time . . .

Kenyon rearranged the last vase of flowers, taking a step backward and surveying her handiwork. "Perfect," she said softly. The cloying fragrance from pale pink roses wafted through the living and dining rooms, mingling with the same scent from a half dozen fat candles burning behind glass chimneys placed strategically on tables and the fireplace mantel in the living room.

Returning to the kitchen, she turned down the flame under a pot of simmering collard greens with smoked turkey wings, then slipped a pan filled with buttermilk biscuits into the preheated oven.

She had planned to have the food for the bridal shower catered, but changed her mind once New Orleans native Jeannette asked her to prepare shrimp-and-crab gumbo, dirty rice and fried okra. After purchasing the ingredients for the three dishes, Kenyon decided to prepare the entire menu of macaroni and cheese, fried okra, a black-eyed pea salad, biscuits, and desserts of sour cream pound cake with fresh berries and homemade vanilla ice cream. Rounding out the menu was a large glass bowl filled with Southern Comfort punch.

Whenever she hosted a dinner party at her Central Park West apartment, it was a catered affair; however, it had been a long time, too long, since she'd actually prepared food for her friends. The last time had been a housewarming celebration at Shumba's loft.

Shumba had done most of the cooking, baking breads, making sauces and cakes from scratch. His mother had taught him and his two sisters to cook as soon as they were tall enough to look over the table. Cynthia Humphries began her own cooking career testing recipes for magazines before deciding to write cookbooks.

Glancing up at the clock on the kitchen wall, Kenyon grimaced. It was four forty-five. If she didn't hurry, she still would not be dressed when her guests arrived.

She made her way to her bedroom, removing the heated rollers from her blown-out hair and tossing them into a large plastic box. Combing the curls, she pinned them up off her neck, applied a light cover of makeup, then changed her smock and drawstring slacks for a black silk midcalf slip dress and a pair of black silk sling-strap heels. Her bare arms and legs glistened from the oil in her scented body cream.

Checking her face one last time in the mirror over a triple dresser, she inserted a pair of diamond studs in her pierced lobes. The stunning gems, like the paintings in her apartment, had been part of Kenyon's late-mother's estate. Dorothy Kenyon had made certain that her only grandchild received every significant item that was a part of her daughter's heritage.

The doorbell rang, signaling her guests had arrived. Kenyon left the names of the invited with the concierge, eliminating the need to announce each one.

Newlywed Jeannette and Raymond Palmer were the first to arrive. Within minutes two more couples walked into the apartment. Kenyon greeted them warmly and hung up their coats, but before she could usher them into the living room the doorbell rang again.

She opened it and stared up at Shumba Naaman. Her pulse throbbed with excitement, and she had the answer to the question which had taunted her for nearly a week. There was no way she could walk away from him a second time. A delightful shiver of wanting raced through her limbs, leaving them trembling with excitement.

"Please come in."

Slowly and seductively Shumba's gaze slid over her face and continued downward before coming back to her face, his widening smile mirroring his approval. "Thank you." Stepping into the foyer, he handed her a large decorative shopping bag. "There's something for Jeannette and something for you in that bag."

"You didn't have to get—"

He placed a finger over her lips, stopping her protest. "We'll discuss it later."

And it was hours later before she and Shumba would be given the opportunity to talk.

Jeannette, Raymond, Shumba and Kenyon sat in the intimate paneled library, drinking cups of freshly brewed cappuccino. The brilliant glow from a full moon lit up the space, making artificial light unnecessary.

Jeannette licked a dot of froth from the rim of her cup. Staring out the window, she shook her head. "I can't believe I'm leaving all of this," she stated wistfully, "and my friends."

"Atlanta is a beautiful city," Kenyon replied.

Raymond Palmer, a tall slender man in his early forties, winked at his bride. His premature gray hair appeared white in the silvered light. "Don't let Jeannette fool you. Right now I'm willing to bet that she has more friends in Atlanta than I do, and I've lived there all of my life."

"That's because I've been dating you for . . ." She counted on her fingers. "Almost six years."

"Six and a half," Raymond countered.

"Six," Jeannette insisted. "I met you a month after Kenyon started seeing Shumba. Tell him, Kenyon."

She stared at the petite, dark-skinned woman who had recently affected a close-cut hairstyle. "I don't remember," Kenyon lied smoothly.

Shumba stared at Kenyon's profile, stunned by the perfection of the bones of her face. His artist's eye quickly committed the curve of her cheekbones, nose and chin to his memory. The up-swept hairstyle showed off the fluid line of her long neck, reminding him of a graceful swan.

"I remember," Shumba stated, his golden gaze fixed on Kenyon, and his wonderfully modulated baritone voice caressing the heavy silence. "Jeannette's right. Kenyon and I met the two of you at Tavern-on-the-Green one Saturday night. And when I saw Jeannette at work that Monday, she told me that it was the first time she'd gone out with you."

Raymond whistled softly. "Damn," he drawled. "You have a mind like a steel trap."

"Tell me about it," Jeannette crooned, her New Orleans drawl still apparent although she'd spent the past fifteen years living and working in New York City. "Shumba used to glance at stock and price quotes at the start of the business day and memorize every one. That's why he was called the Wizard of Wall Street. And speaking of Wall Street"—she raised her delicate china cup—"goodbye and good riddance. And instead of frying my brain cells watching someone else's money, I'm going to decorate my new home and fill it up with a lot of babies."

Raymond rose to his feet, and the other three occupants of the room also stood up. "Speaking of home, it's time Jeannette and I headed out. We're scheduled for an early morning flight out of Newark."

Jeannette, placing her cup and saucer on the Biedermeier-style center table, sniffled, vainly fighting tears. Kenyon placed her own cup on the table and extended her arms to her best friend. The two men watched as Jeannette and Kenyon tearfully said their goodbyes.

Raymond, again, thanked Shumba for the sculpted reclining terra-cotta figure he had given them as a wedding gift. The nude figure bore no facial features or definable genitalia. The style was reminiscent of several African cultures whose deities were asexual.

Jeannette and Raymond would return to Atlanta with the sculpture and more than a dozen envelopes filled with gift certificates to the some of the world's finest shops. Mr. and Mrs. Raymond Palmer had been given the option of choosing tableware from Cartier, bed dressing from Ralph Lauren or floor coverings from Schumacher. The gifts were as elegant as the small circle of people who had maintained a fast and loyal friendship over the years.

"I'm going to miss you," Jeannette cried.

"Don't be so melodramatic," Kenyon scolded in a soft voice. "You're only going to Atlanta, not Antarctica."

Pulling back, Jeannette wiped her eyes with a tissue. "When are you coming down to visit?"

Kenyon laughed. "Don't you and Raymond want to get used to being married?"

Jeannette flashed a lopsided smile. "We've done just about *everything* a married couple would do except live together."

"I hear you, girlfriend. But seriously, I'll try to make it next spring. I have a project that I'm working on, and it should be completed sometime around early March."

Jeannette kissed her cheek. "I'm going to hold you to that date." Walking over to Shumba, she rose on tiptoe and kissed him. The top of her head came to the middle of his chest. "My invitation extends to you, too. Don't be a stranger."

"I'll try not to be."

"I'm warning you, Shumba. Don't make me come to New York and get you."

It was his turn to laugh. "I'm scheduled to exhibit some of my work at an Atlanta gallery in May. I'll make certain to look you up."

"Would you mind if Raymond and I hosted a reception for you?"

Kenyon knew Shumba was embarrassed by Jeannette's offer. He never had been one to draw attention to himself. As the Wizard of Wall Street he had avoided the spotlight wherever possible.

"I'll let you know," he replied noncommittally. Extending his hand, he congratulated Raymond and wished him well.

Shumba waited in Kenyon's library/sitting room while she saw Jeannette and Raymond to the door. When he'd entered her apartment, he had been awed by the black-and-white oil by Ellis Kenyon in the foyer. Awe became astonishment when he recognized some of the priceless works of her late-grandfather hanging in the living room. Not once had she ever mentioned that she owned any of his paintings.

He'd tried reassessing his reaction to seeing Kenyon again and failed miserably. It was as if they'd never parted. Except for her weight loss and the change in her hairstyle, Kenyon Bryant was the same.

She'd moved from a tiny Greenwich Village studio apartment to a Central Park West high-rise luxury building with oversized rooms, yet her taste in furnishings was the same—simple and elegant.

She'd left a high-powered Wall Street position as financial analyst to set up her own company, and it was apparent that she had continued the success with the purchase of the apartment and the elegant Neoclassical and Art Déco furnishings.

Four years. He had wasted four years not going after her, but he intended to make up for lost time. And this time he would not let her go.

"Shumba." Turning around at the sound of his name, he stared at the gaily wrapped box she cradled to her chest. "Should I open this now or wait until you leave?"

He walked to where she stood at the double doors to the library. Taking the box, he moved into the living room. The smell of roses hung in the air, the sputtering candles fighting valiantly to remain lit. Some of them had burned beyond their five-hour limit.

Sitting down on a sofa, he pulled her down beside him and handed her the box. "Open it now."

Kenyon was too aware of the man sitting too close to her. His charcoal-gray trousered thigh brushed intimately against the silk of her dress, and she could feel the soft whisper of his warm breath caress her bare shoulder. She could also feel the heat from his golden gaze on her face as she bent over and deftly removed the invisible tape holding the paper together.

Her eyebrows lifted in surprise when she pried the top off the box to find a smaller one wrapped in the same paper. She went through the action twice more, laughing.

"This reminds me of those little painted wooden dolls who get smaller and smaller as you remove the outer one," she said with a wide smile.

Shumba nodded, sweeping several lengths of braided hair over his right shoulder. Tonight he'd secured his hair in a length of leather, opting not to have the wealth of braids move freely around his shoulders.

Kenyon opened the last box and went still. It was the gold Inca

Rochelle Alers

queen he had tried to give her at his loft. Her head came up slowly, and she stared up at him.

Her measured gaze took in the deep-set gold eyes staring back at her. She noted the delicate length of his straight nose and the strong sensuality in his firm mouth. She reveled in the liquid gold in skin pulled tightly over sculpted cheekbones and the softly curling reddish-brown braided hair that had become his crowning glory.

Could he see what she was feeling? Did he know that she still loved him?

A slight smile softened her full lips. "Thank you, Shumba."

Tilting his head at an angle, he arched his eyebrows. "You accept?"

Nodding, she said, "One thing my mother and grandmother did teach me and that was how to be gracious. I accept."

Leaning forward, he pressed his mouth to hers, increasing the pressure slightly before pulling away. "You're very welcome."

Placing the gold statue on the cushion, Kenyon quickly came to her feet. She didn't trust herself to sit beside Shumba and not fall into his arms. It would be easy, so easy to invite him to stay—to spend the night.

Shumba stood up and slipped both hands into the pockets of his trousers. Kissing Kenyon again was a mistake. His body had reacted so quickly that he feared losing control.

"Do you need help cleaning up?" he asked, not recognizing his own voice.

"No," she replied quickly. "I'll take care of everything in the morning."

Shumba gave her a skeptical look, but decided not to press her. "Everything was delicious."

"I had a wonderful teacher."

"As did I," he replied, referring to his mother. His expression grew serious. "Would you mind if I called you and invited you out every once in awhile? Just to talk."

Tilting her chin, Kenyon stared up at him. "What would we talk about?"

"Art of course."

Mixed feelings surged through her, and her emotions seemed out of control. Shumba kissed her twice, and it didn't mean he wanted more than that. Sharing a kiss didn't mean they would become lovers again.

"No, I don't mind."

The smile that softened his features made him appear a lot younger than his thirty-seven years. "Thank you," he whispered politely.

Kenyon walked to the foyer and retrieved his top coat from the closet. She watched as he slipped his arms into the cashmere garment, it fitting perfectly across his wide shoulders.

He smiled down at her, opened the door, and within seconds he was gone. Kenyon locked the door and leaned against it.

Shumba had gotten her to accept his gold queen, and she would see him again. This was one time when both of them had come out winners.

Seven

Kenyon awoke Sunday morning to the sound of sleet tapping against the windows. Snuggling under a down-filled comforter, she promptly went back to sleep.

It was nearly one o'clock when she finally left her bed. She brushed her teeth, showered, and slipped into an old sweat suit to begin the onerous task of cleaning up after the party revelers.

Preparing a cup of instant coffee to fortify herself, she filled the kitchen sink with hot, soapy water and soaked dishes, glasses and silver.

Soiled tablecloths were stacked for the dry cleaners, tabletops were dusted for smudges and fingerprints, and the vacuum cleaner picked up discarded bits of food and dirt.

Two hours later Kenyon, preparing to heat a portion of gumbo and rice for her dinner, heard the telephone in her office ring. Anyone who had her number knew never to call her at that number on the weekend. Shrugging, she ignored the ringing. The answering machine would pick up the message.

She spent the remainder of the afternoon putting up holiday decorations; she hung a decorative evergreen wreath with a colorful kente-cloth bow outside her door, and placed electric candles with orange bulbs in the window of every room. All she needed was Christmas carols to get her into the holiday season.

She called her grandmother at six thirty, knowing the older woman never answered her phone during "60 Minutes."

"Hello, Grammie."

"Hello, baby girl. How are you doing?"

"Fine. How are you?"

"Not bad for an old lady."

Kenyon smiled. Her grandmother had said the same thing for as long as she could remember. "Are you getting ready for my visit?"

"I've been ready for months," Dorothy Kenyon replied. "What I'd like to get ready for is a wedding. I'd like to see a great-grand-child before I go on to glory."

"Grammie," Kenyon wailed.

"Don't you Grammie me, Kenyon Dorothy Bryant. I just don't understand it. You live in a city with millions of young men, and you can't find a date"

"It's not that I can't *find* a date. It's my prerogative that I don't choose to date anyone right now."

"You're thirty-five years old. What are you waiting for?"

Why do I let her do this to me? Kenyon raged silently. "Look, Grammie, I have to go."

"Why? Are you going out on a date?"

"Soon." She had promised Shumba she would see him.

"That's what I want to hear. Are you still coming in on the twenty-second?"

"Yes, Grammie."

"What time should I expect you?"

"I'm scheduled to arrive in Boston around ten. I have less than an hour to make the connecting flight to the Vineyard."

"I'll be there waiting for you, baby girl."

"Thanks, Grammie."

There was a moment of silence. "There's no need to thank me, Kenyon. I love you."

"And I love you, too."

Kenyon hung up, her eyes swimming with unshed tears. Dorothy Kenyon was the last link with her past. She had been her parents' only child, and it appeared as if she was destined not to have any children.

Maybe she should've married Shumba. Maybe she should consider dating Jesse. The maybes attacked her relentlessly until she entered her office to check her calendar and prepare for Monday.

The flashing red light on the answering machine reminded Kenyon of the call earlier that afternoon. Pressing a button, she listened to the familiar masculine voice. It was Shumba, inviting her to take in a movie with him. He left his number, saying if she was interested then she should get back to him before six.

"See, Grammie, I had a date," she said aloud, grinning.

Picking up the telephone, she dialed Shumba's number and got his answering machine. She thanked him for thinking of her and left her private number.

She had another week before her trip to the Vineyard, and Kenyon was certain she would see Shumba again before she and Jesse attended his New Year's Eve fête. Very certain.

Kenyon walked into the conference room at Crayton Creations, flashing a friendly smile at the members of III-D-Tee. Three of the four young men rose quickly to their feet, while the fourth leaned forward but did not stand.

"Good morning, gentlemen. Please be seated," she ordered in a soft voice; unbuttoning the jacket to her pale gray suit, she slipped onto a chair at the head of the oval table.

"Is this going to take long?" growled Darrell Royce, the most aggressive, talented and recalcitrant of the quartet. "We're supposed to be at the studio by one."

"No," Kenyon replied, the narrowing of her eyes was the only indication of her annoyance. "I can assure you that what I want to talk to you about will not take that long."

She had met with each young man individually and outlined their personal investment prospectus. David Baker, Deacon Simms and Tyrell Williams were attentive, asking pertinent questions, while Darrell had slouched on his chair, sulking. He'd interrupted her invariably, saying," *I want to take care of my own money."* Kenyon had quickly reminded him that he'd agreed to the clause in his contract which read that 25 percent of all income would be set aside for investment purposes. Darrell's glare had been threatening, but she stood her ground. She wasn't going to let a temperamental twenty-two-year-old neophyte frustrate or thwart her with his audacious behavior and outbursts.

Placing her manicured hands on the table's highly polished surface, she smiled. "A realtor has approached me with an offer from a client who wants to sell a block of abandoned stores and apartment buildings."

"Where is it, Miss Bryant?" David questioned.

"Around the corner from you and Deacon." They lived in apartments in landmark 1901 brownstone structures in Harlem.

David jumped to his feet, giving Deacon a high-five hand-shake.

"How much is this scheme going to cost me?" Darrell snapped. "I don't want to be no super of no buildings."

Kenyon struggled to contain her temper. "It's not going to cost *you* that much because it will be a collective effort. All of you will invest equal shares. And to answer your point about being a superintendent—you won't be. As an owner of the properties, you'll hire a building manager to clean up and contract with a company to make repairs.

"I've looked at the properties, gone over an engineer's report, and worked up the figures on what it would cost for renovations to bring everything up to code. I—"

"What do you think?" Deacon cut in. "Does it look good?"

She smiled for the second time since walking into the room. "If you decide to invest, I think you're on to a good thing. You'll have income from two sources—business and residential. But you also could have income from business *and* business."

"Business and business?" Tyrell asked. He was the least talka-tive of the four.

"The apartments can be sold as cooperative units. People usu-ally take good care of what they buy. Rentals bring in transients, who may or may not take care of the property. So if you sell the units, and depending upon the price, you may recoup your initial investment within two years."

Four pairs of eyes were fixed on her, and Kenyon knew they

were receptive—even Darrell. What she was prepared to offer them was an opportunity to generate income even when their recording careers ended.

"David and Deacon, the both of you live in the neighborhood so I want to know firsthand what kind of businesses are needed. Tyrell and Darrell, I want to know what type of business establishments, whether they are part of a major chain or franchise, would you like to see come to Harlem. I want you to think about it, and if all of you are willing to put up the money to purchase the property, then we'll meet the first week in January to discuss your findings."

"Hold up, Miss Bryant," Darrell ordered.

She arched her eyebrows. "Yes, Darrell."

"Why do we have to wait that long?" His voice was soft, almost apologetic.

Kenyon stared at Darrell in surprise, remembering his incessant hostility. "I want you to think about what you're going to invest in."

"You didn't ask me to think about throwing away my money when you had me sign insurance papers," he countered.

"Acquiring insurance is not throwing away money or an option. Insurance is a necessity, and buying a city block isn't. You've got three weeks to think about it. Enjoy your holiday, gentlemen. I'll see you again in the new year."

Gathering her handbag and leather portfolio, Kenyon walked out of the conference room and down the carpeted hall to Mark Crayton's office. She knew what she'd asked the four to consider was totally alien and unfamiliar, but what the members of III-D-Tee had to realize was that they were very wealthy young men—even before they completed their first video.

Mark turned away from the window behind his desk and smiled at her. "How did it go?"

Kenyon flopped down on a worn leather chair beside his massive desk. "It was interesting."

"How?"

She stared at Mark's corpulent frame and shaven head, his golden brown skin glistening like polished brass. His solemn expression and soft voice belied a quick mind and an uncanny ability to recognize extraordinary talent. Mark's success hadn't come overnight, but within the last ten years he'd stopped counting the number of Grammy Awards he'd won as producer of the year.

"They fight like pit bulls about buying life insurance but don't blink an eyelash when they're presented with pooling their resources to purchase an entire city block," she explained.

"That's because they want to be businessmen, Kenyon. What they fail to realize is that singing is a business and not a nonstop party."

"They're going to make it, Mark."

He eased his large bulk down to a high-backed leather chair. "I know they are. They're good kids and they're different. I don't see the slick bravado in them that so many young entertainers have. They've stayed out of trouble, and they're willing to work hard."

Kenyon studied Mark's brooding face. "Are you saying that III-D-Tee are unique?"

Mark met her steady stare. "Not that unique. It's just that I see these boys as the sons I never had."

She knew how much Mark had wanted a son. His wife of twenty-eight years had given birth to five girls.

"Think of all the fun you've had walking down the aisle of the church and giving your daughters away."

"Don't remind me," he groaned. "Do you know what weddings are going for nowadays?"

"Too much," she replied, sorry that she'd brought up the topic. Standing, she reached for her coat, hanging on a coat tree. Mark moved quickly, taking the coat from her and helping her into it. "Tell the realtor that our clients have expressed an interest in the property," she continued, "but that they're also looking at another parcel in Washington Heights."

Mark watched her button her coat. "Why the stall, Kenyon?"

"The owner owes the city more than a million in back taxes on all of his properties, and I believe we can negotiate for a lower figure. It's better for him to sell low than to lose it all."

"When do you intend to let him know that the kids want it?"

"I'll meet with the realtor after the new year. Meanwhile the *kids* have an assignment to research what businesses they want to lease to. I've suggested that the apartments should he cooperatives instead of rentals."

Mark gave her a long, lingering stare, then shook his head. "I can see it all now. III-D-Tee real estate magnates, not pop singers."

Smiling, Kenyon patted Mark's solid shoulder. "And you'll be able to take the credit for their successes."

"Not without you."

She winked at him, then picked up her handbag and portfolio. "I'll call you before I leave for the Vineyard."

Mark nodded and walked her to the door. "Thanks again, Kenyon."

"You're welcome."

She left Crayton Creations' West Forty-first Street offices and took the crosstown bus to the East Side. The sales manager of the lingerie department at Bergdorf Goodman had called her earlier that morning, saying that the nightgown she'd ordered for her grandmother had come in. Dorothy Kenyon only wore silk undergarments and nightgowns.

Caught up in the seductive pull of the crowds, decorations, music and the cold, crisp weather, Kenyon walked in and out of Fifth Avenue department stores, browsing and buying.

It was after four o'clock when she finally walked into the lobby of her apartment building, both hands gripping large shopping bags.

Minutes later she walked into her apartment and dropped the bags on the floor beside her bed. The light on the answering machine on her bedside table flashed off and on. She waited until she'd hung up her coat, kicked off her shoes, and changed from her suit into a pair of black leggings with a loose-fitting sweater before she picked up the message:

Kenyon, I know this is short notice, but I'd like to invite you to accompany me to a birthday celebration Saturday night. If you can't make it, I'll understand.

He didn't have to leave his name. She knew it was Shumba as soon as he'd said her name.

Sitting on a rocker, she pushed several strands of hair behind her left ear, rocking back and forth. She wanted to see him again, but she also wondered what it was Shumba wanted—other than friendship.

His reaction to meeting her again at the gallery was anything but friendly. There was no mistaking his hostility.

But the images of them together at his loft surfaced. His kiss and her response. His hands on her breasts and her body's reaction to his explosive passion. Then his soft healing kiss after she'd accepted his gold sculpture.

His statement: *"The book is now open for Shumba and Kenyon. It's open for friendship and anything else you'd want for us."* She'd said she wanted friendship when what she wanted was to share the love she'd had with Francis.

But Shumba was Francis. His outward appearance may have changed, but he still was the man she'd fallen in love with and had pledged to spend the rest of her life with. And she had promised to love him—forever.

Rising from the rocker, she picked up the telephone receiver and dialed Shumba's number. It rang four times before she heard the deep voice on the other end.

"Good evening."

"Good evening, Shumba."

"Kenyon," he crooned. "Thank you for returning my call."

"I'll go with you," she said quickly.

There was a loud, pregnant silence followed by an audible sigh of relief. "Thank you, Kenyon."

She smiled. "Where is it and what type of attire?"

"It's in White Plains, and the dress is semiformal."

"What time should I be ready?"

"I'll pick you up at four."

"I'll be ready."

"Kenyon?"

"Yes, Shumba."

"Pack a bag to spend the night and bring a swimsuit." There came a distinctive click, then a dial tone.

"Shumba," Kenyon shouted into the receiver. Her heart racing uncontrollably, she pressed the redial button. It rang incessantly on the other end until his answering machine clicked on.

Slamming the receiver down to its cradle, she compressed her lips into a tight line.

"Damn you!"

If he thought she was going to fall into his bed just because she'd agreed to go out with him, then Francis Humphries a.k.a. Shumba Naaman was sadly mistaken.

Eight

The concierge had announced Shumba's arrival, and Kenyon waited for him at her apartment door, the toe of her right foot tapping impatiently. She hadn't heard from him all week, even though she'd left several messages on his answering machine for him to call her.

Her rage at his duplicity simmered for several days before it faded completely while she prepared for her upcoming trip to visit her grandmother.

A secret part of her wanted to relive the passion she'd shared with Shumba, while at the same time she was frightened, frightened that he wanted to exact his measure of revenge.

A recurring dream taunted her as she slept with the images of Shumba making love to her, then his laughter as he left her weeping for him to come back to her.

The dreams were so vivid that she awoke in a panic, her entire body trembling from the nightmarish illusions.

The doorbell rang, and she unconsciously smoothed down the silk crêpe de Chine midnight-blue dress over her flat abdomen before opening the door. The sight of Shumba standing before made her mouth go dry. She opened it wider, and he stepped into the foyer. Shifting slightly, he closed it before turning back to Kenyon.

His long hair was newly braided and hung down his back, a few plaits resting over his left shoulder. His flawless golden-brown skin shimmered, competing with the gold in his sherry-colored eyes.

A sweeping navy-blue topcoat hung open, revealing a white silk shirt with a banded collar and an impeccably tailored dark blue suit.

Shumba sucked in his breath, his gaze inching from Kenyon's coiffed hair framing her face, to her lush mouth, outlined in a vermillion red, and down to the chic dress clinging to her scented brown body.

Two wide bands of dark blue satin crisscrossed her chest and flowed in a slim line of crêpe de Chine, which ended midcalf. Sheer navy stockings and matching blue satin heels complemented her stunning look.

"Exquisite," he breathed out softly.

"Come here," she beckoned, motioning with her forefinger. "You have some explaining to do."

Shumba caught her hand, holding it firmly. "I'll explain in the car, kitten. The driver and the guest of honor are waiting downstairs."

"But—"

"Where's your bag?" he interrupted.

Kenyon pulled her hand out of his loose grip. "Over there." A kidskin carry-on bag sat by the ebony and gilt table.

"Your coat, Miss Bryant."

Seething, she opened the foyer closet and withdrew her black silk opossum-lined raincoat. Shumba stared at the expanse of smooth dark brown skin on her partially bared back before he helped her into the coat.

"Your keys, Miss Bryant." Picking up a small sequined purse, she handed him her keys. "After you, Miss Bryant," he continued. He grasped her bag, opened the door, then closed and locked it behind him. He dropped her keys into a pocket of his topcoat before taking her arm and escorting her down the carpeted hallway to the elevator.

They waited for the elevator, and Kenyon glared at him. "Explain now," she demanded.

"I owe all I've achieved thus far as an artist to two women," he said quickly. "One is whose birthday we'll celebrate tonight and the other is hosting the banquet. Naomi Morrow is an art connoisseur who is a trustee on the boards of the Metropolitan Museum of Art and the studio Museum in Harlem. Shelby Graham is married to Naomi's nephew, and she is assistant curator for the Studio Museum and my agent.

"Shelby and Marshall invited me to attend Naomi's birthday celebration and requested that I bring a guest," he continued.

The elevator arrived and the doors slid open silently. Shumba glanced inside the car, then waited for Kenyon to precede him before stepping in beside her.

She stared up at his well-defined profile. "A guest to stay overnight?"

Tilting his head at an angle, Shumba smiled down at her with a speculative look, realization dawning quickly. It was all he could do to keep from laughing. "You and I will not share a bed, kitten. Shelby and Marshall have enough bedrooms to accommodate their overnight guests."

Kenyon nodded, murmuring, "Thank you."

Something inside of her wanted to share a bed with Shumba—to see if what she and Francis had had would be the same, *and* to find out if what they had had could be even better this time.

The elevator descended to the lobby; the concierge opened the front door for Kenyon and Shumba, and the limousine driver met them as they strolled under the canopy to the waiting car. The driver took Kenyon's bag and helped her into the rear seat. She sat down next to a tiny woman whose smooth khaki-brown complexion was the perfect foil for her expertly coiffed silver hair.

The older woman extended a gloved hand. "Naomi Morrow."

Kenyon flashed a warm smile, taking the elegant woman's proffered hand. "Kenyon Bryant. Happy birthday, Mrs. Morrow."

"Naomi, please. And thank you very much, child."

Shumba folded his long frame into the car, sitting on the seat facing the two women; the car pulled away from the curb, and shifting slightly, he sat opposite Kenyon, his outstretched legs framing hers.

"Naomi," he began, "I'd like for you to meet Kenyon Bryant.

I think you'd be interested to know that she's Ellis Kenyon's granddaughter."

The overhead dome light illuminated the excitement in Naomi's dark eyes. "I met your grandfather one summer when my late-husband and I vacationed on the Vineyard. It was many years ago, probably before you were born," she added. "Charles and I stayed in Oak Bluffs every other summer, and I remembered meeting and talking to Ellis when he and your grandmother hosted an open house to showcase his work. My only regret is that I didn't have the money at that time to purchase a dramatic black-and-white oil that was a complete departure from Ellis's usual landscapes and portraits."

Kenyon noticed the slight smile tugging at Shumba's strong masculine mouth. He knew Naomi was referring to the painting hanging in her foyer.

"Shumba told me that you're on the board of the Studio Museum."

"Yes, I am," Naomi confirmed. "My nephew's wife, Shelby, is assistant curator."

"I have quite a few of Ellis Kenyon's paintings which have never been exhibited."

Naomi leaned closer to Kenyon. "Are you saying that you're willing to loan the museum some of Ellis's work from your private collection?"

"Yes." Kenyon knew it was selfish to hide most of her grandfather's lesser-known paintings from the world. Most of her friends who visited her apartment were not interested in art—except for Shumba—or even knew who Ellis Kenyon was.

Naomi pressed her gloved hands together. "Wait until Shelby hears this. She'll be beside herself."

Shumba crossed his arms over his chest, closed his eyes, and listened as the two women launched into a dialogue about Ellis Kenyon. The heat and the gently swaying motion of the luxurious automobile relaxed him as he stretched out his trousered legs until they cradled Kenyon's stockinged feet and ankles.

His entire being was filled with the soothing sound of her

voice, the fragrance of her perfume and the warmth of her feet sandwiched between his.

He'd been at home when she'd called and left the messages on his answering machine but had not answered or returned her calls because he feared she would change her mind about going out with him. He was not going to allow her time to bow out. And he knew Kenyon well enough that if she committed herself to something, she would always follow through.

Kenyon walked into the brightly lit living room of the house at the top of a hill and recognized her host and hostess immediately. They had been at the gallery the night she was reunited with Shumba.

She stared up at two floors of glass and skylights as a young man took overnight bags up to the second-story bedrooms.

Shumba placed both hands on Kenyon's shoulders and slipped the coat from her body, then removed his own and handed them to another of the hired staff the Grahams had contracted for the evening to see to their guests' needs.

Grasping Kenyon's hand, Shumba led her over to where Marshall and Shelby Graham took turns hugging and kissing Naomi.

Kenyon smiled at Shelby Graham. Her flawless dark brown skin, large, vibrant eyes, and naturally curling short hair set the stage for a beautiful woman in the full bloom of impending motherhood. A flowing pale gray silk smock over a pair of matching slacks artfully concealed the late stages of her pregnancy. Around her slim neck hung a string of large, perfectly matched pearls.

Shumba's left arm curved possessively around Kenyon's waist. "Kenyon, I'd like you to meet our hosts, Marshall and Shelby Graham. Marshall, Shelby, Kenyon Bryant."

She hesitated before accepting Marshall Graham's extended hand. What she'd glimpsed of Marshall Graham from a distance was startling up close. His close-cut graying hair, neatly barbered moustache, and overall classic good looks reminded her of the men in the portraits her grandfather had painted on his canvases, while his all-black attire emphasized his imposing height.

"Welcome to our home," he said with a trace of a southern drawl.

"It's my pleasure," she returned. Turning to Shelby, Kenyon smiled warmly. "Hello. You look beautiful."

Shelby held out her arms and hugged Kenyon, her protruding belly not permitting her to hold her close. "You don't know how much I need to hear that at this stage in my pregnancy."

Marshall arched a sweeping eyebrow at his wife. "I tell you that all the time, sweethcart."

Shelby smiled, resting a slender hand over her silk-covered belly. "That's because you're quite pleased with yourself." Turning to Kenyon and Shumba, she wrinkled her nose. "It's a boy," she announced.

"Nice work," Shumba said, giving Marshall a high-five handshake.

"Don't you dare congratulate him, Shumba Naaman," Shelby warned with a smile. "I'm the one who's going to do all the work in another three weeks."

Shumba knew when to retreat. "Excuse me, but I think I need something to drink."

Kenyon curved her arm around Shumba's waist under his jacket as he guided her over to a portable bar. "Wrong call, darling."

She felt him stiffen and heard his slight intake of breath. The minute the endearment left her lips, she knew she'd made a faux pas.

Shumba stopped several feet from the bar and stared down at her. His luminous eyes narrowed slightly. "Am I, kitten?"

Tilting her dimpled chin defiantly, she gave him a sidelong glance. "Are you what?"

He lowered his head until their lips were only inches apart. "Am I your darling?"

Why after four years was it so easy for her, for them, to lapse back into old habits? She couldn't move, blink, speak, or breathe. It was as if she had never left him. What she felt was so strong and implacable that she feared answering his question. He *was* her darling and she wanted him as her lover—again.

Her chest felt as if it was going to explode if she didn't let out her breath. She finally did, and a rush of moisture flowed from her parted lips as her chest rose and fell heavily.

Her gaze slid slowly over his lean sculpted face. "Right now you are," she whispered against his mouth.

Shumba's eyes widened in astonishment. He'd hoped she wouldn't lie to him, and she hadn't. He knew what she was feeling because what he felt was the same.

He moved his mouth over hers in a gentle, healing kiss. It was only a brushing of the lips, but the banked fires flamed uncontrollably. He kissed the tip of her nose and pulled back.

"Are you certain you don't want something stronger than selt zer or club soda?" he teased, smiling.

Kenyon returned his sensual smile. "Tonic water."

"Tonic water," he repeated. What he needed was a shot of scotch, bourbon or whisky, but opted for a glass of white wine.

Both of them sipped their drinks, staring over the rim of the glasses at each other. Shumba reached for her free hand and held it gently as the Graham house filled quickly with a continuous flow of invited guests.

"Want to go for a walk?" he asked Kenyon quietly.

Thick lashes concealed her innermost thoughts as she stared up at Shumba. "Where?"

"In the garden."

"Have you forgotten it's December?" she asked through clenched teeth, not wanting anyone to overhear their conversation.

"I know what month it is, and I'm aware of how cold it is. The question remains: do you want to walk in the garden?"

Shrugging a bare, slender shoulder, she said, "Okay."

Leaving their half filled glasses on the bar, Shumba led her across the room. He paused briefly to let Marshall know where they were going, then continued out the living room and down a long, narrow hall.

He opened a door, and Kenyon stepped into an oasis. The

"garden" was a greenhouse filled with trees, many pregnant with their ripened yield, flowering tropical and exotic plants and more than two dozen vegetable gardens.

The warm, humid air inside the building settled on her exposed skin, and her damp face glowed with a healthy sheen. Visually examining a Japanese garden, she shook her head in wonderment.

The Graham's living room was decorated with magnificent flower arrangements, and Kenyon was willing to bet that the flowers had come from their greenhouse.

"All of the flowers you see and all fruits and vegetables that will be served tonight come from this greenhouse," Shumba said, reading her mind.

"Who does the gardening?"

"Marshall."

"It's magnificent," she stated, glancing around. "When does he find time to plant, weed, and prune?"

"Before and after classes. He's headmaster for an all-male prep school in Harlem."

"Interesting," Kenyon said, thinking of the positive role model he presented to his students.

They strolled up and down the immaculate broad paths, identifying melons, cucumbers, carrots, tomatoes, eggplants and varying types of lettuce.

Shumba glanced at his watch. They'd been gone for more than twenty minutes. "We'd better get back, or Shelby and Marshall will send out a search party for us."

They returned to the main house, joining seven other guests who were drinking and eating from the platters of hot and cold hors d'oeuvres carried by several waiters.

A half hour later everyone was directed to the dining room for a sit-down dinner. Naomi sat at the head of the table, while Shelby sat across the table, opposite her. Marshall had opted to sit at his wife's right.

Kenyon found her place card and realized she was seated opposite Shumba instead of next to him. The elderly man seated

on her left leaned a little too close for propriety, and she gave
him a half smile when he whispered how much he liked her dress.

She endured his Cheshire cat grin and insipid compliments
through the tropical fruit cup, green salad and the main course
selection of pressed duck, butterflied lamb, baked chicken or
poached salmon with steamed mixed vegetables. By the time
coffee and dessert were served, she gave Shumba a look which
said *rescue me!*

Shumba registered Kenyon's look of desperation and shot her
dining neighbor a warning glare. Perceptively, he straightened,
nodded, and inched away from her.

Dinner concluded, everyone filed out of the dining room and
returned to the living room to enjoy the band, who had set up
their instruments while dinner was being served.

Marshall swung his aunt into a smooth dance step to the melodious strains of "Red Sails In The Sunset," her favorite song.

The band of six continued with a series of slow-dance numbers, and Kenyon found herself in Shumba's arms, her cheek
pressed to his solid shoulder.

She reveled in the slim hardness of his body and the deceptive
strength in his strong fingers cradling her waist. Her left hand
moved from his shoulder to the nape of his neck, her fingers
grazing the wealth of braids falling down his back. Her hand
tightened slightly on his nape and he gasped, his breath hot
against her ear.

Shumba pulled her closer until they were cemented from
shoulders to knees. He wanted her fused to him, he wanted to
be inside of her, he wanted them as one.

Images of making love to Kenyon surfaced, and he was unable
to conceal his growing desire as his maleness scorched her flesh
through the fabric of her dress.

He wanted her! She *had* to know that he wanted her. Kenyon
was like no other woman he'd ever known. Just a glance, just a
slight touch, and his body responded to her as if he had no control
over it.

Kenyon felt his hardness and her own heat growing in the

hidden place between her thighs. She couldn't walk away and leave him on the dance floor. Not in his aroused state.

Shifting slightly, she maneuvered her lower body until there was a modicum of space between them. "Shumba," she whispered hoarsely.

"I know." There was a wealth of desperation in the two words of acknowledgment.

The reveling continued for another two hours, everyone drinking and dancing. Kenyon was more than relieved when she danced with some of the other men, where there was no repeat of what she had experienced with Shumba.

At ten o'clock Shelby surreptitiously disappeared, and Marshall graciously informed everyone that his wife, given her condition, had retired for the evening, and within the next hour most of the others prepared to take their own leave.

Naomi thanked each of her friends for helping her celebrate another year of life, and she promised to return what had become a tradition among the group of lifelong associates.

Kenyon followed Naomi up the staircase as both women made their way to the bedrooms set up for them.

"Good night and happy birthday, Naomi," she said, smiling at the older woman.

"Good night, child," Naomi returned, waving.

Kenyon walked into her bedroom and closed the door. The space was as charming as the rest of the house. A thoroughly modern structure was decorated with blending of a mix of styles. Queen Anne-style chairs with glass-topped, very classic modern tables and antique quilts as wall hangings blended harmoniously to make the entire structure appear lived-in.

The colors of pistachio-green and white predominated her bedroom—from the striped wallpaper to the pale green carpet and the white eyelet comforter over celery-hued sheets and pillowcases.

White wicker furniture created a country ambience and was complemented by colorful green-and-white patterned cushions on a rocker and footstool.

And in that swift moment Kenyon wanted with Shumba what

Shelby had with Marshall. She wanted a home filled with the items she treasured from her past, and she wanted her own belly filled with a child impatient to be born; she wanted Shumba as her husband and the father of her children. And she wanted him more than she'd ever wanted something in her life.

Walking over to the floor-to-ceiling Palladian window, she stared out at the blackness of the night. She could barely make out the tiny lights from faraway structures situated on the bluff overlooking the Hudson River. The sky was cloudy and without the illumination of stars or a moon.

A sadness settled over her, and she knew it had been a mistake to come to Naomi Morrow's party with him. They couldn't recapture their past or the depth of feelings they once shared.

The physical attraction was still alive—it had been apparent from their first encounter, but that was all they had. And Kenyon was mature enough to know that no relationship could survive if based solely on sex.

Nine

Bright sunlight streamed in through the windows, warming Kenyon's face as she slept soundly. She lay on her side, her tousled hair falling over her forehead. Her face was scrubbed clean of makeup, and she looked very young and vulnerable.

Shumba stood at her bedside, watching as she slept, his gaze fixed on the large stones in her pierced lobes. It was as if he was looking at a stranger for the first time.

The diamonds in her ears were at least two carats each. When he'd dated her, he'd offered to buy her jewelry for her birthday or Christmas, but she had balked at the offer. She had accepted the diamond ring for their engagement, and she returned it when she told him she couldn't marry him because she didn't know him anymore.

Who had given her the earrings?

How could he have slept with Kenyon and not known her? How many secrets had she hidden from him?

She never mentioned her grandfather's paintings nor the antique furnishings in her Central Park West apartment

And if they married, would she have ever revealed them to him?

Sitting down on the edge of the bed, he shook her gently. She came awake immediately and sat up. The sheet and blanket covering her body fell to her lap, revealing the bodice to her nightgown made entirely of pale peach lace.

Shumba felt as if the breath had been sucked out of his lungs as he stared at the outline of her breasts through the sheer fabric.

Seeing the direction of his gaze, Kenyon slid down to the mound of pillows cradling her shoulders and pulled the sheet up to her throat. "What time is it?"

"Nine thirty," he croaked painfully.

She frowned. Shumba wore a faded sweatshirt with a pair of equally faded jeans. "Why did you let me sleep so late?"

The ache in his groin was unbearable, and his control snapped. "If you'd slept with me, then I would've gotten you up earlier."

"That's where you're wrong. I don't sleep with you."

"But you did," he shot back.

"Yes, I did. But there were a lot of things I used to do that I don't do now."

Shumba inhaled deeply, then let out his breath slowly. He didn't want to fight with Kenyon all he wanted to do was hold her and love her.

He reached for her, but she pulled away. "Don't, Kenyon. Please, kitten."

She wanted him to love her the way he used to love her. She didn't want to fall into bed with him—that she could do with any man—even Jesse.

"What do you want from me, Shumba? It can't be my body."

"You're right, kitten. It's not your body." He wanted her body, her future *and* her for life.

Kenyon pushed her hair behind her left ear, smiling. She was relieved. He didn't want her just for her body. "Then it's friendship?"

Shumba ran the fingers of both hands through his braided hair. He wanted to shake her until she was breathless. He wanted to tell her that he loved her, but he was frightened; what he didn't want was to ever experience her rejection again.

Lowering his hands, he nodded slowly. "Yes, Kenyon, friendship."

Her smile was dazzling. "Well, friend, if you want me to go swimming with you, then let me get up and put something on that's more appropriate for the task than this nightgown."

Shumba left the bed and walked to the door. "I'll wait outside for you."

Kenyon waited until the door closed behind him then left the bed. She went into an adjoining bath and splashed water on her face and brushed her teeth, then eased her body into a flame-red tank suit and concealed her hair under a bright yellow Speedo latex cap.

Crossing the bedroom and opening the door, she saw Shumba sitting on the carpeted hall floor, waiting. He rose fluidly to his feet and extended his hand.

They walked the length of the hallway, hand in hand, and down the curving staircase in complete silence. Skylights and glass panels along the cathedral ceilings let in the brilliant sunlight throughout the large modern structure designed with connecting buildings.

Shumba led her down the same hallway which led to the greenhouse, but didn't go through the door leading to the tropical oasis in the middle of a White Plains, New York, suburb. They had entered an exercise and weight room.

He smiled at her perplexed expression. "I thought you'd want to loosen up before swimming."

Suddenly it all came back to Kenyon. She recalled the time she and Francis had taken an impromptu four-day trip to Puerto Rico to rejuvenate their sagging spirits after a frantic two weeks of trading where stock prices fell steadily for eighteen consecutive days.

They'd flown from New York late one Thursday evening and arrived in San Juan at midnight. They checked into a private villa and slept for hours. The next day they worked out in an exercise room, swam in a pool, then gave their exhausted bodies over to the expert care of a masseuse.

It had taken only four days, but they returned to New York and their high-pressured positions healed and more in love than before. Two days later Francis had proposed marriage, and she had accepted.

Her dark gaze was steady. "I'll loosen up in the pool."

Shumba shrugged his broad shoulders under his faded sweatshirt. "Suit yourself." He turned on his heel, his bare feet silent, and strode to the door.

Kenyon followed him, and they entered the building housing an Olympic-sized indoor pool. She stared at the Persian-blue tiles surrounding the pool while Shumba shed his shirt and pants. His long, lean body cleaved the water in a nearly splashless entry before she dipped her foot in the water, testing its temperature.

She slid down into the lukewarm water, floating on her back, then turning over and leisurely swimming the length of the pool.

They floated and frolicked in the water like playful brown seals, splashing the other when they came too close. Images of their passionate Puerto Rican escapade was apparent whenever their gazes met, and after a while they both realized that what they'd had could never be repeated.

Kenyon and Shumba returned to New York City late Sunday afternoon without Naomi, who had elected to spend a few more days with her nephew and his wife before coming back to her Upper East Side apartment.

Kenyon had left her telephone number with Shelby, promising that she would arrange for the curator to set up a showing of her grandfather's paintings for a late-spring exhibit at the Studio Museum in Harlem.

She and Shumba were silent on the return drive, and it wasn't until he saw her to her apartment door that she broke the silence, thanking him for a wonderful weekend.

"Will I see you New Year's Eve at my place?" Shumba asked as she unlocked the door.

Glancing at him over her shoulder, she smiled. "Yes. Jesse and I will be there."

Leaning over, he pressed a kiss to her silken cheek. "Have a wonderful Christmas, a happy Kwanzaa, and give my love to your grandmother."

Her large dark gaze locked with his golden one. He disturbed her in so many ways she couldn't begin to list them all. She loved him, he frightened her, the nightmares of him rejecting her, and the passionate, smoldering desire for him that refused to fade.

"I will. And . . . thank you, Shumba."

She opened and closed the door and he was gone.

Dorothy Kenyon stood on the wraparound porch of the spacious white Colonial structure with black shuttered windows, waiting for her granddaughter to emerge from the taxi. She'd spent the past two hours peering through the lacy panels covering the living room windows, anticipating her arrival.

A gentle smile creased her smooth, dark face as a network of tiny wrinkles crinkled her alert brown eyes. Pulling a cashmere sweater tighter around her chest, she moved closer to the top step of the porch and waved at the driver opening the back door of the taxi.

"Good afternoon, Albert."

Albert Henderson helped Kenyon from his battered automobile, then turned and doffed his equally tattered cap to one of the oldest year-round residents on the island. "Good afternoon, Miss Dorothy. I brought your grandbaby in safe and sound."

"So I see, Albert."

Dorothy's smile widened when she finally saw Kenyon. Noticing her granddaughter's expertly cut black hair lifting slightly away from her beautiful face from a cold ocean breeze and recognizing the elegant cut of her wool coat, she felt an inexplicable feeling of pride. Kenyon was the mirror image of her mother at the same age. Dr. Carolyn Kenyon-Bryant had drowned, along with her husband, in a boating accident. Drs. William and Carolyn Bryant were only thirty-five years of age at the time of their death, leaving an orphaned ten-year-old daughter in the care of her maternal grandmother and grandfather.

Kenyon, arms extended, raced up the porch steps and hugged her grandmother. Burying her face against Dorothy's neck, she inhaled her familiar gardenia-scented cologne.

"It's always nice coming back, Grammie."

Dorothy patted Kenyon's head. "It's good to have you back home. Come on in out of the cold, baby girl." She waved to

Albert, who left Kenyon's single piece of luggage and a large shopping bag filled with gaily wrapped packages on the porch and had returned to his taxi. He returned her wave through the open taxi window and drove away.

Kenyon stepped into a living room filled with furnishings and memories from her childhood. It was in this room that she'd learned that her parents' bodies were found washed up on the beach off Nantucket Sound after having been missing for three days.

It was in this same living room where her grandmother had given her the grandest sweet-sixteen party ever celebrated in Oak Bluffs since the early 1900s, when affluent African-Americans began purchasing large tracts of land on Martha's Vineyard

It was in this living room where she and her grandmother had planned a Christmas Eve candlelight wedding ceremony for her and Francis Humphries.

And it was in this very living room where she'd found comfort and solace from her grandmother after she told Francis that she couldn't marry him because she didn't know who he was anymore.

A large live pine tree stood off-center in the spacious room, waiting patiently for the heirloom tree decorations that were pulled out every Christmas for nearly sixty years.

Kenyon smiled at Dorothy. "I'm going to change into something comfortable, then you can tell me all about all the Vineyard gossip I've missed since my last visit."

"There's not too much gossip going around lately. Just that Hamilton Reid's grandson moved back last fall. You do remember him, Kenyon?"

She remembered him too well. Her grandmother had attempted to play matchmaker for years, but Kenyon never liked him well enough to go out with him.

"Yes, Grammie, I remember Edward."

"He's such a fine young man."

"He's a bore, Grammie."

Dorothy puffed up her ample bosom, reminding Kenyon of

a ruffled hen. "Must I remind you that he's a very eligible bachelor?"

"Good for him," she mumbled under her breath.

Dorothy's jaw dropped slightly before she pursed her lips tightly. She could not understand why Kenyon continued to resist getting married. So many of the young men who vacationed on the Vineyard during the summer asked about her. And whenever she returned home for her annual month-long summer vacation, she never attended any of the social gatherings or accepted a date from any of the single men who seemed genuinely interested in seeing her socially.

Her granddaughter had changed, and there were times when Dorothy felt that she didn't know who she was.

Changing the subject, she said, "I just happened to make a batch of gingerbread cookies this afternoon."

"What else did you just happen to make, Grammie?" A teasing smile softened Kenyon's mouth.

"Chicken and dumplings and smothered cabbage."

"Just a little spur of the moment thing?"

"Of course, baby girl."

"If that's the case, then I'd better get settled in quickly."

She retrieved her luggage and shopping bag with the gifts she had bought for her grandmother from the porch and made her way up the staircase to her bedroom to unpack and change her clothes.

Kenyon placed another piece of seasoned wood on the andiron, watching until the wood caught the burning embers from a blackened one before replacing the screen around the fireplace.

She returned to sit on the large camelback sofa with her grandmother, moving over until their shoulders touched.

"It's beautiful," Dorothy whispered as if she didn't want to disturb the mood.

They had decorated the tree, and this year she had opted to let

Kenyon stand on the stepladder to hang the many delicate orna-
ments on the upper branches.

She was in remarkably good health at eighty-two, but Dorothy
didn't want to tempt fate by losing her balance and falling. It
was only after Kenyon's insistence that she'd hired someone to
do the heavy work around the house and yard. However, she still
cooked for herself, took her daily two-mile walk, and attended
church services every Sunday. She probably had a busier social
life than her granddaughter.

Kenyon's gaze swept around the darkened space. She had
turned on the tree lights, lit a fire in the fireplace, and turned off
all of the lamps. The result was shimmering, flickering pinpoints
of light highlighting the faded Aubusson rug on the wood floor,
the framed portraits and landscape paintings of Ellis Kenyon's,
and the original furnishings that were shipped to the island to
decorate the house several years before her grandmother's birth.

"It's so quiet, so peaceful," she whispered, pulling her wool
sock-covered feet up under her.

Dorothy laid her head on Kenyon's shoulder, while pulling a
knitted afghan over their knees. The coronet of white braids
pinned on the crown of her head brushed her granddaughter's
ear.

"Don't you relax in New York?"

Kenyon chuckled softly. "Of course I get to relax. Remember,
I work for myself."

"Your grandfather worked for himself, and that man did not
get to relax until he died."

"Believe me, Grammie, I relax."

Dorothy patted her hand. "I must admit that you look well."

"I am well."

There was a comfortable silence, only the sound of crackling
wood and an occasional shower of falling embers breaking the
hush.

"What really happened between you and Francis?" Dorothy
asked quietly.

Pulling back, Kenyon stared at Dorothy's distinctive profile,
suddenly aware of how much she resembled her maternal grand-

mother. They shared the same dark brown skin, generous mouth and dimpled chin. Her eyes and nose were a softer, more feminine version of her late-father's.

"Why ask now, Grammie? Why after all of these years?"

"Because I'm not the meddling old woman you think I am. You called off your wedding, saying you weren't ready for marriage, and I had no choice but to believe you. Now I'm not so certain.

"I see a change in you, Kenyon, and what I see I don't like. You're more beautiful than you've ever been, but it's all surface. A stylish hairstyle and elegant clothes make for a nice presentation, but that's all it is, baby girl. Your smile is sad, and your laugh is hollow and brittle.

"Your mama did not get the chance to live a long life, but what she did do was live a full life. She wanted to be a doctor like her granddaddy, and she studied hard to become one; she fell in love, married, and had the child she always wanted. I grieved for years after losing my only child because I always thought that parents aren't suppose to bury their children but the other way around. One day your granddaddy told me it was time to stop grieving because our baby had gotten everything she wanted out of life, and when she died she had found that happiness she always sought.

"And what I don't want to do is leave this world knowing that my grandbaby hasn't found her happiness."

Hot, wet tears flowed down Kenyon's cheeks as she listened to Dorothy's monologue. Her grandmother was right. She had changed, and she hadn't found the happiness she walked away from four years ago.

Softly and hesitantly at first, she told Dorothy everything: Francis resigning his position, letting his hair grow, his dietary restrictions, and finally changing his name. She then revealed her reaction to his transformation and how deceived she had been made to feel.

Dorothy patted her back gently. "He didn't deceive you, Kenyon. You've deceived yourself because whatever Francis chooses to call himself, eat, or style his hair, the fact remains that you still love him."

"How could I've brought him back here with his hair standing all over his head in little plaits?"

"The same way you brought him here with his hair cut close to his scalp."

Kenyon pulled away from Dorothy, staring at her as if she had never seen her before. "You—Oak Bluffs proverbial snob! Are you saying that you would've accepted a dreadlock-wearing artist as your granddaughter's husband? Whatever happened to your researching every young man's genealogy to discover whether he had the 'acceptable pedigree'?"

Dorothy rested both hands on her hips. "I am not a snob, Kenyon Bryant. I just wanted to make certain that the boys you dated weren't from a family of thieves or murderers. I needed to know if they were decent and God-fearing. It had nothing to do with whether they were Baptist or Methodist, or whether they earned their money by sitting behind a desk giving orders, or working bending their backs taking orders."

She had never seen her grandmother so angry. "I . . . I didn't know, Grammie." Her voice was soft and quivering. "You didn't think I saw you, but I did when you used to sit in your bedroom holding my mother's photograph, rocking and crying. Your face was so sad that I told myself that I would never do anything that would put that look on your face again."

"I was grieving, Kenyon. Everyone's entitled to a period of grieving."

"And I've had mine."

Dorothy hugged her. "Do you still love him?"

"More than ever."

"You're seeing him?"

Kenyon cradled Dorothy gently and revealed all that had happened since she was reunited with Shumba Naaman more than two weeks ago at a New York City art gallery.

Dorothy's smile was mysterious as she listened to Kenyon, recalling how much her own life paralleled her granddaughter's.

"Ellis wasn't the man I was supposed to marry," she stated,

shocking Kenyon with this disclosure. "My very proper physician father didn't think very much of artists or actors. He called them a 'degenerate lot.' But I loved and believed in Ellis. A month before I was to be married, I eloped with Ellis."

"Grammie!"

"You heard me," Dorothy confirmed with a wide smile. "It was the best decision I ever made in my life. My father wouldn't speak to me until after your mother was born. He came to my house, begging to see his granddaughter, but I wouldn't let him in. It was Ellis who used to go behind my back and take Carolyn to my parents' house. I didn't find out about their secret excursions until your mother started babbling about seeing Grampa. Then I had it out with Ellis, but it took him with his calm thinking to make me see being stubborn wasn't in the best interest of our daughter having a normal, loving relationship with her grandparents."

"What are you saying, Grammie?"

"If you want your young man, then go after him."

Ten

Kenyon had selected her red outfit with the greatest care. The Chinese-style dress with a mandarin collar and long sleeves floated over her slim, curved body like a ribbon of watered silk. She'd secured her upswept black hair with a number of antique jeweled pins that she'd received from her grandmother as one of her Christmas gifts.

Jesse Parker had merely raised his eyebrows in astonishment when he'd removed her coat after they arrived at Shumba's SoHo loft. He found it hard to believe that Kenyon Bryant could improve on her stunning appearance—but she had.

A wry smile touched his attractive mouth. She may have come to Shumba's New Year's Eve/Kwanzaa celebration with him, but their host was the lucky man.

The more than two dozen people gathered at the apartment participated in a combination *karamu,* or feast for the sixth day of Kwanzaa, and a New Year's Eve celebration that became more festive as the year neared its end.

Kenyon saw a few people she'd met when she'd initially dated Francis, but most of them didn't recognize her; and aside from Shumba greeting her and Jesse when they first arrived, she had not gotten the opportunity to speak to him alone.

A roaring fire, kept hot by an inexhaustible stack of firewood, added to the heat of gyrating bodies keeping tempo to taped music floating throughout the duplex apartment. A large brass wall clock, occupying a space under the open stairway, kept time, indicating the minutes and seconds before the new year was ushered in. In less than ninety seconds, it would be a new year, a time for old memories and of those new ones to come.

Shumba weaved his way through the throng, his gaze fixed on Kenyon. He had spent the past week thinking about her, both his mind and body agonizing over her absence.

If she had been in New York, he knew he would've come to see her—uninvited. But her going to Martha's Vineyard had changed everything. He couldn't afford the time to seek her out, because he was nearing the completion date to have the jewelry samples for the European dealer who wanted to duplicate his designs for several wealthy clients.

Not only had Shumba designed certain pieces for the overseas dealer, but he also had received a commitment from Cartier to market his latest creations.

His career was at its zenith—everything had come together at the right time and place. Professionally, for the second time in his life, he had achieved ultimate success.

But it was not his career that he was concerned with—it was his personal life. And there was only one person he'd always wanted to share his life with, and that was Kenyon Bryant.

He'd spent most of the night watching her as she pressed her slender, silk-clad body close to Jesse Parker's, a slowly, steady-building resentment welling up in him.

"Twenty seconds!" someone called out.

Shumba's braided hair whipped around his face as he turned his head and stared at the clock. He had less than twenty seconds to get to Kenyon before the beginning of a new year.

"Excuse me, excuse me," he mumbled, forcibly pushing several people aside.

"Five, four, three, two!" chanted the crowd. "One! Happy New Year!"

The moment the clock struck the new year, Shumba found himself trapped in the grip of a tall, slender woman who pulled his head down and covered his mouth with hers in a single swift motion. In an attempt to free himself from her possessive grip, she stumbled, and he held her tightly to keep her from falling.

Kenyon, stunned, watched as Shumba pressed the woman

closer to his chest, deepening their kiss. Successfully concealing her pain, she turned to Jesse.

Moving fluidly into his embrace, she lifted her face and pressed her lips to his. For a brief moment she relived the kiss she had shared with Shumba, offering Jesse what she had offered Shumba. Jesse, caught off guard by her unexpected passion, returned the kiss as his tongue parted her lips.

As quickly as it had begun, it was over. She pulled back, her eyes wide with shock, her face burning with shame.

"Take me home, Jesse." Her voice was a tremulous whisper.

He placed a hand on her shoulder. "Kenyon."

"Now," she demanded.

Kenyon stood at the elevator door while Jesse retrieved their coats, trembling. How could she have been such a fool? She had come to Shumba's house because she'd promised him she would come. She also came because she wanted to tell him that she still loved him, and if she had to beg him to give her another chance she would—however, her timing was wrong and the setting was wrong.

A determined look glistened in her eyes. She would not fail the next time.

She and Jesse left without saying goodbye to their host, garnering a taxi after waiting on the frigid New York City sidewalk for more than fifteen minutes.

Jesse held her gloved hand protectively within his until they reached her apartment building. "I'm not going to come up with you," he informed her. "I have another stop to make before I go home tonight."

Kenyon smiled and nodded. "Thank you, Jesse." Leaning forward, she kissed his mouth tenderly. "Happy New Year."

"Happy New Year, honey."

The concierge opened the door to the taxi and helped her out. She thanked him and strolled to the entrance of the building and into the lobby to the bank of elevators.

It wasn't until she had taken off her clothes, removed her makeup, and pulled a nightgown over her naked body did she realize that she had unconsciously made a New Year's resolution: she was going to become Mrs. Shumba Naaman.

Kenyon replaced the portable telephone in its cradle, a slight frown forming between her eyes. The realtor for the owner of the Harlem properties said his client would not lower his asking price.

"Damn!" she mumbled, flipping a curl of black hair behind her left ear. There had to be a way to put a little pressure on him. All she was asking, on behalf of III-D-Tee, was a 10 percent reduction.

The phone rang and she picked up quickly, thinking maybe the realtor had changed his mind.

"Kenyon Bryant."

"Happy New Year, kitten."

"Shumba," she whispered. The new year was a week old.

"You and Parker left the party so quickly the other night that I never got a chance to wish you a happy New Year."

"Jesse had somewhere else to go," she half lied.

"Are you busy right now?"

"Not really. What I'm trying to do is figure out a way to get someone to come down on the price of a parcel of property."

"Where's the property?" Shumba questioned.

"Harlem."

"Business or residential?"

"Both." Kenyon bit down on her lower lip. She could almost see the wheels turning in Shumba's head. "He owes a lot in back taxes."

"Why didn't you say that. Give me the block, lot and section, and I'll call you back."

"What are you going to do?"

"I still have my contacts on the 'street.' Give me the info, kitten."

She read off the numbers to Shumba, her heart racing. Within minutes he'd reverted back to the trader who could shift millions of dollars around the world while memorizing every transaction he'd ever made.

"I owe you again," she stated quietly.

"And one of these days, I'm going to call in my chips," he teased. "Let me see what I can do for you."

"Thanks."

"Don't thank me yet because what I may ask from you, you may not be willing to give."

"Try me."

"I'll talk to you later."

She hung up and stared out the window across Central Park. Closing her eyes, she exhaled, reliving the soothing sound of Shumba's voice. She'd been so caught up with her work that she thought of him only when she was in bed.

Opening her eyes, her gaze fell on the single sheet of paper Mark Crayton had faxed to her earlier that morning. He needed the name of an artist who could design a series of promotional ads for three of his groups. The groups were scheduled to tour the States and Canada in a fifteen-city summer concert extravaganza.

"Shumba!" she said aloud. If he accepted the assignment, then she would have paid him back for the gold statue. She would have to come up with something else if he was able to get the realtor to agree to lowering the price on the Harlem property.

She did not have to wait long for Shumba to get back to her. He called, saying he was coming up to see her. What he had to tell her could not be repeated over the telephone.

Kenyon opened the door, and Shumba stepped into the foyer, his broad shoulders filling out the doorway. The smile on her face revealed her deep feelings for him, and she fought the overwhelming desire to fall into his arms, while making a fool of herself when she confessed that she loved him and had never stopped loving him.

She extended her hand. "Let me hang up your jacket."

"It's all right. I'll hang it up." He hung the supple tobacco-colored leather jacket in the closet near the door as Kenyon surveyed his black wool turtleneck sweater and matching tailored wool slacks. He had secured his braided hair in the leather thong, and she much preferred that he leave it to fall randomly over his shoulders and down his back.

"I've prepared some tea. Would you like some?"

"Yes, please." He rubbed his hands together. "There's a bite in the air, and I wouldn't be surprised if we get some snow before the day's over."

"Have a seat in the living room. I'll be right back with the tea."

She disappeared into the kitchen, berating herself for sounding parochial and stilted. *I've prepared some tea. Would you like some?* She hadn't sounded that sophomoric since she was seventeen.

Kenyon measured a scoop of loose tea leaves into a hand-painted teapot with boiling water, then set it on a tray with two matching cups and saucers.

She felt the source of heat, but could not turn around. Shumba stood behind her, his chest pressed against her back.

"Do you need any help?"

She swallowed several times. "No."

He didn't move. "Your clients can offer for the property. The owner is willing to drop the price 10 percent."

She placed the tray on a countertop and spun around to face him. "You did it! How did you pull it off? How can I thank you?"

Amusement flickered in the gaze that met hers. "Yes, I did it. And to answer your second question, I contacted an old friend who's with the City Collector's office. His files turned up a sizable tax lien against the property you're interested in. He made an *unauthorized* call, alerting the owner that the city was going to take over his property within thirty days. The rest you know.

"Now to answer your third question." Lowering his head, and the warmth of his breath sweeping over her mouth, he said, "You can begin to thank me with this." He brushed his lips over hers teasingly, setting her nerves on edge.

"And this," he continued, his voice dropping an octave. His mouth moved to her throat, and continued its downward exploration to the opening of her oversized man's shirt

Kenyon pressed her palms against his sweatered chest. She couldn't think with his mouth on her bared flesh. "Shumba," she moaned.

"What, kitten?"

"What . . . what are you doing?"

One arm tightened around her waist and brought her flush against his middle. Raising his head, he stared down at her parted lips, the gold in his eyes glittering like brilliant points of sunlight.

"I'm taking payment for services rendered," he said, giving her a half smile.

Her hands slid up to his shoulders, and she locked her fingers together behind his neck. Tilting her head back, she returned his smile. "I have a counteroffer," she stated softly.

Shumba shifted his eyebrows, his smile fading. "What is it?"

"I need an artist to design several promotional ads for three singing groups. Are you interested?"

His arms dropped, and she felt his loss immediately. Reaching up, he covered her hands and extracted them from his neck.

"What exactly do you need?"

"I want you to design a logo, select the colors, and create a theme based on their very different singing styles."

"When you do need them?"

"As soon as possible. They're all touring this summer."

Shumba hesitated, measuring Kenyon for a moment. He wanted to make love to her while she wanted to talk business. But if it meant being with her, then he was more than willing to talk business.

"Do you have a press kit on them?"

"Yes." Turning, she picked up the tray and handed it to him. "If you take this into the library, I'll get the information you need."

He bowed slightly from the waist. "Yes, ma'am." Chuckling, he walked out of the large full-service kitchen and into the library.

Placing the tray with the teapot and cups on the Biedermeier-style center table, he pushed aside several hardcover books. Again he was astounded by the furnishings in Kenyon's apartment. Elegant and tasteful. Just like the woman.

He walked over to the floor-to-ceiling window and stared out at the bare trees sweeping across the park. Night had fallen, and streetlights shimmered eerily on roadways and sidewalks, creating unusual and unfriendly shadows. But inside Kenyon's apartment he found warmth and safety.

"Shumba."

He turned at the sound of his name. Kenyon stood at the mahogany double doors, holding a stack of papers against her breasts.

She didn't move as he crossed the small space and stood over her. The soft, sweet smell of her hair and body floated up to him as he tried analyzing the mysterious look in her large dark eyes.

His right hand came up slowly, and his thumb outlined the shape of her sensual mouth before his fingers swept through her hair.

The fingers of Kenyon's free hand curved around his wrist, and she held on to Shumba's arm, squeezing gently. She was tired of fighting her own emotions, she was tired of fighting him.

He swept her up into his arms, and the files she'd cradled to her chest floated to the carpeted floor unnoticed.

"May I, Kenyon?" he asked hoarsely.

She buried her face against his chest, inhaling the musky scent of his cologne. She wanted his warmth, his strength and the passion he'd always wrung from her.

"What?" She didn't even recognize her own voice.

His gaze, riveted on her face, moved slowly over her body. He didn't want Kenyon to see his fear, his indecision. *Please don't reject me,* he prayed silently. *Not again.*

Placing a slender hand alongside his lean jaw, she smiled. "What, Shumba?"

"May I make love to you?"

An intense awareness of their strong physical needs raced from Shumba to Kenyon, heating their blood and increasing their passions.

Closing her eyes, she nodded. "Yes."

Relief shook him from head to toe, and Shumba's broad shoulders were heaving as he breathed in deeply. "Where's your bedroom?"

She opened her eyes and her heart lurched. In the brief second when her gaze met Shumba's, she thought she saw a glimmer of love.

"I'll show you."

Eleven

Shumba carried Kenyon into her bedroom, not seeing the romantic floral chintz bed covering or peach-and-white striped silk drapery in the golden lamplight.

He held her aloft with one arm while pulling back the comforter. Placing her on the bed, his body following, he kissed her tenderly. There was no need to rush—they had four years to make up for.

Slowly, methodically, he unbuttoned her shirt, baring skin as he went from her throat to her hips. His fingers fanned out over her flat belly, and she inhaled sharply.

"I won't hurt you, kitten. I won't hurt you," he repeated, crooning softly.

Kenyon nodded and smiled. "I know you won't, darling."

Shumba removed her shirt, socks, and leggings. He stared at the swell of her breasts above the lace cups of her bra, the narrowness of her waist and the womanly flare of her hips.

Reaching over, he tugged her silk panties gently off her hips and down her long legs. Her bra followed and Kenyon lay naked before his gaze.

He rose from the bed and stripped off his own clothes, watching Kenyon as she watched him. She chewed her lower lip while clenching and unclenching her hands. Was she nervous, or had she changed her mind? Turning back to his slacks on a chair, he withdrew a foil packet from the pocket and placed it on the bedside table.

"Turn off the light and come to bed, Shumba."

Needing no further urging, he flicked off the lamp and lay down beside Kenyon.

She turned to him, draping a leg over his thighs. The feel of her nakedness, the press of her breasts against his arm, and the heat emanating from the area between her legs broke his control. He moved over her, kissing her deeply while his hands explored her silken flesh.

Kenyon felt her blood heat and course through her veins like heated steel as she returned his kisses. She curved into the hard angles of his body and gasped. His hair-roughened chest sent sparks of fire through her breasts, bringing the nipples to a pebbly hardness.

She took her time rediscovering Shumba's body. What had been solid bulk was now lean muscle. Closing her eyes in the darkness, she memorized every line, every hollow of his physique.

Shumba touched Kenyon everywhere but there—the hot, pulsing, wet area between her thighs. He wanted the fiery passion she'd aroused in him to last. However, her hands were everywhere—scorching his back, buttocks and chest. Her delicate fingers sent electric shocks through his groin where the blood pooled heavily in his manhood, and unable to prolong the spiraling passion racing out of control he reached for the foil pouch on the table.

Kenyon welcomed him into her body, gasping as he filled her with his hardness. She set a rhythm and he followed, rolling his hips heavily against hers. The cadence changed, quickening, and together they found a tempo that made them one.

Their passionate lovemaking swept away the pain, disappointment and the resentment of years past. All that mattered was now; all that mattered was the two of them.

Together they climbed the heights of ecstasy, lingering on the precipice until they tumbled back to earth and reality.

Shumba withdrew and Kenyon turned her back, pulling the sheet up over her moist body. Her racing heart slowed as she sucked gulps of air into her labored lungs. She closed her eyes and slept the sleep of a sated lover.

* * *

Kenyon woke up at dawn, alone. Flicking on the bedside lamp, she stared at the imprint of a head on the pillow beside her own. Bile rose in her throat when she realized that Shumba hadn't even bothered to wake her before he left.

Her nightmare about him leaving her was not a nightmare after all. It was déjà vu.

Pulling her knees to her chest, she squared her shoulders. Well, it wasn't as if they both didn't get what they wanted. And hadn't she been just a little curious to know whether Shumba was as good in bed as Francis?

She had her answer. Shumba was better than Francis.

Pushing back the sheet, she swung her legs over the side of the bed. She took a step, then stopped. The tenderness between her thighs was a poignant reminder of what she'd shared with her former lover as she proceeded, taking gingerly steps, on her way to the bathroom. She was certain that a leisurely soak in the whirlpool bath would help soothe her sore muscles.

She flicked on the bathroom light, and then she saw it. Taped to the mirror was a piece of paper she recognized as her business letterhead.

She pulled it off the mirror, reading Shumba's neat print: *Kitten—I'm sorry I couldn't stay the night. I'm scheduled to be on a flight to London at 10:00 A.M. I'll call you when I arrive. Love—S.*

P.S. I have the press kits.

A relieved smile crinkled her eyes. He hadn't walked out on her. She reread the sentence: *I'll call you when I arrive.*

She would wait for his call.

Kenyon's anticipation turned to annoyance before shifting to apprehension. Shumba had been gone a week, and she hadn't heard a word from him. The tapes on her answering machines contained messages—but none from Shumba Naaman.

At first she thought he had forgotten her. Had he become *that* engrossed in his buying and selling of artifacts? Had he embraced the out-of-sight out-of-mind ideology?

One night she awoke suddenly, thinking that perhaps something had happened to him. What if he couldn't call her?

She waited until what she considered a reasonable time and called his apartment. The answering machine clicked on after two rings, politely telling the caller to leave a message and it would be returned. She hung up without leaving a message.

One thing she would not do and that was chase him. She had never pursued any man—not even Francis Humphries.

A second week passed without a word from him, and Kenyon's stubborn pride wavered. What if something had happened to Shumba, and he couldn't call her? What if he lay sick or injured in some European hospital?

The questions and doubts plagued her constantly as she set up a meeting to begin the process of purchasing the block of property for III-D-Tee.

She had set up a holding company for the transaction, and she had been given power of attorney as the purchasing agent.

The closing date was set for Friday, February 13.

Kenyon walked into the office of what once had been one of the most powerful landlords in Manhattan. She glanced at the furnishings in the reception area, noticing that what had been opulence was now shabby elegance. Overzealous purchasing, rising taxes, a falling economy and a shift from the wretched excess of the eighties had toppled a mighty real estate empire.

She was directed into a conference room by a young secretary who appeared barely out of her teens. Her long acrylic nails were airbrushed with every color in the spectrum.

An elderly man rose from his sitting position behind a worn

rosewood conference table. A warm smile revealed aging yellow teeth.

"Good morning, Miss Bryant. It may be Friday the thirteenth, but it's a lucky day for my client."

Kenyon shook his proffered hand. "And for mine, Mr. Kirby."

John Kirby and Kenyon spent the next three hours reading and signing documents. It took another half hour for her to draw checks for past due taxes and monies for the various escrow accounts.

John offered to buy her lunch, and she accepted his invitation. She had come to respect the man who was a throwback from another era where deals were cemented with a handshake and not high-powered lawyers over high-powered lunches.

She and John said their goodbyes on the sidewalk outside a restaurant on Park Avenue South. At the last moment he leaned forward and kissed her cheek.

His still bright-blue eyes twinkled mischievously. "That's for Valentine's Day."

Her gloved fingers touched her cheek where he'd kissed her. "Thank you." Leaning down, she returned the kiss to his leathered jaw. "Goodbye, Mr. Kirby."

Making her way to the bus stop, Kenyon bit down on her lower lip. Valentine's Day. She had forgotten about the holiday the way Shumba had forgotten about her. It had more than a month since she last saw or heard from him.

Disappointment had lingered the first two weeks of his absence, but faded. She was an adult, she was mature, and she had her memories of Francis and Shumba.

She rode the uptown bus, staring out the window. Store windows were gaily decorated with red hearts, flowers and banners, reminding lovers of their special day.

Her grandmother's words rushed back to haunt her: *If you want your young man, then go after him.*

Did she want her young man? Did she want Shumba?

Yes, screamed a silent voice. She loved him, and she wanted to spend the rest of her life with him.

She had to get off the bus! Pressing the yellow tape, she stood

p. The driver glanced at her as she rushed down the aisle and aced down the steps.

Kenyon looked around. She was at Sixty-second and Madison Avenue. The gallery—she was only blocks from the art gallery where she met Shumba in mid-December.

She made it to the gallery at the same time a tall, slender blond man locked the door. Waving frantically, she mouthed that she wanted to talk to him.

He unlocked the door and opened it slightly. Dark gray eyes swept appreciably over her face. "We're closed, miss."

"I know, but I wonder if you could tell me about an artist who exhibits here," she said quickly.

"Who?"

"Shumba Naaman."

The man smiled. "What about him?"

"When is he going to exhibit again?"

"Look at the showcase, miss."

The door closed and was locked again, but that didn't matter to Kenyon as she stared at the large white printed sign in the empty window. Shumba Naaman had a showing for the next day.

Twelve

The telephone from the lobby rang shrilly throughout Kenyon's apartment. She picked up the receiver and listened to the concierge's voice. He told her that a Mr. Shumba Naaman wanted to see her.

She hesitated, her heart pumping wildly. She wanted to see him, but on her own terms. She had wanted to be the one to see his shocked expression when she walked into the gallery.

"Send him up."

Pulling the belt to her robe tightly around her waist, she waited by the door.

Three minutes later Shumba strode into the foyer, a wide grin splitting his handsome face.

He thrust a large bouquet of blood-red roses at her. "Happy Valentine's Day, kitten."

Her eyes narrowed as she folded her hands on her hips, refusing to take the flowers. "Don't you dare kitten me, Shumba Naaman. You disappear for a month, and I'm supposed to be your kitten?"

"I left the note saying I would call you when I arrived," he argued, taking in everything about her in one sweeping glance. It was apparent she was preparing to go out. She had curlers in her hair, and her face was made up.

"That was five weeks ago!"

"Exactly, darling. I'm here and I've called."

"What happened when you got to London?"

Realized dawned. "You misunderstood. Not when I arrived in

London, but when I got back." He stared down at the shimmer of tears in her eyes. She thought he'd left her.

"Kenyon, darling, I would never leave you. Not ever."

She flung herself against him, her arms going around his neck. "Why didn't you call me?"

Shumba inhaled the scent of her skin and hair. "I couldn't. If I had, I would've come back. I had to stay and complete my commission."

Pulling back, she smiled up at him, loving everything she saw, everything she felt. "You have a showing tonight."

His gaze lingered on the diamonds in her ears. "Are you going with Jesse Parker?"

"No. I'm going with you because I love you, not Jesse Parker."

Shumba didn't appear surprised at her confession. "I know you do, Kenyon. Parker told me you did."

Her delicate jaw dropped. "He did what!"

"We had a talk—man-to-man. I had to know if there was anything going on between the two of you before I made my move. I'd never go after what belongs to another man."

"I'm not a trophy to be passed around." She tried to sound insulted.

"No, you're not. You're a prize, kitten. My prize. Now, can I implore you to get dressed. I don't want to be late for my own showing."

Kenyon walked into the brightly lit gallery with Shumba, nodding at the owner, who merely raised his pale eyebrows when he saw her.

"Hello, again."

She smiled attractively. "Hello."

Shumba glanced from Kenyon to Hans Gustave. "You two know each other?"

"We've met," they chorused, smiling.

Shumba dropped a kiss on Kenyon's curling hair. "I'll be right back."

Hans took her coat, visually admiring her lithe body in a black sheath as she walked around the gallery, studying several painting on the whitewashed walls.

Her gaze shifted to Shumba as he leaned over a small glass case. His dramatic black attire, towering height and his braided hair rippling down his back sent a wave of erotic pleasure through her body.

He knew she loved him even though he hadn't said that he loved her. That didn't matter anymore. What mattered was that they would never be apart again.

Shumba returned to Kenyon, his right hand reaching into the breast pocket of his unconstructed jacket. Withdrawing a long, flat case he handed it to her. "I want you to wear this for me, Kenyon. Maybe one day it will mean as much to you as your earrings."

She touched her right ear. "These were my mother's. My father gave them to her on their tenth wedding anniversary."

He felt the heat rise in his face. He thought a man had given them to her. A slow smile softened his tense jaw. "I'll have to come up with something quite unique for our tenth anniversary, but I'd like for you to have this for our engagement. That is, if you'll marry me."

Her hands shook slightly as she raised the lid of the black velvet box. Her shaking increased as she stared down at the most exquisite necklace she'd ever seen. Swirls of dull yellow gold were hammered and linked together with two diamond-encrusted interlinking hearts. It had been designed with the look of jewelry from ancient African kingdoms.

"Help me put it on," she urged.

Shumba took the necklace and secured it around her slender neck. "You are the perfect model for the Kenyon Collection, kitten."

Turning slowly in his embrace, she smiled up at him. "You've named it for me."

"I love you that much, kitten."

She closed her eyes and pressed her mouth to his. "And I love you enough to want to spend the rest of my life with you."

Shumba deepened the kiss. "You won't have to worry about that. You will."

They were still in each other's arms when the gallery began filling with the curious, who had come to see the unveiling of Shumba Naaman's new line of jewelry called the Kenyon Collection.

Epilogue

Kenyon turned over to her right, expecting to encounter her husband's hard body but found the space where he had been. Opening her eyes, she stared at the outline of the depression where he had lain next to her throughout the night. A smile touched her lush mouth as she stretched her arms above her head, the flowing sleeves of a sunny yellow silk gown sliding down her slender limbs like fluttering butterflies.

She loathed leaving the warm bed, but she knew she couldn't linger too long before visiting the bathroom. Sitting up, she swung her legs over the side of the bed and slowly made her way to the adjoining bath. It took her less than twenty minutes to complete her morning toilette.

Her chin-length hair secured at the back of her head with an elastic band and her body swathed in a white terry robe, she returned to the bedroom.

A slow smile crinkled her eyes as her gaze met Shumba's. He stood with his back to the window, a profusion of braided hair flowing over his broad shoulders. He extended one arm, and she walked into his embrace.

Tilting her head, she pressed her mouth to his in a tender joining. "What are you hiding behind your back, darling?"

Shumba's sherry-colored eyes studied her face with an agonizing slowness. "I can't get anything past you, can I?"

"No you can't," she replied between soft nibbling kisses.

Pulling his left hand from behind his back, he handed her a single red rose wrapped in cellophane. "Happy Valentine's Day, kitten." Stapled to the clear plastic was an envelope. She arched a questioning eyebrow. "Open it, Kenyon," he urged.

She sat down on a cushioned wicker rocker, raising her bare feet to a matching ottoman. Laying the rose across her lap, she detached the envelope from the cellophane and withdrew a single sheet of paper. The page was filled with Shumba's precise handwriting. She glanced up at him before her gaze returned to the letter:

My Wife, Lover, Friend:

It was one year ago today—on Valentine's Day—that I asked you to share your future with me, and it has been a year filled with more happiness than I could've ever thought possible.

The times I tell you that I love you don't convey the depth of my feelings for you. You are the flame that fires my soul, the peace that soothes my heart, and the woman in whose arms I want to breathe my last breath.

I love you now, I'll love you tomorrow, I'll love you forever.
Shumba.

Tears welled up in her eyes and overflowed, staining her flawless cheeks. Shumba walked to her side and knelt down beside the rocker. Lifting her right hand, he fastened a delicate gold bracelet with two diamond-encrusted interlinking hearts on her wrist.

Smiling through her tears, Kenyon wound her arms around his neck, pulling him close. "Thank you, my love."

His mouth tasted an ear before moving to her neck. "I'm the one who should be doing the thanking. Thank you for your love, your passion, your understanding, and most of all for our child." He splayed his fingers over her distended belly, feeling the strong movements of the baby impatient to be born.

"I don't think she wants to wait for March," Kenyon whispered softly, staring down at her husband's hand.

"Neither do I," he stated with a wide grin. Leaning over, he kissed his wife. He deepened the kiss as she tightened her grip on his neck. Sweeping her up into his arms he carried her to the bed.

The letter and the single red rose lay on the carpeted floor as they lay on the bed together, their hearts beating as one.

The early morning light coming through the windows caught the blue-white fire of the diamonds in the hearts of gold on Kenyon's wrist as she lay at Shumba's side, her eyes filled with love for the man she'd planned to spend the rest of her life with.

"Happy Valentine's Day," she said with all of the passion she felt for him at that moment.

"Thank you, kitten," Shumba managed to say before her delicate hands began a heated exploration of his chest under his T-shirt.

It was later, much later, that Kenyon whispered in Shumba's ear that he should take her to the hospital.

Carolyn Dorothy Naaman made her dramatic appearance into the world on February 14 at eleven fifty-five P.M., presenting her parents with the perfect Valentine gift.

Masquerade

Donna Hill

Joi Holliday slid her unfashionable glasses farther up her button nose. Sighing, she pushed aside the romance manuscript she was reviewing and lightly massaged her temples. The heroine had finally let the hero catch her, and the chapter ended with a rapturous love scene with them both echoing words of undying adoration.

Why was it that all of the heroines always found the perfect hero? *Humph. Fiction.* Those things never happened in real life. At least not her life.

At twenty-six, she'd never been truly in love. She longed for the warmth, love and security that she read about every day as part of her job, and heard her friends and colleagues discuss with fervor. Sure, she had all of the trappings of success: a nice car, a duplex apartment in the Village and a great job as senior editor at her father's romance publishing company. However, as much as she was reluctant to admit, she lived vicariously through the exciting lives of the characters whom she read about. She couldn't help but wonder just how much of what the authors wrote were excerpts of their own lives.

She stood up and stretched her petite five-foot four-inch body, removing her glasses in the process. Maybe if she were taller, she mused, or fashionable like the women who graced the covers of *Essence* and *Today's Black Woman* . . . Joi lowered her arms and smoothed her dark brown suit jacket. A slow smile illuminated her honey-brown face. If only she could have a relationship with someone like Marcus Speller. Ummnn. Well, it wasn't that she didn't have plenty of opportunity, but Marcus worked for her—for her father actually—-as a freelance reviewer and copywriter. Besides, he probably had a little black book that rivaled the Yellow Pages. Definitely off-limits. Anyway, she was certain she wasn't his type. He looked like the kind of man who dated only cover models, or high-powered women executives. Everything that she wasn't. *At least she could dream.*

She crossed her small but airy office to turn on the stereo, her short, shapely legs covering the distance in quick strides. Instantly the sounds of CD 101.9, the local jazz station, filled the air with "Mr. Magic" by Grover Washington, Jr. "Yeah, right," she said with a sardonic chuckle. Well, at least she had her private affair with the Internet. While surfing the net about a month prior, she'd located the Sociable Singles Network, an on-line dating service. She'd been communicating with one guy for about three weeks. He seemed really wonderful, almost perfect, and he loved to read. Probably too good to be true. Unfortunately he wasn't Marcus Speller.

Speaking of Marcus, she thought, he should be arriving shortly to pick up his work for the week. Her pulse began to race with anticipation.

Marcus smoothly weaved his cream-colored Acura Legend in and out of the mid-town Manhattan traffic. The digital clock on the dashboard read eleven-fifteen. He was due to pick up his stack of manuscripts in fifteen minutes.

As he drove, he wondered what Joi would be wearing today. Probably another drab outfit to camouflage that fine figure. He was certain she wore those schoolmarm clothes to keep the men at bay—which, as far as he was concerned, didn't work. Joi Holliday was a delicate bud waiting to bloom.

Unfortunately he could never be the one to make it happen. He had pretty strict rules about crossing the lines of business. The last thing he needed was to try to make a play for her and lose his job as a result. The freelance work he did for Holliday Publishing was the foundation of his bread and butter. He certainly didn't want to offend the boss's daughter. He shook his head. Then again, if Joi would just give him the slightest bit of rhythm, he would gladly toss his rules out of the window.

Momentarily he pulled up in front of the building on Third Avenue. As usual, there was not a parking space to be had. And as usual, he drove the extra two blocks to the garage. One of these days he was going to get lucky, he vowed, zipping up his leather jacket against the frigid January wind. He braced his body against the chilling zephyr and walked back to the offices of Holliday Publishing.

"Hi, Marcus," Claire Daniels, the receptionist greeted.

"Hi, yourself," he grinned, flashing a brilliant white smile and a perfect dimple in his left cheek. "Is Ms. Holliday in?"

"Yes. She's expecting you. Let me buzz her."

"Yes, Claire?"

"Marcus Speller is here, Joi."

"Send him in." As usual, with the mention of Marcus's name, she got a sudden hot flush and her pulse beat a bit faster. With shaky fingers, she picked a piece of lint from her brown wool skirt, took a long breath, and put on her best professional face. She slid her glasses back in place.

By the time Marcus knocked on her open door, she was seated behind her desk, pretending to read an unreadable manuscript.

She looked up at the sound just as Marcus peeked in. Good heavens, he was a dead-ringer for Malik Yoba from "New York Undercover," she sighed in silence. *Indescribably delicious!*

Unbidden, a smile lifted her full lips, and Marcus's stomach clenched in response. She couldn't possibly know how beautiful her smile is, Marcus concluded. If she did, she'd flash those pearls more often.

"I see you're busy as usual," he grinned, stepping into the room, while unzipping his jacket.

The simple act conjured up all sorts of erotic images in Joi's mind. "Come on in," she said in a voice so steady she surprised herself, especially since her heart was racing a mile a minute.

Damn, he's wearing that African Musk body oil again. It should be illegal. And those jeans. Omigoodness. She pushed her glasses farther up on her nose and pressed her knees together.

"I have a stack of manuscripts for you to read, and I also need back cover copy for the ones I've approved." Joi rattled this all off while shuffling through the notes on her desk, intentionally avoiding his gaze.

"Any good ones in the bunch?" He took a seat opposite her and pulled his jacket open to reveal the broad chest covered in a brilliant knit sweater in kente colors.

Joi stole a furtive glance. Hmmm. She cleared her throat. "The two that I've bought I think are real winners. I've only skimmed through the other three . . . but you know what I like . . ."

Her voice seemed to trail off—suggestively—? he wondered, at which point their gazes collided. In that moment Marcus wished he could take her comment literally. He reached across the desk to gather up the stack, and their fingers brushed.

Even behind the lenses of her glasses, Marcus noticed the inner flame that seemed to ignite in Joi's eyes.

She almost gasped out loud when the corner of his mouth curled up in a half grin, his dimple winking at her, apparently oblivious to the effect of his touch. What in the world was wrong with her today? This was worse than usual. It must be the after-effects of that erotic love scene she'd read earlier.

"I'll have these back for you by the end of the week." His voice seemed unusually low, almost provocative, Joi thought. But of course she was imagining things. Marcus always sounded like Barry White. Fortunately the similarity ended there.

Marcus Speller was six feet of hard-packed muscle. He had a smooth Hershey-chocolate complexion that was so rich you just wanted to run your tongue across it to get a taste.

Does she realize how sexy she is when she runs her tongue across her lips like that, Marcus wondered, watching the pink bud glide across her partially opened mouth.

Joi blinked, jarring herself back to reality and pulled her tongue back into her mouth. *Lordhammercy. I just know I wasn't doing what I think I was doing.* "It would be great if you could fax me the back cover copy as soon as possible," she stated in a rush. "Those are the next books up, and I need to get a quick turnaround."

"No problem. I'll tackle those first." He took the papers and placed them inside his leather backpack.

Joi leaned back in her seat, quietly observing his precise movements. Then suddenly she felt bold. "Marcus?"

He looked up, expectation lighting his dark brown eyes.

"We've worked together for more than six months," she began. "But I've never asked you—why do you enjoy this kind of work? I mean . . . you could have your choice of freelance jobs with your background. Why the romance market?"

He grinned that soft sexy grin and her stomach fluttered in response. "If nothing else, I'm a businessman. I studied the fiction market as a whole. Romance is, by far, the most lucrative. The genre produces more books per month than any other, which equals more work for people like me." He leaned a bit closer, and she subtly inhaled his scent. "Besides, what better way to discover what makes women happy than by reading about what they're looking for?" He gave her a conspiratorial wink.

Joi felt waves of heat infuse her blood. She pushed her glasses farther up the short bridge of her nose. "I see," she said over the knot in her throat. "Well, I guess that's about it," she expelled on a long breath. She pushed her chair away from the desk and stood up.

Marcus stood up as well, towering above her. "I'll have the copy back to you by midweek." He just crossed his fingers that his fax machine would hold up until he could replace it with a new one.

"That would be great." She smoothed the folds of her brown suit jacket, and Marcus noticed the slender, delicate hands. He'd bet money they'd feel like smooth satin moving across his skin. He blinked away the vision.

"I'll have these back to you on Wednesday," he uttered softly. He moved toward the door, then over his shoulder he said, "Have a great day."

"I just did," she mumbled under her breath, then louder, "You, too."

Marcus hustled down the two blocks toward the garage, thinking about Joi Holliday. He knew she was the perfect woman for him: compassionate, beautiful, intelligent, businesslike but still sexy in her understated way. Beneath all that drabness was a sleeping beauty waiting to be awakened by her prince. He chuckled as he stuck his key in the ignition. He was beginning to think like those folks in the romance novels he reviewed.

However, his reality was inescapable. On the outside people would think he could have any woman he wanted. For the most part, it was probably true; if he was willing to settle for the airheads, golddiggers or the "I need a father figure for my kids" type of woman, then he would be set. That's not to say that there weren't good women out there, he just happened to attract the wrong ones.

But if it were up to his notorious matchmaking sister, Charisse, she'd have him "hooked-up" with somebody if it killed her. Being one of the most sought-after photographers in New York, Charisse was in constant contact with a bevy of beautiful women, who she had no qualms in presenting to her bachelor brother. She wanted him to be as happily married as she was. Charisse had tried everything, he mused, nearing his loft apartment in the West Village—from blind dates to dating services. He'd gotten so fed up with her meddling that he'd actually signed up with one of those on-line services just to get Charisse off of his back.

He had to admit, as he opened the door to his apartment, the service was fun. He could converse with any number of women, reveal to them what he was really about, what he wanted and expected without the usual hassles. If any of them got turned off, they simply did not reply to your e-mail. An added plus was that the whole experience gave him tons of material for a great article on the subject.

There was one woman, though, who'd especially sparked his interest. They'd been e-mailing each other for several weeks. They'd scheduled another chat session for 9 P.M. He had plenty to do until then, and hopefully the work would keep his mind off of Joi.

"Ready for lunch?" Monica asked, peeking her head through Joi's open doorway.

Joi peered around her computer screen and smiled. She and Monica Lorde, the company's publicist, had been friends for more than ten years. Monica was the only one who knew the real Joi Holliday, inside and out. More often than she cared to admit, she wished she was more like her vivacious friend. Monica had a steady flow of admiring males beating a path to her door. She and Monica were about as different as two people could be. Where she was short and petite, Monica was tall and statuesque. Monica wore bold colors in all of the latest styles. Joi's wardrobe consisted of navy blues, browns, forest greens and some white blouses for variety. Yet they were closer than two sisters. That's why Joi was eager to tell Monica about the masquerade ball that the group on the Internet, Sociable Singles, was sponsoring.

"So let me get this straight," Monica said, while pointing her fork and chewing a succulent cherry tomato. "You get a costume, meet some strange guy through this on-line service, and then meet for the first time at a masquerade ball?"

Joi nodded.

"How in the devil are you going to know who this character is?"

"We describe ourselves on the computer and let each other know what we're wearing. The beauty of it is, it's not like a real date. If we hate each other's guts, it's not like we're joined at the hip for the night. He doesn't have to take me home, and I don't have to make excuses why he can't come in." She sat back with a satisfied grin. She wouldn't dare tell Monica the whole story—that she'd described herself as totally the opposite of what she really looked like. She really didn't think she could handle being turned down sight unseen. The problem was, how would she explain all this on the night of the ball?

Monica cocked her right eyebrow, a move she'd honed to a fine art, and looked at her friend with skepticism.

"Why do you do this?" she suddenly asked as if the absurdity of it had just hit her.

"Do what?" Joi volleyed, pretending confusion.

Monica dropped her fork with a loud clink and exhaled. "Go through these backdoor routines to meet men?"

Joi pursed her lips. Her brow crinkled. "I'm not like you, Monica. You know that. I don't have your flair for clothes or your gift of gab." She looked down at her half-eaten crab salad. "I'm just the way I am. Unfortunately the men I'm attracted to aren't attracted to me."

"Girl, I'm about tired of this woe-is-me B.S. When's the last time you took a good look in the mirror? If you'd take off them damn Coca-Cola bottle glasses and hike up those long-ass skirts, you might catch something."

"Yeah, a cold—right after I trip over the crack in the street that I couldn't see," she chuckled.

Monica suddenly burst out laughing, envisioning her girl-friend's scenario. "Whew," Monica croaked, trying to catch her breath and wiping the tears from her eyes. "You're probably right." She took a big gulp of Pepsi. "But seriously, why don't you let me take you shopping? I know you have plenty of money 'cause you sho 'nuff don't spend it on clothes!" She shook her head. "And let's see about getting you some contacts while we're at it."

"Hate contacts. They hurt my I-balls," Joi dragged out in an exaggerated drawl.

"Then at least get some frames that were manufactured in this decade."

"We'll see," she grinned, secretly excited. Maybe it was about time she gave fashion a chance. She wondered what Marcus's reaction would be, or her Internet lover when they met at the ball, or her father's . . .

"What are you daydreaming about?" Monica questioned, halting Joi's ruminating.

"Oh," she sighed, "I was thinking about Marcus, and wishing that he was the guy I get along with so well on the Internet."

Monica reached across the table and clasped her friend's hand. "Why don't you give Marcus a chance to really get to know you? Girl, whether you realize it or not, you are gorgeous. Sometimes I'm kinda glad you don't get all fly—you'd steal the men right out from under me, *or over me,* depending on my mood," she giggled.

Joi shook her head. "Like Barry White says, 'Sho you're right.' "

"I'm serious." She lowered her voice to a whisper. "Just because your father married a gorgeous woman who walked out on him is no reason for him to believe you'll turn out like her." She sucked her teeth in annoyance. "He has you believing that your looks are some sort of carnal sin instead of an attribute to be admired and enhanced."

Joi looked down and practically spoke into her plate. "My mother's looks are what destroyed my parents' marriage and my father. She used them to lure men, whether it hurt my father or not," she spat with vehemence, the old wounds seeping open.

"Did it ever occur to you that maybe, just maybe, your father's version isn't totally true?"

Joi's soft brown eyes darkened behind the lenses. "Why would my father lie to me?"

Monica gave her a steady look. "Maybe to hide his role in the demise of the marriage—and to make himself out to be the victim in order to turn you away from your mother to punish her."

"That's ridiculous," Joi hissed between her teeth, tossing the napkin on the table. She signaled the waitress. "I don't want to talk about this anymore."

"Hon, you need to discuss this. I've been telling you this for years. You need to see everything for what it really is. The bottom line is, Joi, you look exactly like Lydia Holliday, and your father could never deal with it."

Joi swallowed down the truth of Monica's words. How many times had she stared at her deceased mother's photograph and seen the uncanny resemblance. Instead of feeling some sort of connection—kinship—it made her feel dirty and unlovable. Maybe she did use her bland clothing and plain ponytail hairstyle as a cover so that her father would love her and not be reminded of Lydia.

"I've really got to get back. I have a stack of work on my desk." She wouldn't meet Monica's eyes.

"Joi? No hard feelings? You know I love you, and I'd never say anything to hurt you, girlfriend. I'd never do that."

"I know," she answered on a whisper. "Maybe a part of me even believes what you say. But there's that other part of me that can't accept it."

Monica nodded. "How about this?"

Joi looked up with a questioning gaze. "What?"

"Let's just forget I opened my big mouth. Who am I to tell anyone how to live their life? You do what makes you happy. We just have different drummers, that's all. If you decide to change your mind about shopping, you know where to find me."

"Thanks. I'll think about it."

And she did think about it even as she signed on to the Internet that night and clicked on to the Sociable Singles web page. She wondered what she would look like in a short, sexy black dress or lingerie from Victoria's Secret.

Within minutes she'd entered the private chat room where her cybermate was already waiting.

"Sorry I'm late," she typed.

"No problem. I just got here myself. I had a pretty busy day. What about you?" he keyed in response.

"The usual. My girlfriend was trying to talk me out of the masquerade ball. She thinks it's weird."

"It's no more bizarre than folks who get all geared up and haunt the singles bars and nightclubs."

"That's the way I feel."

"We seem to feel the same way about a lot of things: politics, the arts, relationships."

She could almost feel the gentleness in his response.

"I think about you a lot," she confessed, feeling bold behind the computer screen.

"I dreamed about you last night," he replied.

"Did you? What was I doing?"

"Making me very happy!" he typed, his strong fingers flying across the keyboard. "Did I make you blush?"

"Of course. You always do when you type like that."

"I wish we could meet. I mean before the ball. The curiosity is keeping me up at night," he teased.

Her heart began to pound. "I'd really rather wait. Expectation is half the fun."

"If that's true, then I'm having a blast! Let's do something different," he suggested. "Since I have to wait to see you, indulge me. Describe what you're wearing," he typed.

Joi's imagination went into overdrive. He'd probably run like a bat out of hell if she described her brown wool suit and plain white cotton undies.

"Well, I have on a short black jersey knit dress and sheer black hose." *Black was sexy.*

"Sounds delicious. But somehow I don't imagine you in black."

"Really? Why?" Her heart raced.

"I envision you in something soft but conservative. I don't see you as flashy, just elegant in an understated way—the kind of woman a man wants to rush home to at night."

"Are you disappointed?"

"Not at all, just surprised."

He'd bewildered her again. As much as she believed that men were interested in glamour and glitz, the more he proved her wrong. Maybe he *would* like her just the way she was.

"But I bet you could change my whole way of thinking." There was a long pause after his reply. "Are you still there?"

"Yes."

"Did I hurt your feelings?"

"Of course not. But I've got to be signing off. I'm beat."

"Sure. Oh, by the way, did you ever get the e-mail connection set up at work?"

Joi suddenly perked up. "Yes, I almost forgot. The program was installed just before the end of the day." She quickly keyed in her e-mail address for her computer at work.

"Now we can converse during the day from time to time."

"That sounds great. I can't wait to try it out. Send me something tomorrow before lunch," she keyed, growing excited at the thought of her "Internet lover" sending her secret messages at work.

"Sure. Look for something about ten o'clock. That's when I usually take my morning break."

"Working for yourself must be interesting," she typed. "You set your own hours, no one to answer to . . ."

"It has its good and bad points, mostly good. I just have to work twice as hard to keep the checks coming in."

"Does it ever get lonely with no co-workers to talk with?"

"At times. But for the most part, I'm so busy my days fly by. Now that I can connect with you during the day, even those brief moments of loneliness will be eliminated."

In that moment Joi felt warm and desired, and she thought of Marcus and how he and her cybermate seemed so alike.

"I have to admit," he continued, breaking into her thoughts, "since we connected I feel different. I look forward to the evenings when we can talk. We have so much in common."

"I know," she replied. "It's as if we've known each other for years."

"Yeah, it's like that for me, too. I'm looking forward to actually meeting you in two weeks. I'll finally be able to put a face and voice together with your wonderful personality."

What would he do when they finally met, and he saw that she wasn't the sultry beauty she'd described—that she became tight-lipped and witless when she was around men? Although he'd said he didn't expect her to be flashy, she was hard pressed to believe it. He probably wanted her to think that looks weren't what interested him the most. It was so easy to live behind the

screen and type out her fantasies, have the conversations that
burned within her like molten lava pour from her fingertips, pre-
tend that she was desirable and that her handsome prince was
only a keystroke away. Well, she'd just have to deal with it when
the time came—either that or just not show up for the ball and
sign off from his life for good.

"I know we promised to keep our identities and backgrounds
private—until we met—but won't you at least tell me your real
name?" he typed.

For a moment Joi had the urge to tell him everything about
herself: her name, what she did for a living, and what she really
looked like. But caution told her not to do it. She still wanted
just a little distance, a little more time with her fantasy. Suppose
he decided to pay her a surprise visit at work before she was
ready? No, she couldn't tell him. Not yet.

"All in good time," she typed. "I think it's so much more
exciting this way. And besides, the old saying goes, good things
come to those who wait. I'm willing. Are you?"

"Since I've met you, I've learned to be a very patient man.
But you sure have my imagination working overtime."

Joi laughed. To think that she could be the source of a man's
fantasy was incredible. She wasn't ready to lose that feeling.

"I'm always happy to provide work for those in need," she
quipped. "And on that keystroke, I will say goodnight."

"Until we connect again." He signed off and Joi followed suit.

A soft smile eased across her face. For those few moments
each night that she'd spent connecting with him, she felt totally
beautiful. Now back to the real world.

She pushed away from her computer, stripped out of her suit
and into her exercise clothes. She went through her regular five-
minute routine warm-up to the beat of "Shoop" by Whitney
Houston.

Briefly she caught her reflection in the full-length mirror that
hung on her bedroom wall. Without the long skirts and frilly
"grandma blouses," her short stature took on a petite femininity.
Her legs, no longer sheathed in dull brown hose, were clearly

defined, each smooth muscle delineated by years of exercise and athletics.

Her skimpy, body-hugging leotard revealed firm, full upright breasts, a taut flat stomach, a tiny waistline that defied explanation and a behind so round and tight she'd never have a problem with sitting too long.

But Joi saw none of this. She simply worked out because she was generally health conscious. With her often unpredictable schedule, it was impossible to get to a health club on a regular basis, so she never had the opportunity to compare her near perfect form with those who were trying to achieve what was already hers.

After her warm-up she worked out until a thin sheen of perspiration glistened like dew on her honey-brown skin. Finishing, she took a long, steaming shower.

Under the pulse of the water, her body seemed to vibrate. Visions of Marcus Speller appeared like an apparition in the mist-filled stall.

Joi closed her eyes, letting the vision settle over her. Her soapy hands glided across her body. "I dreamed of you last night," Marcus was saying.

"Did you? What was I doing?" she whispered in response.

"Making me very happy."

Her eyes flew open. Marcus never said that. I.D. #23875 did, less than an hour earlier.

Joi turned off the shower, draping a towel around her sculpted body. "If only Marcus would say those things," she wished aloud.

Marcus switched off his computer and stretched his long, lean body along his king-sized bed. Propping up his knees, he braced the manuscript against his bare thighs to read. This one wasn't too bad, he concluded, making his notations. But knowing Joi's taste in romance novels she would never buy it. The storyline was much too conservative. He shook his head. For someone who presented herself as this very staid, almost prudish woman, Joi's taste in novels was truly sensual, almost erotic.

Instinct told him *that* was the real woman behind the disguise. If only he could find a way to penetrate the facade, he knew what would be awaiting them both.

Joi arrived at the office earlier than her usual 8 A.M. She had a ton of work to complete, and a new writer had an appointment with her at nine thirty. Not to mention the weekly editorial meeting at ten o'clock.

Within an hour she'd line-edited a solid portion of a historical romance set in the late 1800s and began her editorial letter to the author. She always admired a historical writer's ability to research the details necessary to come up with the backgrounds for their novels and bring them to life without the story becoming inundated with facts and figures. What was additionally appealing about this novel was that the characters were all African-American, and the story wasn't about slavery!

Beyond her open door, she heard the sounds of the office coming to life as the staff of more than fifty began to filter in. In the three years that she'd worked for her father's company, there had been very little turnover, which was a rarity in the publishing industry. Overall, Paul Holliday was a fair employer, although not the easiest person to get close to. She could attest to that. She'd been trying for more than fifteen years.

After her mother left when Joi was only ten, her father was never quite the same. He became withdrawn and sullen, rarely giving compliments or encouragement—never love. In the big brownstone that they shared in Brooklyn, she always felt so alone that she had to battle for any tidbit of attention. Her father selected her clothes, her friends, the books she read and the places she went. It wasn't until she was twenty years old that she had her first perm. Until now, she'd never minded her father's handling of her life. She'd been comfortable. It made her feel that he cared about her. But if the things that Monica said were even

remotely true . . . No, it couldn't be. Monica always had a way
of dramatizing everything. Her intercom buzzed, interrupting her
musing.

"Ms. Holliday, your appointment is here."

"Send her right in." Her reflections on her life would have to
wait.

"I know my contract doesn't allow for my input on the cover,"
Naomi Fields was saying. "But would you please keep an eye
on things for me?" Her large hazel eyes set in a perfect heart-
shaped face implored her.

Naomi was a first-time author with the talent that would take
her places in the industry. Joi had every intention of seeing to it
that she got whatever she needed. Nothing gave her greater pride
than to see one of her authors rise to stardom.

Joi gave Naomi an encouraging smile. "You know I'll do whatever I can, Naomi. *Caress* is a fabulous debut novel, and I intend
to see that it gets first-rate treatment."

Joi felt Naomi's breath of relief. "I really appreciate that, Joi.
Will I see the artwork before it's complete?"

"I'll see what I can do. I'm not making any promises."

"Fair enough." Naomi rose. "I know how busy you are, so I'll
let you get back to work."

"Well, I do have a ton of paperwork and a meeting in about
fifteen minutes. Oh, you'll be happy to know your manuscript
is with our copywriter, who's writing the text for the back cover
even as we speak. It was picked up yesterday."

"Sometimes I still can't believe this is all happening. I've
wanted to be a writer for as long as I can remember."

Joi smiled. "You've always been a writer, Naomi. Now you'll
just be a published one!"

Out of the corner of her eye, Joi caught the flash of a blinking
light and heard the soft beep, both indications that she had e-mail
waiting. Suddenly she was in a hurry for Naomi to leave. Joi
came around her desk and gave Naomi a quick hug. "Everything

is going to be fine," she assured, ushering her to the door. "You just keep writing and let me worry about everything else."

"I'll try," she promised.

As soon as Naomi was safely on her way down the corridor, Joi hurried back to her computer and clicked on her e-mail. Seconds later the royal-blue screen was filled with text.

"Good morning, my unseen vision of loveliness." The sweet greeting brought a smile to her lips. "I hope you had as tough a time as I did getting me out of your head. I was totally unsuccessful in banishing you from my mind.

"How are things going so far? I must say that I've accomplished a lot this morning. I finished writing a really tough article and read through an unspeakably awful manuscript. But, hey, it's all part of the job. Listen, I know this may sound wild, but I have a proposition for you. Since it's still about two weeks away for the ball, I thought we could have a preliminary date . . ."

Joi's heart immediately began to thunder. *A date?*

"I know what you're probably thinking, but it's not what you think. We'd actually be dating on-line: music, food, atmosphere, the works. Be ready. I'll have everything prepared. Until then . . ."

Joi stared at the screen in total disbelief. An on-line date? How could that be possible? Yet the idea was so intriguing. Her overactive imagination swung into full gear. The possibilities were endless. She began to smile. Her Internet lover was becoming more interesting every day.

Tucking the thought of the date in the back of her mind, she prepared for her meeting.

After the departure of the three editors, Joi and her father were the only ones remaining in the conference room.

"How are things with you, Joi?" Paul Holliday asked. "We haven't had a chance to talk in a while." He crossed the room to the concealed bar behind the bookcase and poured himself a glass of Perrier. Emptying the contents from the tiny green bottle into the narrow glass, he topped the sparkling drink with a twist of lemon.

Joi adjusted her glasses and smoothed the pleats in her green wool skirt. "Everything is fine." Her words were barely loud enough to cover the short distance between them.

Paul didn't notice. As far as he knew, his daughter was always soft-spoken, low-key and unobtrusive; the way a woman should be . . . the way he wanted her to be. No man would be interested in Joi Holliday—wallflower. If he could assure that, he would always have her love. He couldn't lose his daughter, too. A part of him knew that his possessiveness of his daughter was wrong, but it was just so hard to let go.

He turned to her and smiled one of his rare smiles, and her heart seemed to do a little dance of pleasure. How she longed for those smiles from her father, for a few words of encouragement.

"You're handling the new line excellently, Joi. The books are leaping off of the shelves, I've been told."

Joi beamed with pride. "Thanks. I'm really enjoying it. I have a great team, and everyone is working really hard."

"That's good," he replied offhandedly, his fertile mind already strategizing his next promotional move.

At fifty, Paul Holliday was the definition of distinguished. His unlined, caramel-colored face was capped with a full head of soft salt-and-pepper waves. He had dark, piercing eyes and a full mouth, outlined with a thin mustache. Even at five feet, nine inches, his solidly built frame and expensive clothing created the illusion of great stature.

Joi began making moves to leave, realizing that their brief moment of communication was over. As much as she didn't want to admit that Monica was right, a part of her knew that her relationship, or lack of one, with her father was the reason why it was so difficult for her to establish relationships with men. What could she do about it, was the question.

"How are things in that apartment of yours?" he asked suddenly.

Joi blinked. "Fine," she mumbled, knowing where this was leading.

"I honestly don't see why you're living alone in this crime-infested city when you have a great big house at your disposal, and me to share it with."

I'd still be alone, she thought. Moving out on her own had been the cause of countless debates over the past year and a half. It was the first decisive move she'd made on her own, and her father had yet to accept it.

"Dad, we've been over this at least a hundred times. I'm fine where I am, and I like the freedom."

Her father pinned his dark eyes on her face. "Freedom! To do what?"

For one inscrutable moment, Joi felt like Dorothy in *The Wizard of Oz* being quizzed by the specter just before Toto pulled the curtain and unveiled the Wizard as a fake. She lightly shook her head to dispel the images. "The freedom to do what I want—or nothing at all," she replied, surprising herself with her retort.

With her heart hammering, she held her breath for a verbal lashing but instead witnessed the rapid-fire change of emotion that raced across her father's handsome face: annoyance, outrage, surprise and unbelievably acquiescence.

"I see." He cleared his throat. "If that's what you want." He tossed down the last of the Perrier and set the glass down on the table. Through sheer force of habit, not necessity, he checked his watch. Paul Holliday never needed to check the time. Every aspect of his life was precise. The Swiss could set their clocks by the accuracy of Paul Holliday. It was simply his way of indicating that you were now an item ticked off on his agenda as completed.

"I have another meeting to attend." He walked toward the end of the table and gathered his notes and briefcase. "I'll see you next week." He turned toward the door, then stopped, still keeping his back to her. "It would be nice if you stopped by for dinner one night," he uttered.

Was that gentleness she heard in his voice, or did she want to hear it so badly she'd only imagined it? Before she had the chance to formulate a response, he was gone.

After completing hours of reading and editing, Marcus decided to call it quits for the day. Donning his leather jacket he headed for a walk up West Fourth Street. He had a taste for pizza and decided to drop in on Uno's, his favorite spot since he moved into the Village. The food was good, the service was top rate, and they made the best virgin daiquiris in town.

Stepping into the semidarkened restaurant, Marcus was quickly seated at a small banquette, beating the after-work rush by mere minutes. He scanned the menu, then the crowd. He took a double take. Two tables away was Joi, seated with another woman who turned the heads of every man who passed.

Joi was seated in profile, giving Marcus the opportunity to absorb her understated beauty without being observed. Although her dining companion was stunning, in his eye and mind there was no comparison. Joi's beauty radiated from within, and her diminutive features only enhanced it. He debated with himself about whether or not he should go over and say something, when she turned and caught him staring.

Joi nearly choked on her pizza when her eyes locked with Marcus's.

"What in the devil is wrong with you?" Monica asked over a mouthful of pizza. "You look like you've seen a ghost."

"That's him," she whispered.

"Who?"

"No! Don't look."

"Don't look where? Who are you talking about?"

"Marcus," she hissed. "And he's coming this way."

"Really?" Monica's eyes sparkled with glee. Now she would finally get to see this Marcus that had her poor friend's head spinning.

"Hello, ladies."

Damn, he sounds just like Barry White, Monica thought, and

he looks like that hunk from "New York Undercover." She turned on her cover girl smile full blast. "Hello, yourself." Her appraising gaze sized him up within seconds. Excellent. Just like Joi said. So she does have some taste after all. Now if she would act like she had some sense and give this brother a play, there might be hope for her yet.

"Hi . . . Marcus," Joi mumbled. "This is my friend, Monica Lorde. She's the publicist for the company."

He nodded in Monica's direction. "Nice to meet you, finally. I've heard your name around the office."

"All good, I hope." But before he had a chance to respond, Monica continued in an entreating voice. "Why don't you join us, Marcus? As a matter of fact, I was just leaving. You can keep Joi company. Unless you're expecting someone," she subtly quizzed. She stole a glance around the restaurant, searching for a lone female and found none.

"Actually, I'm not expecting anyone."

"Perfect."

Joi kicked her under the table, and she jumped.

"Something wrong?" Marcus asked concerned.

"No." She grinned weakly. "Just indigestion. The pizza." She patted her stomach.

Marcus nodded in understanding.

Joi rolled her eyes and tried not to laugh.

Monica pushed away from the table and took her purse. "Enjoy yourselves. Joi, I'll speak with you later," she said, adding special emphasis to "later."

"Nice meeting you, Monica."

"You, too." She gave a brief wave and was gone.

Marcus gave Joi a penetrating stare, and Joi swore that she would melt. "Do you mind if I sit down?"

Joi shrugged her right shoulder. "Go right ahead."

Marcus sat down, folded his hands in front of him, and looked around.

Joi was suddenly parched but was too nervous to pick up her piña colada for fear that her hands would shake. She folded them between her knees.

"I've been dropping in here for the past month," Marcus said, signaling for the waiter. "But I've never seen it this crowded so early."

Joi grinned. "You must really like pizza."

He laughed in response. "Yeah, I guess you could say that."

"Do you live in the area?"

"About three blocks away. I moved into the area about the same time I started coming in here. I have a loft on Eighth Street."

Her stomach did a quick somersault. "Eighth Street?" she squeaked. "I live on West Fourteenth."

"We're neighbors" he grinned. Then he began enumerating the things they had in common. "We obviously like pizza. We both like to read romances, and I'd bet money that your drink has no alcohol."

"How'd you figure that one out?" Joi giggled, and Marcus felt his insides pulse.

"I can spot a nonalcoholic beverage a mile away," he teased. "Besides, I don't use alcohol in my drinks, either. Which is another reason why I love this place. They make the best virgin daiquiris in the city."

"Then I have to try one. Which do you recommend?"

"For beginners," he began, pretending seriousness, "I suggest the strawberry. Then you can move up to banana."

The waiter appeared at their table. "I'll have a deep-dish with shrimp topping and two strawberry daiquiris." His eyes slanted across at Joi, and they both laughed.

Slowly she began to unwind, enjoying Marcus's company, his quick wit, his boundless laughter and what seemed to be his interest in her—as a person. In the months that they'd worked together, they had never seen each other outside of her office, and they'd never discussed anything other than business and his next assignment. She was continually amazed to find that they had so much in common.

"I think I must have every recording that The Whispers ever made," Marcus confessed. "Those brothers can blow."

"Can't they?" she enthused. She almost blurted out that The Whispers were to be the special guests at the masquerade ball.

But to reveal that would be to confess to the fact that she was involved in an on-line dating service—the place for dateless cast-aways.

"Maybe we can exchange CD's sometime," Marcus suggested.

Joi's pulse fluttered. "Maybe," she replied evasively. "What else do you do in your spare time?" she asked, needing to change the topic.

"Besides listening to good music and reading tons of manuscripts, I write music for a couple of groups."

"Really?" Her eyes lit up like sparklers. "Has any of your music been recorded?"

"Not yet," he confessed, grinning. "But I'm always hopeful."

"The music industry is such a tough field. Here today and gone tomorrow." She shook her head.

"That's all too true. They don't make singers like they use to, the ones who can stand the test of time like the Dells, the O'Jays, Patti LaBelle and Aretha." He took a sip of his daiquiri.

Joi laughed and followed suit. "You don't seem old enough to even remember them."

"I'm old in spirit." He chuckled. "Not to mention that my father was an avid music collector. He must have every album ever made by anyone! And until I took so well to writing, music had been my major in college."

Joi was shaking her head in wonder.

"What?"

"This is just too incredible."

"What?"

"My father is a collector also. I played piano and sang—it seems like since I was born."

He looked at her curiously. "Then how did you get into publishing?"

"My father felt that it would be best if I had two majors: music—and since I had a love for reading and writing—journalism. He was already well established in the publishing industry, so when he started the romance line, I took it on. But I never lost my love for good music. It's a backdrop for everything that I do."

"What are some of those things, Joi Holliday?" Marcus asked, his dark eyes searching, his bottomless voice caressing.

Joi felt weightless, her thoughts and emotions spinning within the powerful maelstrom of his gaze, drawn by the magnitude of his voice. "A . . . a lot of things," she began, hesitating. She took a long breath, then tossed her fears aside and plunged in. "I listen to music when I cook, read, think, eat, work, exercise." She started to laugh. "Just about everything."

"Everything?" he asked suggestively. He saw her whole body tighten and knew he had crossed the invisible line. "That would about cover everything," he said with a grin, attempting to recover their camaraderie. "What's your favorite type of music?"

"I like everything, but I'm a fiend for jazz," she replied, relaxing again.

"Maybe I could entice you to accompany me to The Bottom Line one night. They always have great artists appearing." He knew he was pushing his luck, but he didn't know if or when this opportunity would ever present itself again. What was the worst that could happen?

She swallowed hard. This was a moment that she'd dreamed of. The man of her fantasies was actually asking her out. She'd obviously died and gone to heaven. "I . . . I don't know . . ." she stammered almost apologetically.

"I know——you're seeing someone. Listen, you don't have to explain. I shouldn't have been so presumptuous. I apologize."

Damn girl. Think! You're blowing it. She heard Monica's voice as clearly as if she were yelling in her ear. "Um, it's not that. What I was going to say was that . . . I don't know . . . much about The Bottom Line. I've never been there."

Marcus leaned across the table, his relief almost palpable. "I'm sure you'll like it." The left corner of his mouth lifted in a half smile. "I'd be honored to be the first to escort you."

She smiled. "Thank you for the offer." She looked at her hands, toward the door and on the table—anywhere but in his eyes. "I've really got to be going. I didn't realize how late it's gotten."

For the first time since he'd arrived, Marcus looked around

the restaurant. The after-work crowd had changed to the dinner crowd predominated by the younger set that inhabited the Village. He checked his watch. Eight-fifteen. He had forty-five minutes to get ready. As much as he was reluctant, he had to leave as well.

"It's been a pleasure spending time with you, Joi. Really. You're an entirely different person outside of the office."

She nodded. "Thanks. I've enjoyed your company, too." She stood up and picked up her coat. Marcus came around the table and helped her put it on. *He's so close.* The scent of him went sailing straight to her brain. She felt her knees begin to wobble.

"Are you okay?" he asked, bracing her shoulders with strong fingers.

"Y-es," she nodded. "I guess I got up too fast."

"Do you want me to walk you home?"

"No! I mean, no, I'm fine. It's a short walk," she concluded on a tremulous smile.

Marcus felt his insides shift, and he wanted to just lean down toward her upturned face and kiss those soft, pouty lips until she begged him to stop.

He's going to kiss me, Joi silently prayed, and then the moment was gone.

"If you're sure," he uttered in that unbelievable voice. He ushered her toward the door, and before he was willing, they were heading in opposite directions.

Joi walked home in a trancelike euphoria. She'd spent the past three hours with the man of her dreams. And the most amazing thing, he really seemed to like her. For a moment there, she actually thought he was going to kiss her. But that would have truly taken her fantasy to the next level. Of course he was being nice to her and feigning interest, she was his employer, of sorts. Then again, he didn't have to offer to take her out—just to be nice.

She released a heavenly sigh as she floated into her apartment. Then reality kicked in. She couldn't have a relationship with

Marcus. He was an employee of her father's company. Relationships between employer and employee went against every company policy and her own ethics.

She plopped down on her couch. So much for dreams. At least
she still had her Internet lover—until he actually met her—that
is. Speaking of which, it was almost time for her to sign on. He
did say he had plans for the two of them. Her spirits slowly lifted
until a smile replaced the stern set of her rich mouth. Hopefully
the "date" that he'd planned would take her mind off of Marcus
Speller.

Quickly she hung up her coat, changed into a soft cotton T-shirt
and comfortable jeans and went into the small room that she'd
set up as her office. Turning on her computer, she quickly tapped
into the Internet, opened the Sociable Singles file, and went
straight to the private chat room.

"I'm here," she keyed.

"Right on time as usual, my unseen vision of loveliness."

She was feeling better already. "So, my prince, what is this
plan for a date that you've cooked up?"

"As a matter of fact, I hope you're ready to leave. I have reservations for two. Our table awaits."

She laughed. "Where?"

"At one of my favorite haunts—Uno's. I hope you like pizza
with all the toppings. Sit back and imagine this: cozy banquettes,
upbeat music, just the right lighting, quality service and me."

Joi would have sworn that her heart momentarily stopped beating, then resumed at a rapid-fire rate. A hot flush swept through
her body. She shook her head and squeezed her eyes shut. She
obviously wasn't reading correctly. Opening her eyes, she pushed
her glasses farther up the bridge of her nose and peered intently
at the screen. No, there was no mistake. If she didn't know better,
she'd swear her Internet lover had spied her in Uno's.

Slowly her breathing returned to normal. "Just a coincidence,"
she said aloud.

"Are you there? I hope you're not disappointed. I thought it
would be fun to do something just a little offbeat. I'm sure you've
been to plenty of fancy restaurants, with guys that were trying

to impress you with their gold cards. But . . . if you'd prefer we go someplace else, I'd be happy to arrange it."

"This is fine," she finally typed. "It's funny that you would pick a pizza emporium. It's one of my favorite foods."

"That's because we're always in sync. Now, just relax . . . Hey, they're playing, 'And the Beat Goes On,' by The Whispers. A real classic."

Joi started to laugh, letting her mind and spirit get carried away with the moment. This was going to be fun. And it was.

For the next hour they exchanged stories, pretended to eat pizza with every type of topping imaginable. Joi nearly fell off her chair when he suggested that she try a strawberry daiquiri. There was so much about him that reminded her of Marcus: his sense of humor, music, favorite food and his ability to make her feel good. Maybe this was the man for her after all.

"I've had a great time tonight, my unseen vision of loveliness. This is just a prelude to the real thing."

"I've enjoyed myself, too. It was almost like being there!" A soft smile illuminated her face.

"Until we connect again . . . stay special."

Joi turned off her computer, leaned back in her chair, a dreamy expression outlining her face. She shook her head and smiled. She'd definitely stepped into the modern age of technology with both fcct. Shc hadn't bccn on a date in more months than she could count, and her first one was in cyberspace. Now that was progress.

Thoroughly pleased, Marcus shut down his computer for the night, and with the bulk of his work for Holliday Publishing completed, he decided to return the numerous calls that were held in limbo on his answering machine. As he listened to the messages, his thoughts began to wander, and his evening spent with Joi was rekindled. He had been a breath away from kissing her. Only good sense had intervened. Yet he couldn't help but wonder how she would have responded, how her lips would have felt against his own, unadorned by lip glosses and colored sticks.

"Don't forget about tomorrow night," the familiar voice was saying on the answering machine, jarring him out of his ruminating. "We'll be expecting you at eight o'clock sharp. Please don't be late, Marcus. And wear something besides those jeans."

Damn. He'd completely forgotten about going to his sister Charisse's house for dinner. He flopped onto his back across his bed, throwing his arm across his eyes. Why in the world did he ever agree to dinner anyway? He knew it was just another one of her setups. Unfortunately there was no way to get out of it. He'd never hear the end of it if he didn't show up. He'd just have to deal with it. He shuddered to think who would be the "mark" this time.

Paul Holliday stoked the fire in the fireplace, then crossed the large den to the bar and fixed a Perrier with lemon. He smiled as he thought back to a night three weeks earlier that was so similar to this. It was the evening he'd met Lana English—the woman who was slowly changing his life . . .

He'd felt totally out of his element. In all his fifty years, he'd never been on a blind date. At this stage in his life, he didn't know how to behave on a date. But it had been too late to back out. In a spell of loneliness he'd given in to his brother David's insistence to accompany Lana English, an old college friend, to a promotional function at the Marriot Hotel. She was in town to put together an event for a Valentine's Day ball, his brother had said. David, the proverbial optimist, was confident that it would be the perfect match: the romance mogul on the town with the woman who held Cupid's bow. "If I wasn't a married man," David had said with a wink and a smile, "I'd take her myself. She's one helluva woman."

With those thoughts weighing down on him, Paul must have changed his suit at least three times, trying to get the right look.

He didn't want to come on too conservative, but he didn't want to look like some guy on the make, either. He was as nervous as a pimple-faced teen on a first date. If there were any justice in the world, the evening would be short and uneventful, he thought. To top off his anxiety, she was one of those nineties women who didn't mind picking up the guy on the first date. So *he* was the one who'd paced the floor and checked the clock. Had things changed that much since he'd been on the dating scene? He'd wondered what other notions she had in her head. She was probably one of those women who . . . but he didn't have time to complete his thought. The doorbell rang.

"It's showtime," he'd mumbled as he went to the door and pulled it open.

"Hi. I'm Lana English," she'd greeted in a soft southern drawl. "I hope I'm fashionably late." She'd smiled, extending a gloved hand. And Paul immediately knew what his brother meant. His fears seemed to melt away, and his stony heart shifted in his chest. Then, as if on cue, the sound of Roberta Flack's "The First Time Ever I Saw Your Face," floated to the couple at the door. With her standing there, a bubbly smile of welcome lighting her face, his fears and his loss were replaced with the first beginnings of hope.

And that hope continued to infuse him day by day. As he waited for Lana's characteristically late arrival, he marveled at the impact she'd had on his life in such a short space of time. In some ways it frightened him. Since Lydia had walked out on him so many years ago, he'd refused to allow any other woman to get close to him. Sadly that included his precious daughter, Joi. He saw that now, as a result of the blooming relationship with Lana. She'd added a new dimension to his life. Her place in it had allowed him to see himself from a new perspective. Her openness and love of life helped him to see how he'd deprived his daughter, how he'd allowed his hurt to control his life and ultimately Joi's as well. He would find a way to change that. Slowly he was beginning to understand that Joi was not Lydia; that all women were not out to "get what they could from a man," and that Joi deserved a life of her own.

Tonight he and Lana planned to stay in and listen to his collection of Miles Davis tunes. Whatever else happened, he was finally ready.

Marcus had been up for hours. He needed to get as much done as early as possible since his evening was accounted for. He was all prepared to send the back cover copy to Joi's office, as promised, when his fax machine blew. It literally ate up the pages that he'd inserted into the slot. Cursing, he attempted to salvage what he could of the documents, but already knew it was impossible. He discarded the shredded papers, then back at his computer, he printed out a fresh set. It had been acting crazy for weeks, but he'd hoped that it would hold up long enough for him to get a replacement. Now he had no other alternative. He'd have to make the investment. The machine was his lifeline, especially when it came to deadlines for the countless articles that he penned for the local papers.

Slowly a smile replaced the frown that was etched on his face. This catastrophe was really a blessing in disguise. Now he'd have a chance to see Joi again. Maybe if he worked it right, he could time his visit around the lunch hour and talk her into joining him. He grabbed his jacket, backpack and keys and headed out of the apartment with a lightness in his step.

Joi was engrossed in her latest manuscript when the flashing light and soft beep alerted her to a message on her computer. Her heartbeat quickly picked up its pace. She put the manuscript aside and keyed in her e-mail code.

"Good morning, my unseen vision of loveliness. I hope you had a great time last night, I know I did. But believe me, it's only the beginning. You seem to occupy so many spaces in my life lately. Everything that I do has thoughts of you in it. I can only hope that I meet all of your expectations and more when the time comes. I know you're probably busy, and I have a deadline to meet. We probably won't get to chat this evening, but if I can, I'll leave a message for you. Until we connect again . . . stay special."

Joi hit the edit key and highlighted COPY, then PASTE, then PRINT. Moments later she printed out a copy of her morning message. Looking over the dark print on the stark white paper seemed to bring him just a bit closer to her, making him real. Closing her eyes, she held the paper to her breasts and smiled, trying to imagine her prince, and the only vision she could conjure was that of Marcus. The sudden ringing of the telephone jarred her out of her daydream.

Flustered, she put down the paper to take the call from none other than her father.

"Daddy? Is something wrong?" Paul Holliday never made trivial phone calls. In fact, he never called at all. Her heart began to pound.

There was a loud clearing of his throat. "I'm sorry to bother you."

Instantly her guard went up. *Her* father apologizing! "You're not bothering me."

"I just wanted to call . . . and say hello . . . see how things were going."

Joi's dark brown eyes widened like two saucers. "Uh, everything is fine. We, we're going to press on the next book, I . . ."

"Not with the business, Joi. Believe me, I know everything is perfect over there. What I mean is, how are things with you?"

"Me?" she squeaked.

"Yes." Paul took a deep breath. "Are you happy, Joi—I mean really happy?"

For several moments Joi sat speechless. She couldn't remember the last time, or if ever, her father asked if she was happy.

"Yes, of course I'm happy," she stuttered. "Why? Daddy, is something wrong? Are you all right?"

She heard his soft chuckle. "Sweetheart, I'm probably all right for the first time in many, many years. You have a good day, and we have to try to get together soon." He hung up before she could respond.

Joi sat with the phone in her hand, the sound of the dial tone humming in the air. She shook her head. What in the world had come over her father? It was so unlike him to utter words of endearment. Though she understood that her father loved her, he was never a demonstrative person. She always assumed that he showed his love just by caring for her since her mother left. He saw to her needs, made sure that she was clothed, fed, educated. He could have sent her to live with relatives in a two-parent household, but he didn't. A young man in his prime, he took on the responsibilities of raising a little girl into womanhood. He may not have been the best of fathers, but he was hers. For that she would always be grateful, regardless of what Monica and others might think. Perhaps his views and his ways of raising her were nearly puritanical, but she'd survived. She'd tried so hard over the years to please him, to gain a smile, a warm word. For the most part, she'd given up, believing that things were just the way they were. Her dad would never be like Bill Cosby. But he was hers.

Unbidden, her eyes filled. A single tear trickled down her cheek.

A soft tapping on her open door shook her. Quickly she dabbed at her eyes, hidden behind the lenses of her glasses. Then she had to wipe them again. Like an apparition, Marcus was standing in her doorway, a look of disquiet darkening his gaze.

"Joi? Are you all right? I could come back—"

"Marcus," she cried in alarm. "No." She jumped up. "I mean, yes, I'm fine. I think I have an eyelash in my eye." She hurried around her desk, her midcalf navy-blue skirt swirling around her legs. "Have a seat. I'm just going to run to the ladies' room." She whizzed past him, catching a whiff of that darn body oil. Just what she needed, she thought, doubly perturbed—weak knees to go along with her racing heart and tear-stained face. This was one of those moments when she was thankful that she didn't wear makeup. She'd really be a sight.

Marcus briefly followed her hasty departure, his own curiosity and concern heightened. Something was obviously wrong. This was not the Joi Holliday that he knew. She'd been crying. There was no doubt about that. The question was, why?

Taking a seat, he wished that Joi felt comfortable enough with him to talk about what was bothering her. He removed his backpack and placed it between his feet. As he did so, he spotted a sheet of paper beneath the desk. He reached down to pick it up and put it back on the desk when the text caught his attention.

He felt the pulse begin to pound in his ears like a roaring tide racing to shore. He read over the words of endearment in total disbelief. It couldn't be. Not Joi. *His* Joi. The impact of the thought suddenly hit him. Yes, he did think of her as his, as ridiculous as that might be. Now what was he going to do? He didn't have time to think about it any further. He heard Joi's voice in the hallway. Quickly he put the revealing sheet of paper back on the floor where he'd found it.

"Sorry to keep you waiting," she said with a shaky grin. She rounded the desk and sat down. "Just like I said, an eyelash." She took a breath and gazed at him. The look she received in return stunned her. It was the same look that the countless heroines she'd read about saw in the eyes of their soon-to-be lovers: *longing*.

For a brief moment their gazes fused together. In that instant Joi felt transported to that special, warm place that she'd only read about. And then the spell was broken

"I know I was supposed to fax these to you"—he handed her the back cover copy—"but my machine went berserk and ate up the pages." He gave her a lopsided grin, and her stomach took a nosedive. "That's the reason for my unannounced visit."

"You don't need an appointment to see me," she practically whispered. She adjusted her glasses and swallowed. "I mean . . . it's no problem. You're almost a full-fledged staff member." How she wanted to walk into his arms, become cocooned in the depths of his eyes, and tell him of her conversation with her father and how it made her feel. But, of course, she couldn't do that. She was his employer. If only—

"Joi," he said softly. He reached across the table and placed his large hand atop hers. Heat raced through her body, charging her heart. "What is it? I mean, I know that we're not real close, but I've been around you long enough to know when something is wrong." He leaned closer, and involuntarily she felt herself being pulled toward him like a moth to a flame. "I just want you to know that . . . you can talk to me . . . if you want to. I'm a great listener. Remember"—he grinned that lopsided grin—"I read romances to discover what it is that women want and need. And right now, I think you need someone to talk with." He leaned a fraction closer. His voice was barely above a whisper. "I'm here."

Once again they were close enough to kiss, so close that she could almost count the silken hairs of his long lashes. So close that—

"Oh, I'm sorry," Monica said in an embarrassed gush.

The two sprang apart as if zapped by lightning.

Monica arched an eyebrow. "Since I was in the building today, I wanted to tell you about the media plan for *Caress.* I guess I'll stop back later." She smiled wickedly. "Good to see you again, Marcus. Ta-ta," she waved and was off.

Marcus expelled a long breath and moved farther back in his seat, pulling his hand away in the process, and Joi felt a sudden emptiness envelop her. Instead of being embarrassed by Monica's inopportune arrival, she was disappointed that the intimate moment was lost.

Clenching his jaw, he looked down at the floor, the telltale note of endearment staring back at him. "I've got to get going," he said, standing abruptly.

Joi's eyes followed the length of his body, resting on his searching eyes. "Thank you for your offer, Marcus. I just may take you up on it."

Her smile was so sweet that Marcus was only a heartbeat away from saying to hell with propriety and just take her in his arms and kiss her like he'd been longing to do. Of course that was out of the question.

"My offer is still open for The Bottom Line." He moved toward the door, then stopped and turned back to her. "I hope to hear from you, Joi. Soon." Then he was gone.

Joi's heart was thundering so loud in her chest, she thought it was going to explode. Her hands started to shake. Her breathing came in rapid pants. "Lordhammercy, I just got a peek at heaven," she muttered.

"What?"

Joi's head snapped toward the door to find Monica standing there with a self-satisfied grin on her face. She strutted into the room. How—was the big mystery to Joi—when the pencil-thin magenta skirt that Monica must have oiled onto her body barely gave her enough room to move her long legs.

Monica flounced into the office, took a seat, and was magically able to cross her legs. She leaned forward. "Did I hear you mention heaven?" She tapped a perfectly manicured nail against her teeth. "It wouldn't have anything to do with that rather fine-looking brother that just left here? Who by the way seems very well endowed, judging by the fit of those jeans."

"Monica!" Joi snapped, her honey-brown face burning with embarrassment. "Is that all you ever think about?" she hissed.

"We . . . ll, not a . . . ll the time." She grinned.

Joi rolled her eyes. She refused to indulge her risqué friend by laughing like she really wanted to do. "Didn't you say you wanted to talk with me about the promotion for *Caress?*" She folded her hands in front of her, a clear indication that she was not in the mood for chitchat.

"Don't get all bent out of shape because I interrupted your little necking session," Monica teased, enjoying the look of pure outrage race across Joi's unadorned face.

"If you weren't my dearest friend," Joi said from between clenched teeth, "I'd snatch that weave right out from the roots!"

Monica erupted into a fit of uproarious laughter, drawing the attention of staff passing by the open door. "Girl, wouldn't that be a sight?" she hooted, doubling over with laughter.

As much as Joi tried to maintain a stern countenance, she couldn't stop the bubbles of laughter that rolled up from her belly, tumbling out and mingling with Monica's.

"Whew," Monica breathed, slapping her palm on the desktop. "That was a good one. Pass me a tissue, girl, before I have mascara running all down my face," she stated, breathless.

Joi pulled a tissue from the box on her desk and handed it to Monica—who gingerly dabbed beneath her eyes—then she took one for herself.

"We were supposed to be talking about *Caress*," Joi said, regaining a semblance of composure. She took a breath. "What's your plan?"

Monica immediately switched gears. She was now all business. Monica Lorde was a primary reason why the new romance line was doing so well. Her promotional ideas were second to none. Having gone into business for herself five years earlier, the Monica Lorde Agency had some of the top clients in the industry. The key to her success was the personal touch that she gave to every account. The fact that they were friends didn't hurt, either.

"The first thing I want to do is work out a photo spread which includes the author stretched out on the beach that she describes in the opening chapter. Of course she will be caressed by one of the drop-dead gorgeous male models." She sat back and smiled in triumph. She could tell by the sparkle in Joi's eyes that she was loving the concept.

"Where do you come up with this stuff?" Joi asked in wonder. "I love it. But," she added, pointing a finger at Monica, "I don't want to start a precedent. The next thing you know, every author will want to be on the cover of their book."

"Don't worry. I'll control the fallout. What I'll stress to each of them is that each book will be unique in design and concept. I'll promise to pay just as much attention to their covers as I did with *Caress*."

"It sounds fabulous, and I know Naomi will be thrilled. She was so worried about her cover. Actually, she's perfect for it, and she looks so much like Iman, the model, she could be her twin sister."

"I know. That's what gave me the idea. We get the look without the cost. There's no way that Holliday Publishing could afford five minutes of Iman's time."

"I hear you. It sounds good to me." Then Joi brushed her hands in a gesture of dismissal. "You just handle it."

"Everything is taken care of. As a matter of fact, I have a dinner meeting with a dynamite photographer this evening." She checked her watch and let out an expletive. She jumped up from her seat. "Speaking of meetings, I have one in about five minutes. I'll call you later," she said in a rush, dashing for the door.

"Bye," Joi called to her receding back.

Now that she had a moment to regroup, she tried to piece together her unbelievable morning. She was still in a quandary about her father and his uncharacteristic phone call and conversation. For the life of her, she couldn't imagine what had brought it on. Then the impromptu visit by Marcus nearly did her in. Thoughts of Marcus brought to mind her Internet lover and the sweet message he'd sent earlier.

The message! Her eyes raced frantically across her desk, then she began rifling through the stacks of papers on her desk. Nothing!

Oh, where could it be? She pushed away from her desk and scanned the floor beneath. "There it is," she breathed in relief. She reached down and retrieved the paper from the floor. The last thing she needed was for someone to get their hands on it. How embarrassing would that be—to have a staff member find out that she was receiving love notes on the Internet. The thought made her shiver.

Taking the sheet of paper, she folded it and tucked it safely away in her purse, which reminded her of how empty her evening would be. Slowly slipping into a state of melancholy, she didn't see Marcus standing in her doorway, but the unmistakable sexy scent of him put all her senses on "hunk alert." She almost gushed out his name before she made visual contact. Instead she dug down deep for control and slowly looked up, feigning astonishment.

"Marcus," she said with just the right amount of surprise. Her heart rate picked up its pace, and that old familiar heat raced

through her veins. She didn't know how much more of this her
body could continue to take in one day. She adjusted her glasses.
"Did you forget something?"

He stepped into her office, and for the first time that Joi could
recall, he seemed nervous.

"Would you mind if I closed the door?"

Close the door! Joi swallowed—hard—and blinked back her
incredulity. She was trying so hard to stop a grin from streaking
across her face that her jaws began to ache.

"Sure, come on in."

"I was down the hall talking with Claire, and when she left
for lunch, I realized how late it had gotten. I thought, maybe, if
you didn't have plans, we could go to lunch together."

First the love note, then Marcus's surprise visit, now this. My
day is getting better by the minute. Is this almost like a date, she
wondered fantasizing . . .

She took so long to respond, Marcus thought she'd taken his
invitation the wrong way and was trying to figure out how to tell
him a polite no.

"Actually, I had a few thoughts on the manuscripts you'd given
me," he said, attempting to salvage as much of his pride as possible. "I figured"—he shrugged his broad shoulders—"if you
had time, I could run them by you. I'd like to hear what you
think."

If you knew what I was thinking . . .

Shaking herself from her daydreaming, Joi looked at her
watch. "That sounds like a great idea. And your timing is perfect,
I'm starved. I'd like to . . ." *do all sorts of things to you,* "take
you up on your offer." She smiled, and Marcus's heart settled
back in place.

Joi came from around her desk and reached for her coat
hanging on the coat stand, but not before Marcus did. Their
fingers intersected, grabbing the coat and each other at the
same time. Joi could have sworn that the lights in the office
flickered.

There was a flurry of throat clearing, averting of gazes and the standard "excuse me—sorry," until Marcus said, "Let me help you with that."

Joi, thankful to turn her back, let Marcus help her into her beige wool coat. He was standing so close, she could feel his warm breath tickling the back of her neck. If only he would do what the heroes always did: lean just a bit closer and scorch her neck with hundreds of tiny kisses, she thought.

Unobserved, Marcus took the moment to truly take in the full picture of Joi Holliday. She stood just barely beneath his chin—in heels. Her soft copper-toned hair looked silky to the touch and smelled as fresh as spring. It was pulled back in her usual ponytail, held away from her neck by an intricately designed leather clip with what looked to be a reproduction of a slave ship leaving the infamous Gori Island. He smiled. How unlike the Joi he thought he knew, to boldly display something as powerful as a slave ship. What other secrets were there to discover about the shy, retreating Joi Holliday?

As he eased her into her coat, he savored the brief contact that his hands made with her body. When his fingers trailed upward and rested on her slender shoulders, he felt her shudder.

Instinctively he moved closer, and he could have sworn he heard her sigh. But of course that was ridiculous.

"Cold?" he asked.

"Just for a minute," she said, thankful for the excuse he provided. "Did you have someplace in particular in mind?" she asked, turning around to face him. She looked up into his eyes, and her heart slammed against her chest.

How he wished he could tell her everything: who he really was, what he knew. But he couldn't do that, at least not yet. "It's your call," he said instead. "What do you have a taste for?"

"There's a great soul food restaurant about two blocks down," she suggested, reluctantly moving away to get her purse from her desk.

"Sounds perfect."

* * *

"You have some appetite." Marcus chuckled, observing Joi's plate, which was loaded with collard greens, sweet potatoes, corn bread and fried chicken. "Where do you put it all?"

"I have to keep my strength up," she quipped. "Actually, I burn a lot of it off when I exercise at night. Because of my height I have to be very conscious of my weight. Believe me, this is a treat for me." She grinned shyly. "My regular diet consists of bunny food: salads and vegetables and naturally pizza," she grinned. "By the way, sir," she added, pointing her fork at his plate, "you're no slouch yourself."

"It takes a lot to fill this body," he said. The simple statement seemed to charge the air with electricity. Their gazes magnetized and held. "You don't look like you'd need to exercise," he said softly. "You're perfect . . . just the way you are." His eyes grazed over her face.

Joi felt the familiar slow burn begin in her stomach then fire upward to flame her face. *He thinks I'm perfect?* The very idea was mind-boggling. She was the first to break eye contact. She cleared her throat, took a long swallow of fruit juice, and adjusted her glasses. "You said you had some ideas on the manuscripts," she said for lack of a suitable response to his compliment.

His ego slowly dissolved into bite-sized crumbs. Idiot, he thought, berating himself. He'd have to find a better way to get her to see what was really happening without losing his pride in the process. "I was listening to 'And the Beat Goes On' last night and eating pizza," he began in a deliberate tone, and Joi nearly choked. "It got me to thinking about *Caress* for some reason . . ."

Joi couldn't even concentrate on what Marcus was saying. Her thoughts were spinning. Last night she was on-line, pretending to listen to the same thing and eating pizza with . . . *Impossible!*

"So what do you think?" he asked in conclusion.

Joi blinked back to the present. "It . . . sounds great. Why don't you write something up, and I'll submit it at the next editorial meeting."

"No problem. I'll get to work on it over the weekend."

They continued to consume their meal in momentary silence.

"Speaking of the weekend," Marcus hedged, "do you have any plans?"

"Um, not that I can think of offhand. Why?"

He smiled slowly "Because my offer to take you to The Bottom Line is still open. I could check the *Village Voice* and see who's appearing this weekend. That's if you're interested in going." He held his breath.

"This weekend?" she squeaked.

He nodded.

"Could I let you know by Thursday?" Her heart thundered in her chest.

"No problem. Just don't forget, okay?"

"I won't." *Believe me I won't.*

As fast as her fingers could punch in the numbers, Joi called Monica's office, only to be informed by her assistant that she was out of the office for the remainder of the day. She needed some advice in a hurry. As much as she wanted to go out with Marcus, she felt that it was totally inappropriate. If her father ever found out that she was dating a staff member, he would have a natural fit, not to mention the other members of Holliday Publishing. What was she going to do?

Stumped, she sucked on her bottom lip. Her limited experiences with the opposite sex left her totally unequipped to handle this delicate situation. She leaned back in her seat. The only thing to do—the right thing to do—was to tell him she couldn't make it. Wasn't it? Oh, what did she know?

A relationship with Marcus Speller—as much as she might want one—was totally out of the question. What she needed to do was concentrate on her friend on the Internet. He was the man for her. He seemed to be everything that Marcus was without the complication of being an employee. Yes, she decided, she would tell Marcus that she had other plans that she'd forgotten, or she had to shampoo her hair, or whatever it was that women gave as excuses. She had to maintain a professional relationship with him. That's all there was to it.

Maybe it was good that she didn't speak with Monica. She would never let her live it down if she told Monica that Marcus formally asked her on a date and she planned on telling him no.

That night, without her cybermate to chat with, she simply signed on to the Sociable Singles page and got an update on the ball. Everything was going according to plan, she read. The ball was set for Valentine night, with the festivities to begin at 7 P.M. at the *Spy Café* in SoHo. The current tally was one hundred fifty, with more confirmations coming in daily. They were anticipating an additional one hundred people within the next week. It was important, the message continued, to have a meeting place and a clear description of your costume so that those who had connected with someone would be sure to find them. For those that did not find a mate on-line, there would be plenty of unattached eligibles for everyone. There was a color print of the layout of the café on the screen, with arrows pointing to specific locations.

Joi was impressed. This was really going to be some event. She moved out of the group mail file and into her personal mailbox to see if her cybermate had left a message as promised. Smiling she found the short but sweet note.

"I'll see you in my dreams. Expect a note from me tomorrow. Stay special."

At least she had that to look forward to, she thought. The next obstacle she had to deal with was her erroneous self-description. She sighed and turned off the computer. She'd just handle it when the time came.

Leaving her small home office, she went into the living room and turned on the stereo. The soothing sounds of Al Jarreau filled the apartment from the speakers in each room. Humming along, she went into her bedroom and changed from her work clothes into her exercise outfit.

Maybe if she pushed herself hard enough, she'd be too tired to dream of Marcus and what could never be. She wondered what he was doing with his evening.

* * *

"Marcus, I'd like you to meet Naomi Fields," Charisse said as Marcus entered her sunken living room.

Naomi raised her mascaraed eyes and rested them on his face. A slow smile of welcome lit her picture-perfect features. "I've been telling Naomi all about you, Marcus," Charisse continued as he made his way into the room.

Marcus crossed the salmon-colored carpet and took Naomi's outstretched hand. "Nice to meet you, Naomi." He cast his sister a sidelong glance. "I'm sure my sister has been exaggerating, as usual," he said with meaning.

"I don't think so at all," Naomi replied in a silken voice.

"I was just telling Naomi that you were one of the readers, as well as copywriter for her book," Charisse interrupted. "I thought it would be great if you both met," she added sweetly. "Why don't you two get acquainted. I'm going to check on my husband and dinner." She whisked out of the room.

Marcus sat down on the far end of the modular sofa.

"I think you did a wonderful job with the copy," Naomi complimented, looking directly into Marcus's eyes.

"Thanks. It was easy. You wrote a fabulous book."

Naomi blushed. "I just hope the readers feel the same way." She crossed her long legs, giving Marcus a spectacular view of toasted-almond thighs.

Marcus cleared his throat and purposefully averted his gaze. The move was not lost on Naomi, who demurely pulled on her short skirt.

"How long have you been writing?" he asked after a long strain of silence, already knowing the answer. Joi always gave him a brief biography on each of the writers whenever she gave him a manuscript. She felt that it gave him a better idea of their style and capabilities, which ultimately made his job easier. Joi was the only editor he'd ever worked with that did that. *Joi.* That was just one of the many things about her that made her special.

"You haven't heard a word I've said," Naomi said, pulling him from his daydream.

When he focused on her face, she was smiling.

"I'd know that look anywhere," she said. "Whoever she is, she's a lucky lady."

Marcus began to chuckle, shaking his head in embarrassment. "Is it that obvious?"

"Very," she grinned. "So how about this? Let's give your sister what she wants."

"You knew?"

"Of course. Single woman—single man—left alone to 'get acquainted.' "

Marcus eased around the glass and chrome coffee table to sit beside her. "You've got yourself a deal. It'll serve her right."

They sat head to head, planning their steps for the evening.

When Charisse returned with her husband, Clay, in tow, she couldn't have been happier. Finally she'd found someone who her very eligible brother found interesting. Hallelujah! She was so thrilled, she practically floated to the door when the bell rang.

"Monica. Welcome. Come on in, we were waiting for you to get dinner started."

"Sorry I'm late," she apologized ."It's been one of those crazy days." She turned toward her escort as they crossed the threshold. "Ronald, this is Charisse Daniels. Charisse, Ronald Martin."

Ronald took Charisse's hand. "Pleasure."

"I'm glad you both could make it. Let me take your coats. The living room is straight ahead. Go right in and introduce yourselves."

Monica stepped through the archway that led to the living room, and her eyes locked on to what appeared to be a very intimate conversation between Marcus and Naomi.

Sheer agility was the only factor that saved Ronald and Charisse from tumbling over Monica when she came to an abrupt halt at the top step.

When Clay entered the foyer from the left, it took all he had to keep from laughing at the precarious sight of three adults pressed back to front, teetering on the brink of collapse. One false move by Monica and the whole group would go down like a stack of dominoes. He rushed over to assist Monica.

Charisse, bringing up the rear, was the first to recover. Stepping away from Ronald's back, she mumbled an apology.

"Sorry," Monica said. "I guess my heel got caught," she stated loud enough to draw the attention of Marcus and Naomi, who sat with their backs to the door.

Marcus turned, and the shock that registered on his face qualified as a Kodak moment.

Ronald stepped from behind Monica to stand at her side. "Are you all right?" he whispered, slipping his arm around her waist.

"Just fine," she said, smiling through clenched teeth.

Clay and Charisse passed a curious look between them, then shrugged it off.

Monica stepped down and into the living room. "Naomi, good to see you. And Marcus," she said, "what a surprise."

"You've met my brother?" Charisse asked.

"Yes. We've bumped into each other once or twice," she said sweetly. "I never made the connection that Charisse was your sister."

"Most people don't," he said, standing to shake Monica's hand and Ronald's in turn.

Monica made the last of the introductions, and they all filed into the dining room.

Now what was he going to do? Marcus worried. If he pretended to go along with the charade that he and Naomi had cooked up, he'd fool his sister as planned, but Monica was sure to say something to Joi. If he told Monica the truth, then he would have to reveal how he felt about Joi—and he was sure Monica would rush back and tell—which would probably ruin any chance he had with Joi.

However, he didn't have much of an opportunity to display his feigned attraction for Naomi. Monica strategically placed herself between he and Naomi at the dinner table, for the most part controlled the flow of conversation, and corralled Naomi after dinner to discuss her campaign strategy for *Caress,* much to Charisse's dismay.

Marcus was tickled by the pinched look on his dear sister's face. "The best laid plans," he breathed in her ear as they passed each other at the bar.

She rolled her eyes as hard as she could without sealing them shut and returned to her place next to her husband.

The three women soon became embroiled in a conversation about photography sessions, selecting a male model and location and wardrobe for Naomi, who was beaming with excitement.

Banished from the machinations of beauty and fashion, the three men resorted to talk of sports, of which Marcus soon grew weary. He rose, arching his back to get the kinks out. "I'm going to be heading home," he said to his brother-in-law. He extended his hand to Ronald. "Good meeting you, brother. Maybe I'll see you again."

"Same here," Ronald replied.

Marcus turned toward the women and received three distinct looks: Charisse was quietly fuming, Naomi looked apologetic, and Monica flashed him a self-satisfied smile. "Good night, ladies. Glad to finally meet you, Naomi. Good luck with the book."

"Thanks. You did a great job on the copy."

"Monica, it was a pleasure to see you again." He smiled.

"Likewise."

He leaned down and kissed his sister's cheek. " 'Night, sis," he said aloud, then only loud enough for her to hear, "Better luck next time." He eased away, chuckling silently. He knew full well that if they were alone, she would have popped him right upside his head.

"I'll walk you to the door," Clay offered.

Marcus shrugged into his coat and slipped on his gloves.

"I wish there were something I could do, buddy," Clay chuckled, giving Marcus a hearty slap on the back. "But Charisse is determined to get you married off if it kills her."

"Don't I know it." Marcus chuckled . "I'm used to it by now."

"How's that on-line dating thing going? Are you still planning to do an article on it?"

Marcus wasn't surprised that Clay knew. Charisse was always hard-pressed to keep a secret, and he and Clay had always been

ARABESQUE ROMANCE BOOK CLUB

120 BRIGHTON ROAD

P.O. BOX 5214

CLIFTON, NEW JERSEY 07015-5214

Accepting the four introductory books for $1.99 (+ $1.50 for shipping & handling) places you under no obligation to buy anything. You may keep the books and return the shipping statement marked "cancel". If you do not cancel, about a month later we will send 4 additional Arabesque novels, and bill you a preferred subscriber's price of just $4.00 per title (plus a small shipping and handling fee). That's $16.00 for all 4 books for a savings of 25% off the publisher's price. You may cancel at any time, but if you choose to continue, every month we'll send you 4 more books, which you may either purchase at the preferred discount price. . . or return to us and cancel your subscription.

Check out our website at www.arabesquebooks.com

BOOK CERTIFICATE

Yes! Please send me 4 Arabesque books for $1.99 (+ $1.50 for shipping & handling). I understand I am under no obligation to purchase any books, as explained on the back of this card.

Name

Address _____ Apt. ___

City _____ State ___ Zip ___

Telephone ( )

Signature

Offer limited to one per household and not valid to current subscribers. All orders subject to approval. Terms, offer, & price subject to change.

Thank you!

AN02OR

THE EDITOR'S "THANK YOU" GIFT INCLUDES:

4 books delivered for only $1.99 (plus $1.50 for shipping and handling)

A FREE newsletter, Arabesque Romance News, filled with author interviews, book previews, special offers, BET "Buy The Book" information, and more!

No risks or obligations. You're free to cancel whenever you wish . . . with no questions asked.

3 QUICK STEPS
TO RECEIVE YOUR "THANK YOU" GIFT
FROM THE EDITOR

Send back this card and you'll receive 4 Arabesque novels! These books have a combined cover price of $20.00 or more, but they are yours to keep for a mere $1.99.

There's no catch. You're under no obligation to buy anything. We charge only $1.99 for the books (plus $1.50 for shipping and handling). And you don't have to make any minimum number of purchases—not even one!

We hope that after receiving your books you'll want to remain an Arabesque subscriber. But the choice is yours to continue or cancel, anytime at all! So why not take us up on our invitation to receive 4 Arabesque Romance Novels, with no risk of any kind. You'll be glad you did!

An important message from the ARABESQUE Editor

Dear Arabesque Reader,

Because you've chosen to read one of our Arabesque romance novels, we'd like to say "thank you." And, as a special way to thank you, we've selected four more of the books you love so well to send you for only $1.99.

Please enjoy them with our compliments, and thank you for continuing to enjoy Arabesque...the soul of romance.

Karen Thomas
Senior Editor,
Arabesque Romance Novels

like brothers. However, he couldn't give Clarisse total satisfaction in having talked him into trying the service. He'd used the explanation that he'd try it out to get an angle on a story, which eventually happened. How would be have known how it would turn out.

"At first I did it just to get Charisse off of my back and to get some ideas for a story at the same time. But once I got into it, I got a kick out of it." He slightly averted his gaze. "As a matter of fact, I met someone."

"Yeah?" Clay's light brown eyes rounded like saucers.

Marcus nodded. "We've been talking for weeks. Or should I say typing. So far we seem totally compatible." He wasn't quite ready to tell Clay everything.

"Sounds great. I have to admit, brother, I was a bit skeptical in the beginning. I always felt those things were for losers. Not a brother like yourself. But I'm finding out every day that's not the case at all. I have a couple of buddies at work that are on-line." He lowered his voice and leaned toward Marcus. "If I wasn't married to your crazy sister, I'd try it myself."

They both laughed, knowing Clay would have hell to pay if Charisse even smelled such a thing.

"Well, good luck, bro," Clay said as Marcus stepped out of the door.

"Thanks. I'm going to need it."

It was almost eleven o'clock by the time Marcus reached his apartment from the upper west side of Manhattan where his sister lived. Bone tired, he got out of his clothes, dropped them on the bedroom floor, and headed for the shower. He knew a hot shower was the only thing that would keep him awake for the next hour.

More than an hour later, he'd crafted his message to his satisfaction. Turning off the computer, he went to bed and dreamed of Joi.

* * *

Joi had been in bed for more than an hour. She'd tried every position short of standing on her head, and she still couldn't get to sleep. The conversation with Marcus was still playing on her mind.

As much as she'd thought she'd made a decision about the date, she was still in a state of flux. From everything she'd heard, The Bottom Line was a pretty popular place. She was liable to run into any number of people who knew them both.

She emitted a heavy sigh and flopped onto her side. She squeezed her eyes shut and attempted to go to sleep, but visions of Marcus and vague images of the man behind the screen teased her all night long.

Joi arrived at her office tired and irritated. If she'd had two full hours of sleep, she'd had a lot. Her eyes felt as if little cement bricks were attached to her lashes.

Mechanically she went through the motions of preparing for the day: setting up her reading material, checking her appointment book and production schedule, and checking for any overnight voice-mail messages. With those things out of the way, she turned on her computer and was thrilled to find a message waiting for her.

"Good morning, my unseen vision of loveliness. I felt lost not being able to converse with you last night. I hope you had a pleasant evening. Mine on the other hand was one for the books.

"I think I told you when we first connected that I had a sister whose goal in life is to get me married. I had to endure another of her setups last night. Nice girl, but definitely not my type. However, we did have a bit of fun at my sister's expense. We pretended to be thoroughly interested in each other, and it would have worked until another guest arrived and positioned herself between us for the rest of the evening. It was quite comical. My sister was livid, but dared not say anything for fear of offending this woman who had just hired her for a major photo job. Anyway, enough about me. I wish you would reconsider going out with me before the ball. I checked the *Village Voice* today, and The Whispers and Regina Bell will be at The Bottom Line this week-end . . . I'm making plans to go, I wish you would, too . . ."

Suddenly all of the air seemed to evaporate. Joi couldn't breathe. She scrolled back up the screen and read the text again. No, there was no mistake. What in the world was going on? This was too much of a coincidence to be a coincidence. First, Marcus asks her to go to The Bottom Line, and then her cybermate does as well. They were so much alike, they could easily be the same person.

Her heart thumped. Suppose . . . no . . . but what if . . . ? How would she find out? She leaned back in her seat and stared at the screen. A slow smile inched across her face.

If this is Marcus, and I'm beginning to believe it is, then I also have the feeling he's somehow found out who I am. But how?

At this point it didn't even matter how he'd found out. If he knew who she really was, that meant he really did care about her "as is," without the fluff and frills. She frowned. Could her father have been right all of these years? But she didn't have time to think about it further, when Monica rushed through the open door.

"What in the world are you doing here? Don't you have your very own office uptown?" Joi taunted.

"Listen, girlfriend, when you hear what I have to say, you'll be thankful I did drop in."

Monica flopped down in the visitor's chair and launched into her story.

It took all Joi had not to burst with happiness. She'd been right. Marcus and her Internet lover were the same person, and some-how he already knew who she was. His recent message left no room for doubt.

"Are you listening to me?" Monica demanded, cutting into

her thoughts. "I'm telling you that Naomi is one hot little number. But I didn't give her a New York minute to get her hands on Marcus." She sat back in the seat, thoroughly pleased with herself. She folded her arms and crossed her legs. "Aren't you going to thank me? I was trying to keep your slot open until you came to your senses."

"Monica," Joi said slowly, staring intently into Monica's eyes. "Marcus and the guy I've been talking with on the Internet are the same person." She began to explain how she'd arrived at her conclusion.

Monica's expression went from bewilderment to shock to outright hilarity. She burst out laughing. "I'll be damned! If this doesn't beat all." She pointed a finger at Joi. "Only you," she chuckled. "Well, you always wanted some fairy-tale romance to drop in your lap. Well—here you have it. You couldn't have done better if you'd written the script." She shook her head in amusement.

"If you're finished," Joi said, her voice dripping with sarcasm.

Monica cleared her throat and reached for a tissue from the box on Joi's desk. She dabbed gingerly at her eyes. "And there I was making a complete fool of myself, thinking that I was saving him for you!" She burst into another fit of laughter.

"I'm glad you find all of this so amusing. But meanwhile I need a plan."

Monica slowly pulled herself under control. "A plan? What in the devil for? You're crazy about him, he's crazy about you. To hell with policy and procedures—just go for it." She sucked her teeth in annoyance.

Yes, she did have the company policy to deal with, but the knowledge that Marcus really cared about her was enough for her to face the consequences.

Joi leaned forward, resting her elbows on the desk, a sly grin playing across her expansive mouth. "But he doesn't know that I've figured it out. I think it will be fun to see just how far he's willing to go—to win my heart," she concluded on a lofty note.

Monica's right eyebrow arched. Now she was interested. "Aren't you the clever one," she teased. "I knew if you hung around me long enough, some of my good qualities would rub off. This sounds like my kind of mission. What can I do to help?"

Joi had everything figured out. All of that romance reading was finally going to pay off. Now, to put it all into action. This was the first time she'd ever played the "hard to get" role. But Monica assured her it would be a cinch. "Just be yourself," she'd teased. They'd planned to meet after work to get phase one into motion.

Joi took a deep breath and tried to calm her jangling nerves. She flipped through her Rolodex and plucked the card with Marcus's home number. She attempted to dial his number three different times and chickened out. Suppose she forgot everything she'd planned to say? Suppose she lost her voice in midsentence? Suppose . . .

The knock on her door caused her to jump. She looked up, and her heartbeat fluttered. "Marcus."

"Hi. Sorry to drop in on you like this, but Claire wasn't out front so I just tried my luck and hoped you'd be in." He stepped into the office.

She sat up straighter in her chair. "No problem. Come on in." She adjusted her glasses and smiled.

Marcus reached behind him and removed his backpack, then took a seat. "I finished up my comments and corrections on the rest of the manuscripts." He pulled them out of the bag and placed them on her desk.

The manuscripts were only part of the reason why he'd come. The real reason was damage control. He needed to find out how much she knew about last night. And if she did know, he needed to feel her out.

"Thanks," she said, wanting desperately to reveal what she knew, but she was determined to play it out until the night of the ball. "I wasn't expecting these until tomorrow. Now I can get a head start." She gave him a long, warm smile, and Marcus had the unsettling feeling that there was more to it than what met the eye.

Marcus leaned back and unzipped his jacket. "I ran into Monica Lorde last night at my sister's house, of all places."

Joi did an Oscar-winning job of showing surprise. "You're kidding." She fixed a slight frown on her face. "I didn't know you had a sister," she said coyly. "But then again, we don't really know that much about each other's personal lives." She smiled sweetly.

Marcus shifted in his seat and gave her a curious look before proceeding with his story. He cleared his throat

"Charissa—my sister—is the photographer that Monica hired to do the layout for *Caress.*"

"Monica did mention that she was meeting with the new photographer, but that's all she said."

"As a matter of fact, Naomi was there as well." He paused to gauge her reaction. She gave him a steady look in return.

"Sounds like you all had a party. Small world." She chuckled. "Isn't it?"

"I hope everyone had a good time." She began shuffling some papers on her desk.

"It would have been a very pleasant evening if my loving sister wouldn't have tried to play matchmaker between me and Naomi."

"You and Naomi?" Her pulse beat escalated. What would his version be?

"Yeah." He rested his right ankle across his left knee. "My sister believes it's her sworn duty to find the woman for me. I have to endure her little setups at least once every couple of months."

By degrees she began to feel better. He wasn't interested in Naomi. She stifled her grin. "Sounds like some evening. How long has your sister been a photographer?"

He smiled. "For as long as I can remember. She's been snapping pictures since she's been able to hold a camera. There wasn't much work for her in Florida, so she moved up here about six years ago, and her career just took off."

"It must be great to go through the year without worrying about boots, winter coats and snow tires. Don't you miss it?"

"Believe me, since I moved to New York two years ago, I've had many moments when I wanted to catch the next thing smokin' back to Florida. These winters are killers." As he spoke, he noticed a change in Joi. She seemed more animated, not so reserved and withdrawn. She was actually looking directly at him instead of her hands, the door or the papers on her desk. It was almost as if she was encouraging him to talk—open up—like someone who was interested.

"So why do you stay?" she asked on a gentle note.

He breathed deeply. "Charisse and I are the only family we have. Both our parents were only children. That leaves us. Charisse feels strongly about family, and she's been trying . . . Well, that's another story. Anyway, I know that's why she tries so hard to find someone for me. She has her husband, Clay. For whatever reason, she thinks I'm lonely." His pulse quickened at the gentleness of her gaze.

"Are you lonely?"

It was a few moments before he replied "At times. But I try to keep myself busy. There's a big difference between being alone and being lonely."

Joi nodded in understanding. "My father can't seem to see the difference between the two, either," she said on a thoughtful note. "He automatically assumes I'm lonely living on my own."

"Are you?"

"Only if I think about it real hard."

His voice dropped an octave. He leaned slightly closer, and Joi seemed to gravitate in his direction. "It seems we have more in common each time we talk. I was wondering if you'd changed your mind about my offer to go out?"

"I . . ." She stopped in midsentence and looked up. "Dad."

Marcus turned in his seat to gaze up at hard brown eyes.

"I didn't realize you were busy." He stepped into the office.

Marcus stood and extended his hand. "Marcus Speller, Mr. Holliday. I do the freelace copywriting and some evaluations."

"Marcus . . . Mr. Speller . . . has been with us for about six months," Joi said, finding her voice. Was that a smile she saw playing around the edges of her father's mouth? No. Couldn't be.

"Is that right? I'm sure you're doing a good job, or I would have heard about it."

Paul remained standing, giving Joi and Marcus a sense of being evaluated. "In any case," he continued, "it's good meeting you. If you're doing a good job, keep it up. If not, don't let me find out." He patted Marcus on the back and turned his attention toward Joi.

"I'd better be going." Marcus picked up his backpack. "I'll pick up next week's batch on Friday. Unless you have something now."

"I do." On wobbly legs, she stood up and went to the row of shelves—which had been divided into little cubicles—-behind her desk. Each cubicle contained a manuscript to be read. There were probably forty manuscripts waiting to be read at any given time in Joi's office.

She pulled a manuscript from the top shelf and another from directly beneath it. "These have been here for three weeks. If you would go over them and submit your evaluation as soon as possible, I'd appreciate it."

Marcus was acutely aware of the change in Joi. She'd stopped looking at him. The softness of her voice had reverted to the precise, deliberate businesslike tone.

"I'll get right to it. I'll leave my invoice with Claire on my way out."

"If she's not there, just leave it on her desk. I'll be sure she processes it right away," Joi said.

He turned toward Joi's father and extended his hand. "Glad to finally meet you, Mr. Holliday."

"Pleasure. I'm sure we'll be seeing more of each other."

A quick questioning look passed between Joi and Marcus.

"I'm sure."

Once Marcus was gone, Paul turned a smiling countenance toward his daughter. "Seems like a very pleasant young man," he stated, finally taking a seat. "How long did you say he's been working for you?"

"Six months," Joi said, alarms blaring in her head.

"You two should know each other very well . . ." His comment trailed off.

Joi sat up straighter, moved a few papers on her desk, and adjusted her glasses. "Yes, we do . . . professionally," she emphasized.

He pursed his lips and nodded. "I was only inquiring because I thought perhaps you'd like to bring him with you to dinner Saturday night."

"Excuse me?"

"Dinner. Saturday." Now Paul was beginning to look uncomfortable.

Joi stared at him for several moments.

Paul sighed heavily, then looked directly into his daughter's eyes. "Yes, I'm inviting you to dinner Saturday evening. I was hoping if you weren't busy you'd be able to make it." He cleared his throat. "There's someone I'd like you to meet."

Joi's eyebrows shot up in surprise. "Who?"

"I'd rather you met her in person. But in the meantime, her name is Lana."

"I see," Joi said in lame disbelief. Her father and a woman? She couldn't recall any significant women in her father's life for all of the years he'd raised her and beyond. At least the few she did run across were referred to as business associates. Until now, he'd never extended a dinner invitation to meet any one of them. She was stunned into silence.

Paul made a short job of collecting his things, purposely avoiding eye contact with Joi. "Give me a call and let me know if you can make it. I was thinking seven o'clock." He draped his coat over his arm. "Feel free to . . . bring someone." He started to leave, then stopped. "Perhaps Mr. Speller would like to join us *if* you extended the invitation." He walked out, leaving Joi with her mouth open.

She couldn't dial Monica's number fast enough.

* * *

"What?" was all Monica kept saying at the end of each of Joi's sentences.

"I know you're not deaf, girl, so stop saying 'what'!" Joi snapped in jest.

"My ears can't believe what they're hearing. That's the problem."

"I know what you mean, and I was right here."

"Your father and a woman. It's about time. No wonder he's mellowing out." She chuckled. "But seriously, this may be a blessing in disguise. At least you don't have to worry about company policy. Your father has apparently kicked it under the rug. So the excuse about your being Marcus's employer won't hold up anymore. You already know he has a thing for you, so invite the man for dinner so we can check out this Ms. Lana up close and personal."

"We?"

"You know what I mean."

"Ugh. Unfortunately I do," she grumbled good-naturedly.

"So—what are you going to do? You didn't tell me if you got to put your plan into action."

"First of all, I'm still going through with the plan. Dinner will just be a little added icing on the cake."

"Oooh, girl, you're starting to sound more like me every day!"

"You know what, Monica?"

"What?"

"I think I'm starting to sound more like myself," she said softly.

The Plan

On her way home, Joi finished up what she and Monica couldn't during their lunch hour. Loaded down with bags, she dropped them at the foot of her bed, completed an hour of exercise, then turned on her computer.

Within moments she was surfing the net. She checked the time at the bottom of the screen: 7:30 P.M. She and Marcus—hmm, that sounded nice—wouldn't connect before nine. Her fingers flew across the keyboard.

"Hi, cybermate. Just wanted to check in. I won't be able to connect with you later. I have plans. But I did want to tell you that if the offer is still open, I'd love to go with you to The Bottom Line on Saturday. Let me know. But if you've already made plans, I'll understand. Leave me a message. Bye for now."

Joi sat back and looked over what she'd typed. She pressed the SEND key and she knew her message had been instantly transferred to Marcus's mailbox. She smiled. This was going to be fun.

All that activity stirred her appetite. She turned in her swivel chair and rolled herself over to the four-drawer file cabinet. Flipping through her freelancers files, she pulled the information sheet on Marcus, jotted down his home phone number, and returned the file to the drawer.

This time she wasn't going to back out. She took a breath and punched in Marcus's phone number. The phone rang four times. She was sure the answering machine was going to intercept the call, when Marcus's low, melodic voice come across the line.

"Hello?"

"Hi, Marcus. This is Joi."

Marcus sat straight up in bed, scattering the stack of manuscripts across the African print quilt.

"Joi. This is a surprise. What's up?"

Be brave. "I was just wondering—if you haven't had dinner yet, maybe we could meet at Uno's."

Marcus blinked back his surprise. "Sure. As a matter of fact I was just thinking about picking up something from the deli," he said, making a quick recovery. "But Uno's is even better."

"Does a half hour give you enough time?"

"Plenty. If I get there first, I'll get the table—same goes for you," he added, and Joi could hear the smile in his voice. Her heart raced.

"Great. See you then." She hung up and grinned like a schoolgirl.

Marcus dashed around his loft in preparation for leaving, all the while wondering what brought on the change in Joi. Why was she asking him to go out? But this wasn't a date—not really, he rationalized, pulling his favorite cream-colored cable knit sweater over his head. It was just two business associates getting together for something to eat. He put one leg into his jeans and stopped. What if she was setting him up to let him down? Her office wasn't appropriate—not with her "open door policy." Maybe she was going to let him down easy in a public place.

Damnit, he knew he should have played it slow and easy with Joi. That surprise visit by her father was probably the icing on the cake. There was no telling what her father said to her after he'd left. He shook his head, annoyed with himself.

Well, he concluded, he'd just have to deal with it. But from the moment he'd found out that Joi and his Internet connection were the same person, he was more determined than ever to win her heart—totally. Their compatibility proved that they belonged together. If she was planning on putting a halt to his slow advances, he didn't know what he'd do next. All be did know was that whatever and however long it took, Joi Holliday was destined to be his.

Marcus arrived at Uno's in record time. He secured a quiet table in the rear of the restaurant and purposely took a seat with his back to the door. He tapped his foot in impatience, checked his watch, and finally ordered a virgin banana daiquiri. Intent on sipping his drink and keeping his mind off of the evening ahead, he focused his attention on the menu and didn't see Joi when she entered and approached their table.

Joi took the brief moment to stare at him, and her stomach did a quick somersault. Standing above him, she saw the slight waves in his close-cropped almost black hair. His muscular neck stretched down and out to broad shoulders and tight biceps that bunched against the fabric of the sweater each time he moved.

Sensing someone standing near him, he turned, looked up, smiled briefly at the very striking woman then turned back around. Not a second later, his head twisted back so fast—he was a sure candidate for whiplash.

"Joi?" he expelled incredulously.

"Hi, Marcus," she answered sweetly, her jaws killing her from having to contain her laughter.

"Joi," he repeated, knowing he sounded ridiculous but not able to help himself. He gathered his wits along with his manners and finally stood up.

Joi smiled and very slowly slipped out of her lemon-yellow trapeze coat to reveal a form-fitting dress of crêpe de Chine in a bold burnt orange, accentuated around the turtleneck collar with a multicolored chiffon scarf that draped dramatically across her shoulders, then fell to meet her dress just above her knees.

Knees! He actually saw knees. Beautiful knees attached to the greatest pair of legs he'd seen in ages.

His eyes slowly rose upward and rested on her mouth that had just the barest hint of color—so faint it was almost indiscernible.

And her hair. She had so much of it. It tumbled in a cascade around her shoulders in glistening chestnut-brown curls. Who was this woman?

"May I sit down?" she asked, breaking through his wall of shock.

He slightly shook his head. "Of course. I'm sorry. It's just . . ."

She smiled "It's just what?" she asked in a silken tone he'd never heard in her voice before, as she eased into the seat he held.

"Nothing."

She nodded as if she understood. Her sides were killing her She wanted to laugh so bad it hurt. If he could only see the look on his face. But she had to admit, when she gave herself a final look in the mirror, she was shocked. She'd stared at her reflection for a good ten minutes before she could truly believe what she saw. Yet she knew, deep inside, that the person facing her in the mirror was no different from the one that faced her every day. This one just had more pizzazz.

Marcus forced his mind to clear. Get it together, brother. It's not like you've never seen a beautiful woman before. You always knew that Joi was stunning beneath the camouflage. It was just unnerving to see her in full bloom. No wonder she didn't walk around like this every day. Men would be falling all over themselves.

"Have any idea what you want to order?" he asked.

Joi slowly crossed her legs and Marcus felt that undeniable surge in the lower part of his anatomy. He shifted in his seat.

Joi casually picked up her menu and held it in front of her face to hide her smile. This was too funny, she thought. "I'll take a deep-dish with everything," she said, returning the menu to the table.

Marcus signaled for the waitress.

"Two deep-dishes with everything," he told the smiling young woman.

"What will you both be having to drink?" she asked, staring longingly at Marcus.

He looked at Joi and grinned. "Two virgin banana daiquiris."

Once the waitress was gone, Marcus leaned back in his seat, pursed his lips, and folded his arms across his broad chest. He stared pensively at her. "You want to tell me what this is all about?"

She gave him a wide-eyed innocent look. "What are you talking about?"

"This!" He extended his hands toward her in accusation—totally flustered by this new self-assured Joi Holliday.

"If you mean why did I ask you out—well, because I thought it would be nice. We had such a great time the other night, and this was my way of saying thank you. Is something wrong with that?"

He gave her a long look. "Of course not. But there's no *reason* to thank me," he asked more than stated. What he really wanted to know, but didn't have the heart to ask, was if this was the big kiss-off.

Joi wiggled her hips just a fraction to get more comfortable, and Marcus's hormones went on a rampage. He picked up the napkin and dabbed at the thin film of perspiration he knew was forming on his top lip.

Joi reined in her laughter and relished in the feel of power that she had. Never before had she felt in control of a situation with a man. It was a heady sensation, and suddenly she understood what it was that her father feared for so long—falling under the spell of a woman and feeling totally vulnerable. But she realized something else as well. The "spell" was not one of beauty, clothes and makeup—it was the adrenaline of self-confidence that radiated from within. The clothes, the hairdo, the makeup were only artifices. Who she was, at that moment, was the same woman she had always been.

The waitress returned with their drinks. "I suppose you're right," Joi said finally, taking a sip from her drink. "About thanking you," she added, to clear the quizzical look he gave her. "But I did have a great time. How was your day?" she asked, changing the topic.

"Not bad. I got a ton of work finished and made some headway on an article I'm working on."

"What is it about?"

"Internet dating," he said, measuring his words. He hoped that it would open the door to the topic and ultimately to them.

She suddenly felt hot as her pulse beat faster. Now it all made perfect sense. What other reason would a man like Marcus Speller have to be interested in her? He'd led her on purposely, to get fodder for an article! Even she, a seasoned writer, could not find the words to describe the depths of her humiliation. She felt like a complete fool. No wonder he'd asked her *what was this all about?*

She cleared her throat and focused on the red-and-white checkered tablecloth. "I see. Sounds interesting."

"I've found out a great deal about the whole trend and the types of people who use the service," he offered gently, sensing the change in her demeanor.

"What type of people are they?" she snapped.

"Not what everyone thinks, for starters." He leaned slightly forward, attempting to engage eye contact. "They're not the lonely hearts—the unwanted. They're just people who are trying to find that special someone, by establishing a friendship first—sight unseen."

She looked up at him then and saw the compassion in his eyes. Slowly she smiled. "That's good to know," she said in a soft voice.

"Have you tried it?" she asked and held her breath, while his eyes held hers.

"Yes, I have."

"And?"

"And . . . I found a wonderful woman."

Her heart began to race. "What is she like?"

He smiled. "It's funny. She seems to be a lot like you."

She swallowed hard and her spirits soared. "Are you saying that you think I'm wonderful?"

"Don't you think you are?" he countered.

She lowered her gaze. "I guess I don't think about it much."

"You should. Because you are."

"I hope everything works out with the two of you," she said, ducking the compliment.

"So do I," he uttered as the waitress placed their food on the table.

They talked of other things, skirting any further discussions of relationships and intimacy.

"I'd like to walk you home," Marcus said, helping her into her coat.

She looked over her shoulder and up into his eyes. "I'd like that, too."

As they strolled toward her apartment, the chilly night air was the perfect ruse for Marcus to put his arm around her shoulder.

"You're shivering," he said, pulling her close. He was elated that she didn't pull away.

"The temperature dropped," she offered as an excuse. There was no way that she would tell him it was the nearness of him that set her to trembling.

Shortly they stood in front of her building.

"This is where we part ways," Marcus said, smiling down on her upturned face, wanting to kiss her.

"I was wondering"—she hesitated—"I mean, if you're not busy . . . would you like to go with me to my father's house on Saturday night? He invited me for dinner and suggested that I bring a guest. I know you said you were sort of—kind of—involved with this woman on the Internet, but if it wouldn't interfere with—"

"I'd love to go," he said softly, cutting off her rambling. "I don't have plans for Saturday, and I can't think of anything I'd like better." He braced her shoulders. "On one condition."

Her eyes sparkled with pleasure. "What's the condition?"

"That you go with me to The Bottom Line on Friday night. I won't take no for an answer."

She thought about the message she'd left on his e-mail and wondered what he would do when he read it. "Then you won't get no for an answer." She grinned.

He leaned down and gently kissed her cheek. He wanted more, but he could wait.

"Good night, Joi. I'm glad you called." He looked deeply into her eyes. "I'll see you Friday." He turned to leave.

"What time?" she called.

He looked over his shoulder. "Be ready about nine."

"I will," she grinned, floating up the stairs. "I will."

Marcus couldn't remember the last time he'd felt this good. There was no doubt that Joi was very interested in him and not on a professional basis. He still had plans to tread slowly. He had no intention of messing things up.

Pulling off his clothes, he prepared for bed, and for the first time in a while he looked forward to the weekend. He would be spending it with the woman he loved.

Loved? The thought stopped him cold. Was he in love with Joi or in love with the idea of winning her heart? Thoughtfully he sat down on the edge of his bed.

Joi was a challenge, there was no question about that. She was unique, and no other woman had affected him the way she had. She could come across as shy, and homespun, someone you wanted to wrap up and take care of day and night. Or she could be the femme fatale that she was tonight, turning him on with just a twist of her hips.

She was bright, funny, career oriented, beautiful inside and out and she wasn't man hungry. It was obvious from her conversation on and off screen that she had never really been involved in a serious relationship. His ego grew by leaps and bounds. She was letting him into her life. He felt certain that no other man had the honor before him. And if he had anything to do with it, none would after.

Yes. He was in love with Joi Holliday.

"I'm looking forward to meeting your daughter," Lana said, snuggling closer to Paul.

Paul didn't respond. How could he explain to her that he had no idea if Joi would accept his invitation. How could he tell her that the relationship he had with his daughter was far from perfect.

"Paul? Is something wrong?" She turned on her side to look at him.

He sighed heavily. "I think there are some things you need to know, Lana, about me and Joi."

Slowly he began the painful story of his breakup and subsequent divorce from his wife, her death some years later, and his way of handling his pain.

"I thought I was doing the right thing by Joi. I was so hurt by what Lydia did, I felt that if Joi somehow lacked the confidence in herself and considered her beauty to be more of a handicap than an asset . . . I wouldn't lose her as well."

Lana reached up and gently stroked his cheek. "It didn't work, did it?" she said knowingly. "Instead of keeping her close, you shut her out, and she wound up with no one and neither did you."

He turned to stare into her wise eyes. "How did you know?"

"I've been there," she confessed. "When my husband left me for another woman, I was devastated. All I had left was my son, Anthony. I did everything in my power to bind him to me. It nearly destroyed our relationship."

"What did you do?"

"When he finally moved out, he told me that he had lived my life for me for fifteen years, and now it was time for each of us to find a life of our own. I probably walked around in a daze for weeks after that, and then one day what he'd said to me finally sank in. That's when I got involved with the Sociable Singles Network and began event planning. It gave me the perfect opportunity to meet people, get others together, and enjoy my life. I've been very happy."

He nodded. "I know I've made some mistakes over the years," he said "Since I've met you, I've realized how empty my life has been, and how I've lived my life has affected my daughter. In my own awkward way, I've tried to make amends to her. I'm hoping that this dinner will be a new beginning for us—*if* she decides to come."

"She'll come," Lana assured. "She'll come."

Paul turned on his side to face her. Stroking her smooth cinnamon-toned cheek, he asked, "How can you be so sure?"

"Your daughter loves you, Paul. She wants you to love her back. She'll be here. I have a very strong feeling that Joi will find her own way, just as Anthony did. Despite the both of us." She smiled and kissed his warm lips.

First thing the next morning, Joi called her father to tell him she'd be there for dinner, Marcus would accompany her. If she didn't know better, she'd swear her father sounded excited.

Replacing the receiver on the cradle, she recalled her "semi-impromptu" dinner with Marcus. She was still reeling from happiness. But she had to remember to play it cool. For the moment he believed he had the upper hand. In less than one week she'd prove him wrong. She couldn't wait to see the look on his face.

The phone rang, pulling her away from her perfect daydream. Instinct told her it was Monica calling to get the scoop hot off the press.

"Joi Holiday," she sang into the mouthpiece.

"It must have been better than I thought," Monica replied. "And I want every intimate detail."

Joi could envision her friend leaning back in her seat, crossing her long legs, and tapping her air-brushed nails with impatience.

"To make a long story short, he's still trying to figure out what's going on."

"Don't even try the 'to make a long story short' routine. I want to hear everything. I want to be like Ma Bell, the next best thing to being there!"

They both laughed loud and long until Joi finally pulled herself together and gave Monica the details that she craved.

"Ooooh, chile, tell me that part again about how you kind of wiggled in the seat and he started wiping his face."

Joi cracked up again. "I will not. Ten times is plenty!"

"All right. All right," Monica conceded. "What are you wearing to The Bottom Line tomorrow?"

"I'm not sure yet."

"Well, don't forget the plan."

"I won't."

"And what about Saturday at your dad's?"

Joi snickered. "My father and Marcus are in for a treat."

"Oh, Joi "Monica whined. "Can't you make up an excuse for me to be there? I don't want to miss this."

"You'll just have to this time. Five is definitely a crowd."

"Hey, I can bring a date."

"Forget it, Monica."

"Yeah, okay. Just make sure you get a good description of Ms. Lana. My curiosity is killing me."

Marcus read the computer message one last time. "Unbelievable," he muttered. "One minute, no date. The next minute— two."

He shook his head. Even though he knew Joi and his cybermate were the same person, he had to let one of them down or he'd give himself away. He thought about that again. Now he was beginning to think crazy.

If he told the "real" Joi—no, he'd look like a fool. If he went to meet his cybermate, Joi would feel ridiculous when he turned up at the club. He'd have to go with the "real" Joi. He'd think of an excuse. Then he reread the message. She'd clearly given him an out, and he was going to take it.

Quickly he typed out his regrets, apologized profusely, and sent the message to Joi's office computer.

"Just as I thought," Joi said to Monica over lunch. "He backed out of the date with the 'other me.' "

"Of course. It's all in the plan." She grinned.

* * *

Shortly after Joi arrived at her apartment that evening, the superintendent rang her bell.

She opened the door to the wizened man, who barely reached her shoulders. "Hi, Mr. Mitchell." Then her eyes rounded in delight. "My package!"

"Came this morning," he puffed. "I held it for ya," he added with emphasis.

She got the hint. "Just a minute." She went to the hall closet, pulled a dollar from her coat pocket, and returned "Thank you," she said, handing him the dollar.

"No problem," he said, flashing a perfect row of yellow teeth. "You take care." He turned and ambled down the hallway.

Joi chuckled and closed the door, then hurried into the living room to open the box.

Tearing open the top, she pulled away the pink tissue paper to reveal her costume for the ball. A smile of pure joy lit up her face, and her dark brown eyes shimmered with delight.

"Perfect," she breathed, gently lifting the exquisite fabric from the box to hold in front of her.

Running to her bedroom, she stood in front of the full-length mirror. Standing there with the fabulous costume in front of her, she felt every bit the role she would play. Valentine's Day could not arrive fast enough. But first—the weekend.

"If you ask me one more time do I have it together, Monica, I'm going to scream. I swear I will," Joi said through clenched teeth.

"Just checking," Monica admonished, taking a last look at Joi's outfit. "Lookin' good, girl," she said finally. "Not too hot but not too cool."

Joi turned toward the mirror, checking her reflection. "I'm pleased," she said smugly.

"Now if you'd just let me convince you to get some contacts."

"These new glasses are perfect. I saw them in the *Essence* catalogue and fell in love with them."

"They're definitely a step up from those other ones. They give you a whole new look."

Joi checked her watch. "You'd better be getting out of here," she cautioned. "Marcus is due to pick me up in a half hour."

"You're right." Monica began gathering her things. "The last thing you need is for him to see me here and think I'm spying."

"Aren't you?"

"Very funny." She leaned down and gave Joi a quick, tight hug. "Good luck, girl. You knock 'em dead."

"I'll try," she said, and Monica heard the tremor in her voice. She sat down on the edge of the dressing room table. "What is it, Joi?"

Joi looked up at her friend, and her eyes sparkled with tears held in abeyance.

"I'm scared. I feel like such a fraud." She lowered her head. "Afraid of what my father will think. Afraid of making a fool of myself in front of everyone, especially Marcus. I—"

"Listen, Joi," Monica consoled gently. "You'll be fine—tonight and tomorrow and the day after. Marcus is so taken with you, you could show up in a burlap bag. As for your father, he's long overdue for a wake-up call. Besides, Paul Holliday has too much class to act ugly at his own dinner party."

Joi giggled at that and sniffed back her tears. "You're probably right," she conceded. "Thanks."

"Anytime." She hopped down from the edge of the table. "Call me the instant you walk through the door," she ordered, hustling out of the room.

"Can I at least take my coat off first?"

"Absolutely not," she called over her shoulder, punctuating that directive with a definitive slam of the door.

Joi shook her head, took one last look at her reflection, then got up. Entering the living room, she turned on the stereo to her favorite jazz station, and the apartment was soon filled with the sounds of Wynton Marsalis, followed by Natalie Cole's rendition of her father's classic "Unforgettable."

Joi felt herself relax, her mind and body unwind as she allowed the music to enter her soul. With her head resting against the soft cushioned headrest of the couch, she closed her eyes and imagined the evening ahead.

Just as she stood on tiptoe with her eyes closed and her lips puckered for a searing good night kiss, the doorbell rang.

Her eyes snapped open, and her heart began to race. Her wrist flew up in front of her face to check her watch "Eight thirty. It's him! He's early. Oh, God" The bell rang again. She popped up from the couch like a jack-in-the-box.

"Okay, just be cool," she warned herself. She took a deep breath and crossed the room to the door. Fixing a smile on her face, she unlocked the locks and opened the door.

Marcus leaned down and planted a feather-light kiss on her lips. Her knees felt weak.

"Hi," he whispered. Then his eyes trailed along her length. His lids lowered appreciatively. "You look . . . wonderful," he said in admiration.

She smiled the shy, endearing smile that set his pulse racing.

"Thank you." She stepped back. "Come in and make yourself comfortable. I just have to get my coat and bag."

Marcus followed her inside and was pleased to see how Joi lived. The apartment, though small, had an airy feel to it. On one wall a beautiful mahogany bookcase held what looked like hundreds of books from every genre. The whitewashed walls were adorned with a stunning array of notable black artists, including works by Tom Feelings and Charles Bibb. Hand-carved African statues stood at majestic attention in three of the four corners of the room. The huge bay window that looked out onto a garden was bare save for the soft floral pouf valances that edged them.

"I'm ready."

He turned from the window, and his heart started that old familiar thumping when his gaze rested on her. He smiled, and it took all of his willpower not to cross the short space that separated them and take her into his arms. In time, he reminded himself.

He shoved his hands into his pants pockets, pushing back his

camel-colored cashmere coat to reveal a tan turtleneck sweater
and full pleated slacks of the same color, split across the middle
with a copper-toned snakeskin belt. Shoes matching his belt completed the *Ebony Man* outfit. The entire combination did serious
justice to his smooth complexion. This was definitely a different
Marcus from the backpack-toting, jeans-wearing guy that came
to her office. She thought he looked good the other night. Tonight
he was even more edible than usual—if that was possible.

"You certainly are," he said under his breath. "We should have
enough time to have dinner before the show."

"Great. What time does it start?" she asked while he helped
her with her coat. She held her breath to keep from trembling as
she felt his hands moving across her upper body.

"Regina Bell opens the show at ten. She'll probably sing for
an hour and then . . ."

"The Whispers," they said, laughing in unison.

"I'm glad we did start out early," Joi said. "This line is unbelievable."

Marcus chuckled. "It's always like this when big names appear
here. It shouldn't be too much longer." He looked down at her
and smiled as he watched her try to peer over the heads of the
people in front of them. She looked perfect tonight. She'd chosen
a very stylish navy pantsuit with a fitted jacket over flowing
accordion-pleated pants. Instead of cascading tresses, or her signature ponytail, her hair was done in a stylish French roll. Tiny,
teardrop earrings were her only jewelry except for her watch.

The line began to move. "Here we go. Stay close," he advised.
He took her hand, and when her eyes flew up to meet his he said,
"Just making sure I don't lose you."

The barest hint of a smile pulled at the corners of her mouth.

Moments later they were seated at a table less than ten feet
away from the stage.

"This is perfect." Joi exhaled on a long sigh of contentment, looking around the huge open room and the throngs of people who poured through the doors.

Marcus angled his seat a bit closer. "I know you're going to have a great time." He looked into her eyes. "I hope this will be the start of many more evenings together."

Joi was the first to look away. She could hardly contain her happiness. *Many more evenings together.*

The show was more fantastic than she'd imagined. Regina Bell brought the crowd to its feet more times than she could count. But she was truly transported to heaven when The Whispers took center stage and crooned their soulful tunes of love. So it was only natural that she found herself leaning against the hard lines of Marcus's body, swaying in time to the music. And it was over all too soon.

"I had a great time," Joi said as they approached her apartment door. "Thank you so much."

"I should be thanking you."

She looked quizzically at him.

"The evening was truly a pleasure, Joi. It's been a long time."

"A long time for what?" she asked softly, staring up into his eyes.

"A long time since I've been in such wonderful company."

She lowered her gaze. "For me, too," she admitted.

"I hope it won't be the last time."

"I'll see you tomorrow."

"It's not soon enough. But I guess I'll have to wait, won't I?"

"So will I," she said softly.

"Good night, Joi." He leaned down and ethereally kissed her cheek. She waited expectantly, and he fulfilled her expectation. Cupping her face in his hands, he slowly lowered his head and pressed his moist lips to hers. The kiss, so sweet, so fleeting beat against her heart like the first burst of spring. Reluctantly he eased away, his gaze locking on to her face.

"Until tomorrow." He turned and walked away.

* * *

Joi talked so much in the past hour, telling Monica about her evening, that she was totally dehydrated. "Yes, I'm sure I didn't leave anything out," she insisted.

"Just checking," Monica replied. "This is just too good. Your fairy-tale romance seems like it's really coming true, girlfriend. I'm so happy for you."

"I have to keep pinching myself to make sure I'm not dreaming."

"If it is a dream, I don't want to wake up, either. This is long overdue. I feel like it's all happening to me."

Joi laughed. "If it was you, you wouldn't be a bundle of nerves like I am."

Monica leaned back against the couch, and for a moment Joi thought she looked uncomfortable. "I've never admitted this to anyone. And I swear if you ever tell, I'll deny it."

"What are you talking about? Who would I tell? *You're* my best friend."

Monica sighed. "Everyone thinks that I have it all together."

"You do."

Monica shook her head in denial. "Not really. It's all a lot of smoke and mirrors." She leaned forward a bit. "I'm scared every day. I get up in the morning and wonder if I'm going to make it. I worry that I'll have on the wrong outfit or my hair isn't just right, or I won't have a witty comment to make at the right time. And if that were to ever happen, everyone would see the scared little girl beneath the weaves and the makeup." She chuckled mirthlessly. "I envy you, Joi. I envy your ability to just be you. I envy the idea that a man who seems as wonderful as Marcus likes you just the way you are, without all the 'extras.' I don't even know how to act without putting on a performance."

Joi looked at her in shocked disbelief. "I . . . I don't know what to say. I never knew you felt that way."

"Joi, whether you realize it or not, your father did you a favor all of these years—as much as I tried to convince you otherwise.

He put you in a position to present yourself to the world for who you are, just as you are. People aren't drawn to you because you have the greatest wardrobe on the block, the fanciest car or the quickest wit. They're drawn to you because you're just a down-right great person. That may have never shown through if you'd allowed your physical beauty to outshine what was important."

A hot exultant tear trickled down Joi's cheek. She swallowed hard and bit down on her lip. She reached across the short space and clasped Monica's hand in hers. "You're the best friend anyone could ever hope to have. With or without the hair, the nails, the clothes. You bring sunshine wherever you go. That's something special. Don't ever think differently."

Monica sniffed loudly and gave a crooked grin. "Thanks. I needed that."

"Anytime, girlfriend. Anytime."

Monica brushed her hand across her damp cheeks. "Whew, a good cry is food for the soul. Now, let's get you together for your big night so I can get out of here. I have a hot date with Ronald."

They both laughed, hugging each other, and headed for Joi's bedroom.

The Dinner

"He's not always the easiest person to get along with," Joi warned as she and Marcus approached her father's house.

"Don't worry so much," Marcus consoled. "Everything is going to be fine. How bad could he be?"

"That remains to be seen," she replied drolly. They walked up the three steps to the front door, and Joi rang the bell. Several moments later Paul opened the door.

"Joi. Mr. Speller. Come on in. Glad you could make it." They stepped across the threshold, and Paul kissed his daughter's cheek. She nearly jumped in shock. He patted Marcus heartily on the back.

Paul led the way to the living room, and Marcus gave Joi a quick wink and an assuring squeeze on her arm.

They entered the well-appointed room, and Lana rose from the couch to greet them.

"Joi, Marcus I'd like you to meet Lana English. Lana, my daughter, Joi, and her friend, Marcus Speller."

Joi crossed the room and extended her petite hand, first to Joi and then to Marcus. "I'm happy to finally meet the both of you. I've heard nothing but good things."

"I hope they're all true," Marcus joked. "Good to meet you also."

She was nothing like she'd imagined, Joi realized. Lana English was a small woman, just about her height. She wore her salt-and-pepper hair in a short, early Halle Berry haircut. Her finely sculpted face had little to no makeup to accentuate the smooth cinnamon-toned complexion. By societal standards she was average looking, but she exuded inner radiance that highlighted every aspect of her being. Joi liked her instantly.

"It's a pleasure," Joi said with sincerity. She turned a quick glance in her father's direction, and the smile that softened his face filled her heart.

"Dinner was absolutely delicious," Joi said, delicately wiping her mouth.

"Lana didn't want me to say this, but she fixed everything," Paul announced, his voice filled with admiration.

"You really turned out a feast, Lana," Marcus commented.

"Thank you. Cooking is a hobby of mine."

"Well, you could definitely give up your day job," Joi said.

Lana laughed. "Actually, my day job and cooking work hand in hand."

"How so?" Marcus quizzed.

"I plan events. Very often I cater the events as well."

"As a matter of fact, Lana's in town to plan a Valentine event," Paul interjected.

"That sounds like fun," Joi said. She took a sip of water from the crystal goblet.

"I think it's going to be fabulous. It's for a masquerade ball."

Joi nearly choked on her water. "Masquerade ball?"

"Yes. I'm involved with an organization called the Sociable Singles Network. They asked me to plan their first masquerade ball."

Now it was Marcus's turn to choke. "Is that right," he sputtered.

Paul looked from Joi to Marcus. "Are you two all right?"

"Yes," they chimed in unison.

"My water went down the wrong way," Joi said.

Marcus gave a halfhearted shrug and focused his attention on his cherry cheesecake.

Lana went on to explain about the network, her involvement, and all the plans being made for the ball.

Joi listened with a smile painted on her face, and Marcus expertly hid his surprise.

"Are you planning on attending, Dad?"

"No. You have to be a member to attend," Paul said. "Lana tried to pull some strings, but the organization is very strict about the membership rule."

Lana smiled apologetically.

"Sorry I'm going to miss it," Marcus said quickly.

"Yes. It sounds like fun," Joi chimed in.

The conversation gradually drifted to the state of the world, upcoming elections and to the show Marcus and Joi had attended the previous night.

"I understand from Joi that you're a music hound," Marcus said after Joi and Lana left the room.

Paul chuckled. "I've been collecting for years."

"My father is a music aficionado, too."

"Great pastime," Paul said, taking a seat on the leather lounge chair opposite the love seat where Marcus sat.

"I guess I inherited the craving."

"You're a collector?"

"I'm sure my collection is not as extensive as yours," he said, angling his head in the direction of the rows of albums, cassettes and CD's. "But I can hold my own," he smiled.

The mention of music was just the catalyst that Paul needed. They launched into a lengthy discussion of the history of music, talked of their favorite performers and their extensive collection of the old jazz greats, completely forgetting about the women in the kitchen.

"Your father was worried that you wouldn't come tonight," Lana hedged, looking sideways at Joi to gauge her reaction.

"I was a bit worried myself," she confessed, feeling free to talk to Lana. "My father and I haven't had the closest of relationships over the years."

"I gathered as much."

Joi looked at her with surprise in her eyes.

"Can I be candid with you, Joi?"

Joi put down the dish she was holding. "Of course."

Lana took a breath. "Your father has been a very lonely man over the years, and even though I've known him for only a short time, we've become . . . very close. He feels that he had not always done the right thing by you. But he loves you dearly. It's just hard for him to express it."

Joi lowered her gaze and adjusted her glasses. "It took me a long time, Lana, but I've slowly begun to realize that. My father did what he felt he had to do. He had a lot to deal with over the years, and he handled it the only way he knew how."

Lana smiled and reached out to touch Joi's shoulder. "I'm glad you understand."

"I'm glad he has you in his life," she said softly. "He deserves some happiness."

"And so do you, my dear," she said sagely. "So take it."

"Thank you for a wonderful evening, Mr. Holliday," Marcus said as they stood by the door. "Lana, it was truly a pleasure meeting you. Call me anytime you plan to cook!"

Lana laughed then kissed his cheek. "I certainly will."

"And anytime you want to talk music, you know where to find me," Paul said, shaking Marcus's hand."

"I'll remember that."

Paul moved toward his daughter, smiling with a bit of uncertainty. She moved toward him, and they embraced. "Thank you," he whispered in her ear.

"Be happy," she responded in kind. She turned her gaze toward Lana. "I hope to see you again," she said pointedly.

"If I have anything to do with it, you will."

They turned to leave, but not before Paul whispered to Marcus, "Make my baby happy."

"I intend to," he said.

"See, it wasn't bad at all," Marcus said, pulling up in front of Joi's building.

She turned to him and smiled. "You're absolutely right." She shook her head. "I don't know who that charming man was tonight pretending to be my father," she joked, "but I hope he stays around."

"I have a very strong feeling that whatever change has taken place in your father has a lot to do with Lana."

"I know. I feel the same way." She paused a moment. "She and I had a nice chat in the kitchen. She cares about my dad a great deal. I'm really happy for him."

"Everyone deserves a bit of happiness."

"That's what Lana said."

"What else did she say?" Marcus whispered, his voice a bare rumble. He leaned toward her.

Joi swallowed as Marcus reached for her glasses and removed them. "She said . . . I should take my happiness," she breathed.

"Did she?" He leaned closer and cupped her face in his hands. "I hope . . ."—the pads of his thumbs brushed across her lips and she trembled—". . . you know where to look." His warming gaze caressed her face, milliseconds before his lips touched down on hers.

Blazing, unimaginable heat seared through her veins, cutting off her air, accelerating her heartbeat. She felt dizzy when the tantalizing tip of his tongue parted her waiting lips and did a mind-numbing exploration of her mouth.

All of her senses became heightened. The heady scent of his body oil swirled through her brain. She could feel every hair on her body, visualize the pulse that raced like a surging tide through her. The tips of her fingers that brushed along his clothing seemed to have become perfect conductors of electricity. She could see—with her eyes closed—every nuance of his darkly handsome face. Had this been what she'd missed—longed for? How sweet was the wait.

Marcus groaned softly as he eased away. Still holding her face, he lowered his head, pressing it against hers, drew on his willpower to control the unbelievable desire that threatened to explode. "I won't apologize for that," he said, his voice a low throb.

"I don't want you to."

He looked into her eyes, wanting to say so much, but knowing he should wait just a while longer. The right corner of his mouth lifted in a grin. "You'd better get upstairs." He pressed his lips to her forehead. He made a move to get out of the car.

"I'll be fine," she said. "There's no reason for you to come up." She didn't dare tell him that if he did come up, there was no telling when he would be coming back down. Not with the feelings that were running unchecked within her.

"Are you sure?" He looked for some sign in her eyes to tell him he'd done nothing wrong and everything right. Her gaze was unreadable.

She nodded and focused on her folded hands.

"I see." Gingerly he handed her glasses to her.

"Thank you," she mumbled. Fumbling with the lock, she opened the door and hurried to the building's entrance. Briefly she turned, stopped, waved good night, then pushed through the glass and wood door.

For several moments Marcus sat motionless in his car. He went over every detail of the evening in his head, right up to and including that mind-blowing kiss. Nothing added up to Joi's abrupt change in attitude. He looked at the building one last time, put the car in gear, and drove home.

Joi's phone was ringing the moment she set foot in the door. She had a good mind not to answer it, knowing it was Monica.

But if she didn't, she also knew that Monica would keep calling until she answered.

Might as well get it over with. She stripped off her coat, tossed it in the chair, and picked up the extension in the hall. "Hi, Monica."

"How did you know it was me?"

"Lucky guess." She chuckled. She sat down and kicked off her shoes.

"Well, don't keep me in suspense. How did everything go?"

Joi took a long breath, then began to tell Monica about her evening, leaving nothing out except the relentless throbbing that pulsed between the thighs.

"You didn't invite him upstairs?" Monica cried incredulously.

"No, I did not."

"Would you mind telling me why, for heaven's sake?"

"I'm not ready to cross that line yet, Monica," she stated clearly. "We still have some loose ends to tie up."

She could hear Monica sigh. "I guess you're right," she conceded. "Only you know what's best for you."

"I'm still learning," she said sincerely.

For the next few days leading up to the ball, Joi and Marcus continued to communicate over the Internet, each keeping their secret. They hadn't seen each other since the night of the dinner at her father's house, and it was just as well, Joi concluded. She was one huge ball of nerves.

"What if he flips when he finds out I knew and didn't say anything?" Joi moaned. "He'll think I was trying to make a fool of him."

"So what will be his explanation?" Monica cut in. "He knows who you are, or at least you think he knows." She shook her head. "Maybe you should have told him when you suspected."

"I had to be sure of Marcus's feelings for me," she said softly, brushing her hair upward and twisting it into an intricate pile on top of her head.

Monica sat down on the edge of Joi's bed. "How you feel about him is the real question," she stated gently.

Joi turned in the swivel dressing table chair to face her friend. "All I know is I've never felt this way about anyone before in my life." She took a deep breath and exhaled. "Every time I think of him, I get breathless. My heart is always racing. I can't eat. I daydream all the time. When he steps into a room, I get hot flashes. My hormones seem to be on permanent supercharge. And I've never felt better."

"Sounds like you've finally fallen in love." Monica smiled with pleasure. "You have all of the classic symptoms."

Joi giggled and briefly covered her face with her hands. "If this is love, I don't want the feeling to ever end." She sighed wistfully, then suddenly her eyes widened. "What if he doesn't feel the same way? What if he never feels the same way . . . What if—?"

"What if you just get a grip, get dressed, get to the ball, and find out once and for all."

The Ball

In the limo drive to the Spy Café, Joi tried to envision the evening ahead. As part of the plan, she'd deliberately described a completely different costume from the one she was wearing. Marcus would be looking for Cinderella. But a lot had changed since she'd told him she'd be coming as Cinderella. She no longer felt like the hopeless young girl waiting for a prince to come and make things right. She didn't have a fairy godmother to help her out. She didn't want magic, and she didn't need rescuing. She held the power to control her destiny. And she would.

As the car approached the café, Joi's heart began to race. She hadn't returned any of Marcus's calls since the night of the dinner. Other than the brief messages they shared on-line, they'd had no contact.

Thinking about it now, Marcus's communication with her had been brief and static. Maybe she'd gone too far in holding him off. He was trying to reach out to her, and she hadn't taken his hand. What if he didn't show up? What if—

"We're here, miss," the driver from the network said. Sociable Singles had gone all out, arranging for transportation for any member who'd requested it. Joi peered through the smoke-tinted window and saw limos and town cars lining the street.

The driver came around, opened the door, and helped her out of the car. For several seconds Joi stood stock still, a heartbeat away from hightailing it back home. But good sense and powerful emotions took over. She'd come this far, she wouldn't back down now. She was sure of her feelings for Marcus Speller. She knew she had what it took to win his heart and his love. And above all, she was ready to take her happiness.

"Thank you." She smiled graciously.

"Have a pleasant evening."

"Oh, I intend to." She walked toward the bank of revolving glass doors and stepped inside.

The past few days had been the most difficult days of his life. Never before had he felt so desolate as he had when, time after time, Joi did not take or return his phone calls.

He stared out of his bedroom window, looking down at the steady stream of traffic. The limo that the network had sent had come and gone without him. The only reason why he bothered to order the car was because he knew tonight he'd reveal his true feelings to Joi. He also knew the last thing he'd want to do at the end of the evening was drive.

He turned away from the window and crossed the room to where his costume was spread out across the bed.

He chuckled without humor, and thought about the halfhearted messages he'd sent to her during the past three days. Since their last night together, some of the enthusiasm had gone out of him. His heart wasn't in it, and he'd started to feel as though she was just stringing him along.

He pushed aside his costume and dropped down on the bed. *"Joi."*

Joi was devastated. The ball had been in full swing for more than an hour, and there was no sign of Marcus.

It was becoming painfully obvious that he had no intention of showing up. Couples were hugging, laughing, and mingling everywhere that she looked. If she ever felt out of place before, those times could never compare to this.

Tears burned her contact-lens eyes and threatened to spill down her cheeks. Taking small gulps of air, she struggled to hold them back. She'd done an excellent job of ducking Lana, who seemed to be thoroughly enjoying herself. But when the M.C. announced that The Whispers were taking the stage, that did her in.

She rushed past the enthusiastic crowd that surged toward the stage, excusing herself along her way to the rest room.

Miraculously she found herself alone. "But of course you're alone," she said to her reflection. "What in the world made you think you could have a man like Marcus Speller hot on your heels?"

She sniffed and wiped her eyes. She looked at herself long and hard, and one by one all of the reasons why Marcus would want her enumerated themselves in her mind.

Slowly anger replaced her hurt and disappointment. How dare he stand her up? she fumed. How dare he make her hurt the way she was hurting? He deserved to know how she felt, and she deserved the satisfaction of telling him once and for all.

Pulling herself together, she dabbed at her eyes and tucked away a stray strand of hair. Taking a fortifying breath, she walked out with the intention of leaving.

She headed directly to the coat-check room when the strains of The Whispers' classic hit "Lady" filled the ballroom.

Again tears filled her eyes, and she could barely swallow over the knot in her throat. She wrapped her arms around herself while she waited, as if she could hold back her hurt.

"You can't leave without dancing with me," came the deep, sonorous voice from just behind her left side. His scent floated around her, and her heart began to thunder and her pulse pounded unbelievably loud in her ears. Fear mixed with surprise, relief and joy kept her immobile. But the tremors began the instant the large strong hands rested on her shoulders and turned her around to face him.

She looked up and opened her mouth to speak, but the words wouldn't come.

"Dance with me," he urged in a ragged whisper. He held out his hand and waited. When she placed her petite hand in his, it was then he realized he'd been holding his breath.

He guided her around the groups of party-goers and circular tables to the center of the floor.

The lights were romantically dim, the room illuminated by a single shimmering sphere of light that hung from the ceiling, throwing off tiny, sparkling pinpoints of light as it slowly spun around.

She moved into his embrace as if drawn by some inner connection. She felt his relieved sigh and smiled as she rested her head against his chest.

They moved as one person, as if they'd always danced this way together, gliding effortlessly across the floor.

Joi was in heaven. He'd come, she thought ecstatically. He did care.

He pressed her closer to him, inhaling the fresh scent of her hair. She was absolutely breathtaking as Cleopatra, Queen of the Nile. The original queen ruled and conquered with brains as well as her dark beauty. But even she could never compare to the queen he held in his arms.

They were perfect together, he thought, never wanting the moment to end, but wanting more than this. And with that longing came the undeniable realization that he would always want more and more of Joi Holliday.

The music ended, the crowd erupted into deafening applause, and Joi and Marcus still held each other, captured in their private world.

"You don't look anything like the woman you described," Marcus said in her ear, swaying with her to a beat that only they heard. "I was expecting a tall Cinderella."

She arched her head back and looked up at him, stunning as the warrior hero, Othello.

"I have no idea what you're talking about. Obviously you have me confused with someone else," she challenged.

He tossed his head back and laughed. "You, little lady, I would know anywhere"—his voice softened—"with my eyes closed." Gently, he removed her mask, and their eyes met in a gentle embrace.

A smile of pure happiness lit her face. "How long have you known?" she asked pointedly.

He grinned. "I could ask you the same thing. I could also ask you why you needed to paint yourself as someone else."

She turned her head away, and he turned it back with the tip of his finger. "Let's get out of here," he said, looking deep into her eyes. "We have a lot of explaining to do to each other."

In short order they'd retrieved their coats and were out in the biting February night.

Marcus put his arm around Joi and hugged her to him. "My car is right on the corner," he shouted over the wind. And he suddenly realized it was the first time in months that he'd actually found a parking space! His luck was finally changing.

"Where do you want to go?" Joi asked, hugging herself inside the still warming car.

"I haven't eaten a thing, and I'm starved," Marcus stated. He turned toward her, his smile beaming with mischief. "Why don't we go to our favorite spot, order everything to go, and have the date that we pretended to have on-line?"

Joi grinned and lowered her eyes, remembering their "first date" and the fun she'd had. "Your place?" she asked in a shy voice.

"Perfect." He squeezed her hand and put the car in gear.

Marcus's dining room was constructed much like the Japanese. Low wooden tables set on a platform were surrounded by overstuffed pillows for seating. Recessed lighting softly illuminated the space, creating intricate shapes and shadows along the cool cream walls and hardwood floors. The room was separated from the rest of the apartment by three sliding doors, each leading to another area of the apartment.

It was the home of a romantic, Joi realized as she took in the atmosphere. It was designed for comfort and intimacy. The living area was decorated with a long soft couch of cool beige with a matching love seat. A small grouping of huge floor pillows near the state-of-the-art stereo system and in front of the magnificently refurbished fireplace begged guests to bury themselves in their softness. Scented candles sat in hand-painted clay pots, filling the air with the soft scent of vanilla.

Then another thought hit her. How many other women had come here and been wined and dined into submission? How many others had been treated to this romantic retreat? He'd confessed that one of his main reasons for reviewing romance novels was to find out how women ticked. *Humph.* His living arrangements were a blatant testament to that.

She turned on her heel at the sound behind her, her eyes blazing with irrational hurt, until her gaze focused on Marcus.

He stood in the center of the dining room, precariously balancing a tray of drinks, plates and utensils on one hand and two boxes of pizza on the other. Her anger evaporated as quickly as it had come.

"Don't move," she instructed and hurried to his side, her flowing robe of gold lamé fanning out around her teal-colored gown.

"You look magnificent," he said in wonder. "Like a true African queen ready to bring her man to his knees."

She smiled, taken aback by his bold statement. *Her man.*

"Let me help you with those," she finally said. She took the boxes of pizza and placed them on the low wooden table.

Together they arranged the table, and Marcus added a spray of wildflowers to the glass bowl that served as the centerpiece.

The soothing voice of Peabo Bryson crooned in the background while they ate and talked.

"Are you going to tell me how you found out?" Joi quizzed, taking a sip of spring water with a twist of lemon.

Marcus tilted his head to the side and leaned on his elbow. "I suppose I was being nosey," he began. "I was in your office . . ."

* * *

When he'd concluded, Joi shook her head and laughed. "That must have been some shock."

"Believe me, it was. But then when I thought about it, it seemed so right. All the time that I was communicating with you on-line, I felt I was connecting with the Joi I knew. There were so many similarities.

"What about you?" he asked, reaching across the table to brush a crumb from her lips with the pad of his thumb. Instantly she felt a warmth flood her body at the contact. Inwardly she sighed and forced her thoughts to clear.

"I started putting it together when your messages began relating to things we'd discussed on line." She chuckled lightly. "I decided to play along." She looked away and shrugged. "I guess I needed to be sure."

"Sure of what, Joi?" he gently probed.

She turned to look directly at him. "Sure that it was the real me you were interested in and not the image I'd created on-line."

"Joi, sweetheart." He rose from his semi-reclining position and came around to kneel beside her. "I fell in love with you—the Joi that seems shy but has this fire burning beneath her cool exterior."

"In love?" she asked incredulously, her heart hammering like mad.

"I fell in love with the Joi that could make me smile every time she pushed her glasses up on her nose, or wore those long skirts but loved the hot love scenes. Yes, sweetheart, in love." He caressed her cheek, easing closer. "I fell in love with the woman who made me think about her for hours on end and compared her to every other woman I met."

His eyes grazed across her face. "You are the most special, the most beautiful, woman I've ever known, inside and out." His lips teased hers, and her eyes fluttered close. He spoke close to her mouth, punctuating each sentence with titillating strokes of his tongue across her lips. "There's nothing you can ever do to disguise the wonderful woman you are. What's most beautiful about you, Joi, is how good you make others feel in your presence. Don't ever trade that for a ton of fancy hairdos, makeup jobs and designer clothes. I love you as you are—whatever way you want to be. With or without glasses," he grinned.

He took his finger and wiped away the rivulets of tears that ran down her smooth cheeks. Then he cupped her face in his hands and captured her lips in a kiss that nearly stopped her heart.

His mouth took possession not only of her lips but her soul. Rivers of heat infused her, so hot and intense she felt the room begin to sway. She clung to him for support, her slender fingers gathering the fabric of his shirt in her fists.

Marcus's moan pulsed through her body, and when she trembled with need, he drew her closer, cutting off all space between them.

Like the conquering warrior Othello, he pillaged her mouth with his rapier tongue, seeking out and finding all of the sweet hidden treasures and staking his claim.

She swayed against him, wanting more—wanting to burrow her way beneath his skin. She couldn't get close enough, not like this, she thought dizzily.

He stroked her body, glorying in the satisfaction of finally having her as his own. His heart beat a song of happiness, knowing that tonight was only the beginning of so many more.

Marcus eased back, groaning her name, then covering her face with tiny hot kisses.

His eyes burned into hers. "I want you, Joi. Tonight and for always," he said in a ragged whispered. "But I want you the right way." He grinned shyly. "Be my valentine, sweetheart. We'll celebrate every day of the rest of our lives, loving each other."

Joi's voice shook with breathless emotion. "What are you asking me, Marcus?"

"I'm asking you to be my lady, lover, soulmate—my wife."

She bit down on her lip to keep it from trembling, then flew into his arms. "Only if you'll be mine," she whispered, delirious with joy.

Like the jewel she was, Marcus eased her down against the pillows, snuggled her close to him, and talked of their future together.

One Year Later

When Marcus's article on Internet dating had hit the newsstands, it was such a success that editors from magazines, newspapers and even television producers began banging down his door with job offers. Although he still freelanced periodically for Holliday Publishing, he worked with another editor as Joi had moved up the ranks to develop a new line of women's fiction.

As for her father, Paul and Lana were officially "living together." Paul had conceded that Lana was her own woman—a free spirit—and if living together was the only way he could have her in his life, then so be it. She and her father had talked, like they'd never talked in all of her growing up years. He'd finally told her the truth about her mother—that she'd left because she was no longer happy in their marriage. And he finally admitted that his obsession with his work and his life had contributed to the demise of his marriage. Lydia was the first thing he'd ever lost in his life. He'd had no intention of losing again. Although the decision was mutual, he'd still hurt, and he'd used his pain as a shield against the world—but no more, he'd promised Joi.

Joi stood in front of her husband of five hours, ethereal in a simple gown of white silk and satin.

Marcus watched his prize, transfixed as she loosened the chignon from the nape of her neck, allowing her hair to fall free around her shoulders, haloing her clear complexion, devoid of makeup.

One by one she unfastened the tiny ivory buttons that ran down the length of the dress's front, letting it fall open, revealing the white silk teddy beneath, then spreading in a pool of milky white around her feet.

She was bold, regal and as sensual as the queen she'd portrayed a year ago to the day. She raised her arms, extending them to him, beckoning him to her. Slowly Marcus crossed the short space of their hotel bedroom and wrapped himself in the warmth of her embrace.

This is what he'd waited for, he thought—lifting his wife effortlessly into his arms—this joining as man and wife. He laid her on their king-sized marriage bed and for several moments simply stared down at this unbelievable gift he'd been given.

They'd promised each other there would be no more secrets, no more hiding behind masks of doubt and uncertainty. Joi knew, beyond a doubt, that she could be herself with him, whatever that self was, and he would love her just the same.

Joi looked up at her husband and smiled. All was right with their world. Then without warning she grabbed him by his shirt and tugged. "Come to me, my conquering hero. I've waited my whole life for this moment, and I don't intend to wait another second longer."

Marcus smiled wickedly. His eyes darkened with desire as he stretched his long hard body alongside hers. "And you won't have to," he groaned, nuzzling her semi-exposed breasts with his hot mouth.

Joi expelled a shuddering sigh when his tongue traced a pattern around her distended nipples. "Happy Valentine's Day," she moaned, ripping the buttons from his tuxedo shirt.

"The best is yet to come," he promised. "Now and for all of the tomorrows."

To the sweet sounds of The Whispers' love song "Just Say Yes," Joi and Marcus found a rhythm to last them a lifetime . . .

To Love Again

Janice Sims

Who can know the
human heart,
a fragile thing at best?
And love, that supernal
spirit forever fuels our quest

As . . .
Slowly wisdom colors
memories, clears away
the smoky glass.
Broken dreams restored,
hearts mended, vision
crystal-clear at last.

—The Book of Counted Joys

Prologue

"Darling, I'm back!"

Alana Calloway stared, mouth agape, at the tall immaculate figure of her late husband, Michael. Dressed completely in white—an expensive linen suit and Italian loafers to match—one moment he hadn't been there and the next, there he was, smiling at her, displaying dimples in both clean-shaven, pecan-tan colored cheeks. His dark brown eyes held an amused glint and a luminous aura surrounded him.

"I must say," Alana murmured, still awestruck, "you look good for someone who's been dead for a year. What kept you?"

I know I'm losing my mind, she thought, *but in case this is real, I want to be able to say I asked at least* one *intelligent question.*

It was in the middle of the night and they were standing in the bedroom of their Daly City home. The hardwood floor gleamed. The furnishings were Scandinavian: spare but artistically pleasing to the eye. A breeze tossed about the sheers at the windows and the piquant fragrance of jasmine filled the air.

Michael walked toward her with his large, brown hands outstretched. Alana's heart skipped a beat. Would he be able to touch her or would his spectral hand pass through her solid form the way they depict ghosts in films? Or would his caress be cold, dead and horrifying?

"I would have been here sooner but it's difficult to get a visa unless you died a saint." He grinned infectiously as he grasped both her hands in his. He was warm, real, alive!

"You've lost weight," he observed, concerned. He looked down into her cognac-colored eyes. "But you're still my beautiful butterfly."

Alana continued to fix him with a disbelieving stare.

"How is this possible?" she cried. "Are you a ghost?" Her eyes devoured him. This may prove to be her last chance to see him. She reached up and touched his face, her hands moving down to his muscular arms, felt through the fabric of the linen suit.

Benevolence shone in his dark eyes.

"I suppose you could say that," he told her lightly. He brought her right hand to his lips, gently kissed the palm. "I don't have much time. These things are tricky at best—visitations, I mean—so I must be swift."

He looked her in the eye, his expression grave. "Much will be revealed to you in the next few days. Through it all, try to remember that I love you, Lana. I always loved you. But I was only human . . ."

Suddenly, Alana could no longer feel his touch. It was as though his body had become insubstantial, vaporous. She could still see him although his form was transparent and steadily fading.

"Michael, what's going on?"

Michael shrugged helplessly. He apparently had no control over the occurrence and was as shocked by it as she was.

"My time is up," he said resignedly. His voice sounded as though he was speaking to her from down a well. "Your time is only beginning. Remember me fondly, Lana."

With that, he vanished, leaving Alana standing alone in the middle of the room. Her voluminous nightgown whipped about her slim legs as the formerly light breeze became a gale and the aroma of jasmine grew stronger, over-powering.

"What's happening?" she shouted, her voice's volume small and ineffectual against the howling intensity of the wind-storm.

One

Turning over in bed, Alana Calloway looked at the lighted dial of the alarm clock through half-open eyes. She had to get up or she'd be late for her meeting with Margery Devlin. Two days before the Annual Valentine's Day Charity Ball and Margery would be on pins and needles, fussing with last-minute details: making certain her San Francisco mansion was sufficiently replete, being critical of every little transgression, being sure that the appearance of the household staff was immaculate.

Alana wasn't in a festive mood. The one year anniversary of her husband's death was yesterday and she could think of a million other places she'd rather be on Friday, February fourteenth, but Margery was her surrogate mother, and she felt honor bound to be present.

Judging from the sunlight streaming in through the slits in the draperies, the day promised to be bright and clear. That alone buoyed her spirits. She stood and went into the large walk-in closet. Grasping the lapels of a man's navy sports coat, she lovingly fingered the material, then bent her head to breathe in the lingering scent of the woodsy aftershave that permeated it.

Taking the coat off the hanger, she put it on and wrapped her arms around her body. The coat's hem practically fell to her knees because Michael had been at least seven inches taller than Alana. With her eyes closed, she could almost feel his two strong arms holding her against his broad chest. If she concentrated, she could remember the deep timbre of his voice whispering, "Good-morning, Lana."

Tears filled her eyes. "Michael," she cried morosely, "what were you doing in an Oakland neighborhood in the middle of the night? And when they ordered you to hand over your money, at gun-point, why didn't you just give it to them and not try to fight them? Couldn't you forego your police training for just one instant? No. You had to fight back. Why couldn't you think of me and how miserable my existence would be without you? Couldn't you think of me? I hate you for leaving me alone like this!"

With a sob, she replaced the coat. Her daily ritual completed, she slowly walked to the kitchen to put on the coffee. While it perked, she took a hot shower. The phone rang as she lathered up. Unwilling to leave the warm shower, she let the machine answer it. She could hear the anxious voice of the caller from the bathroom.

It was Genero, her assistant. "Alana," he said, sounding as though he had been sprinting, "would you please tell your mother that your people perform better when she isn't breathing down our necks? Little-Miss-Hollywood is getting on my last nerve and sister doesn't want to go there."

Alana smiled. Genero and Margery were both high-strung. No wonder they were getting in one another's hair. Genero was the coordinator in her catering business. She was owner and the supervising chef, but Genero made certain her instructions were carried out to the letter. Meticulous to a fault, he was easily flustered and turned into a tyrant when excessive pressure was put on him. Margery knew exactly which buttons to push.

Quickly rinsing off and toweling dry, Alana sat on the bed as she dialed Genero's cellular phone number.

He answered at once. "Hello!"

"Well, *you* sound pleasant," Alana said, laughing.

"Alana, thank God," Genero breathed, his voice softening. "You can't get here fast enough to suit me. Margery is making our lives miserable. Changing recipes. Questioning the staff's abilities. Clovis is wielding his cleaver menacingly. If you love your mother, you'll speak with her at once."

"Put her on," Alana said calmly.

"Alana, where did you ever find this, this person!" Margery demanded imperiously. "I think you ought to—"

"Margery," Alana cut in, "I want you to leave Genero to his work. He knows what he's doing. I would not have left him in charge if he didn't."

"But—" Margery began.

"Please, Margery. I would like this affair to be the most highly praised fête of the year. Unless you put your trust in me, I don't think we'll be able to pull it off."

"Oh, very well," Margery conceded. "I'll let the little man win this go-round."

"Little!" Alana heard Genero exclaim hotly before Margery hung up.

Sighing heavily, Alana rose and went to the kitchen to pour herself a large cup of java. She had a feeling she was going to need it.

Wrapped in a white terrycloth robe, she stood at the sliding glass door that led out to the balcony of her Pacific Heights apartment. The reflection in the glass was that of an attractive young woman with flawless café-au-lait skin, wavy, coal-black shoulder-length hair, large, wide-spaced, sable-colored eyes with golden flecks in them, a short, pert nose under which was a full mouth with sensual contours.

She occupied the entire top floor of a stately Victorian home owned by a retired University of California English professor, Jonathan Crenshaw. She had lived there for about a year, having taken the converted apartment shortly after Michael's death. She'd been lonely rattling around in their large Daly City home.

Daly City had been ideal for them because it wasn't very far from San Francisco, where Michael worked as a police detective, first class, and Alana had her fledgling catering business. Margery had wanted Alana in San Francisco, where she would have been able to see her on a daily basis. But Michael had balked at the idea, saying that newlyweds needed their space. Alana had felt bad about the decision because since her parents' untimely demise in a head-on car crash ten years ago, Margery was the closest thing she had to kin.

The balcony overhung Jonathan's backyard and offered an unobstructed view of their neighbor's orange clay tile roof. She glanced down and thought she spied Jonathan's silver head below. Opening the sliding glass door and stepping onto the balcony, she placed her coffee cup on the weathered redwood railing and bent over it to call out to him.

"Good morning, Jonathan."

The still handsome septuagenarian beamed at her, revealing dimples in both suntanned cheeks. He removed his big straw hat as he returned her greeting. "Good morning. You look particularly well rested and lovely today. Is there a reason? . . ."

Eyebrows arched in confusion, Alana said, "What?"

"Someone sent you a beautiful bouquet of red red roses," Jonathan informed her, smiling. "Not wanting to disturb you in case you were sleeping in, I left them outside your door. Is there a new beau in your life?"

"If there is, this is the first I've heard of him," Alana said jokingly. "Roses you say? I can't imagine who would send me roses. No one has sent me flowers since . . ." She stopped. She was about to say, Michael sent me those orchids on our first anniversary. "Since Godzilla was a lizard," she said instead. That was one of Michael's favorite sayings, meaning a great length of time had passed.

Jonathan laughed and replaced his hat. He squinted up at her. "Make sure you tell the eternally gorgeous Miss Devlin that her number one fan sends her his best. And I want to hear all about your new beau, my dear," then as an afterthought added, "Oh, yes, your mail arrived. I put it through the slot in your door."

As Alana went back inside, she glimpsed Jonathan's tall, fit figure bent over his beloved roses, pruning away the unwanted growth which would in turn leave room for the flowers to thrive.

She went into the living room to scoop the mail up off the floor. There were a couple of bills, a lingerie catalog, a magazine and a letter written on fine linen stationery. There was no return address on the letter and her own address had been typewritten. Tearing it open, she gingerly unfolded the letter, expecting to read a short missive from a close friend. Instead, the note read:

My darling Butterfly . . . It's time you learned to love again . . .
It's time you learned to love again.

Alana's hands trembled as she reread the note. The breath
caught in her throat, and she found her legs wouldn't hold her
up. She gratefully sat down on the Shaker bench which stood
near the front door. This is some cruel joke, she thought, it has
to be. She looked down at the paper, then in a fit of anger, balled
it up and tossed it into the wastebasket next to the bench. Who
would want to hurt her this badly? Reading Michael's personal
endearment for her evoked bitter sweet memories. No one, absolutely no one on this earth, called her "butterfly" except her
dead husband.

A chill ran down her spine. She stood and retrieved the piece
of paper. She would make a detour before driving to Nob Hill.
She'd phone Margery from the Caravan and tell her she was going
to be delayed; but first, she had to get dressed.

Ten minutes later she was heading out the door attired in a
midnight-blue raw silk pantsuit. Tailored to fit her slim, slightly
muscular figure, it accentuated her trim waist and nicely rounded
derriere, but she had not chosen it because she knew it heightened
her sex appeal—she'd chosen it because it had been within easy
reach when she'd gone into the closet in search of something to
wear. In the last year Alana hadn't put much thought into ways
in which to attract the opposite sex. As far as she was concerned,
she was still in mourning.

Just outside the door she nearly tripped over the huge bouquet
of roses. She'd completely forgotten Jonathan had told her they
were there. She bent to scoop up the fragrant gift. Inhaling the
sweet aroma, she sighed. She hoped that whomever had sent
them wasn't connected to the letter. She needed something positive to attach her emotions to today.

Removing the card, she read: *Love is a spirit longing to be*
free. Fear is the jailer and faith holds the key. It was signed, Your
Secret Admirer.

Alana held the roses close as though they were a loved one
she was giving a warm embrace. A satisfied smile brightened
her features making her heart-shaped, brown face appear child-

like, almost ethereal. The flowers had to be from Nico. Who else could make her feel so wonderful with just a few words written from his heart?

She turned on her heels to take the flowers into the apartment. She was glad she'd made up her mind to go see him this morning. Not simply because she needed his help but because she also needed his strength.

Sunglasses on, purse firmly in hand, she stepped back out of the house on Lombard Street into another beautiful San Francisco morning. As she approached the champagne-colored Caravan with her company's Vesta insignia on the side: a painting of a lovely black woman dressed in a toga, a few grains of golden wheat in one hand and an egg beater in the other, she pointed and pressed the remote keyless entry button.

She slipped onto the leather seat, fastened her seat belt and turned the key in the ignition. She sat there a moment as the engine warmed up.

Reaching down for the cellular phone, she absently dialed Margery's number. What could she say to her that would not make her worry needlessly? Margery, being an actress, was given to reacting dramatically to any sort of change in plans. Alana was going to be delayed? Why? She was going to drop by the police station to see Nico? Why?

Alana found herself wishing anyone other than Margery would answer the phone. She was relieved when Maria, Margery's personal assistant, answered in her Spanish-accented voice. "Hello, Devlin residence. Maria Martinez . . ."

"Hi, Maria."

"Alana, where *are* you? You know how Margery gets when things don't go her way and right now she's arguing with Genero about the menu. He tried to tell her that all the food has already been purchased for the menu you all settled on months ago but she doesn't want to listen."

"I'll be there in about forty-five minutes. I have to swing by the police station for a few minutes first. Hang in there, Maria."

"You know me," Maria said, laughing suddenly. "Margery

can growl all she wants to. I'll keep my cool. Are you certain nothing's wrong, Alana? You sound peculiar."

Alana supposed since she and Maria had been friends a long time, the other woman could detect subtle changes in her tone of voice. They were around the same age, Maria having recently turned twenty-eight. At the age of eighteen, Maria had come to work for Margery soon after her family came to the United States from Mexico. Alana had just moved in with Margery during that time period and the two became fast friends. Alana had been a bridesmaid in Maria's huge Catholic wedding in Santa Clara and had held her hand when Maria had been in labor with Mariana, now five. Carlos, Maria's husband of seven years, had been out of town on business and hadn't been able to make it back home on time.

"I'll tell you all about it when I see you," Alana promised her friend. "I should be there at around eleven."

"Okay," Maria reluctantly agreed. "I'll give Margery your message. See you later."

"All right. Thanks, Maria."

Eight-fifty Bryant Street was bustling with activity, even at nine fifty on a Wednesday morning. The San Francisco Police Department never closed. Keeping the peace in a city that spans one hundred thirty square miles and was the home of over seven hundred thousand people was a daunting task.

Nicholas Setera, one of the city's finest, was busy taking down the statement of a drug addict he and his partner, Jack Pullman had arrested twice before. It wasn't the junkie they wanted, it was his supplier. Pete Bodis, alias Peanut, committed burglary to support his drug habit. He was arrested this time for a smash-and-grab. He threw a rock through the window of a pawn shop and stole a portable TV.

Nico cleared his throat and looked at Peanut over the computer monitor. His brown eyes were stern as he shoved the arrest form across the desk for the addict to sign. "You must like our accommodations, Peanut. You keep coming back for more."

Peanut was slumped down on his chair. His brown, pock-marked face wore a sullen expression and he looked like he hadn't had a decent meal or a bath in weeks. He sat up, preparing to sign the form.

Nico slammed his hand down hard on the desk, atop the form. "You're pitiful. Don't you give a damn about anything anymore?"

Peanut's eyes widened with fear and his hands dropped to his lap. Oh God, he thought, Setera has that look in his eyes. He knew he wasn't going to be taken to his cell without a sermon. He'd gladly spend twice the allotted time behind bars if only he didn't have to hear what a mess he'd made of his life. That was cruel and unusual punishment.

The muscles worked in Nico's strong, square jaw as he eyed Peanut. "How long have you been on that crap? Three, four years? Your first arrest, not by yours truly, was in ninety-four. Before that you were an orderly at San Francisco General. You had a wife and two kids. Whatever became of them? Do you ever see your kids?"

Peanut didn't reply. His eyes were riveted on his hands.

"You're twenty-nine and you look fifty-nine," Nico stated flatly. He ran a hand over his short, curly, jet-black hair. His heart wasn't in this. He knew Peanut was just as much a victim as he was a criminal. Nine times out of ten if a man hadn't become an addict, he would have been a law-abiding citizen. Who knew what circumstances in his life had induced him to try narcotics as an anesthesia to his problems. However, Nico also knew he'd be remiss if he didn't try to reach the addict on some level. A life wasted is one life too many.

"It's too late for me," Peanut said in a voice so low that Nico had been unable to hear him.

"What?" Nico asked evenly.

Peanut met Nico's gaze. "I'm a dead man." He tried to moisten his cracked lips. "Ain't no hope for me."

"There's always hope, Peanut. I've known addicts in worse

shape than you are who turned their lives around. You can do it. It will be the hardest thing you've ever done in your life, but it's not impossible. I'll help you as much as I can. I have friends who work with addicts. They can help you get clean, if you really want to be clean."

Nico's last statement hung in the air. He waited, hoping that the decimated human being sitting across from him would respond positively. Even a nod in the affirmative would be a step in the right direction.

"How?" Peanut asked plaintively, his voice cracking. Unshed tears sat in his bloodshot eyes.

Rising, Nico bent over the desk and grasped Peanut's hand, firmly shaking it. "One step at a time, my brother, one step at a time."

He grinned as he sat back down and began typing a message to John Goldman, director of the South Market Rehabilitation Center. John was a good friend, and though it was difficult to find space for all the addicts who needed a place to dry out nowadays, he felt certain John could pull off a miracle. Nicholas Setera was a man who believed in miracles.

By the time Alana reached Bryant Street, she had almost talked herself out of seeking Nico's help. The last time they'd been together, about a month ago, they hadn't parted on the best of terms. In fact, Alana had thrown him out of her apartment.

It had begun innocently enough. Both Alana and Nico were free for the evening. He was off duty and she didn't have any parties to cater, so she'd invited him over for a home-cooked meal.

Before Michael's death, Nico was a frequent guest in their home. She and Michael and Nico and whomever the woman of the hour was would often double date. They liked to dance and on weekends went to some of the trendier San Francisco night spots, sometimes closing the places. But they were also the type of people who could enjoy a quiet evening at home barbecuing steaks and playing bid whist.

Michael and Nico had been partners for five years. They worked Vice. Their personalities were complementary: where Michael was hotheaded, Nico was a calming force. When Alana met Michael, she was welcomed into their group. So it wasn't surprising that she grew to love and admire Nico like the brother she'd never been blessed with.

Alana had prepared *arroz con pollo,* Nico's favorite main course. When she opened the door to greet him, the aroma of the Cuban dish assailed his nostrils. As if under a spell, he handed her the dozen red roses he'd brought her and headed straight back to the kitchen.

Alana shut the door, a smile on her face. She was always pleased whenever someone reacted favorably to her cooking. In the kitchen, she placed the flowers in a vase as she watched Nico examine the contents of the pots.

"Mmm . . ." he said rapturously. "Are you hiding my mama somewhere on the premises?"

His downward sloping, velvety-brown bedroom eyes regarded Alana with new found respect.

"I'm innocent, Officer," Alana told him, grinning.

Placing the top back on the pot, Nico turned to take her into his arms. He danced her around the tiny kitchen.

Alana laughed happily. "Okay, I admit I *did* get the recipe from Mama Setera."

"I knew I smelled Cubano magic in those pots," Nico told her triumphantly.

Nico was Cuban-American of African descent. He and his parents were among the hordes of Cubans who, because of poverty and political persecution, fled the island nation in the early eighties. He had worked hard to claim his share of the American Dream, earning a bachelor's degree in criminal justice, serving two years on the Greater Miami police force.

Five years ago, when he was thirty, he joined the San Francisco police department. He made detective two years later.

Now, he reached for the vase that Alana was still holding in her arms and placed it on the counter. He then hugged her with gusto. "You have made me so happy," he said, his deep voice lapsing into a Spanish accent as it did when he was angry or excited, or in this case, ecstatic.

Their eyes were locked. "It only took a phone call," Alana said. "Mama Setera was pleased to know that her baby boy is being well fed so far away from home."

Alana should have known something had changed between them by the passionate expression in Nico's warm brown eyes. However, in the heat of the moment, she misread his signals and shrugging out of his embrace, she pleaded the need to get back to preparing dinner and pressed him into service by asking him to set the table. Something to keep his hands busy.

The dinner conversation was warm and animated as always. Nico declared that the *arroz con pollo* was "Muy delicioso."

After dinner, as they stood side-by-side at the sink washing dishes, Alana suddenly felt the fine hairs on the back of her neck stand at attention. Admittedly it was a singularly erotic sensation, but it unnerved her to realize her close proximity to Nico was causing the reaction. She glanced at him sideways. He was watching her intently, his sexy eyes speaking volumes. Her heart thumped excitedly. He smiled. She flushed. Her golden-brown skin was tinged red from her neck to her ears.

She looked away first, going to the pantry to get a clean dish towel. She didn't really need one, but the trip afforded her a few seconds' respite from his overpowering sexuality.

When she turned back around, Nico was still watching her. She wondered if it was possible for a man to seduce a woman with just his eyes. She felt herself weakening under his gaze.

"Would you excuse me?" she said a bit breathlessly. She handed him the dish towel. "You start drying. I'll be right back."

In the bathroom she splashed cold water on her face and neck, hoping it would cool the embarrassing heat that threatened to consume her. Her big brown eyes held a frightened expression in them. She was *attracted* to Nicholas Setera. Her husband's best friend. *Her* best friend, for God's sake.

Okay, to be honest, she'd always been attracted to him. The

man was a splendid specimen. But that was simply aesthetics. She could admire a work of art without becoming emotionally attached to it. Couldn't she?

She sat on the toilet seat and tried to reason her way through her dilemma. She missed intimacy. It had been nearly a year since Michael was taken away from her, and hence it had been a very long time since she'd been with a man. Not that she missed sex so much. It was just that she and Michael shared a very passionate sex life, and once you've had that, to be totally bereft of it makes one even more aware of what you were no longer getting.

Being in Nico's presence was a constant reminder. He exuded sensuality. No, the man fairly reeked of it. It was present in the shape of those bedroom eyes and the sooty lashes that framed them. It was in the way his wide, mobile mouth turned up at the corners when he smiled. The play of the muscles in his back when he was walking out her door. The symmetry of his long, tanned body. The strength of his hands. Even his feet with their neatly manicured nails and graceful arches were sexy. She made a mental note not to go to the beach with him anymore. In warm weather the beach was one of their favorite places to frolic. Now, however, she didn't think she had the willpower to watch him come out of the water, his trunks clinging to him. What was wrong with her? She had to gain control over her thoughts before she returned to the kitchen and Nico's scrutiny.

"Alana! Are you all right?" Nico asked, knocking on the door.

"I'm fine. I'm just reapplying my makeup," Alana lied, attempting to stall for time.

"Don't do that on my account, I think you're beautiful without it," Nico said innocently enough.

Beautiful? He'd never called her beautiful before. Wasn't there a law against using that word to describe a pal? "You look . . . decent" or "You won't frighten small children," were acceptable. But beautiful? Nah. He'd definitely crossed the line of decency.

Livid, Alana quickly dried her face, came out of the bathroom, and plowed right into Nico, who was standing in the hallway. Nico reached out to steady her on her feet, and she angrily jerked her arm free of his hold.

TO LOVE AGAIN   225

"You should be ashamed of yourself," Alana said accusingly, storming past him.

Puzzled, Nico placed a hand on his chest as if to say, "Who me?"

"You know what I'm talking about," Alana tossed over her shoulder.

"Ay!" Nico exclaimed in exasperation as he caught up with her in the middle of the living room.

They faced one another. Nico stood with his arms crossed at his chest, looking down into Alana's upturned face. He sighed. She impatiently tapped her right foot on the carpet, awaiting his apology.

Nico's voice was low and controlled when he spoke. "You are . . ." rolling his r's, "upset with me because I think you're beautiful?" he said incredulously.

Alana tried to discern whether he was actually oblivious to his effect on her or if he was being obtuse. His eyes raked over her, sending her temperature skyward once more.

"That's what I'm talking about," she said, backing away from him. "You've got to stop looking at me like that."

Nico had grinned at her. His sexy eyes looked her up and down. "Like what?"

"Like you're the Big Bad Wolf and I'm Little Red Riding Hood, that's what."

Nico closed the space between them in a couple of steps. Grasping her by the shoulders, he pulled her hard against his chest. For a millisecond, Alana thought of resisting him, but although her mind was strong, her body was decidedly weaker.

She fit easily in his embrace. At that moment she could have been convinced that she'd been born to be in his arms.

"Don't be afraid of your feelings, Lana. It's me, Nico. I would never hurt you," Nico said in her ear. *"Querida. Mi corazon."*

Alana, being fairly fluent in Spanish, knew what those words meant: Darling. My heart. She didn't want to think about what his words would portend though. For the time being, she was giddy with happiness, completely lost in the sensual quality of their bodies touching.

One of his hands was at the base of her spine, igniting sparks of sexual longing that she'd held in check for far too long. His other hand was in her hair, at the back of her neck, gently massaging her there.

"*Te quiero,* Lana," he murmured huskily. I love you. I want you. They meant the same thing in the midst of passion. Nico bent his head to kiss her, and she met his mouth with the full force of her emotions. A little gasp escaped from between her lips as they parted to allow him access.

He was gentle, not wanting to be too aggressive. Yet he was thorough, exploring her with the intensity of a lover with more than kissing on his mind. It was foreplay on the most intimate level.

The hand that had been caressing the back of her neck moved downward to the hem of her blouse, then, to rest on her hips. Their bodies pressed closer, and Alana's five-feet seven-inch frame wrapped itself around his six feet. Without missing a beat, they walked crablike over to the couch and fell onto it, Alana on top of him.

That's when she felt his arousal, and her feverish mind registered what she was doing: making out on her living room couch with her husband's best friend. She hastily got up off of him, straightening her blouse as she did so.

"Oh, my God, Nico. This can't happen. We can't do this. It isn't right."

Nico got to his feet. After tucking in his shirt, he looked into her eyes. "Lana, this may not be the best time to tell you this, but I've been in love with you for a very long time. At least two years before Michael was killed. I would never have told you if Michael had lived, God rest his soul, but Michael is no longer with us."

He stood close to her, his hand on her arm. His warm brown eyes were pleading as he continued, "I know you love me, Lana. I've seen it in the way you look at me. And tonight, when we touched as lovers do, I felt the power of your desire. Please don't make me wait any longer. I need you."

"I need . . ." Alana began, but couldn't finish. What *did* she need? To make love to Nico with such abandon that all the pain of the last thirteen months would be forgotten . . . if only for one night? That wouldn't be fair to either of them.

"I need time to think this through," she said at last. Her large brown eyes were filled with remorse. She knew she was hurting him, but it was better to give herself time to decide what her true feelings for him were than to jump into a relationship and find out later that he'd only been a convenient stand-in for Michael. She was too fond of Nico to use him in that manner.

Sighing, Nico allowed his arms to fall resignedly at his sides. He walked over to the door and placed his right hand on the doorknob. His eyes were on her face. "Are you throwing me out?" There was a glint of humor in his brown depths.

"I'm throwing you out," Alana confirmed, unable to hold back a gentle smile.

"Forever?" he said. A dimple appeared in his left cheek.

"You're the best friend I have," Alana replied honestly. She frowned. "Of course not forever."

Nico opened the door and turned to look back at her as though he was trying to commit her present facial expression to memory. "I won't phone you until you contact me," he promised. "I love you, Lana."

"I love you," Alana returned.

He left without another backward glance.

Two

After Peanut was taken to a holding cell, Nico went to the officer's lounge to get himself a cup of decaffeinated coffee. He didn't drink the real stuff because, at the end of a long day, it left his nerves jagged around the edges—hence making it nearly impossible to get a good night's rest.

As he walked back into the outer office, a large, open room that was the workplace of the dedicated men and women who comprised the Vice squad, he saw Alana coming through the door. He nearly spilled his coffee as he spun on his heels and went back into the lounge. Another officer, Eric Bilkis, a big, burly redhead was coming out of the lounge at that instant and collided with Nico.

"Hey, man, haven't you ever heard of turn signals?" Eric joked.

"Sorry, Red. There's a lady out there I'm not keen on seeing, if you know what I mean," Nico told him.

"You bachelors," Red said, grinning. "Now if you treated a lady like a lady should be treated, you wouldn't be hiding in lounges."

He craned his neck, looking out over the office. "Which one is she? The blonde at Gardner's desk? The brunette talking to Brewster?"

"No," Nico replied, his eyes on Alana's face. She didn't look happy. She was probably there to tell him to stay out of her life. He couldn't bear to hear those words coming from her mouth. "It's the beautiful lady in the blue suit."

"You need your head examined, my man," Red said as he watched Alana with admiration. Then, "Hey, she looks familiar. I know I've seen her before. Wait a minute. Isn't she Michael Calloway's widow?"

"Yes," Nico hesitantly admitted.

"You dog!" Red guffawed. "You *need* to be hiding."

"Get your mind out of the gutter, Red," Nico warned through clenched teeth. "I hold that woman in the highest esteem and would be willing to fight anyone who doesn't."

Eyebrows arched in surprise, Red said, "Oh, it's like that, is it? Well, okay, it's about time you took the plunge, Setera. No more making us married guys look like wimps because we jump when our wives say jump. Now you've got a ring through your nose. I'm liking this. Maybe I should go tell the little lady where you are. You'd have more privacy in here than out there."

"That's quite all right," Nico said. "I'll go to her."

He took a good swig of his coffee, poured the rest of it down the sink, then tossed the empty container into the trash. Mentally steeling himself, he left the lounge with a smiling Red looking after him, giving him the thumbs-up sign.

That was the problem with being friends with so many of my co-workers, Nico thought. They're always giving me unsolicited advice. Not that he wouldn't have had the nerve to face Alana without the prodding. After seeing the expression on her face, the blatant fear, he wouldn't have made it through the day without finding out what was on her mind.

A modicum of his own anxiety dissipated when Alana turned, saw him, and smiled at him. Perhaps she hadn't come to lower the boom after all.

She approached him in a rush and fell into his open arms. Her full mouth was turned up in a sensual smile. "I was beginning to wonder where you were. I thought that maybe you'd gone undercover."

Her brown eyes were searching his face. "You wouldn't do that without informing me, would you?"

"No, Alana," Nico said quietly. His voice, alone, assured her. Relieved, Alana sighed. "Thanks for the roses. They were beautiful and the poem, too." She looked deeply into his eyes. "I missed you."

"I missed you," Nico returned the sentiment. He hugged her tightly, not caring that they'd become the center of attention in the busy office. "How have you been?"

"Lonely. There were many times I'd pick up the phone to call you and replaced the receiver because I still have so many unanswered questions. And now this . . ."

Alana reached into her shoulder bag and retrieved the letter she'd received in the morning's mail. She handed it to Nico, who read it.

"Butterfly was Michael's pet name for me," Alana explained. "He called me that because of—"

"A butterfly shaped birthmark you have on your bottom," Nico supplied effortlessly.

Alana's smile faded. She felt her cheeks grow hot. "He told you something that personal?" she whispered.

"You'd be surprised by what partners talk about on a stakeout," Nico said, taking her by the hand. "Let's take a walk, shall we?"

As he passed his desk, he paused to remove his jacket from the hat tree near it. As a detective he wasn't required to wear a uniform, and today was wearing a tailored blue suit with a crisp, white, long-sleeved, buttoned-down shirt that he'd rolled up at the sleeves. He unrolled the sleeves, buttoning them at the wrists, and slipped into the jacket with a little assist from Alana.

They went outside, around the side of the building, and found a wooden bench in the shade of a palm tree. Sitting down, Nico regarded her with a concerned look in his eyes.

"When did you get this?"

"It was in today's mail," Alana replied.

"It has a Los Angeles postmark. Whom do you know in L.A.?"

"I have a few acquaintances in the business in Los Angeles," Alana said. "And then there's Bree . . ."

"No," Nico said with conviction. "Bree wouldn't do this."

"I agree," Alana said. "If this had come from Bree, she would have signed her name with a flourish. She and Georgie have both told me they think it's time I started seeing someone." Twins, Briane and Georgette Shaw were Alana's oldest and dearest friends. They had grown up together.

"The L.A. postmark doesn't have to mean it came from someone in Los Angeles, just that it was mailed there. Someone close by could have had a friend mail it from L.A.," Nico observed.

"So you believe it's meant to frighten me, and that we should be looking for someone with a sinister agenda?"

"No, no," Nico said quickly. "First of all, who but an acquaintance of yours or Michael's would know his pet name for you? I believe it's a practical joke. Their using Michael's endearment for you was a tad much, but maybe it was simply an attention-grabbing device."

Alana agreed with Nico's reasoning, but something else occurred to her and she wondered if he'd also thought of it.

"Nico, those unanswered questions I referred to earlier, maybe you can help me answer a few of them."

Nico knew where she was going. They'd discussed it before, and he'd always steered her away from it. But now, after everything that had happened between them, he wasn't so inclined to protect his dead partner from Alana's probing questions. He couldn't hide the truth from her forever. And now he had a stake in the outcome.

He frowned as he glanced down into her upturned face.

"You're not going to bring up your suspicions about Michael being unfaithful again, are you?"

"The events leading up to his death just do not make sense to me, Nico. What was he doing in an Oakland neighborhood at three o'clock in the morning? Also, why did he tell me he was going to a poker game? I haven't met anyone yet who could corroborate that lie. And another thing: for months before his death Michael was drawing away from me. He was cold, abrasive. He was like a man with a lot on his mind, things he definitely didn't want to share with his wife. I swear, Nico. I think he was cheating on me."

Nico grasped one of her hands, squeezing it gently. "Alana, I know Michael loved you." Looking into her eyes, he continued.

"You say he was secretive, distant, he snapped at you for no reason at all. Maybe he was involved in something he shouldn't have been, but it didn't have to be an illicit affair. He could have been doing something illegal."

Michael being on the take was more difficult for Alana to believe than his having an affair. The Michael she knew was honest and steadfast. The product of a broken home, he seemed to value his home life all the more for it. A man who had never known his own father, he often talked of being a parent, a good parent, to his and Alana's future children. He was a handsome man. She imagined women threw themselves at him. His resolve could have weakened.

"Do you have any evidence to back up these allegations?" Alana asked of Nico's comment about her husband.

"Do *you* have any evidence to back up your suspicions?" Nico countered.

Standing, Alana took the slip of paper with the message on it out of his hand. She shoved it deep into her shoulder bag. "No, but I plan to get some," she replied, looking down at him, her dark eyes determined.

Nico rose also. "And how are you going to go about doing that?"

"Using photos of Michael, I'm going to canvass the neighborhood until someone comes forward and talks to me," Alana informed him. "A cop got killed in their neighborhood. Maybe someone saw something and was afraid to talk to the police about it. Maybe they won't be as reluctant to talk to me."

She slung her bag on her shoulder, preparing to leave.

Grabbing her by the arm, Nico turned her around to face him. "Sweetheart, that's a bad idea. That neighborhood has seen its share of violence. There is no way I'm going to let you do something so foolhardy."

Sending him a challenge with her eyes, Alana said, "And how do you suppose you're going to stop me?"

"I'll handcuff you to your bed if I have to," Nico answered. The image proved too enticing. Clearing his mind, Nico frowned at her. "I'll help you," he said at last. "If you have to know what Michael was doing before his death, I'll find out for you."

Smiling, Alana was pleased Nico hadn't called her bluff. There was no way she would have done what she'd threatened to do. Thank God she knew him so well. She had been counting on his deep sense of honor and duty to come to her rescue. "I'd appreciate your help," she said, meeting his gaze. "But I'm coming along for the ride." She offered him her hand to shake on it. Nico reluctantly took it. "I'm your new partner, Detective," she told him.

Nico held onto her hand as he pulled her close against him. "Not so fast, there are a few rules the junior partner must abide by because if she doesn't, the boss—and that's me—will call the whole thing off."

"I'm listening," Alana said, her warm breath against his cheek.

"We're in this together. We make decisions together. You have to promise me that you won't do anything without thinking it through. No going off half-cocked. You got me?"

"Yes," Alana said softly. She wished he would release her because his nearness was doing crazy things to her libido. Their eyes met and held.

"Now that you know the rules, here is my stipulation for offering my help. When this is over and you know, once and for all, why Michael was behaving strangely just before his death, you and I will settle things between us, Alana."

"Agreed," Alana breathed.

On tiptoe, she planted a sisterly kiss on his cheek. Nico, however, caught her by the shoulders and soundly kissed her on the mouth. "I didn't promise to play fair," he murmured against her ear.

He released her and Alana stumbled backward, turning the heel over on her right pump. Straightening up, she grinned at him. "I'm fine," she assured him. "Okay. Call me when you're ready to get started. The sooner, the better. If I'm not at home, I'll be at Margery's."

"I'll do that," Nico said, smiling. "Drive carefully."

* * *

"I don't know," Maria said, exasperated. "She wouldn't say. She just said she was going by the police station, and she'd explain everything when she arrives. *El fin.*"

She turned and walked out of the room, leaving her inquisitors looking at each other with questioning expressions on their faces.

"What do you suppose Alana is up to?" Margery asked of her best friend, romance novelist, Antoinette Shaw.

Toni frowned, causing wrinkles to appear in her smooth brow. "You worry entirely too much about Alana. She isn't a child any longer."

"I agree. If left to her own devices, Alana will get over her grief soon enough," Genero spoke up. He sat back on the overstuffed chair in Margery's elegantly appointed bedroom. The three of them had gone upstairs to question Maria about Alana's message, away from the prying eyes of the myriad workers downstairs.

"She could be dropping by the police station to make up with Nico after their misunderstanding," Toni offered reasonably. "Alana isn't one to hold a grudge."

"That would be fabulous, wouldn't it?" Margery enthused, rising from her comfortable position on the bed. She was wearing one of her silk jogging suits. It was aquamarine with one bold fuchsia stripe down the front of it. Petite at five-three, she always wore three-inch heels. Today she was wearing a pair of white leather backless sandals by her favorite Italian designer. On a woman of lesser style and panache, the outfit would look ridiculous, but on Margery the combination was stunning. She wore her black hair in a short style, swept away from her lovely heart-shaped face.

"That they should finally succumb to their feelings for one another would be ideal," Toni readily agreed.

Antoinette Shaw was quite the opposite of Margery where physical attributes were concerned. They were both forty-eight, however, Margery who was in the limelight, never discussed her age. If pressed, she'd say, with complete sincerity, "Thirty-nine and holding." Whereas, Toni, who was an ex-activist, being involved in the Civil Rights Movement in the sixties and a vocal opponent of the Vietnam War, was a realist and approached aging with both eyes open. Personally, she thought she'd never looked or felt better. She was statuesque, at five-eight, and had a voluptuous figure. Not overweight but definitely not under. She had high cheekbones, large, very dark, almost black eyes and a full mouth which she'd always used to full effect. She got her skin coloring, a creamy golden brown, from her mother who was of French Creole and African-American ancestry.

"Love will prevail," Genero said, smoothing a shiny lock of hair from his face. He had the indigo skin of his forebears, who had been West Indian born. He never discussed his lineage. It wasn't that he was ashamed of being Jamaican. On the contrary, he was quite proud of his people. It was just that he'd found, since coming to America, that people responded more positively to the mystery that was Genero. Only his closest friends—and he counted Margery, Toni and Alana among them—knew where he came from and what he was about. All others were left to wonder, oftentimes in awe, about him. He liked it that way. What mattered was that he was one of the best chefs in California and one day he would own the most popular restaurant in Beverly Hills. At twenty-seven he had plenty of time to work toward his goal. He considered his stint with Alana as a stepping stone. He respected her prowess as a chef, and he liked her as a person.

"I hope they do make up," Margery said prayerfully. "My darling Alana has been mourning a man who doesn't deserve her loyalty. However, I couldn't come out and tell her what sort of person he was, I'd only succeed in alienating her. I couldn't bear that. She's my daughter. But I know several things have been nagging at her these past few months and if things work out as we wish, she and Nico could make me a grandmother by next year."

"Don't get carried away," Toni cautioned her with a grin. "A wedding first, then we'll think about grandchildren."

Toni and Genero went to sit next to Margery on the big, four-poster bed, flanking her.

"It'll all work out," Toni consoled her.

"Of course it will," Genero added brightly. He got to his feet. "I should get back down there," he announced. "God knows what Clovis has added to the vichyssoise. For some reason, he seems to believe substituting onions for leeks is acceptable. I keep telling him that leeks have a milder flavor than onions. One must not overpower the taste buds."

Alone, Margery and Toni looked at one another and burst out laughing.

"I love that boy," Margery said confidentially. "But we have got to get him interested in something other than cooking."

"First things first," Toni said, wiping the tears from her eyes. "We need to find out what's going on with Alana before we can think of turning our attention to Genero."

Standing, she paced the room, looking quite regal in her African-inspired caftan. "Little did we know, thirty years ago, where a small promise would take us . . ."

Toni was referring to the pact that three eighteen-year-old college freshmen had made one night as they sat, cross-legged on their dormitory beds.

It was December, nineteen sixty-seven. The three friends had been too poor to afford to go home to their respective southern states for the holidays, so they'd decided to keep each other company.

Antoinette Shaw and Constance Moore were roommates, and Margery lived down the hall. They'd become fast friends when they'd met in June and when they found out that all three were southern belles: Antoinette hailing from New Orleans, Margery from Tupelo, Mississippi and Constance, from Birmingham, Alabama—the coincidence only cemented their friendship all the more.

So as they sat, bemoaning their difficult state of affairs, they began to talk, as young girls will, of how much better their respective futures would be.

Anyone looking on would have spied three lovely women-to-be dreaming impossible dreams. Making promises they would not be able to keep. However, if they could have peered into the hearts of those three, they would have been pleasantly surprised for Toni, Connie and Margery possessed a strength of will that would propel all of them to greatness.

Constance had been blessed with a voice only the gods could have bestowed upon her. She was a voice major who was already making a name for herself. Dame Judith Iverson, the lead soprano with the Metropolitan Opera, having heard Connie sing during a visit to California State, had written the aspiring opera singer a letter expressing interest in becoming her mentor. Connie had gratefully accepted, and Dame Iverson had responded by insisting that Connie spend the summer with her in New York City, where Connie could study voice alongside some of the most promising singers in the country.

Antoinette was a born poet. Already published by a small literary house at eighteen, she saw the world as a place to be schooled and took every opportunity to learn something new. This attitude sometimes got her in trouble though. If not for that mind-set, she might not have become involved with Charles Edward Waters, the son of a wealthy Boston businessman, and wound up expecting twins by the end of her freshman year in school. A Catholic, she didn't even consider not having her girls, even when she found out she could not depend on Charles Edward Waters for support.

Margery, the petite bundle of energy from Mississippi, would be the next Dorothy Dandridge even if it killed her.

As the youngest child in a family of eight other siblings, she was used to being ignored. But the way Margery looked at it, that simply meant you had to try harder. So try, she did. As she would tell countless reporters later in life, her career began in church. Sundays would find the Devlin family in St. John Baptist Church, praising God and tiny Margery waiting for her chance to shine. From the age of three, she recited poems that left the congregation genuinely moved. By the time she reached puberty, she was director of the Christmas pageant. No one else had Margery's flair for the dramatic. She could take the meager props the destitute church could ill afford and turn them into a magical wonderland. Churchgoers often filed out of one of Margery's productions with tears streaming down their contented faces. It wasn't surprising to anyone in Tupelo when Margery Devlin won a scholarship to study acting in far off California.

That night, in sixty-seven, they made three promises to one another. Number one: to always be there for one another when they were needed. Number two: to be supportive of each other's careers wherever possible. And lastly, to take care of each other's offspring should anything happen to one of them, God forbid.

As the years passed, Constance became a principal singer with the Metropolitan Opera. She married Dr. Garth Shelby and gave birth to Alana Margery Antoinette Shelby. With hard work and determination, she'd made all her dreams come true. Then on a stormy October night in 1987, while leaving a party, she and Garth were killed by a truck driver who had swerved to avoid hitting another car that had stalled on the highway.

Both Margery and Toni had been at the apex of their careers. Margery was the most sought-after African-American actress in Hollywood, having won an Oscar for her role as a long-suffering mother in the drama, *The Living Is Easy*. She was at the much dreamed of point in her journey where she could pick and choose roles and be paid an exorbitant amount for doing something she loved. Unfortunately her personal life wasn't going as well for she was in the process of divorcing her husband, actor Daniel Lincoln, for adultery.

Toni, an award-winning novelist, was the darling of the San Francisco literary world. The mother of twin teenaged daughters, Georgette, a superior student, and Briane, another Margery who was following in her auntie's footsteps by becoming an actress. Toni had chosen singlehood, being unable to give her heart to another man after having it trampled on by Charles Edward Waters, who had never tried to be a part of his daughters' lives.

Following the loss of Alana's parents, Margery and Toni agreed that she should go to live with Margery in San Francisco. It helped that Connie and Garth had left very clear instructions in their wills that Alana should be taken care of by Margery and

Toni, the particulars to be decided by the two friends. So for the first five years after her parents' deaths, Alana was the charge of her two doting aunts. Then five years ago, Toni moved back to New Orleans where she could keep an eye on her elderly parents.

"I feel so guilty, having to resort to subterfuge," Toni said, turning to look at Margery.

"There is nothing wrong with looking out for your child's best interests," Margery said stoically. "We won't *do* anything per se. We'll simply observe and see what develops. Watch and hope."

"It's already been over a year and she's still having those dreams. I know because she told me about the last one. What I don't know is why the guilt? What reason does Alana have for feeling guilty?"

"Who knows?" Margery shrugged, sighing. "Maybe they argued just before he went out and got himself killed. Widows often experience guilt associated with their husbands' deaths. It isn't uncommon."

"I wish she would confide in us more," Toni said wistfully. "She needs someone to talk to. When I suggested she see a therapist, she just laughed. Aunt Toni, she said, I'm not a basketcase. I'm simply grieving in my own way. Can't you respect that?" Toni mimicked Alana's voice almost perfectly. "Of course I can respect that."

"She's always been loyal to those she loves," Margery reminded Toni. "Losing her parents like that was hard on her and then to lose her husband to a violent death. He was the only man she ever considered herself in love with. She may never be fully over him." She glanced over at Toni, her eyes filled with amusement. "Remind you of anyone?"

"I am not still in love with Charles Edward Waters," Toni disavowed. She turned away, going to stand at the French doors and peer out at the hills behind Margery's home. "If anything, I'd like to get my hands around his scrawny neck and squeeze. I didn't need him, but the least he could have done was to be a father to his daughters."

"The last time I saw him," Margery said, coming to join Toni at the French doors, "he wasn't a bit scrawny. He was as vital and handsome as he was nearly thirty years ago, maybe even better looking. You know how black men tend to grow into their own after a certain age? Well, the man is ripe, darling. And now that he is no longer married, maybe . . ."

"Maybe nothing," Toni said with finality, her dark eyes flashing fire. "Girl, you'd better control those matchmaking tendencies of yours because if Charles Edward and I were ever *accidentally* thrown together again, someone would be dead in a matter of minutes and it wouldn't be yours truly."

"All right," Margery placated her. "I'm sorry I even brought it up."

The intercom on the wall near the bedroom door buzzed, and she walked over to it and pressed the TALK button. "Margery here."

"Red alert," Genero said cheerfully. "Alana has arrived and is presently giving Maria the four-one-one."

"We'll be right down," Margery replied crisply. Then to Toni, "Come on, let's go see how far the game is afoot, my dear Watson."

"After you, Sherlock," Toni said, smiling.

"We're going to have to let you go, Karen," Miss Ekert said, looking down her bifocals into Karen Robinson's stricken face. "I'm sorry, but the company is downsizing. I'm afraid your position has been eliminated."

Karen hadn't been cognizant of a word past the phrase "let you go." She was mentally calculating the cost of the gas she'd used to come to work this morning only to be fired. Let go. Such a pleasant-sounding euphemism. Why didn't she call it by its true name? Fired, canned, eviscerated. God knows, her gut felt like someone had just stuck a knife in it.

"But you told me only last week, that I was doing an excellent job," Karen said hopefully.

"You are a good receptionist, Karen," Miss Ekert said, her

voice sympathetic. "But that isn't the point. The company's losing money, we've got to unload unnecessary luxuries and unfortunately your position is a luxury. Anyone coming into this real estate office can be greeted by any available agent."

"I'll take a cut in pay," Karen offered, close to desperation. "But I need this job."

"We thought of that option," her boss said sadly. "We still couldn't swing it. I'm very sorry. I'll give you the best letter of recommendation I can compose, Karen. I'm truly sorry."

"Sorry" doesn't put food in my son's mouth, Karen thought with acrimony. But what do you care? You come to work in a Benz, dressed in designer outfits every day.

Miss Ekert placed a sealed number-ten envelope in Karen's outstretched palm.

"We were able to provide you with two weeks of severance pay, plus this week's check. I hope that helps," Miss Ekert said, sounding as though she'd been more than generous. She managed a weak smile. "You are not required to work the rest of the day. Unless, of course, you want to." There was a hopeful tone to Miss Ekert's voice that enraged Karen.

"No," Karen said, barely able to contain her anger. She got her purse from the lower drawer of her desk. Two years. Two years and this was how they treated her? She'd given her all to this job. She never wore a sour expression. Her voice was always pleasant and professional. She was the first person customers saw when they walked through the door, and she made certain they were not put off. On several occasions, she had overheard customers praising her because of her cheerful attitude. Now she looked at Miss Ekert with lackluster eyes. "I'll just get out of your way. There are a few hours left in the day. I should put my time to good use by looking for another job."

"I haven't had time to write your letter of recommendation," Miss Ekert said regrettably. "I'll do it right now."

She began walking toward her office, which was in the rear of the building.

"That's all right," Karen called after her. "I have an up-to-date resumé. I'm sure that if whoever hires me is interested in my previous place of employment, they will phone you."

She had forced back the impending tears and was more composed as she stood in front of Miss Ekert and reached for her hand. She smiled as she shook Miss Ekert's thin, pale hand. "I've enjoyed working here the past two years. Good luck with the downsizing. I hope it keeps you afloat." About as well as a dingy with a hole in it the size of a watermelon, she thought.

That image must have brought an elated glint to her brown eyes because Miss Ekert breathed a sigh of relief and pumped her hand enthusiastically. "I'm so happy we could part friends, Karen. It pains me so to let you go."

"Yes, I'm sure it's hard for you. But don't worry about me. I'm young and smart. I'll find another job."

A couple of the agents, both attractive blondes, came over to say their farewells.

"I'll miss you, Karen," the taller one said, but her smile didn't reach her eyes.

"Take care of yourself," said the other.

Karen simply smiled and turned to leave.

Her vision was blurred by tears as she walked around the building to her car. As she got behind the wheel of the 1980 Toyota Corolla, she hoped it would start. It needed a lot of work done on it. For the last few months, she'd been driving on a wing and a prayer. She turned the key in the ignition. It started right up. She laughed hysterically. At least she would be saved from one more indignity today.

Three

When Alana arrived at the house on Nob Hill, she was met at the door by a curious Maria who dogged her steps all the way to the kitchen. Alana knew Margery's kitchen as well as she knew her own, so she went directly to the pantry, where she hung her purse on one of the hooks provided for the kitchen staff's belongings.

She had removed the letter with the intention of showing it to Margery and Toni.

She unfolded it and gave it to Maria to read. "I received that this morning. Some prankster thought it would be amusing to send me a message that would remind me of Michael."

Puzzled, Maria looked up at Alana after reading the note.

"Who would do such a thing? Even if you don't take it seriously, what kind of person would think of sending you such a message, and why?"

"Someone who's bitter?" Alana proposed, meeting Maria's eyes. "Suppose you were in love with a man, then he gets killed, and you read in the paper that he's survived by a wife. How would that make you feel?"

"Angry, used, humiliated," Maria replied disdainfully. "I would want to dance on his grave."

"Yes, but what good would it do?" Alana said, keeping her voice low. "He's already dead."

Maria smiled. "I see what you mean. He's gone but his wife is very much alive and probably living it up on his death benefits. Why not share some of your misery with her?"

As they talked, Alana walked around to the various posts in the kitchen where her employees were busy preparing the cuisine for the upcoming party.

She paused next to Clovis, who was chopping up leeks.

"Hello, Clovis, how are you today?" she said.

Clovis, a tall, dark-skinned native Californian, grinned at her, revealing large white teeth in his mustachioed face.

"I'm doing well, thank you. You're just in time to witness the fact that I'm using leeks and not onions in the vichyssoise. For some reason, Genero accuses me of doing otherwise."

"You're doing beautifully," Alana praised him. "I'll be sure to mention to Genero that I saw the leeks with my own eyes."

She kept walking, but before she could pause at another workstation, Maria grasped her by the arm. "Wait a minute," her friend began. "Why do you suppose she waited so long to start in on you? Why wait over a year?"

"It will soon be Valentine's Day," Alana said, sounding quite sure of herself. "The holiday for lovers. It's the time of the year when people all over the country turn their attention to romance. Maybe she has no one in her life. Maybe Michael was the man she thought she'd be with for the rest of her life."

"You're making a lot of assumptions," Maria said, looking serious. "What if you're wrong and Michael was never unfaithful to you? Then what?"

Before she could answer, Margery and Toni came into the room and descended upon Alana.

"Darling. There you are, finally," Margery exclaimed. Alana had concluded, years ago, that it was impossible for Margery to enter a room without seeming as though she was walking onto the stage of a packed theater.

Alana kissed her proffered cheek. "Don't get your pantyhose in a bunch, Little Momma. I'm fine. I just needed to talk to Nico before coming here."

"About what?" Margery asked petulantly. "What could be more important than my party?"

Don't lay it on too thickly, Toni thought. Margery really could be a ham when she wanted to be.

Alana looked over at Maria, who handed Margery the letter.

The color drained from Margery's face when she read it. She silently passed it to Toni, who, untrained in the dramatic arts, managed to retain her coloring.

"And what did Nico make of it?" Toni asked.

"He believes it's harmless. A reminder from a friend that I need to get on with my life," Alana replied, watching Toni's face. Her aunt wasn't one to hide her emotions. If she was afraid for Alana's safety, Alana would be able to read it in her facial expression.

Toni's placid features revealed nothing aside from curiosity.

"How exciting," Genero put in as he walked up and took the note from Toni. "A mystery. We'll help you solve it, Alana. It'll be fun. Sort of like that scavenger hunt we did for the Morrissey party last year. Who will find the culprit in the least amount of time?"

"No, no," Alana said, shaking her head. "May I remind you that we have two hundred guests arriving in a little under forty-eight hours? Someone must be here to make sure our plans are carried out, and that someone, dear Genero, is you. That's why I hired you. I know how much you love a mystery, but your services are required right here."

Twisting his handsome face into a frown, Genero handed Alana the note and turned away. "I never have any fun."

"Back to my question," Toni said. "Does Nico think anything needs to be done about this?"

"As a matter of fact," Alana began, "Nico and I are going to investigate the matter together. He promised to phone me as soon as he gets some free time."

Alana could have sworn she saw Margery give Toni a meaningful look and then the two aunts smiled at each other. Of course, they could have been pleased because she and Nico were back on speaking terms. They were aware that she had not seen him for over a month.

"Well," Margery said, clapping her hands, "then that's settled. Genero will remain here and oversee the party, while you and Nico reenact an episode of 'Murder, She Wrote.' Although how you could leave me alone with that little man in my hour of need, I'll never know. Haven't I been good to you? Or do you harbor some secret resentment of your dear aunt?"

Sighing, Alana placed a protective arm around her diminutive surrogate mother. "Little Momma, have I ever let you down? I have everything planned to the last detail. Genero is a godsend. My people are thoroughly professional. And I promise you, I will be in and out of here at least twice daily until the night of the party. And I will be the first to arrive when the festivities begin."

"All right," Margery conceded, sounding like a child who was being coaxed out of a temper tantrum. "But you have to promise me that once you find the person behind this, you will put forth your best effort to go forward with your life, my love."

"That's why I'm doing this," Alana said, reasonably. "I realize it's time I did something positive about my suspicions instead of letting them fester. So, yes, I do promise."

She stood patiently while first Margery, then Toni, hugged her hard enough to almost require CPR afterward, then she continued her rounds, making certain the party preparations were being executed satisfactorily.

"Alana and Nico spending time together will make them realize how much they need each other," Toni said to Margery once they were alone. "So far, things are going beautifully."

"She's definitely headed in the right direction," Margery agreed happily.

As Nico maneuvered his black vintage 1966 Stingray through the afternoon traffic, heading toward the ocean, his mind was on Alana and how he was going to handle their makeshift investigation. Foremost in his thoughts was the conviction that he had to be totally honest with her. Which meant he had to confess to knowing about Michael's affair.

That knowledge had been eating away at his insides for some

time now. He'd found out about Michael's indiscretion quite by accident.

One night after signing out at the station, Michael suggested they go grab a bite to eat but Nico had made other plans, so he begged off. By happenstance, they were both going to Oakland, and as Nico crossed the San Francisco-Oakland Bay Bridge, he spotted Michael's car up ahead. At that moment he decided to follow him. Michael had recently started bringing up other women in their conversations. Michael was big on hypothetical situations. He'd often begin his sentences with, "What if . . ."

Nico didn't think Michael would have the nerve to come out and tell him he was having an affair because he knew Nico adored Alana. Nico was continually telling Michael how fortunate he was to have Alana. Deep down, Nico felt that Michael got a kind of perverse pleasure out of telling him all about his marital woes. Shortly before his death, his major complaint about Alana was that she wanted to wait another year before conceiving a child. She didn't feel her business was on a good enough footing and wanted to concentrate on her work before becoming a mother.

That night, Nico played a hunch through to the bitter end. Staying several car lengths behind Michael in order to avoid detection, he trailed him to an apartment complex in Oakland.

Sitting in his car, he watched with fascination as Michael was met at the apartment door by a young, attractive woman who threw her arms around his neck and kissed him on the mouth. Nico recalled thinking how domestic the scene looked. She could have been Michael's wife greeting him after the close of a busy workday. The smile on Michael's face was warm and inviting. Like he had every right to be kissing a woman who wasn't Alana.

Nico knew then that his partner had a secret life. In Daly City, he had Alana who, in Nico's estimation, was the perfect wife. In Oakland, he had that pretty woman who'd enthusiastically fell into his arms. Undoubtedly neither woman suspected what Michael was up to. It took an unusual type of woman to willingly share her man with another woman. No. Michael was furiously juggling two lives. As with all secrets, it was just a matter of time before the truth came into the light. Nico's sole concern was how long he could protect Alana from the knowledge and when she learned of Michael's infidelity, how he could lessen the blow for her.

When Michael was killed, Nico saw no reason to tell Alana of her husband's proclivities. He thought her grief would take a natural course and she'd eventually go on with her life. Not being able to get inside her head, he had no way of gauging her true feelings. So all he could do was bide his time and be there for her should she need him.

Sometimes, Nico found himself wishing he could turn back the clock to the moment he'd met her.

He and Michael had been club-hopping that night, nearly four years ago. They'd been sitting at the bar in a blues club drinking cold beers when Nico heard a delightful feminine laugh. He thought it odd that he should be able to distinguish that sound from the cacophony of the band and the many other voices around him but he had and he followed the sound until his eyes rested on a lovely golden-brown skinned woman with shoulder-length tresses that reminded him of a raven's wing. She looked up suddenly and their eyes met. She smiled at him. He smiled back, automatically coming up off his chair. Her smile was all the encouragement he needed.

So entranced by her was he, that he hadn't even noticed his partner, sitting right beside him, had also made eye-contact with her. Michael was already across the room before Nico was out of his seat.

By the time Nico reached Alana's table, Michael had pulled up a chair next to her and proceeded to charm the three women seated around it.

In a matter of minutes, Michael and Alana were up dancing and Nico was left at the table with Bree and Georgie Shaw.

"He doesn't waste time, does he?" Georgie had commented dryly. She'd told him she was an attorney. She'd just passed the California bar examination. "On her first try," her sister, who was an actress, had added proudly.

"No," Nico said regrettably. "Michael isn't one to let grass grow under his feet."

"Is he nice?" Bree inquired sweetly. Nico had been somewhat taken aback by that question. How was he supposed to reply? Michael was his friend. "No, frankly, he's a womanizer of the first order." At least that would have been closer to the truth. However, they were out for an evening of fun and not armed with the gift of divination, Nico had no way of knowing that months later, Michael and Alana would be married. "He's the best," he'd said then.

Later, as the evening waned, he'd gotten his chance to dance with Alana. However, by that time, it was obvious she was smitten with Michael.

It was difficult for her to draw her eyes away from Michael's handsome face as Nico pulled her into his arms for a slow dance.

"Are you two good friends?" she asked, her voice husky.

"We've known one another since the police academy," Nico had told her. "That was almost two years ago."

"You're both great-looking guys," she'd said, looking up at him with those clear brown eyes. His heartbeat thundered in his ears. Could she be interested in him?

"Why aren't you in a relationship?"

Nico had gone on to explain the life of a cop to her: the long hours, the imminent danger that had a way of making you hesitant to bring another person into your life. She'd listened intently and her next words told him everything he needed to know about her. "It takes a special kind of person to do what you do and retain your innate humanness," she had said, her voice low.

"Stop that," he'd joked. "Or you're going to make a grown man blush."

She'd laughed a deep, throaty laugh that he'd found altogether delightful. He'd lost his heart there on the dance floor.

In the intervening years, he'd simply fallen more in love with her. He thought of transferring to another city more than once but realized he couldn't bear to be away from Alana for any great length of time. So he made up his mind to be the best friend to Alana that he could possibly be. When Michael showed his true colors, he would be there to look after her. He was helpless to do anything other than wait for the inevitable.

Michael's death had shocked them all. Nico had certainly never imagined such an abrupt conclusion to Alana's marriage. A whole new set of rules applied here. He vowed to remain silent about Michael's other life. When not on duty he comforted Alana, listened to her curse the Fates for putting her husband in the line of fire of murderous carjackers.

Months after Michael's death she was still trying to rid herself of his ghost and now that someone had created a mystery for her in the form of the letter she'd received this morning, Nico had only one option: to confess everything.

Four

"What are you doing home so early?" Geraldine Robinson asked of her daughter as Karen walked through the door of her apartment. She'd dropped by the grocery store on the way home because Michael needed milk for his cereal in the morning.

Her mother was sitting on the sofa, folding clothes. Michael was playing with his toy soldiers a few feet away. Geraldine dropped the towel she was folding back into the laundry basket and went to her daughter. "Karen?"

Karen continued into the kitchen, where she placed the bag on the small table and began putting away the foodstuffs: the milk into the refrigerator, the green beans into the cabinet next to the stove. Finished, she faced her mother.

"They fired me, Ma," she said. Her bottom lip trembled as she fought back tears.

Geraldine, a stout woman in her early fifties, enfolded her only child in her arms. "My poor baby," she cooed. "Tell Momma everything."

Karen looked up into her mother's clear, compassionate brown eyes and silently thanked God for her.

"Miss Ekert said that the company is losing money so they had to cut back, which meant they could no longer afford to keep me. She said they could do without a receptionist," she told her mother, her voice listless.

Holding her at arm's length, Geraldine looked up into her eyes. "You had outgrown them anyway," she said positively. "A few more credits and you'll have your business degree. I have a little money set aside. We can make it until you find something else. Don't think of this as the end of the world, baby. Think of this as an opportunity to expand your horizons."

"It just came at a bad time," Karen replied, sniffling. "I was counting on that job to help pay my tuition for my last semester in night school. Now I'm going to have to postpone school for a while until I can find another job, a job that pays well enough so that I can afford to continue going to school. Sun Realty really messed with my plans, Ma."

"A little setback isn't going to do you in, child," Geraldine prophesied. "You've had disappointments before . . ." She glanced lovingly at Michael. "But look how far you've come. When you got pregnant with Michael, you could have gone on welfare like any number of other women, but instead you stayed in school and kept working, knowing that in the long run, fending for yourself was going to help you provide a better future for your child." She gently squeezed one of Karen's hands. "I was proud of you then, sugar. And I'm still proud of you. What that man did to you . . ." She blew air between her full lips in an exasperated gesture. "Well, some women would've just up and died from the humiliation, but not you. You survived. You're strong, baby. That's how I raised you to be." Her eyes held a humorous expression in them. "Remember when Michael was born, and you wanted to give him up for adoption, for all of fifteen minutes, and I talked you out of it? Have you ever regretted your decision?"

"Not for a minute," Karen answered, looking at her son with her love for him glowing in her eyes. "He's the best thing that ever happened to me."

"And you're the best thing that ever happened to me," Geraldine said with conviction. "Momma will be here for you. The Lord will provide."

Karen burst into tears then, but they were not tears of regret at losing her job, or tears of anger at an unfeeling system, but tears of relief at knowing she always had someone whom she could talk to when she was at her lowest.

"Go ahead and let it out," her mother advised her. "Then I

want you to go wash your face and come back out here wearing a smile. We've got work to do."

Karen felt something tugging on her dress's hem and looked down to see Michael with a worried look in his large, golden-brown eyes. Eyes just like his father's. "Why are you cryin', Ma?" he said in his small voice.

Karen knelt and pulled him into her embrace. "Mommy's a little sad because she lost her job today, sweetie. But it's nothing for you to be sad about because everything's going to be all right."

At two years of age, Karen knew there wasn't much Michael understood about the grown-up world. He knew a job was the place his mommy went every day except on the weekend. And he knew that on the weekend, he had his mother all to himself. She made pancakes for him Saturday and Sunday mornings. They would sleep late and watch cartoons in bed and when they got up, she took him to fun places like McDonald's and the zoo where he saw all sorts of wonderful animals. His favorite were the monkeys. They always made him giggle.

"Can I have pancakes in the morning?" he said, looking up at her expectantly.

Karen laughed happily. "Yes, sweetie. I'll make pancakes for you tomorrow morning."

By late afternoon Alana was becoming a bit anxious to hear from Nico. Following Margery and Toni's brief interrogation, she'd rolled up her sleeves, put on an apron, and pitched in with the food preparation. When it was at all possible, she liked working alongside her staff. More often than not, however, her expertise was needed wooing the clients and in the initial planning of an event.

She was helping Gina, a young single mother who'd been with Vesta for a couple of years, stuff eggrolls. Gina was telling about the latest adventure in her daughter, Laura's life. "Just before I left her at the day care center, she turned to me and asked,

'Mommy, do you know why boys like to hit me and pull my hair?' " Gina's dark brown eyes were animated as she continued. "No, I told her. No, honey, I don't know why. Then she looked at me with a thoroughly innocent expression on her tiny face and said, 'Miss Stephens says it's because I hit them first.' " Gina laughed. "Well, I didn't know what to say to that. My three-year-old, a bully? I didn't realize she had an aggressive bone in her body."

"Maybe it would be a good idea if you visited the day-care center one day, just to observe," Alana suggested, stifling laughter. "It could be she's defending herself. Have you had a chance to talk to Miss Stephens about it?"

"No, I'm going to do that this afternoon," Gina said as she wiped her hand on a dish towel. She picked up the large baking sheet they'd been placing the finished eggrolls on and passed it to Clovis, who covered it with plastic wrap and carried it to the walk-in freezer. The day of the ball, they would be removed from the freezer and deep fried.

"When you've got kids, it's one thing after another," Gina complained, turning back around to face Alana.

"Still," Alana said, smiling at her, "I envy you. You have a beautiful child, and you're engaged to one of the nicest men I know. You're a fortunate person, Gina."

"Yeah," Gina concurred, her full lips curved in a wistful smile. "I guess I am at that. But it sure has taken me a while to get here. You know what a living hell my first marriage was. The one good thing that came out of that was Laura. The experience also taught me to stand on my own two feet. It was a hard lesson but one I needed to learn." She laughed. "I lucked out with Gary, but still, I'm never going to depend on another person to support me."

"Girl, you are fierce!" Alana said proudly.

"No, girlfriend," Gina said seriously. "You are the one. You have been my role model."

"Get out of here," Alana said, hands on her hips.

"When you hired me two years ago, I thought I'd be here maybe four, five months. But when I saw you in action, I said to myself: I could learn something here because this woman has her stuff together." Gina cleared her throat. "Uh huh. I sure did. And I was right. I've learned more about catering from you in two years than I could have working in a restaurant in twice as much time."

"That's because you applied yourself," Alana politely informed her. But she was grateful for the compliment, which she knew to be genuine. Gina Evans was not the kind of person to kiss-up to the boss. She was a straight shooter who would rather incur your wrath than bite her tongue.

Hearing a collective sigh from the four women in the room, Alana looked up and saw Nico coming through the swinging doors.

He had gone home between there and work and had changed into a pair of black jeans, a blue denim shirt and a maroon T-shirt underneath. Alana glanced down and saw he was wearing his favorite black motorcycle boots. I am not riding on the back of his Harley Davidson tonight, she thought briefly.

"Hello, Nico!" said the chorus of feminine voices.

"Hi, ladies," Nico said. He blushed.

Alana quickly washed her hands and dried them on a towel.

"I'm leaving now. I'll see you tomorrow morning," she told Gina. "Give that little bully of yours a kiss for me."

Walking toward Nico and taking him by the hand, she led him out of the kitchen. "You know," she said jokingly, "you really should have someone announce you before you come into a room full of women. Hunk alert, hunk alert!"

Nico grinned at her, showing perfect white teeth in his golden-brown, square-chinned face. His downward sloping, warm brown eyes regarded her with keen interest. "Do I detect a note of jealousy in your voice?"

"Who, me?" Alana said noncommittally. She wasn't about to fall into that trap. "Besides, you're supposed to be using your detecting skills to locate the person behind that rather cryptic note."

They were alone in the hallway, and Nico took the opportunity to pull her into his arms. "You smell like ginger," he said as he caressed her back. Alana felt her body relax in his embrace. There

was no use fighting it. She was growing ever fonder of his nearness. She looked up into his eyes.

"How was your day?"

Nico laughed. "I've longed to hear you ask me that. Only I
wanted it to be when I came home to you."

Alana's stomach muscles tightened at the sound of the uncon-
cealed longing in his voice. Her heartbeat speeded up. She
pressed her face against his muscular chest. He smelled of soap
and water and sandalwood.

There was no adequate response to such an intimate comment.
She reached up and gently touched his cheek, then she wiggled
out of his hold. "Hang on, I forgot my shoulder bag."

She left him standing there while she went back into the
kitchen to get her purse, which she'd left hanging in the pantry.

The clamor immediately ceased when she walked through the
twin swinging doors of the kitchen. A sure sign that she was
being talked about in her absence. "Forgot my purse," she said
to no one in particular. All eyes were on her as she retrieved the
purse and quickly walked back out. The voices resumed as soon
as the door closed behind her.

That was strange, she thought, then shrugged it off. A handsome man came by to pick her up. People were always intrigued
by romance. There was no harm in their thinking that she and
Nico were an item.

Nico, with Margery and Toni keeping him company, was waiting for her in the foyer.

"Oh, there you are, darling," Margery said, coming to take
her by the arm. "Nico was telling us that you and he are in the
middle of an investigation. You *will* tell your aunt all about it
tomorrow, won't you?" She kissed Alana's cheek. In a lower
voice she said, "You can always change your mind about going
through with this. Let it go, dear. What good would it do you to
find out something you'd rather not know? Haven't you endured
enough heartache?"

Alana returned her kiss. "I need to know, Little Momma. I'm
sure you can understand that."

Margery nodded, keeping any further comments to herself.

"You take good care of our girl," Toni demanded of Nico after having pulled him aside.

Nico had long admired and respected Toni. He remembered reading about her exploits as a boy in high school. He never imagined he would actually meet her one day. But about three years ago Alana had invited him to Thanksgiving dinner with them. He was amazed when Antoinette Shaw strode into the dining room carrying the turkey. He had been enamored of her ever since.

"Don't worry, Toni," he said now. "I'll guard her with my life."

"That's all I expect," Toni said lightly. But she meant it and he knew it.

Alana came to claim him then, and they left.

"I hope my aunts weren't putting you through the third degree," Alana said as they descended the front steps.

Nico placed a protective arm around her. The weather had turned chilly, as San Francisco afternoons do in February. "I brought an extra leather jacket for you," he told her. Alana's gaze went to the Harley Davidson waiting in the driveway. "And why, pray tell, did you bring that machine?"

"It's good for getting in and out of afternoon traffic," Nico said, defending his beloved motorcycle. "And it's small and not as noticeable as your van or my car would be. Afraid your 'do' won't survive the night air?"

He got on the motorcycle and put on his helmet, fastening it under his chin. Ignoring his comment, Alana quickly slipped into the aforementioned jacket and straddled the seat behind him. "The only thing missing is my biker-chick outfit."

"Complete with the leather chaps?" Nico said, smiling.

"And the removable 'Mom' tattoo on my right forearm," Alana added, her grin infectious.

"I'd like to see that," Nico returned easily. "But for now, hold on to me."

"Where are we going?" she asked as she donned the helmet.

"Someplace where we can talk. I have a few confessions to make."

"Oh goody, confessions," Alana said in a playful mood. She put her arms around his waist, locking her fingers. "I can't wait. What, you use foreign coins in the drink machine at work?"

"It's much more serious than that," Nico said as he kick-started the huge Harley.

Nico took Van Ness Avenue all the way down to Geary Street, then turned onto Park Presidio Boulevard. At that point Alana had no difficulty discerning that they were headed into Golden Gate Park. The Japanese Tea Garden was one of their favorite destinations. The serenity of the intricately landscaped garden made it one of the most visited points of interest in San Francisco.

The park itself covered one thousand acres that, over the years, had been divided into recreational fields, picnic areas, paths for walking and museums.

After parking, Alana and Nico walked through the beautiful, painstakingly carved gateway and strolled hand in hand past pools filled with giant goldfish.

Deciduous trees grew all around them. Footbridges over pools of water. Paths bordered by dwarf trees and large stone statues that stood like sentinels at Shinto shrines.

Alana always felt at peace in these tranquil surroundings. She wondered, however, why Nico had chosen this particular place to make his confession. Perhaps the quietness of this garden would cushion the blow of his revelation?

They chose a bench near the entrance to one of the shrines and sat down.

"Make it fast," Alana said. She had the feeling this was not going to be something she wanted to hear, and she wanted to get it over with as swiftly as possible.

Nico bit his bottom lip. He narrowed his eyes as he regarded her, opened his mouth to say something, then shut it again. Sighing, he reached for one of her hands and held on to it as though he gained strength from her touch.

Alana arched her eyebrows in an impatient gesture. "Come on, tell me, Nico."

"Oh, God," he began. "Alana, this is the hardest thing I have ever had to do." He took her other hand, and Alana had the feeling that he was holding on to her in order to prevent her from fleeing once she heard what he had to tell her.

"First, let me tell you about the Michael Calloway I knew," he prefaced. "When we first met, in the police academy here in San Francisco, I liked him right away. He was gregarious, the life of the party. People flocked to him. He became my best friend, and I was proud to call him my partner. But almost immediately after you two were married, he grew frantic. Something was eating him. It was like he'd changed into a whole different person." He paused and glanced down at their clasped hands. "But I knew that wasn't true. Michael hadn't changed. I had. He was still the man who loved women." Alana flinched and he held on to her more firmly. "You knew that about him before you married him, did you not?" His Spanish accent was surfacing now. Alana gave an almost imperceptible nod. She knew. "As I was saying," he continued, "Michael hadn't changed his spots, but I was no longer tolerant of his behavior because I was . . ." He looked her straight in the eyes. "Because I was in love with his wife."

Tears sat in Alana's big brown eyes. "Nico, don't."

Nico brought her right hand up to his mouth and kissed her fingers. "Let me finish, please." He looked down again, unable to see those tears in her eyes without wanting to take her in his arms and kiss them away. "One night, Michael and I were out getting a sandwich and, as it often did, the topic of conversation turned to your marriage. I was uncomfortable talking about your problems. Now, you know why. He was upset because you wanted to postpone having children."

Alana nodded, remembering. "Yes, he wanted to start a family right away."

"I sided with you," Nico told her. "Michael blew up and accused me of being in love with you, and I didn't deny it. That's when he shoved me and the fight began. At any rate, he told me that he was cheating on you and that you were too naive to realize it."

"Why didn't you come to me?" Alana asked, her voice low, controlled. "Maybe I could have salvaged my marriage."

"Come to you with what?" Nico said. "It would've been my

word against his, and whom would you have believed? Besides, I had a hidden agenda: I wanted you."

"Okay," Alana said. She breathed in deeply and exhaled. "You've confessed. But really, Nico, you have nothing to feel guilty about. Michael told you he had other women but you didn't have proof, so you really don't know whether he was telling the truth or just being a blowhard."

"I *do* know," Nico said quietly. "I followed him to her door. I watched as she greeted him, they kissed, and he went inside."

Alana felt sick to her stomach. She wrenched her hands free of his grasp and got to her feet. Looking down at him, she shouted, "Who is she?"

"I never pursued the matter," Nico said truthfully. "What was I supposed to do, come to you with an address and you go over there only to have your heart torn to shreds? He's dead now, Alana. Let it rest."

Seeing all the curious eyes turned their way, Alana sat back down and lowered her voice considerably. "So why tell me all this now?"

"Because you came to my office and threatened to find her on your own if I didn't help you," Nico reminded her.

Alana bowed her head sadly. "True enough."

Nico moved closer to her and placed his arms around her shoulders. "He loved you in his own way," he said in his calm manner. "Just not the way a husband should."

"Well," she said after a long pause. "We've come this far, we'd just as well go all the way."

Nico's bedroom eyes bespoke his confusion.

"I want her name and address. I want to talk to her face-to-face," Alana announced.

Nico stood, picking up his helmet as he did so. Seconds passed as he simply looked down at her, then he turned and calmly walked away from her. Alana gathered up her purse and her helmet and followed him. "You can't deny me, Nico. You owe me."

Nico's expression was thunderous when he faced her. "I owe you?"

"For keeping all of this a secret for so long," Alana explained.

He quickened his pace. He was already through the gate and heading toward the parked motorcycle.

"Nico!" she called.

He was on the motorcycle and turning the key in the ignition when she caught up with him. She quickly got on behind him.

"Are you a masochist?" she heard him say as he gunned the motor. She held on tightly as he sped out of the parking lot. "I will not give you her name and address," he said with finality.

Alana rested against him, letting the pain of his revelation wash over her.

As he drove, Nico could feel her body tremble in the throes of a crying jag. God knew, there was very little he would deny her, but how long was he expected to watch her being consumed with the loss of a man who didn't show her the respect she deserved? Maybe he was missing something here. It was impossible for him to put himself in her place. What could possess her to want to talk to the woman who had been her husband's lover? He didn't understand it. Perhaps he never would.

He pulled into the parking lot of a Mexican restaurant and shut off the engine.

Alana slid off the seat and waited for him to join her.

"I'm sorry," she said before he could even utter a word. "You don't owe me a thing, Nico. You've been a prince throughout this whole sorry mess." Her soft brown eyes were contrite as she looked up at him. Her hand went to her face to wipe away the residue left by her tears. "I'm such a fool. It's not as if I didn't suspect Michael had someone else. I mean, a woman knows these things. But to actually have my suspicions confirmed. Well, that's a whole different ball game."

"Don't apologize to me," Nico said, his voice harsh.

Alana stepped backward. "You're angry—"

Nico quickly caught her by the arm. He smiled. "No. I'm not angry with you. I'm angry with myself. I don't know what I was thinking, coming to you with the proof you've been looking for and then refusing to go a step further because I don't agree with your line of reasoning." He let go of her. "I can't know what you've been going through since Michael was killed. I only know what I've observed. And my perceptions have been colored by my love for you. So you tell me, Alana. Tell me why you feel the need to meet with this woman."

People were going in and coming out of the restaurant around them, and there was a brisk winter breeze making its presence felt. Alana had been growing cold standing out in the open, but now she felt a warmth from within. To be loved by a man of Nico's caliber was an unexpected pleasure. It was funny—up until a few minutes ago, she had thought Michael had been the love of her life. As it turned out, what they had shared was built on lies and illusions. His lies. Her self-delusion. But here was a man who was offering her his heart and soul, with no excess baggage attached.

"I think it's because I feel the need to be totally rid of him," she said softly. "It's like being immersed in ice water. It's a shock to the system, and it numbs you. I don't want to wonder about them any longer. Once I meet her, and if she's willing to talk to me, I know I'll be able to put everything associated with Michael behind me."

They had removed their helmets and their gestures were dramatic as they talked. To anyone looking on, they appeared to be arguing. Ultimately, a Mexican gentleman with a handlebar mustache, wearing a large, white apron with the words, *El Jardin Abundancia* emblazoned across the front, came outside and called, "Hey, lady, is that guy bothering you?"

Alana paused in mid-sentence and smiled at the man. "No. Everything's fine here. Thanks for asking."

"All right," the fellow said. "You coming in to eat? Today's special is the tortillas."

Turning to Nico with a wry smile on her lips, Alana said, "Were you planning on feeding me tonight?"

Nico eyed the small restaurant with skepticism. "I was going to take you someplace nicer," he said in a low voice.

"We'll be right in," Alana told the proprietor.

The man grinned at her and went back inside.

"Okay," Nico said grudgingly as they began walking toward the restaurant's entrance. "But don't blame me if you have a sudden attack of Montezuma's revenge and spend half the night in the bathroom."

Laughing, Alana put her hand through his arm, urging him forward. "Some of the best cooks are found in the most unlikely places," she said from experience.

The decor of El Jardin Abundancia—the abundant garden—restaurant consisted of original oil paintings on the walls of beautiful flower and vegetable gardens, red table cloths on the tables and hanging plants. "It's clean," Nico observed. "I'll give them that much."

"And the air smells good," Alana said as they claimed a booth near the picture window.

They sat down opposite each other and deposited their helmets on the seat beside them. Nico reached across the table and playfully traced the outline of Alana's jaw. He sighed. "They say good things come to those who wait," he murmured, as though he was talking to himself. He raised his gaze then, his liquid brown eyes caressing her face. "Do you want to know when I first knew I was in love with you, Alana?"

Alana lowered her eyes, her sooty black lashes resting above high cheekbones. Moistening her lips, she looked directly into his eyes. "Let me guess. Was it the time we went to Lake Tahoe and your date, the supermodel, refused to go into the water and Michael was glued in front of the t.v. watching basketball, which left the two of us?"

Leaning forward, Nico grinned at her. "What makes you think it was that time? As I recall, you wore that white one-piece, and by the time we finished one game of water polo, you, and it, looked like something the cat dragged in."

"Is that right?" Alana said, feigning hurt feelings. "Well, if I remember correctly, you and Sheena—"

"Shana," Nico corrected her.

"You and 'Shana' went for a stroll in the woods and returned covered with poison oak. I've spent many a spare moment wondering how you managed that in a vertical position."

"You thought about that, huh?" Nico asked, his left eyebrow arched in amusement. "Actually it was all quite innocent. She picked up a leaf, admiring its beauty. The girl was used to limousines and champagne. What did she know about the woods? I took the leaf from her. You know how quickly poison oak spreads."

"Yeah." Alana laughed. "By the time you two got back to the cabin, you were covered in red welts and scratching like crazy."

"We've gotten off the subject," Nico said seriously. "Which, I think, was your intention. Why does my telling you I love you make you so uneasy?"

Alana grasped one of his big hands across the tabletop. "You mean so much to me, Nico. I think you know that. I definitely couldn't have made it through the last year without you." She gently held his hand and met his gaze. "I'm afraid that if we take our relationship a step farther, that we'll end up spoiling what we already have. You know how it is between couples who've become intimate and something goes wrong. Chances are, they are *not* going to continue being friends." Cocking her head sideways, she placed his hand on her cheek. "I want you in my life forever, Nico. Not just for a moment."

"Don't compare me to him, Alana," Nico told her evenly. His dark, hooded eyes bored into hers. "I knew it was inevitable, your reluctance to allow yourself to fall in love again after your experience with Michael. But I'm not like Michael, Alana. We were total opposites. His not knowing his father did something to his psyche. I, on the other hand, have a great relationship with my dad. We love and respect one another. My Papa taught me the most difficult lesson a father can teach his son. He taught me to love the woman I choose to spend my life with. My father has never been untrue to my mother, not after forty years of marriage. Not after six children, a mortgage and the ups and downs of life, in general. They remain as in love today as they were when they were first married at the base of Cuba's highest mountain, Pico Turquino, forty years ago."

"Good evening," the waitress, a pretty Mexican girl in her late teens said, as she stopped next to their booth. "My name is Lucy, and I'll be your waitress tonight." She paused, her broad smile revealing straight, white teeth. "We're happy you could join us. The special tonight is—"

"Tortillas!" Alana and Nico responded in unison to the delight of Lucy who laughed happily.

"I see you've met my uncle Rudy," she said.

Five

The City by the Bay was awash with light and brimming with activity as Alana and Nico made their way across town on the Harley Davidson. Alana was content to sit behind Nico, her arms wrapped around him, her cheek pressed against his back. For the moment she had given up the idea of seeking out Michael's mistress. She was tempted to let it go, as Nico and Margery had urged her to do. What would she accomplish anyway? Michael was beyond redemption. And the woman, whoever she was, would probably be hostile toward her, especially if she had known Michael was a married man and had still opted to be with him.

But what if she was also a victim? Michael could have deceived her, too. They could have both been his unsuspecting dupes. That possibility hadn't previously occurred to her. If there was a chance that they had both been played for fools, she wanted to know about it. Logically, the only way to find out was by meeting with the other woman.

So when Nico walked her to her door, she gave him a hug and said in his ear, "I know you don't want me to pursue this, but I've decided I'd like to meet her."

Holding her at arm's length, Nico peered down into her face. "I had a feeling you would," he said, his voice low. He smiled at her. "How do you want to handle it?"

Frowning, Alana considered it. "Let me get back to you on that, okay? Bree's flying in from L.A. in the morning, and I promised Georgie I'd go with her to pick her up at the airport."

She smiled at him, her eyes bright. "Have you picked up your tuxedo yet? You do remember that you're my date for the ball?"

Nico grinned. "That date was made before we, well, you know," he said, referring to the first time they'd kissed and the subsequent results of their actions. "Do you still want me?" He stepped closer to her. "It would be my pleasure to escort you. Do you want me, Alana?"

Alana's pulse rate accelerated, and she felt the heat beginning to rise somewhere in the vicinity of her lower regions. Want him? Yes, she wanted him. She wanted him with a ferocity that alarmed her.

She inhaled silently and exhaled with a groan. Their eyes met, and seeing the humor in his told her he'd chosen his words specifically to get a rise out of her. He smiled. She rolled her eyes. "You are the biggest flirt, Nico Setera," she said accusingly as she stepped backward. "Yes, Setera. I'd like you to take me to the ball. I want you to be dressed to the nines. I want you to be on time. And I want you to drive the Stingray, not the Harley. For now, that's all I *want* of you. So say good night."

"Good night," Nico responded, still smiling at her expense.

Alana tiptoed to plant a kiss on his cheek, and Nico kissed her on the forehead, his mouth lingering there for a moment longer than necessary. "Things have a way of changing," he said.

The next morning Alana rose from her comfortable bed, went into the closet, removed Michael's jacket from its hanger, threw it onto the floor and stomped on it. Then she found a cardboard box and dumped everything belonging to her dead husband (that she'd formerly been reluctant to part with) into it and hauled it to the curb. Thursday was garbage pick-up day.

She was just completing her task when Georgette Shaw, one of her dearest friends, pulled up in her 1965 powder blue Mustang convertible. Georgie, with her long braids flowing behind her, walked up to Alana and gave her a brief hug. "Hey, girlfriend.

What in the world are you doing? Why are you jumping up and down in that box?"

Stepping out of the box, Alana smiled at Georgie. "I was just getting rid of some of Michael's things, that's all."

"And having fun doing it," Georgie observed with a grin. She placed an arm about Alana's shoulders as they walked to the house. "What happened? Did you and Michael argue in one of those too-vivid dreams you have about him? Do you want to talk about it?"

They climbed the stairs to Alana's apartment side by side, and once inside, Alana retrieved her shoulder bag and came back out to the living room where she'd left Georgie.

"We can talk on the way to the airport," she said. "If the flight is on time, Bree and Pierre will be wondering where we are."

"The dog or the man?" Georgie said as they left the apartment.

Turning around to look at her, Alana said, "What do you mean, the dog or the man? I'm talking about her poodle."

"Then you haven't heard," Georgie said with a scowl. "My sister's latest Don Juan happens to be named Pierre St. Martin. He is a wannabe who has latched on to her in hope that some of her good fortune will rub off on him."

"She's bringing him?" Alana asked. She wanted to meet him. Bree's relationships were always interesting even if they were invariably short-lived.

"She is," Georgie confirmed with a grimace. "We spoke last night. She says she can't bear to be away from him for two whole days. Love's in full bloom. I tell you, Alana, I don't think anything Mom tried to teach that girl about self-respect ever sank in."

"Well, we'll just have to make the best of it," Alana said in her role as mediator. "Believe me, Aunt Toni will have him running back to La La Land, with his tail between his legs, in a matter of seconds if she gets one inkling that he's mistreating Bree. So don't worry about it."

In the car Georgie turned to smile at her. "You're right. The Terminator will handle that situation. What's going on with you? Have you experienced satori concerning your husband?"

As Georgie pulled away from the curb, Alana fastened her seat belt and relaxed. "You could say I've experienced a sense of sudden enlightenment about my husband." She went on to tell Georgie everything she'd learned about Michael over the last twenty-four hours.

"I can't say I'm surprised," Georgie said once Alana was finished. "But I am sorry to hear it, girlfriend. My sympathies are with you. I just regret Michael isn't still with us so that we can plot a proper form of punishment for him. Now *that* would be good therapy for you."

Alana smiled at her friend who, as an attorney with the public defender's office in San Francisco, was well versed about crime and punishment.

She and Georgie and Bree had known one another all their lives. Georgie and Bree were two years older than Alana so they'd always regarded her as their baby sister. The sisters were fraternal twins. Georgette was born three minutes before Bree which, throughout their formative years, was the catalyst that made her the leader, and instigator, in their relationship. Her rule often made Bree resent her sister, however not to the extent that their bond became irreparable. They loved each other and remained loyal sisters in every sense of the word.

Alana envied them their closeness because she had no siblings. And on several occasions she'd used that argument to shame the sisters into settling disputes. They were lucky to have one another, and she made sure they remembered it.

As they approached San Francisco International Airport, Alana admonished Georgie to be nice to Bree's new beau. "Who knows?" she said. "Your first impression of him could have been flawed."

Georgie gave her a knowing look and laughed. "Okay. We shall see what you think of him."

After leaving the car in short-term parking, they entered the terminal and spent ten minutes trying to locate Bree among the crowd of travelers. San Francisco International Airport is one of the world's busiest airports, so they were fortunate when they heard Bree calling to them from across the room.

Alana had to admit Georgie had been correct about Pierre St.

Martin. He and Bree were standing near the luggage carousel
awaiting the arrival of their bags. They were both dressed casually—Bree in jeans and a golden-hued silk blouse and her favorite pair of Doc Martens. He was also wearing jeans, a T-shirt and
a leather jacket with leather boots, all in black. He wore dark
glasses and his long, natural black hair in dreadlocks. There was
something innately cocky about his stance as he stared off into
space, a look of utter boredom on his handsome face.

The sisters hugged fiercely, then Alana gave Bree a hug and
a peck on the cheek. "Hi, sweetie, you look gorgeous as always,"
she said.

She wasn't exaggerating. Bree was beautiful with her large
light-brown eyes, unlike her mother's or Georgie's, who had very
dark eyes. Alana supposed Bree inherited her eye color from
their long-dead father, killed during the Vietnam War.

Bree had the pecan-tan skin that paler women burned themselves on beaches in hope of acquiring. Her mouth was full and
her nose long, well-shaped. She wore her thick, black luxurious
locks in a short, tousled style that was all the rage in Tinseltown.
She was extremely popular as an actress in Hollywood, being
one of the most sought-after performers in television. She jokingly referred to herself as the queen of the small screen. She'd
made several television movies and was well-known as the black
detective, Jody Freeman, who always got her man. The Jody
Freeman movies were action-packed comedy-dramas that always
drew a large viewing audience.

That wasn't to say that her sister was plain. Georgie held her
own in the looks department. They were opposites in how they
perceived beauty, however. Bree was more glamorous—it was
her job to look good, after all. Georgie adopted a business look
for the courtroom and had a more casual approach to apparel for
everyday. She fancied jeans and loose tops and her hair was invariably in braids. She'd worn it in that style since college, and
now it hung down her back, almost to her hips.

They were both five feet, eight inches tall, Bree being rather
slim and willowy, Georgie, more voluptuous, like her mother.
They were both athletic. Bree enjoyed running and swimming.

Georgie also ran and had a third-degree black belt in judo, an interest introduced to her by her friend, Sammy Chan, who owned a dojo there in the city.

"Georgie, you remember Pierre . . ." Bree said, her well-modulated voice enthusiastic. She was praying her sister would also remember her manners.

"Yes, how are you, Pierre? Welcome to San Francisco, I hope you enjoy your stay," Georgie said politely.

"Hello again, Georgie," Pierre said. He had the southern twang of a Texan. Alana couldn't imagine him growing up with the name Pierre St. Martin in West Texas. The other kids would have ridiculed him mercilessly. Pierre St. Martin had to be a stage name. Bree used Briane Miller when her true name was Briane Marie Shaw.

"And this is my dear friend, Alana Calloway. Alana owns a catering service here in San Francisco," Bree explained.

Alana offered her hand in greeting. Pierre removed his glasses as he smiled at her. His eyes were a pale shade of green in his dark brown face. "Hello, Alana. Bree has told me so much about you, I feel as though we're already friends."

Charming *and* handsome, Alana thought. No wonder Bree is enamored of him. Who wouldn't be?

Bree was busy taking Pierre, her ebony-hued toy poodle, out of his traveling cage. Pierre possessed a pugnacious nature and was extremely protective of Bree. The only people he'd taken a liking to over the years was Alana, on whose lap he was known to curl up on and take a nap; Toni, who, he'd learned, had no patience for his imperious moods, and Toni's mother, Marie Shaw, who had such an angelic aura about her that all creatures tended to be drawn to her.

Now as Bree held him in her arms, he was wiggling his tail and pushing out of his mistress' arms, eager to go to Alana. Alana took him, and he immediately began licking her face. "I've missed you, too," Alana said with affection.

"I don't believe it," the human Pierre said. "He actually likes someone other than Bree. That dog hates me."

"You and I *do* have something in common, after all," Georgie said as she reached down and picked up one of Bree's many bags. "Head 'em up and move 'em out, you guys. Mom and Margery are waiting."

"We're staying with Aunt Margery?" Bree asked. "I told you we had reservations at the Fairmont."

"Yes, well, our little Margie wouldn't hear of it," Georgie told her. "She insisted that you stay with her. She and Mom are in hog heaven having all three of us home."

"Oh, dear," Bree said worriedly. Then to Pierre, "But don't you worry, darling. They're really wonderful women and you *have* been dying to meet Aunt Margery."

Alana wondered if Bree made it a habit of stroking Pierre's ego or if she was truly nervous about his meeting her mother and aunt. Over the years Bree had played at relationships. Could it be she was serious about Pierre St. Martin? As they crossed the terminal, she decided Bree's anxiety was real. She wanted them all to like her new paramour.

Pierre put up a valiant effort to assure Bree everything would be all right. Even Georgie seemed impressed by his sincerity. Maybe I was wrong about him, she thought.

Bree's apprehension was unfounded, however, because when they arrived at the house on Nob Hill, Toni and Margery were on their best behavior.

Hugs and kisses were the order of the day. Margery even gave a pat to the head to the canine Pierre who had been most unkind to her the last time he'd visited.

"Hello, you little rug rat," she said happily. "Left any presents in anyone's shoes lately?"

"Auntie," Bree said. "He only did that because he senses that you don't like him."

"Then he's very intuitive for a birdbrain," Margery returned good-naturedly. She then relinquished custody of the dog and gave her undivided attention to his human namesake. "I'm very pleased to meet you, young man. Where did you get those interesting eyes?"

Pierre blushed profusely. Margery had a way of reducing full-grown men to whimpering babes. They were putty in her hands. She'd worked years at perfecting her craft.

"I, I," he stammered.

"Don't worry, darling," Margery said as she took him by the arm and led him out of the foyer into her home. "With a face like yours, you don't need to speak."

"I'm sorry, Miss Robinson, but we haven't any job openings at the moment. I'd be glad to take your application, and if anything opens up, we'll call you back for an interview," the human resources manager at the fifth business office Karen had visited that morning, regrettably said. "Our company has had to put a freeze on hiring."

Sighing, Karen nodded. "Okay." She placed a neatly filled-out application form on the woman's desk. "Thank you for your time. Have a nice day."

The older woman looked after her with sympathy. "Good luck with your job hunting, dear," she called.

Karen turned to briefly smile at the woman before pushing the glass door open and stepping onto the sidewalk in front of the travel agency's office.

Her fifth rejection. It wasn't that she'd believed all she had to do was apply for a job in order to get one, it was just that she hadn't observed even the prospect of being hired yet.

She tried to maintain a positive attitude as she quickly walked to her parked car. She had one more place to try: a small architectural firm across from the Civic Center was looking for a secretary. She could type and knew shorthand and was schooled in WordPerfect, a computer program which proved helpful to secretaries in the performance of their jobs. She'd never worked as a secretary before, but she was qualified nonetheless.

She liked the cool ambience of the architectural firm the moment she stepped into the office. The walls and floors were done in muted tones of gray and maroon. A pretty African-American receptionist greeted her and invited her to take a seat. One of the

architects, Mr. Prentice, the partner who needed an assistant,
would come out and take her back to his office for the interview
shortly.

Karen sat down on a gray leather upholstered chair facing the
entrance. She was wearing her best business attire: a two-year-old
navy-blue suit whose skirt fell just above her knees. She had not
wanted to wear it because having it on evoked bad memories.
The last place she'd worn it had been to Michael's graveside
memorial service.

Not wanting to be seen, she'd stood apart from the others amid
a copse of trees. Her mother had tried to talk her out of going,
but she was unable to stay away. Even with the realization that
Michael had used her, her love for him compelled her to say
goodbye to him.

It was a chilly, overcast day in February. There was a long line
of cars at the L. A. cemetery: limousines, privately owned cars
of family and friends and the service vehicles of the San Francisco Police Department. Michael had been one of their own,
and they'd shown up in droves to show their respects.

When Karen arrived, in her beat-up Toyota, she had had to
park at the very end of the processional, and by the time she was
close enough to see and hear the service, her shoes were mud-
splattered.

She'd stood about thirty yards away and observed as the minister talked about Michael Calloway. She heard him describe a
man she was not familiar with: a pillar of his community, a devoted husband. Her Michael had been a confirmed bachelor who,
although he loved her, did not propose to her even after she con-
ceived his child. They had met in a club in Oakland. He told her
he lived in nearby San Francisco and worked as a security guard.
He never mentioned the San Francisco Police Department. He
most definitely never mentioned his wife.

Karen had learned his true identity when she had read about
his murder in the *San Francisco Chronicle.* The paper did a
touching tribute on the young cop who'd been gunned down by
would-be carjackers. The killer had been apprehended three days

later. The police were not about to let anyone get away with killing a brother in uniform.

Karen followed the whole morbid tale with fascination. She cut out every article the paper ran about him, pasting them in a scrapbook. When Michael's obituary appeared in the paper, along with the time and place his service was to be held, she knew she would be there.

So as she stood among the trees in the drizzle, her tears intermingling with the rain, she watched as the chief of police handed a folded American flag to Michael's widow.

The woman stood and was immediately embraced by a tall man in dress uniform. From her vantage point, Karen could see that Michael's wife was beautiful. She was wearing a designer suit and was smartly coiffured. All those around her were especially solicitous of her, and when the tall man in dress uniform was not at her side, she was flanked by two attractive older women—one of whom bore an uncanny resemblance to Margery Devlin, the movie star.

Suddenly, Michael's wife looked up and stared in her direction. Karen knew she had seen her. She felt incapable of moving, however. Then the woman who resembled Margery Devlin put her hand on the widow's arm and whispered something into her ear. Karen took the opportunity to leave. She'd seen enough.

"Miss Robinson?" a deep male voice inquired.

Karen slowly raised her eyes to the smiling face of a tall, trim, dark-skinned, ruggedly-handsome man in his mid-thirties.

He reached for her hand. She hastily rose to her feet and grasped his hand. They shook, and he laughed deep in his throat. "You were daydreaming. What's the matter, aren't you having a good day?"

He indicated the way to his office with a courtly gesture. They began walking down the hall. "The reason I ask is it's my theory that people daydream more often when they're worried about something."

He talked easily to her, as though he'd known her all her life. Karen was instantly at ease in his presence.

"I'm not exactly worried," she said. "A little apprehensive, maybe."

"About the job?" Scott Prentice asked.

He opened the door to his office and allowed her to precede him. Karen stepped into a large, airy work space with plenty of light filtering in through the oversized windows.

There was a large oak desk near one of the windows, and a few feet away from it stood a huge drawing board with several rolled-up blueprints sitting atop it. Karen assumed that was where he did most of his work.

Scott sat down behind his desk, and Karen took the chair directly across from him.

"Don't worry about the job, Miss Robinson. It's yours if you're willing to work hard and learn as you go."

"Oh, I am," Karen said enthusiastically, leaning forward in her chair. "I'm a hard worker. I'm smart. I'm completing my bachelor's degree in business administration. I know I'd do an excellent job for you, Mr. Prentice."

"Business administration," Scott Prentice said, a smile causing crinkles to appear at the corners of his brown eyes. "You're overqualified for this job, Miss Robinson."

"I'm in a catch-22 situation here, Mr. Prentice. I don't have a degree yet. I'm paying for my education, and I'm a single mother. I have a two-year-old . . ."

"The terrible two's, huh?" Scott said. He turned around the eight by ten photograph whose back had been to Karen atop his desk. Karen looked into the face of a cherubic girl-child with her father's skin color and eyes the exact shade of roasted almonds. The face elicited a smile from her.

"Cute, isn't she?" Scott said proudly.

"A heartbreaker," Karen agreed.

She saw no reason why she shouldn't feel free to display her photos of Michael, so she whipped one out and handed it to Scott.

"He looks like a scrapper," Scott said. "Who keeps him for you during the day?"

"My mother," Karen replied.

"You're lucky," Scott told her. "I get to see Danielle only on weekends and holidays. My ex got custody of her in the divorce."

Karen was pleased to hear no irritation in his voice when he mentioned his ex-wife. She didn't think much of men who maligned the mother of their children. Her experience with Michael had inadvertently taught her that lesson.

"I know that having to see your daughter on weekends and holidays isn't like seeing her every day, but whatever time you spend with her is good. My son never sees his father."

Embarrassed at the thought that she'd carried the conversation to a much too personal level, Karen looked down.

"I agree," Scott said, smiling. "I should be grateful for the time I have with Danielle instead of grousing about the time I don't have with her."

He liked Karen Robinson. She seemed honest, and she wasn't afraid to say what was on her mind although there was a reticence, a shyness, about her that made him wonder. He'd take a chance on her.

"You're hired," he said with confidence. "When can you start?"

"Right away," Karen said, her brown eyes flooded with relief.

"Don't look so thankful," Scott said teasingly. "I may be an ogre to work for."

They rose and shook on it. When his hand touched hers this time, Scott knew he'd had an ulterior motive for offering her the position: he was attracted to her.

Karen continued to smile at him. "You don't look like an ogre to me, Mr. Prentice. At this point, you look like a lifeline. I'll have no problem working for you."

"Then it's settled," Scott said. "Can you really start right away, because I have a proposal that needs to be typed up."

"Yes," Karen replied a little breathlessly. "Just point me to my desk."

* * *

Alana lay her head on the inflatable tub pillow and closed her eyes. The soothing sounds of jazz artist, Cassandra Wilson, playing on her portable CD player came through the earphones she wore and the scent of Orange Flower wafted up from the warm, foamy bath water. She sighed. Nico would be coming over in two hours so that they could discuss how best to approach Michael's mistress. For the present though, all she wanted to do was relax and let the world recede into the background.

She felt her muscles loosen up as she sank further down into the fragrant water. The sensation was like floating. She drifted off to sleep, buffeted in a cocoon of seeming euphoria.

Then, she was in the water at Lake Tahoe. The day was sunny and bright and she and Nico were tossing a beach ball back and forth. She looked around, wondering where Michael was and she remembered he was watching basketball.

Nico threw the ball over her head. As she leapt up out of the water for it and came back down with it, she slipped and went under. She swallowed water and panicked. She couldn't get her breath. The next thing she knew, Nico was pulling her out of the water onto the bank. He gently lay her upon the grass and she was coughing and spitting up water as he straddled her and massaged her lungs from behind, forcing the water out.

Soon, she was fine and sitting up, offering him a wan smile. She went to say something and he silenced her with a raised hand. Then he pulled her into his arms and held her close to him. Not a single word passed between them however, she could feel his love and his relief at not losing her radiating from him. She had never been more content and in her dream-state, thought, "Don't let me wake up for a while, just let me enjoy this."

A hand was on her bare shoulder, nudging her awake.

"Alana, Alana."

It took a moment for her to realize that she was no longer dreaming. With a start, she sat up, splashing water onto the bathroom floor. Nico squatted beside her, smiling at her. "Girl, what are you doing sleeping in a tub full of water? You could drown like that."

Alana was grateful there were plenty of bubbles that served as a blanket to cover her.

"Nico, what are you doing here?"

Nico rose, reached over and selected a large, fluffy white over-sized bath towel from the shelf opposite the tub. He handed it to her. "I arrived early and rang the bell. You didn't answer. I knew you were here because I saw Jonathan downstairs and he told me you were. Thinking something might be wrong, I used your spare key. Once inside, I called to you, you still didn't reply so I searched the apartment and found you here snoozing." He bent down. Their faces were only inches apart. "Let me wash your back for you while I'm here." When he placed one muscular arm, up to the elbow, into the bath water, close to Alana's backside, she hastily slid forward in the tub.

"Where *is* that sponge," Nico said, his downward-sloping brown eyes alight with amusement. Alana grabbed his hand and held onto it.

"Out," she ordered sternly, looking him in the eye. "Get out now or in a moment, you'll be drenched. You only get one warning."

"That could be fun," Nico told her. He stood and began removing his shirt, revealing a washboard stomach and highly developed pectorals.

Alana stared at him. "You're playing while I'm rapidly turning into a prune."

"No one's stopping you from getting out," Nico said. He turned his back to her. "Okay, go ahead and get out."

"The second I rise, you'll turn back around," Alana accused him. "No. You've got to go, Setera."

"Oh, all right," Nico said at last. He walked out of the room and closed the door behind him.

Alana carefully stood and began toweling dry. The door came back open and Nico stuck his head in, "By the way, I brought take-out."

Alana quickly wrapped the towel around her and stepped out of the tub. Angry, she slipped and slid on the wet tile. Nico came forward and pulled her into his arms, thereby preventing her from falling. She threw her arms around his strong neck and held on.

"You are a relentless prankster," she breathed. He smiled at her and she was unable to maintain an angry frame of mind.

The feeling that came over her then was reminiscent of the spiritual sense of contentment she'd had in the dream Nico had awakened her out of. I love him, she thought. I'm in love with Nico. It had taken a jolt from her subconscious in the form of the dream to make her face up to it. That's why she had felt as if she couldn't let go of Michael. While he was alive, she had been in love with his best friend. It had happened at Lake Tahoe. If she had known Michael was seeing someone else, she would have left him then. Consequently, she wouldn't have punished herself with guilt-feelings the last year. Deep down, she had told herself: My husband's dead. He loved me but I didn't love him as I should have. I don't deserve to be happy.

Hindsight, she thought sadly. If I'd known then what I know now, I would've chosen Nico the night we all met.

"What's that frown for?" Nico asked, breaking the silence between them.

Alana brightened. "I adore you."

Nico responded by softly kissing her lips. When the kiss ended, Alana dreamily gazed up into his eyes. Then she felt a draft. Laughing nervously, she firmly grasped him by the shoulders. "Don't move." The towel hung loose between them. Any sudden movement on his part and she'd be standing before him in all her glory. She reached down for the towel and re-wrapped it around her body. "Okay, you can move now."

Nico gave her an enigmatic grin. "I don't think I want to go just yet. You've just said you adore me. If we stand here a while longer maybe you'll admit that you're in love with me."

Alana lay her head on his chest and smiled contentedly.

Soon, she thought.

Six

Nico waited patiently outside of apartment 306 of the Royal Arms Apartments in Oakland. The group of buildings were government subsidy housing, with a difference: the residents had taken it upon themselves to maintain their homes in a decent, respectable manner instead of relying upon bureaucrats to run things. Therefore the grounds were manicured, the walls and hallways were clean and free of graffiti, and there were no drug dealers hanging on corners plying their goods anywhere in the vicinity of the Royal Arms.

Nico had read in the papers that the neighborhood had had some assistance from Muslims in keeping the criminal element out of their complex—a fact that made certain politicians unhappy, but then they didn't live in the Royal Arms. The residents had welcomed any help they could get since, in their opinion, the authorities weren't doing an adequate job.

The door remained closed; however, a gruff female voice called, "Who's there?"

Nico calmly placed his badge in front of the peephole. "My name is Nicolas Setera. I'm a detective with the San Francisco Police Department."

"Badges don't mean nothin' round here," the woman said through the door. "What else you got?"

Nico wasn't in the least perturbed by the woman's cautious attitude. It was a dangerous world, and nowadays being a cop didn't garner the trust in your average citizens' minds and hearts the way it used to.

He gave her the number of the police operator. "Call that number," he suggested. "And ask them to describe me, then if you still don't want to talk with me, I'll gladly leave."

The woman was away from the door for five minutes as Nico stood on the front stoop, observing the activities of her neighbors. Children were playing on the lawn, a man half-heartedly washed his car two doors down. A teenaged couple was apparently walking home from school together—they both had backpacks slung over their shoulders as they held hands.

Hearing the door being unlocked, Nico returned his attention to apartment 306. A plump, middle-aged woman, a smile on her round, dark brown face ushered him in. "Okay," she said lightly. "You check out."

Nico stepped into a neat, modest living room. A toddler was sitting in the middle of the room in front of a television set, watching "Sesame Street." The little boy looked up, saw Nico, grinned, and said, "Hi!"

"Hello," Nico said, smiling.

"Pay attention to the Count," the woman admonished the boy. "You need to learn your numbers."

She looked expectantly at Nico. "What can I do for you, Detective?"

Nico was still focused on the child. He reluctantly looked away from the tyke and gave the woman his undivided attention.

"Mrs.—"

"It's Miss. Geraldine Robinson. Won't you have a seat, detective?" She continued to eye him suspiciously.

Nico sat on a multifloral armchair, and Geraldine sat across from him on the matching couch.

"Do you recall hearing about the murder of a San Francisco police officer in this neighborhood about a year ago?"

Geraldine Robinson sat with her back stiff, her brown eyes never leaving Nico's face.

"Yes, I do remember when that happened. What a shame. A nice young *family* man like that," she said in mock sympathy.

Nico heard the note of sarcasm in her voice and it made him wonder if Geraldine Robinson knew more than she was letting on. His eyes narrowed. "That officer was my partner, Miss Robinson," he said sharply. He watched her face.

Geraldine flinched noticeably. "What exactly do you want from me, Detective—"

"Setera," Nico supplied.

"I'm a busy woman," Geraldine said defensively. "I was in the middle of preparing dinner when you rang my bell."

It occurred to Nico that she was protecting someone. "Did you, or anyone else living here know Michael Calloway?"

Geraldine sighed. All she wanted was to get this police officer out of her house. "No, Detective. No one living here knew Michael Calloway."

Geraldine rose. "I'll show you to the door, Detective. I'm sorry I couldn't be of more help to you."

Suddenly, she froze, a horrified expression on her face. From across the room came the sound of a key being inserted into the front door lock. Geraldine glanced up at the clock on the living room wall. Not *now,* she thought frantically.

"Momma!" Karen called as she walked through the door, her arms filled with packages. "Michael!"

Karen spotted her mother standing, like a mannequin, in the center of the room, her mouth open in shock.

"Momma, what's wrong?" she asked as she approached her. "Mr. Prentice had to go out of town for a couple of days, so he told me to take the afternoon off . . ."

As she passed the etagere, she saw Nico. Her eyes were panicked as they searched the room for Michael, who had gone into his bedroom to get his stuffed Big Bird. "Michael, Michael, come to Mama, baby!"

Sensing her mother's level of anxiety, Karen was almost beside herself with worry for her son. She ran from the room calling to him.

Nico was on his feet, following her. "Miss Robinson? Nothing has happened to your son, believe me. I'm a cop. I'm not here to cause you or your family any harm."

By the time Nico got midway down the hall, Karen was returning with Michael in her arms. The packages she'd been carying were strewn down the hallway. Nico had to step around them to reach her.

"Miss Robinson, there's no need for you to be upset. I just want to ask you a few questions about Michael Calloway."

Standing in the hallway, Karen regarded him with angry eyes. She covered her son's right ear with her left hand. "Why are you questioning us about him?" she asked belligerently. She turned and continuing walking until she'd reached the living room where she sat on the couch, still cradling Michael in her arms. Geraldine had gone into the kitchen to resume dinner preparations, but her ear was strained to hear anything going on in the living room.

"Who are you?" Karen asked, her tone wary.

Nico introduced himself and produced his badge and picture ID. Karen perused them then met his gaze once more.

"Why are you asking questions about Michael?"

"He was my partner," Nico replied. He sat down next to her on the couch, turning toward her. "The thing is, his widow wants to know why he was found in this neighborhood. He wasn't on duty that night, and he'd told her he was going to be elsewhere. You understand?"

"Yes, I understand," Karen said as she rocked Michael in her arms. She looked down into Michael's upturned face. "Would you go into the kitchen with Grandma, sweetie? Ask her to give you a cookie and some milk."

Michael climbed out of his mother's lap and did as he was told.

"He seems like a great kid," Nico complimented her.

Karen smiled. "He *is* a great kid." Their eyes met and held. "How well did you know Michael?"

"Not as well as I thought I did," Nico said cautiously. "Although, we were best friends for a number of years."

"For months after he died, I expected someone to come here asking all sorts of questions. When no one did, I figured Michael had done a good job of keeping us a secret."

Nico sat back as well. He wasn't going to push her. Karen seemed to want to talk. It was as if she'd been waiting for the moment when she could talk to someone about Michael. He was grateful he was that someone.

She laughed self-consciously. "I didn't know he was married until after I read his obituary. I'd known him for three years. I read in the papers that he'd been married for only two. I often wonder which of us he met first and why he chose her to marry over me. Can you answer that?"

"No," Nico said softly. He didn't know what he'd expected to find in Michael's mistress. Someone cold and detached? This woman was neither of those. She appeared intelligent, and from everything he'd observed since stepping into apartment 306, he judged her to be an honest, hard working young mother trying to build a better life for her son.

"I can't tell you why Michael did what he did," he told her honestly. "All I can tell you is that you came as a surprise to his wife. That's why I'm here. She sent me to act as a sort of intermediary between you two."

"So Alana has just found out about us?" Karen asked, her eyes a little sad.

"You know her name?" Nico said, astonished.

"I was at the memorial service. I heard the minister call her name. That was you next to her throughout the service?"

Nico nodded. "Yeah, that was me.

"You care about her," Karen said matter of factly.

"Very much," Nico admitted freely.

"That's good," Karen said. "At least *she* has someone to help her get over that creep."

"She wants to meet you," Nico told her, watching her face for a surprised reaction.

Karen merely frowned. "I don't know," she said in a low voice. "What if she wants to pull my hair out?"

"Alana's not that kind of person," Nico said reassuringly. "She says she wants to meet you so that she can finally purge him from her system. Maybe you can help each other. From your comments about him, it doesn't seem as though you're completely over him yourself."

"Oh, I've been through all the stages of grief," Karen told

him. "At first, I was in denial. Then I blamed myself. Now I'm putting the blame where it should be, on Michael."

"Then you're a little farther along than Alana is," Nico said. "She lived with the hope that she'd been mistaken about his infidelity for over a year. Now she knows he was cheating on her and is experiencing feelings of inadequacy. She thinks that if she'd been a better wife, Michael would not have strayed . . ."

"That isn't true," Karen said forcefully.

"I know it isn't true," Nico said, looking her in the eyes. "Maybe you can convince her."

"All right," Karen said, having made up her mind. "I'll meet with Alana. When?"

Nico reached into his jacket pocket and retrieved the handwritten note Alana had given him to give to Karen if she proved to be amenable to their meeting.

Karen tore it open and read: *It's not my intention to disrupt your life, Karen. And if you choose not to meet me at Le Petite Café tomorrow afternoon at one-thirty, I'll respect your wishes and not try to contact you again. But if you do decide to come, know this: I don't hold any grudges against you. I won't judge you. I won't seek revenge for wrongs done me, either verbally or physically. I simply want to talk to you. Alana Shelby Calloway.*

Karen knew Le Petite Café, she'd been there for lunch on a number of occasions. The restaurant was always crowded at around one. So there would be plenty of witnesses if Alana Calloway decided to attack her. She'd feel relatively safe in that environment.

"Okay," she told Nico momentarily. "Tell her I'll be there."

"That's it," Alana said as she concluded Thursday morning's staff meeting. "I officially declare that all major preparations are complete, and I'm giving you all the rest of the day off. Thank you for a job well done."

Clovis raised his hand to get her attention.

"Yes, Clovis?"

"Alana, about your suggestion that we join the party after the buffet has been set up. Were you serious?"

Alana smiled at him affectionately and glanced at the rest of her crew scattered about the kitchen.

"Of course I was serious. Margery has contracted with another service to provide waiters and waitresses. You guys worked hard to prepare all the food, you deserve to get out there and enjoy yourselves. So, please, wear your best party outfits and bring a loved one. It's Valentine's Day!"

"I'll definitely be there," Gina put in, her brown eyes sparkling with excitement. "I'd never turn down the opportunity to rub elbows with the rich and famous. Maria told me Whoopi is coming. I love her. I've seen all her movies."

"There, you see?" Alana said, hoping Gina's enthusiasm was catching. "Come and have a good time."

"I'd feel out of place," Clovis maintained. "I'm just a cook."

Alana stepped forward and grasped one of Clovis's big, dark hands in both her hands. Looking into his eyes, she said, "Don't you ever let me hear you deride your profession again." She smiled. "Ours is an honorable calling. Everybody has to eat, and few people have your talent for making food appetizing. So never say, 'I'm just a cook,' say instead, 'I'm the best damn cook on the planet,' then you'd be closer to the truth."

The gentle giant smiled benignly. "You always have a good comeback prepared, don't you, Alana?"

"That's my job," Alana said. "I'm the coach, you're the team. I have to keep my team fired up." She looked around the room. "Any more dissenters?"

There was a general consensus that everyone would be attending the ball. "Very good," Alana said finally. "Then go home and get some rest, you're going to need it tomorrow."

After everyone else had gone for the day, Alana made one last round, making certain everything was put away properly; then she gathered her belongings and left the kitchen. She needed to go home and work on Vesta's books. She'd named the company after the Roman goddess of the hearth, since the hearth in the past was the center of the home. She'd vowed that her company would reflect good, wholesome qualities. Vesta would always produce nutritious, delectable food for a fair price, and she would treat her employees like family.

Her cellular phone rang as she began ascending the stairs in search of Margery and the others. She knew that Georgie and Bree, along with the two Pierres, were gone to Fisherman's Wharf to purchase crabs. Bree wanted to have a crab boil tonight. But Margery, Toni and Daniel, Margery's contrite ex-husband who'd arrived shortly after Bree and Pierre, were somewhere in the house.

"How's everything going?" Nico asked, his voice husky.

"Everything's going so well, I just let everyone go home for the day," Alana answered, smiling. She paused on the stairs and leaned against the wall. "How are things with you? Did you catch up with the infamous other woman?"

Nico laughed on his end. "Karen Robinson isn't your run-of-the-mill home wrecker. She seems . . . nice."

"Nice?"

"She claims she didn't know Michael was married until she read it in the papers."

Alana considered that and said, "You're a good judge of character. Do you believe her?"

There was silence for several seconds as Nico weighed his response. He didn't want to be precipitous. Plus, there was the matter of Michael's child. Should he tell her or wait for Karen to do so? "Is there any way we can get together sometime today?" he asked quietly. "I had the early shift so I'm no longer on duty. Besides, I'd like to see you."

Hearing the concern in his voice, Alana felt butterflies forming in the pit of her stomach. What could be so important he couldn't tell her about it over the phone?

"Sure. I'm leaving Margery's in a few minutes. I have to go home and work on the books. Tomorrow's payday."

"I'll meet you there in a half hour," Nico said.

After they'd hung up, Alana ran the rest of the way upstairs and went to Margery's study, which was adjacent to her bedroom. As she'd guessed, Margery, Toni and Daniel were in the book-

Seven

Karen felt her palms grow damp with moisture as she watched Alana Calloway cross the crowded restaurant, making her way to her table. Alana was smartly attired in a dark copper-toned Donna Karan pantsuit and flats to match. Her thick, dark hair was flawlessly done in an upswept style, one lock falling over the right side of her high-cheekboned face. To Karen, she looked as though she'd just stepped off the cover of *Essence*.

What further unnerved her was how Alana had made a beeline for her once she'd entered the restaurant. Had Nicholas Setera's description of her been that detailed?

"Hello," Alana said, standing next to her. "You must be Karen."

Karen got to her feet and hastily shook Alana's proffered hand. "Yes," she replied, nervously looking around them. "How did you know?"

Alana laughed shortly as she sat down opposite Karen's chair. "In case I was held up, I asked John to seat you at my favorite table."

"Oh," Karen said as she settled back into her chair.

Alana decided that Nico had been correct in his estimation of Karen Robinson's appearance. Perhaps three inches shorter than Alana's five-seven, Karen was trim, almost to the point of being reed thin. Her dark brown eyes were almond-shaped and at the moment held an expression of apprehension in them. Her face was heart-shaped and quite pretty in spite of her lack of makeup.

She wore her black hair in a short fashion that was shorn close on the sides.

Face to face with the other woman, Alana thought. The experience wasn't what she imagined it would be. Karen Robinson didn't look like a cold-hearted man stealer to her. Under different circumstances, Karen was probably someone she'd choose for a friend.

"Would you like to order something?" Alana asked.

"No, no," Karen hurriedly replied. "I couldn't eat a thing." Her stomach growled. She'd missed breakfast.

"Well I could," Alana said, motioning to a passing waiter. "Oh, David!"

Seeing Alana, David stopped in his tracks, a tray of drinks suspended in the air as easily as if it was attached to his wrist.

"Gotcha, Alana. I'll be right there."

He continued to another table in his station, deposited the drinks in front of the patrons with a flourish, and turned to head back to Alana's table.

After a quick buss to Alana's cheek, he grinned at her, his green eyes shining in his California-suntanned face. He absently smoothed his blond ponytail back.

"Girl, you look good enough to be on the menu," he said, his smile bringing out the dimple in his left cheek. "Vesta keeping you busy?"

"As ever," Alana told him. "David, Karen."

"Hello, Karen. You look wonderful, too. First time here?"

"Yes," Karen said shyly, unwilling to be more forthcoming.

"Well then, may I suggest the crabmeat salad? It's fresh, it's fine, it's divine."

"I'll take it," Alana replied at once. She'd had a craving for crabmeat since last night when she'd missed out on Bree's crab boil. She and Nico had gone to her apartment where they'd spent most of the night talking.

"Okay," Karen acquiesced.

"And what would you like to drink?" David asked, order pad poised to take down their requests.

"A cola?" Karen timidly said.

"Are you asking me or telling me?" David joked.

"Lay off, you rascal," Alana warned him good-naturedly. "She'll take a cola, and I'll have iced tea. Go do your job, or I'll hire you away from John, then you'll really be sorry."

"Slave driver!" David retorted, grinning at her.

David went to get their salads, and Alana smiled at Karen. "Don't mind him. He was just trying to include you in our usual give and take. You see, this was my first gig after graduating from the California Culinary Academy. I was here for over a year, working under the head chef. I got to know several of the staff quite well. David remains my favorite."

Karen knew she must appear simpleminded, sitting there like an idiot with little to say, but she felt so out of place, it was difficult to think.

Sensing her discomfort, Alana reached across the small, round table and placed her hand atop Karen's.

"I meant what I wrote to you in that note, Karen. I'm not here to heap blame on you. Truly."

Their eyes met and they smiled at one another.

Alana removed her hand and sat up straight in her chair. "I thought we could sort of compare notes, try to piece together the secret life of Michael Calloway. Starting with when each of us met him." She paused, clearing her throat. "I met Michael in ninety-four. June, I think it was. Two friends of mine and I were out dancing at a club here in San Francisco. He walked over to our table and introduced himself. The next night we had our first date."

Karen's demeanor experienced a metamorphosis as she leaned forward. Her eyes were no longer timid. They were somewhat angry.

"I met the b . . . *him* in ninety-three," she said, her tone barely under control. "In December. I remember because Christmas was just around the corner. He gave me a gold bracelet for Christmas."

A little surprised by this revelation, but not completely nonplussed, Alana pursed her lips and said, "Mmm . . . huh." She had come there to get answers to her questions and no matter what Karen Robinson said, she was going to listen.

"We met in a club in Oakland," Karen said. "He liked to dance."

"I would say that's an understatement," Alana remarked dryly.

They looked at one another and laughed uproariously at the absurdity of it all. They'd both met him while out dancing.

Bringing their salads and drinks, David smiled pleasantly.

"Now that's more like it," he said approvingly. "Enjoy your lunches, ladies." He left them to their meals.

"Oh, God," Alana said, coming down from her laughing jag and wiping the corners of her eyes with the white cloth napkin provided for Le Petite Café's customers. "I wonder how many other women he picked up in clubs."

"You think he had time for more than two?" Karen asked, dabbing at her tears with her napkin as well.

"No," Alana said, looking at Karen. "I mean he was already seeing you, and then he meets me, courts me, and convinces me to marry him all in the course of three months."

"You married him after three months?"

"I'd never been in love before. I led a rather sheltered life. I went to an all-girl high school in New York. Then my parents were killed, and I moved here to live with my aunt. I attended California State, then found my true calling: the culinary arts. My mind was totally on getting ahead. Then I met Michael, and he blew me away."

"Me, too," Karen agreed. "I was struggling to get through my first year of college when we met. I came from the projects. In Michael, I saw my way out."

"He seemed so sincere," Alana said, sighing. "I never doubted he loved me. Not until the end."

"Me, either," Karen said. "And the thing is, I avoided men whom I thought to be bad influences: drug dealers, men with no direction. Then to be deceived by him. I was mad as hell when after I got pregnant, he made it plain to me that he had no intention of marrying me. But, as it turned out, my son has been a blessing. He's the only thing I don't regret."

Nodding sympathetically, Alana took a sip of her iced tea.

"What kind of father was he? Michael always raved about what a great father he'd be. He never knew his own father, you know."

"I have to give credit where credit is due," Karen said magnanimously. "He paid the hospital bill and he provided for Michael's needs. I didn't have to hassle him about that." She laughed. "The only time he appeared really happy was when he was holding Michael. The last few months he was alive, he was like a man possessed. Now that I know about you, I can see why."

"Yes, I noticed that as well," Alana told her, meeting her gaze. "It couldn't have been easy for him. Juggling work, two women. Providing for his son. I almost feel sorry for him."

"Almost," Karen put in. "But not quite."

She sat up straight in her chair and regarded Alana with clear, determined eyes. "I know he's dead, and we'll never know why he did what he did, but why do you think he married you instead of me?"

Alana didn't reply right away. Since learning of Karen's existence, she had assumed Michael had met her after their marriage. However, if what Karen said was true, he'd known the other woman at least five months before they'd met. Did Michael love her more? Was that the reason he'd married her?

Unfortunately, only Michael could answer that question. She recalled the last dream she'd had of him. "Remember me fondly," he'd implored.

"Who knows why he chose to marry me?" Alana said at last. "I think maybe he was in love with us both and couldn't decide whom to give up. But it seems to me that if he'd been forced to make a decision, he would've chosen you. You gave birth to his child. Michael never got over being abandoned by his father. I can't imagine his doing the same thing to his son."

"But he lied to me about everything," Karen said, unwilling to attribute such a noble trait to Michael. "It's true enough, he loved his child. However, I think he would have gone on deceiving everyone if he'd lived." She tossed the napkin she'd been nervously twirling between her fingers on to the table. "I should have known he was married by the way he behaved. I don't know why I was so blind."

"You loved him," Alana said simply. "We didn't *want* to believe the worst. It would have destroyed our perfect illusions."

Nodding, Karen smiled. "You're right. I wanted to believe he'd break down and marry me someday. I'd given him a beautiful child. If I could simply be patient, maybe he would eventually do the right thing."

Alana's gaze was steady as she smiled at Karen. "Whatever you do, Karen, don't give up on finding someone who will truly love you. Sometimes finding him is as easy as turning around and looking at the person standing next to you."

"You're talking about Detective Setera, aren't you?"

Alana laughed. "Nico said you were smart."

"It doesn't take a genius to see that he cares for you a great deal. The way he stood by your side the day Michael was laid to rest. His tracking me down so that you would have a sense of closure. You're a lucky woman, Alana."

"I am," Alana agreed.

She bent down and picked up her purse. She rummaged through it for a moment, coming out of it with a long manila envelope. She handed it to Karen. "I feel like passing a little of my luck along."

Karen appeared reluctant to accept the envelope. She looked at it as though Alana was offering her a bomb.

Laughing, Alana placed the envelope on the tabletop. "I promise you, it won't explode."

Karen gingerly touched the envelope, then picked it up. Pulling up the flap, which wasn't glued on, she opened it and removed the contents. Her eyes grew larger with shock and disbelief. "Oh my God!" she exclaimed. "Oh my God!"

"Consider it Michael's inheritance from his father," Alana said, a contented smile on her lips. "That is the full amount of Michael's death benefit . . ."

"But you don't even know for a certainty that Michael is really his son . . ." Karen protested.

"I am certain," Alana assured her. She looked directly into Karen's eyes. "I know what I'm doing, Karen."

She didn't want to go into how Margery and Toni had acquired a copy of Karen's son's birth certificate. For one thing, the story was too long to get into at the moment and for another, she was sure the detective, Bob Dean, had employed illegal practices to obtain the document.

"This is too much," Karen said, her eyes misty. "You don't even know me. What if I'm a disreputable person and I use this for selfish purposes?"

Alana set about eating her crabmeat salad. Between mouthfuls, she said, "You're the mother of his child. You deserve that money. Do whatever you wish with it. It was only sitting in the bank earning interest."

Karen stared at the cashier's check. She had never seen so many zeros in her life. She could finish college, put a down payment on a house. Send Michael to a good college when the time came. For once in her life, she wouldn't have to live from paycheck to paycheck. She felt as if she'd just won the lottery.

"This isn't some kind of mean-spirited joke?" she said. "You're actually giving me nearly a hundred thousand dollars?" She leaned forward, looking into Alana's eyes. "I don't know what to make of you. Are you crazy? Why? Why would you do this?"

Sighing, Alana placed her fork on the tabletop and drank some of the iced tea. With both elbows on the tabletop, she rested her chin in her palms. She smiled slowly.

"That check represents the last of Michael Calloway," she said. "He's gone from my life forever."

"And my son gets a better life," Karen said, catching on.

She laughed, her brown eyes clearing up considerably. The time for weeping was past. A celebration was in order.

"David!" she called.

David, in the middle of serving swordfish to an elderly couple, finished with his unique flair and then hurried to Alana and Karen's table.

"Did I hear one of you goddesses beckon me?"

"I did," Karen said happily. "Champagne, David. The best you have and make it ice cold."

"You're a woman after my own heart," David said, beaming.

Amused, Alana watched as David made haste to do Karen's bidding. Then her eyes rested on Karen's face.

"You're not anything like I imagined you would be," she told Karen.

"You aren't, either," Karen said. The apprehensiveness was now replaced with self-confidence. "But I need to say this, even though I know we have come to an understanding: I'm sorry. I'm sorry for the pain I inadvertently caused you. For the sleepless nights. Worrying where your husband could be. I wouldn't wish that kind of hell on anyone."

"Thank you," Alana replied sincerely.

David returned with the champagne. After placing a crystal wineglass in front of each of them, he pulled out the cork. The sound reverberated around the room, and diners applauded. There was something about champagne that put everyone in a festive mood.

He poured the golden liquid into the glasses, pausing to allow the bubbles to settle, then he placed the bottle in ice, moving the ice bucket close to Karen. "Don't let it tickle your noses," he said, as he departed.

Karen raised her glass. "To the future," she said.

"Without Michael," Alana added.

"May we all live happily ever after."

"And to your son," Alana said, smiling.

"May he grow up to be nothing like his father," Karen declared prayerfully.

"Amen," Alana intoned.

They touched glasses and drank deeply.

"Can we eat now?" Alana said afterward. "I missed breakfast this morning."

Karen laughed as she picked up her fork and dug in. "My mother's going to have a heart attack when I tell her what happened today."

Eight

With a macabre sense of humor, Alana realized that if the house on Nob Hill suddenly blew up she would lose everyone she loved in one fell swoop.

She was standing in the alcove between the kitchen and the ballroom, watching the festivities, which were in full swing. Margery, with Daniel at her side, was laughing at something the mayor had said. Alana smiled. She was sure Margery was warming to Daniel in spite of her protests to the contrary.

Couples danced to the melodious tones of a twelve-piece orchestra. Bree and Pierre, standout performers, were the center of attention. Georgie, with Brian Chandler, her attorney boyfriend, took the spotlight off the thespian couple with their version of a hip hop tango. The crowd cheered.

Feeling a hand at the small of her back, Alana leaned into Nico's warm embrace. His arms went around her trim waist, and he bent his head to plant a kiss on the curve of her fragrant neck.

"What are you doing back here?" he said. "You should be out there with me, putting Bree and Georgie to shame."

Turning to face him, Alana smiled. He looked so handsome in his tuxedo. "Let them have their fun," she said, more than content to remain where she was: in his arms.

Admiring the silver lame gown she was wearing, which fell three-inches above her knees, had spaghetti straps, soft folds at the bustline, and plunged downward in the back all the way to her waist, Nico sighed. "Everyone should see you, just once, in this."

Turning to wrap her arms around his neck, Alana clasped her fingers together as she kissed his chin. "I wore it for you."

"And I'm a grateful man," Nico told her seriously. He kissed her lips. "But you're not getting away with being a wallflower tonight."

Taking her by the hand, he led her into the ballroom.

"Alana," Georgie, wearing a red beaded gown in honor of Saint Valentine, called from the dance floor. "Get over here, girl, and show us how to salsa. Miami style."

"You've been challenged," Nico said, his warm brown eyes looking at her with such sensual vibrancy that Alana felt her body tingle with excitement.

They assumed the stance, her right foot sliding forward on the hardwood floor. Nico removed his coat and flung it into the audience. He saw Toni catch it in midair and smile gleefully at him.

The band went into an upbeat Latin number, and Nico executed a movement which reminded Alana of a matador. Then his hand was reaching for her, and they moved with sensual fluidity as they made the dance their own.

"Oh, my," Margery commented to Daniel from the sidelines. "I haven't witnessed anything that blatantly sexual since . . ."

"You and I were together the last time?" Daniel said hopefully, his arm going around her waist as he pulled her close to him.

Margery lay her head on his chest. "I do miss you, Daniel. But I . . ."

"But you're afraid I haven't changed," Daniel finished for her. "It's okay. Take your time. I'll be here."

Margery closed her eyes and relaxed in his arms. She loved Daniel. She had never stopped loving him. She was no longer that trusting young woman whom he'd taken for granted years before. But some things were still worth the risk.

"Okay, Daniel," she murmured.

His heart beating double-time with pure joy, Daniel gently kissed Margery on the lips. Tears sat in his golden-brown eyes when he looked down into her beloved face. "I'll spend the rest of my life making you happy."

"We'll spend the rest of our lives making each other happy," Margery corrected him. She smiled into his eyes.

To their left, Toni quietly observed the reunion of her best friend with the love of her life. It's about time, she thought. She looked away, only to lock eyes with an interesting-looking gentleman across the room. Wasn't that Spencer Taylor, the famed jazz pianist? He was even more devastatingly handsome in the flesh.

"Georgette," Brian Chandler said into Georgie's ear. "This is all very entertaining, but can't we circulate more? I haven't even met the mayor yet."

Looking into Brian's smooth dark brown, impatient face, Georgie stifled a groan. All Brian thought about was networking. She didn't think the brother had ever let loose in his entire Ivy League life. She was beginning to think he was only with her because she had access to certain people. People whose friendship she would never dream of using for career advancement.

She cast an envious eye at Alana and Nico. To have a man look at her like that . . . and have no ulterior motive.

"Georgette?" Brian said again, this time unwilling to be ignored.

Turning on her heels, Georgie walked away from him.

"Georgette, I'm talking to you," Brian said as he followed.

"Why is it you can't call me Georgie?" she said petulantly. "Would it kill you to be less formal with me, Brian? We're not in the office now, loosen up."

She kept walking. "Brian?" Turning, she realized that Brian was engrossed in conversation with the San Francisco District Attorney.

"Are you glad you came?" Bree asked Pierre as she stood locked in his two strong arms.

"Oh, yes," Pierre breathed. "It's everything you said it would be. I've met so many influential people. Thanks, babe."

"You're welcome," Bree responded. Somehow the feel of his arms was not the same for her. She had been aware from the start that Pierre wanted to act more than anything. And she also knew, from experience, that two actors trying to make a go of a relationship didn't often have positive results. But somehow she'd grown fond of Pierre, and that fondness had matured into love. She suddenly had a premonition of them going their separate ways. She shuddered.

Pierre's hold tightened. "What's wrong, sweetheart?"

"Nothing," Bree said. "Just hold me."

Studying Alana and Nico as they danced in the manner only those who had been partners for years did, Bree wished she would someday know that kind of happiness.

The Latin tune was replaced by a Gershwin song, and Genero tapped Nico on the shoulder, wanting to dance with Alana.

Alana waltzed around the room with Genero, complimenting him on his appearance and the fine job he'd done supervising the party.

Genero shrugged off her compliment. "It was nothing any culinary genius couldn't have pulled off. I wanted to talk to you about your aunts . . ."

"Oh, no," Alana cried. "Not again."

Genero gestured toward a lovely, petite African-American woman in her early twenties, dancing with the commissioner.

"They set me up with her," he said. "She's a chef at The Beverly Hills Hotel."

From his expression, Alana couldn't tell whether he was pleased or not.

"Well, was it a hit or a miss?" she asked, her brows knit together in worry.

Genero grinned impishly. "She's wonderful."

"Then why aren't you dancing with her?" Alana asked, relieved. "Go ask her to be your Valentine. Must my aunts do your courting for you?"

Laughing, Genero bent his dark head to quickly kiss Alana on the cheek. "Are you sure you and Margery aren't blood relatives?"

Left without a partner, Alana made her way off the dance floor. As she wove her way through the crowd, she spotted Gina to her left dancing with her fiancé, Gary Nunn. Gina waved to her, a wide grin on her pretty face. Earlier in the evening, Alana had noticed her showing her favorite actress how to do the Electric Slide.

"Excuse me," Alana said as she bumped into a tall man.

Clovis looked down at her. "Alana, hello. You remember my wife, Alice?"

"Of course," Alana replied, smiling at the handsome, stout woman who was a foot shorter than her husband. "How are you, Alice?"

"Winded," Alice said, laughter in her deep brown eyes. She was wearing a simple white gown that fell to her ankles. It gave her a sophisticated, elegant appearance. Clovis wore a basic black tux. Alana noticed he'd trimmed his mustache.

"Well, you both look fantastic," Alana complimented them.

Alice blushed. "Thank you, Alana."

"Enjoy yourselves," Alana said as she left them.

She made it as far as the very alcove she'd been standing in before Nico had pulled her onto the dance floor where she was waylaid by Maria and her husband, Carlos.

"I think you all outdid yourselves on the food, Alana," Maria told her. "Everything was *delicioso*."

Carlos kissed Alana on the cheek. They hadn't seen one another in some time. He was kept busy by his job as district manager for a fast-food chain.

He was around five-ten, dark-skinned and the epitome of the doting spouse. He was always affectionate with Maria. After greeting Alana, his arm was back around Maria's waist, drawing her close to him. They were both wearing black: Maria in a short, sleeveless sheath that clung to her ample curves and Carlos in a tailored tuxedo.

"Thank you," Alana said cheerfully. Reaching up, she removed a leaf from Maria's hair. "Where'd that come from?"

"Oh, my," Maria said. Tinges of red appeared on her cheeks. "We just stepped outside for some air."

She and her husband lovingly gazed into each other's eyes.

"The air must be especially good tonight," Alana joked. "See you guys later. Have a great time."

She turned around to continue walking toward the buffet tables and nearly stepped on Pierre. Bending to pick the poodle up, she tried to calm his trembling. He had been dodging dancers, more than likely attempting to locate his mistress.

Cuddling him, Alana rubbed his small head. "Poor baby. Who let you out of the bedroom?"

Undoubtedly, prying guests had been upstairs. After looking around the bedroom, they'd thoughtlessly left the door ajar.

"You could have been trampled on," Alana complained. Searching the room for Nico, she saw him dancing with Margery. She would take Pierre back upstairs, then go and convince him to take her home. She liked to party as well as the next person, but tonight on their very first Valentine's Day as a couple, she wanted him all to herself. They still had unfinished business to settle.

"All's well that ends well," Margery said happily as she and Nico did a passable two-step. "You and Alana will get married and give me plenty of grandchildren. Then this old childless soul will never be lonely again."

"As for being old," Nico began. "You will always have a timeless beauty and as for being lonely, I believe Daniel is more than willing to take care of that problem."

Margery smiled up into Nico's handsome face. "You're such a sweet boy. I'm so pleased my darling Alana has finally awakened from her slumber and found *you*."

Toni politely smiled as Spencer Taylor told her of his recent concert dates in Boston. She felt her right foot going to sleep as he droned on about the many celebrities who had come backstage to congratulate him on his splendid performance. It was a pity that a man of such pulchritude should be a brain-numbing bore.

"You are familiar with Charles Edward Waters, the frozen-food king? He is possibly the wealthiest black man in America. He told me he thought my playing equaled the great Duke Ellington's."

Don't believe everything he tells you, Toni wanted to warn him, but didn't. She vigorously shook her leg, trying to get the blood circulating in it.

"You're right," Spencer Taylor said. "Here I am bending your ear when we should be dancing. Shall we?"

It was as good a way to awaken her sleeping member as any, so Toni accepted.

Barry White sang of love from afar on the Stingray's compact disc player as Alana and Nico cruised through San Francisco's streets. The full moon looked as though it was suspended directly above the Golden Gate Bridge.

The ball had been a resounding success. Alana expected to read about it in the society pages of tomorrow's paper. Now Margery could rest on her laurels until she started planning her wedding. Alana had a feeling she and Daniel were more in love than they were when they were first wed nearly twenty-five years ago. She was happy for them.

Nico reached over and gently massaged the back of her neck. "How do you feel? Tired?"

"A little," Alana replied softly, enjoying the feel of his strong fingers on her skin.

"Too tired to go to my place? I have a surprise waiting for you there. We haven't had the chance to celebrate our first Valentine's Day together yet."

"What kind of a surprise?" Alana asked, turning in her seat to look at him.

"It won't be a surprise if I tell you what it is," Nico countered, his deep voice husky.

He stopped the car at a red light, and Alana moved closer to him and planted a warm kiss on his cheek. Nico pulled her into his arms. "Do not do that unless you are willing to pay the price," he warned her provocatively.

"Would you shut up and kiss me?"

"And she's rude too," Nico joked as his mouth descended upon hers.

They were interrupted by the sound of blaring car horns. The light had changed to green.

Alana got back in her seat, fastening her seat belt. Nico hit the accelerator and shifted into second, then third.

"You're going to make me get a ticket yet," he grumbled, looking sideways at her with a smile on his full mouth.

Nico's house was located in the North Beach section of San Francisco in a neighborhood that had once been the home to the city's wealthiest citizens. Today the area was populated by middle-class families who wanted a nice place to rear their children.

It was a bi-level bungalow with big airy rooms that allowed the breezes from the Pacific to circulate throughout. When he'd purchased the house, three years ago, Alana had helped him decorate it. They had compromised between his love for leather and her desire to bring nature inside by going with contemporary furnishings in Italian leather for the living room with natural wood accents.

As they stepped into the foyer and Nico engaged the alarm, Alana laughed softly. "I see Mrs. Bailey was recently here."

"I'm not as bad as I used to be," Nico said, defending himself. "Mrs. Bailey comes in only once a week now and she doesn't have to berate me for leaving my shoes in the middle of the room anymore."

Nico switched on the lights, slightly dimming them. They sat together on the brown leather couch in the living room.

He grasped one of her hands in his, squeezing it gently. His dark, thickly fringed eyes looked down at their entwined hands.

"I need to know something before we go any farther, Alana." He peered into her eyes. "That day when we were swimming in the lake and you got a cramp and went under and I went in after you. Later, when we were certain you were out of danger, you looked at me in such a way . . . I can't begin to describe it. Did I *imagine* that look?"

Alana's heart thumped fiercely in her chest. She never dreamed he had noticed. She had fought to subdue her emotions. For months before that fateful summer day, she had been trying to deny that she was falling in love with Nico. Then after a harrowing experience in the water, she could no longer hide from it. She loved him. She had felt so guilty.

"If I had known Michael was seeing Karen, I would have left him then," she said now. She touched his face with her free hand. "I loved you so much, Nico. But I couldn't hurt Michael. In all his life, he never had anyone who stuck by him. I couldn't abandon him."

Nico knelt before her, holding both her hands in his. His bedroom eyes bespoke his passion. "I know you must have been in torment," he said. "We were both in our own unique hell, wanting each other but remaining loyal to Michael who, unbeknownst to us, was doing as he pleased."

Rising, he pulled her up with him, and they held each other for a long while. *"Te amo,* Lana. I love you with all my heart and soul, my being." Looking into her big brown eyes, Nico took her lovely face between his hands. "I've never loved anyone else, Lana. I'm telling you this so you'll know the intensity of my feelings for you."

"I tried to bury my love for you, Nico. But, no matter how hard I tried, I couldn't do it. Sometimes it was so all-consuming, I couldn't bear to be around you."

"Those were the times you pushed me away," Nico deduced, his eyes taking in the delightful curve of her lips.

"Yes," Alana said passionately, her breasts swelling with desire. He had to kiss her soon or she'd perish with the want of the feel of his mouth on hers.

"Un momento, mi amor," he said, as he released her. He slowly reached into his coat pocket and removed a small, red velvet-covered box. He handed the box to Alana, his hands closing around hers.

"There are some traditions my parents taught me that I cannot ignore," he said, his accent more evident due to the depth of his emotions. "Alana, you know I adore you. Will you do me the honor of becoming my wife and partner in life? Will you allow me to cherish you and protect you for always?"

Nico released his hold on her, allowing his arms to fall to his sides. Alana could not pull her gaze from his wonderful face.

She knew she had heard a proposal, but the whole scene felt surreal to her.

"Alana?"

"I do," she murmured.

Nico grinned. "It's a little early for that reply."

"I will," Alana corrected herself. She screamed and jumped into his arms. "Yes, yes, yes, yes!"

Laughing, Nico set her back down "You haven't even looked at the ring. You might not like it."

Alana opened the tiny box and smiled broadly. The ring was a two-carat diamond solitaire in a white gold setting.

"It's beautiful," she told him. "Thank you."

Nico solemnly placed the ring on her finger, and then they kissed. Coming up for air, Alana said, "When you promised to always protect me, what exactly did you mean?"

"It means I'd gladly give my life for you," Nico said, jutting out his strong square chin. "And I mean that, *querida.*"

"Will you also protect my honor?"

"To my last breath."

Alana laughed softly. "Well, don't be so vigilant tonight, Nicholas Setera, because for the next few hours I just want to be your woman. Make love to me, Nico."

"As you wish," he replied, his voice husky and his eyes never leaving her dear face.

Picking her up in his muscular arms, he carried her upstairs to his bedroom, where they stood at the head of the queen-sized, hunter-green comforter covered bed.

Nico reached up and methodically removed the pins holding Alana's naturally wavy hair in its smooth chignon, dropping them onto the nearby nightstand. Her hair fell in soft waves about her face. Alana, in turn, removed his tie, placing it next to the pins, and then she began to slowly unbutton his pleated, crisp white shirt.

Her sable-colored eyes raked over him. She wanted to record every detail of this moment in her mind's eye so that she'd never forget it. Not the look of passionate longing in his dark, uniquely downward-sloping thickly-fringed brown eyes. Nor the sound of his breathing or the feel of his warm exhalation on her hot skin.

Finished undoing the shirt, she bent her head and kissed his hairy, decidedly muscular chest.

Nico grasped her by the shoulders, halting her slow progress downward. "One good turn deserves another," he said. He walked around behind her and unzipped the silvery gown, and the weight of the material caused it to slip from her silken teddy-clad figure. Alana stepped out of the dress and bent to pick it up. She tossed it onto a nearby chair.

She stood before him in a black teddy, silk stockings and her silver Italian pumps.

Boldly stepping forward, she reached for the clasp on Nico's slacks. He stayed her hand there. "As you can see, I want you very much, *querida*. But unless we want to start a family tonight, you'll have to excuse me for a minute."

Nico kissed her forehead and disappeared into the adjacent bathroom.

When he returned, Alana was lying on the bed after having removed her shoes and stockings. She looked up and was unable to suppress a gasp. Nico was completely nude except for a pair of black bikini briefs. She'd seen him in bathing trunks before, however never in an excited state.

"You should see your expression," Nico said, smiling.

He sat beside her and drew her into his arms. It was the first time their bare skin had ever touched like this, and he could not help trying to experience all the sensations of touch, feel and taste simultaneously. He breathed in her sweet essence. His hands ran over her soft, pliant body and he ran his tongue along the perimeter of her full mouth.

"Nico," Alana said breathlessly. Her eyes were closed. Her head went back as she succumbed to a euphoric feeling of pure pleasure. Nico followed the delicate curve of her throat with his tongue.

"You're exquisite," he whispered in her ear. "So lovely, you take my breath away."

"I feel like this is my first time," Alana told him, her eyes coming open. "I've dreamt of this moment so many times, and now that it's here, I'm so nervous . . ."

"Shhh . . ." Nico said.

He gently forced her back onto the bed, holding her in his strong arms all the while. They lay facing one another.

"Sweetheart, tonight is ours. From this moment, here and now, the past is dead and the future is new territory. We will explore it together."

Alana pulled him close and kissed his square chin, working her way upward to his full mouth. She couldn't believe her good fortune. Nico loved her—and she wasn't dreaming.

Epilogue

Alana rolled over in bed and slammed her hand down hard on the OFF button of the alarm. Forcing her eyelids apart, she read the lighted dial: 3:23 A.M. That hadn't been the alarm she'd heard after all.

She none too gently nudged Nico awake. "Nicholas Setera, wake up. It's your turn to go get Nicky."

Sitting straight up in bed, Nico yawned. "Didn't we just go to sleep?"

Alana laughed as she sat on the side of the bed. "It only feels like it. I'm going to the bathroom. Nicky's waiting for you."

Wiping the sleep from his eyes, Nico yawned again and finally put his feet on the floor.

"He's two months old," he grumbled. "When is he going to start sleeping through the night?"

"You're asking me?" Alana replied, smiling at the sight of her husband stumbling toward the door. "This is my first child too, you know."

"Well, what did the book say?" Nico asked, referring to the child-care manual Alana had read throughout her pregnancy.

"It said by the time he turns three months old, we will probably resemble the walking dead, and judging from your appearance, it was right," Alana said, laughing heartily.

Turning to leave, Nico said, "Well don't look into the mirror when you go into the bathroom because you might run out screaming."

Alana nearly did scream in fright when she saw her reflection in the bathroom mirror. There were dark circles beneath her eyes, and her crowning glory looked like she'd stuck a finger in an electric socket. She smiled at that haggard young woman because, even though she looked less than lovely, she'd never been happier.

She splashed cold water on her face and dried it with a clean towel. Then she cleansed her breasts in preparation for her son's three A.M. feeding, which was nearly half an hour overdue. No wonder he was screaming at the top of his lungs.

She went back into the bedroom and awaited Nico's arrival. She knew he was delayed because he was changing Nicky's diaper. From day one, Nico had been an attentive father. He never shirked his responsibilities, no matter how dirty the job.

Nico entered the room five minutes later, cuddling his son in his muscular arms. Nicky was no longer crying. He found solace in his father's nearness. For Nico's part, he was instantly transformed for the better when he held his son. He could not help marveling at the miracle that was Nicolas Shelby Setera.

He carefully placed Nicky in Alana's arms and sat on the bed next to them. He was wearing only pajama bottoms. Alana wore the top. He loved watching his wife feed their son. She held Nicky firmly against her and Nicky automatically turned his head toward her breast and suckled contentedly. Eight pounds, ten ounces at birth, Nicky had gained over two pounds in his two months on Earth. He was thriving beautifully on his mother's milk.

Alana had been observing Nicky, making certain he was positioned correctly. She could hear him swallowing, feel the slight pulling sensation. He was in his normal rhythm.

She looked up to find Nico smiling at her.

"What?" she asked, curious as to what he found amusing.

"You just took to that as if you'd been doing it all your life," Nico said, his eyes meeting hers. "He looks more like you every day," Nico said as he gently touched his son's head which was covered with an abundance of curly black hair.

"I think he looks like you," Alana disagreed. She grinned. "Of course, everyone thinks he looks like someone else. Yesterday Margery told me she thinks he has my mother's eyes."

"That's understandable," Nico said. "Connie *was* his grand-mother. But when Toni saw him, she swore he has her nose. Now *that's* scary."

They laughed.

Nicky opened his eyes. They were the same warm brown color as his father's.

"We broke his concentration," Nico joked. Then added, "Do you know what tomorrow is?" He looked up at her expectantly.

"Thursday," Alana replied deadpan.

"Does June 15th ring a bell?" Nico said, his finger trailing along her strong jawline.

"Mother's Day is in May," Alana began, seemingly unaware of where her husband's line of questioning was leading. "My birthday's in April. Yours is in July . . ."

"Alana Setera . . ." Nico said, his deep voice rising slightly.

Alana grasped one of his big hands in hers and squeezed it reassuringly. "Do you think I'd ever forget our anniversary?"

Raising her hand to his mouth, Nico kissed her fingers one at a time. His dark eyes mirrored his emotions. He'd waited a long time for this moment. Looking into Alana's eyes and seeing her love for him reflected in them, he knew it had been worth the wait. "Not for a second," he replied confidently.

Rochelle Alers is a native New Yorker who now resides in a picturesque fishing village on Long Island where she draws inspiration to write her novels and short stories. Her interests include music, art, gourmet food, meditation and traveling.

Donna Hill is a multipublished author of African-American romance novels which has garnered her rave reviews and legions of devoted fans. A versatile writer, Ms. Hill's business, health and relationship articles have appeared in a variety of newspapers and magazines. She has done reading and book-signings at sites across the country. She lives in Brooklyn, NY with her family.

Janice Sims lives in Mascotte, Florida with her family. A journalism major, she has always written short stories, inspired by Toni Morrison and Zora Neale Hurston.

SIZZLING ROMANCE BY *ROCHELLE ALERS*

SUMMER MAGIC   1-58314-012-3 $4.99US/$6.50CAN
When Caryn Edwards rented a summer house in North Carolina, she never knew she'd have to share it with handsome developer Logan Prescott. Soon, their mutual distrust dissolves and passion takes over—but can the magic last when the autumn comes?

HAPPILY EVER AFTER   0-7860-0064-3 $4.99US/$6.50CAN
Lauren Taylor's heartbreaking divorce has left her with little more than memories of sensuous tropical nights and long-gone happiness. Now her ex is back in Boston with an offer she can't refuse and a chance to start over with a man she'd lost once before.

HEAVEN SENT   0-7860-0530-0 $4.99US/$6.50CAN
When Serena Morris-Vega visits Costa Rica, she finds herself saving an ailing corporate CEO's life. In the process, she discovers secrets about his true identity . . . and an all-consuming passion for this mysterious stranger.

HIDDEN AGENDA   0-7860-0041-4 $4.99US/$6.50CAN
After Eve Blackwell hires the dangerous and irresistible Matt Sterling to find her abducted son, she must enter into a charade of marriage with him on a journey from Virginia to Mexico . . . but their attraction is too strong to remain a charade for long.

HIDEAWAY   0-7860-0135-6 $4.99US/$6.50CAN
Parris Simmons has spent the last ten years hiding from her past. But when her ex-lover finds her and offers her the protection of his name, she agrees to marry him and their desire reignites—until a dangerous secret threatens to destroy everything they cherish most.

HOME SWEET HOME   0-7860-0276-X $4.99US/$6.50CAN
When Quintin Lord meets his new neighbor, ballerina-turned-caterer Victoria Jones, he is surprised and enchanted by her grace. But love has cost her and she will not put her heart on the line again—until Quintin proves to her that a lasting love is worth any risk.

VOWS   0-7860-0463-0 $4.99US/$6.50CAN
After practical accountant Vanessa Blanchard is seduced by Joshua Kirkland while on vacation, she is left with unanswered questions and sleepless nights of remembered ecstasy. For Joshua, his game of seduction has become a daring race to protect the woman he loves . . .

USE COUPON ON NEXT PAGE TO ORDER THESE BOOKS

Own These Books
By *ROCHELLE ALERS*

__SUMMER MAGIC   **$4.99**US/**$6.50**CAN
    1-58314-012-3

__HAPPILY EVER AFTER   **$4.99**US/**$6.50**CAN
    0-7860-0064-3

__HEAVEN SENT   **$4.99**US/**$6.50**CAN
    0-7860-0041-4

__HIDDEN AGENDA   **$4.99**US/**$6.50**CAN
    0-7860-0384-7

__HIDEAWAY   **$4.99**US/**$6.50**CAN
    0-7860-0135-6

__HOME SWEET HOME   **$4.99**US/**$6.50**CAN
    0-7860-0276-X

__VOWS   **$4.99**US/**$6.50**CAN
    0-7860-0463-0

Call toll free **1-888-345-BOOK** to order by phone or use this coupon to order by mail.

Name _____
Address _____
City _____ State _____ Zip _____
Please send me the books I have checked above.
I am enclosing $_____
Plus postage and handling* $_____
Sales tax (in NY, TN, and DC) $_____
Total amount enclosed $_____
*Add $2.50 for the first book and $.50 for each additional book.
Send check or money order (no cash or CODs) to: **Arabesque Books, Dept C.O., 850 Third Avenue, 16th Floor, New York, NY 10022**
Prices and numbers subject to change without notice.
All orders subject to availability.
Check out our Web site at **www.arabesquebooks.com**